'"You know what's going on, right?" *Ninefox Gambit* asks. Often, you have to say, "Uh, yeah, of course," when the real answer is "I have no idea, but I really, really care." And then you keep reading.'

**Strange Horizons**

'For sixteen years Yoon Ha Lee has been the shadow general of science fiction, the calculating tactician behind victory after victory. Now he launches his great manoeuvre. Origami elegant, fox-sly, defiantly and ferociously *new*, this book will burn your brain. Axiomatically brilliant. Heretically good.'

**Seth Dickinson**

'A high-octane ride through an endlessly inventive world, where calendars are weapons of war and dead soldiers can assist the living. Bold, fearlessly innovative and just a bit brutal, this is a book that deserves to be on every awards list.'

**Aliette de Bodard**

'Ambitious. Confusing. Enthralling. Brilliant. These are the words I will use to describe Yoon Ha Lee's utterly immersive, utterly memorable novel. I had heard very high praise for Lee's short fiction—still, even with those moderate expectations I had no idea what I was in for. I haven't felt this blown away by a novel's originality since *Ancillary Justice*. And, since I'm being completely honest, *Ninefox Gambit* is actually more inventive, boundary-breaking, and ambitious than that.'

**The Book Smugglers**

'Cheris' world feels genuinely alien, with thrillingly unfamiliar social structures and technologies, and the attention to detail is simply stunning. Just don't ever let your concentration slip, or there's a good chance that you will miss something wonderful.'

*SciFi Now*

'A dizzying composite of military space opera and sheer poetry. Every word, name and concept in Lee's unique world is imbued with a sense of wonder.'

**Hannu Rajaniemi**

'There's a good chance that this series will be seen as an important addition to the space opera resurgence of recent years. While Lee has developed a singular combination of military SF, mathematical elegance, and futuristic strangeness, readers may note echoes of or similarities to Iain M. Banks, Hannu Rajaniemi, C. J. Cherryh, Ann Leckie and Cordwainer Smith. Admirers of these authors, or anyone interested in state-of-the-art space opera, ought to give *Ninefox Gambit* a try.'

***Worlds Without End***

'Daring, original and compulsive. As if Cordwainer Smith had written a *Warhammer* novel.'

**Gareth L. Powell**

'That was a great read; very intriguing world building in particular. I now want to sign all my emails with "Yours in calendrical heresy."'

**Tobias Buckell**

# RAVEN
## STRATAGEM

First published 2017 by Solaris
an imprint of Rebellion Publishing Ltd,
Riverside House, Osney Mead,
Oxford, OX2 0ES, UK

*www.solarisbooks.com*

ISBN: 978 1 78108 537 0

10 9 8 7 6 5 4 3 2 1

A CIP catalogue record for this book is available from the
British Library.

Designed & typeset by Rebellion Publishing

Printed in Denmark by Nørhaven

# RAVEN
## STRATAGEM
MACHINERIES OF EMPIRE BOOK TWO

YOON HA LEE

SOLARIS

# CHAPTER ONE

LIEUTENANT COLONEL KEL Brezan's general had just been tapped to deal with the Hafn invasion. Brezan had expected chaos, just not this much of it. General Kel Khiruev had had to scramble her swarm after the Hafn assassinated General Kel Chrenka eighteen days ago. In Brezan's experience, assassinations never made the situation *less* chaotic.

Brezan was one of Khiruev's personnel officers. It was a better position than Brezan had ever hoped for, given the equivocal notes in his profile. As it stood, Khiruev's swarm was immense, in keeping with the threat that Kel Command anticipated. Brezan was impressed they'd scared up so many people on short notice. They'd given Khiruev one of the hexarchate's six cindermoths, its largest and most powerful vessels of war, as her command moth: the *Hierarchy of Feasts*. The swarm contained an additional 119 bannermoths and 48 scoutmoths. Kel Command had informed them that the Hafn had advanced to the Severed March, a region of space that had been quiet for as long as Brezan remembered, and which was therefore less well-prepared for the event than anyone would like. Yet here they were, cooling their heels at a transfer point because Kel Command, in its infinite wisdom, had decided that it was so important to add a single captain with secret orders that it was worth holding up Khiruev's swarm.

Brezan had spent the last seventy-three minutes reviewing the damnable woman's profile and refraining from kicking the terminal.

He didn't care how good she was at calendrical warfare. If he didn't hear from her transport in the next twelve minutes, he was going to recommend that they head out anyway, with a side of telling Kel Command to go hang. The Hafn had already left population centers on eight planets in crystallized ruins. The priority was fighting them sooner rather than later.

Captain Kel Cheris. Her early record showed that she was competent, as infantry officers went, with one oddity, her mathematical aptitude. The Nirai, the faction that contained most of the hexarchate's scientists and engineers, had tried to recruit her on the strength of it. Her heart had been set on joining the Kel, however—something that Brezan knew a little about—and, as the joke went, the Kel never said no to volunteers.

More interestingly, Cheris was a Mwennin, a member of a minority that no one had heard of. Granted, in an interstellar polity containing uncounted systems, this wasn't difficult, but the Mwennin additionally kept their heads down and avoided faction service. Brezan had no doubt that their existence was tolerated only because their numbers were minuscule even in the one system where they had settled, and because, between the heretics and the foreigners that might as well be heretics, the hexarchate had enough trouble to deal with. Still, Cheris had acquitted herself well enough, given her origins.

Brezan couldn't help a twinge of bitterness when he thought about it. He came from an honorable Kel family, an older sister on General Inesser's staff for fuck's sake, but he would never go far and he knew it. Some of the soldiers made disparaging comments about the fact that he was a womanform when they thought he couldn't hear them. But his fellow officers were civil about it, which was all he cared about. Rather, the notes in his profile about impulsiveness and unconventional thinking had impeded his advancement.

Cheris had not been able to stay out of trouble either, for all that her record had previously been good. She had recently been involved with the Siege of the Fortress of Scattered Needles, which had been taken over by heretics colluding with the Hafn. Brezan suspected that the record was leaving out something important, but most of the relevant segments were classified. Even General Khiruev's direct inquiries had been stonewalled.

Even better, Kel Command had fielded the undead general Shuos Jedao at Scattered Needles. No one denied Jedao's brilliance at tactics, but he was also mad, and he had once massacred two armies at Hellspin Fortress, one of them his own. The Kel swarm sent to deal with the Fortress's heretics had been wiped out, probably by Jedao himself. He was supposedly dead for good now, but who knew how true that was. Kel Command had been reviving him through mysterious means to throw at emergencies for the last few centuries, after all.

Cheris had tangled herself in that disaster, and something in that accomplishment had convinced Kel Command that General Khiruev would find her vitally useful. They just wouldn't say how. Brezan would rather they had sent a shipment of extra boots. Because, with all the marching they did in space, the boots would be more useful.

Brezan looked around the cindermoth's command center with its faintly glowing terminals, the impatient officers, beetleform and deltaform servitors performing maintenance. General Khiruev was a dark-skinned woman with an untidy streak of white in her hair and disfiguring scars showing pale along the side of her face where she'd never bothered getting them fixed. Unlike the others, she looked unruffled. On the other hand, the moth commander, Kel Janaia, kept checking her terminal for the time even though her augment's internal clock should have been synchronized with the mothgrid.

Seven more minutes. Shouldn't they have heard from the transport by now? Brezan resisted sending a note to Communications, who wouldn't thank him.

Of course, this was business as usual. It was no secret that Kel Command, being a hivemind, frequently made questionable decisions. A few centuries abusing composite technology would do that to you. Brezan functioned indifferently as part of a composite, one of the reasons he had expected to land at a boring desk dirtside instead of here, but he conceded that that sense of utter humming conviction, of *belonging*, was addictive. At least things weren't likely to get worse.

As it turned out, things were about to get worse.

"Sir, a needlemoth is requesting permission to land," Communications said to the general. "The transport bears one Captain Kel Cheris for transfer."

Who the hell was the captain that she rated a needlemoth, anyway? Brezan had never seen one in person, although they turned up all the time in spy dramas. Scan had put it on the central display. It looked like it'd hold a person and a half, if the scale was to be believed.

"Not late yet," Khiruev said with an equanimity Brezan wished he shared. "Colonel Brezan, make the arrangements."

"Sir," Brezan said. He dispatched instructions to the mothgrid to be passed on to the captain. She'd be staying in one of the nicer guest rooms rather than with the command moth's infantry complement, as befitted her courier status.

Just then they received a report that a Hafn swarm had been spotted on the way to the Fortress of Spinshot Coins. Like Scattered Needles, Spinshot Coins was one of the hexarchate's nexus fortresses, which maintained calendrical stability throughout the realm. Unless everyone adhered to the high calendar and its associated systems of behavior, the hexarchate's exotic technologies—most notably the mothdrive that permitted fast travel between star systems— would cease to function. The nexus fortresses had been designed to magnify the effect of calendrical observances.

The Hafn, not being stupid, were focusing their efforts on the fortresses. That wasn't the problem. The problem was that the Hafn had demonstrated that *their* exotic technology functioned in hexarchate space, where the high calendar was dominant. It shouldn't have been possible, yet here they were. Still, the general had orders to protect the nexus fortresses at all costs. Who knew what the Hafn would be able to pull if they got calendrical terrain lined up on their side?

"Scoutmoth 19 says there are possible scan ghosts," Communications was saying when someone entered the command center.

Brezan started, mainly because he had studied Cheris's profile extensively. While he expected her to report to the command center, the newcomer didn't move like her. The medical records and kinesthetic data had showed that Cheris had the standard body language that Kel infantry were imprinted with in Academy. This woman moved with the deceptive efficiency of an assassin. Brezan began to snap a reprimand. Instead, the words stuck to his teeth.

Captain Kel Cheris was short, with yellow-pale skin, an oval face, and black hair worn in a regulation bob. Those weren't what surprised him. At least they matched the profile.

Besides the jarring body language, he noticed her uniform. Kel black-and-gold, like that of almost everyone in the command center, except her insignia should have been a captain's talon. Instead, she sported a general's wings. Beneath the wings was a Shuos eye. To say nothing of her gloves, Kel-black, but with no fingers.

Brezan froze up. He knew what the insignia meant, what the fingerless gloves meant. Occasionally the Shuos, who specialized in information operations, were seconded to Kel service. They wore the ninefox eye to indicate their faction of origin. But no Shuos general had served among the Kel for four centuries.

No living Shuos general, anyway.

General Khiruev had risen from her seat. "That joke's in terrible taste, fledge," she said in her mild voice. Nevertheless, people flinched from 'fledge': the Kel only said that to cadets, in public anyway. "Fix the insignia and take off the gloves. Now."

During his lifetime, General Shuos Jedao had been one of the Kel's best officers. Then Hellspin Fortress had happened. Brezan considered it proof of Kel Command's psychosis that their response to Jedao going comprehensively insane was to stick him in an immortality device to repair his mind, then add him to the Kel Arsenal on the grounds that Jedao was scarier than they were, so why not weaponize him?

The half-gloves that Jedao had worn in life had been out of fashion in the hexarchate for a good four centuries, and with excellent cause.

"Oh, come now," Cheris said. She spoke with a drawl.

A terrible suspicion curdled in Brezan's mind. Granted, the hexarchate was home to a staggering number of low languages in addition to the high language, but Brezan made a point of getting to know people's origins, even when those origins were as hopelessly obscure as that of the Mwennin. He'd listened to samples of Mwennin poetry-chants—he didn't even like poetry when it was in one of his native tongues—and they had, if anything, sounded like rapid torrents of sibilants. It was possible that the Mwennin had multiple languages themselves, but he doubted any sounded like Jedao's native drawl, which he remembered from the archive videos he'd viewed in academy.

"Doctrine," Khiruev said, "escort her out of the command center and lock her up. I'll deal with her later. If Kel Command intends this as a puzzle, it can wait until things are less hectic here."

The Doctrine officer got up.

Cheris didn't even glance in their direction. "General Khiruev," she said, "I believe you've served at your present rank for fifteen years."

Brezan's suspicion sharpened.

The muscles along Khiruev's jaw went taut. "That's correct."

"I'm Shuos Jedao. I've held the rank of general for a good three centuries and change."

"That's not possible," Khiruev said after a second.

*Stop listening to them,* Brezan begged silently.

"Oh, don't tempt me to make a Kel joke," said Jedao or Cheris or whoever the hell they were, "there are so many to choose from. Why don't you set me a test?" The corner of their mouth tipped up. Brezan had seen the same smile in a four-hundred-year-old recording of a completely different face.

One of Brezan's problems was that he was, despite his competence, a marginal Kel. Brezan possessed weak formation instinct. The injection process wasn't entirely predictable, and sometimes cadets failed out of Kel Academy because they couldn't maintain formation. He had spent his entire time there convinced they'd kick him out. Formation instinct, the emotional need to maintain hierarchy, made

Kel discipline possible and allowed the Kel to use formations to channel calendrical effects in battle, from force shields to kinetic lances. A Kel without formation instinct was no Kel at all.

But for once, his deficit was an asset. He went for his sidearm.

His enemy was faster. Brezan was aware of fragments: the noise of their gun going off. The world dimming at the edges. A sudden shock running from hand to wrist to arm. The bullet singing as it ricocheted off Brezan's gun's slide; the gun itself flew out of his hand. Everyone ducking.

Brezan's hands wouldn't stop shaking.

"Shit," Brezan said with feeling. His ears were ringing. "I have Captain Cheris's profile memorized and her aim isn't remotely that good."

"Overkill is something of a personal defect," Jedao said, not modest in the least.

All the Kel in the command center were watching them. General Khiruev was watching them. A terrible yearning filled her eyes.

Brezan was fourth-generation Kel. He knew what a Kel looked like when hit between the ears by formation instinct. He should have kept his fucking mouth shut.

"General Jedao," Khiruev said, "what are your orders, sir?"

It was an open question who was the worse master: Shuos Jedao, arch traitor and mass murderer, or Kel Command. But Brezan clung to the compass of duty. He dropped the useless pistol and scrabbled for his combat knife.

He wasn't alone. The Doctrine officer was a Rahal, but they were even slower than he was. Soon every Kel in the command center had a gun trained on one or the other of them. People he'd served with for years. He was threatening their new formation leader. The only reason he and Doctrine weren't full of holes already was the novelty of the situation.

Hell of a way to die. At least he wouldn't be around to hear his insufferable sister Miuzan ribbing him about it. He dropped the knife.

"Hold," Jedao said before anyone could change their mind and fire. His eyes were thoughtful.

Brezan recognized the *are you or aren't you?* expression of someone trying to decide from his severely cropped hair whether he was a man after all, or a woman who preferred masculine styles. Ordinarily Brezan would have clenched his teeth. In this instance, however, he enjoyed the petty pleasure of confusing Jedao even in such a small matter.

"What's your name, soldier?"

No point keeping it to himself when the other Kel would rat him out. "Lieutenant Colonel Kel Brezan," he said. He had the petty satisfaction of watching all the Kel twitch at his failure to say "sir." "Staff officer, Personnel, assigned to General Kel Khiruev of the Swanknot. If you're going to shoot me, you might as well get it over with. I won't serve you."

Brezan heard an inner whisper urging him to trust General Khiruev's judgment; to serve the new formation leader the way Kel were made to serve. Damningly, he quelled it with ease. His proper loyalty belonged to Kel Command, not an upstart undead Shuos general possessing a Kel captain.

"You might be a crashhawk," Jedao said insultingly. He was perfectly relaxed, but given how the situation was playing out, he had no reason not to be. "Hard to tell. Still, there are people like you"—his gaze flicked to Doctrine"—and the seconded personnel who don't have formation instinct. I won't be able to rely on them."

Brezan gritted his teeth. There were eighty-two Nirai on the *Hierarchy of Feasts* alone, more in the rest of the swarm, to say nothing of Shuos and the occasional Rahal and a couple Vidona. If Jedao was going to—

"I'm not going to kill them," Jedao said, "but I can't bring them with me, either. I need a list of people to let off. I assume we have sufficient transports for the job. They'll have to have everything but minimal life-support and navigation disabled. Won't buy me much time, but every little bit helps."

Brezan could fight, but he'd die the moment he twitched a muscle. If, for whatever incomprehensible reason, Jedao intended to spare those he couldn't control with formation instinct, there was a chance of getting word to Kel Command. Even if Kel Command was responsible for this mess to begin with, or more likely, Jedao had played some trick to set it up.

General Khiruev and the chief of staff were calmly discussing logistical options to offer to Jedao.

Holes opened in Brezan's heart.

"All right," Jedao said. "I suppose we had better send Colonel Brezan off before we bore them further." He gestured toward a pair of junior officers.

Brezan didn't resist, but he did say, bitterly, "Congratulations, Jedao. You've hijacked an entire fucking swarm. What are you going to do with it?"

He glimpsed Jedao's brilliant smile before the soldiers yanked him around. "I'm going to fight the Hafn, of course," Jedao called after him. "Oh, and give Kel Command my love."

*I am going to kill you if I have to crawl through vacuum naked to do it,* Brezan thought as he was marched out of the command center. He had the feeling it wouldn't be that easy.

# CHAPTER TWO

WHEN NESHTE KHIRUEV was eleven years old (high calendar), one of her mothers killed her father.

Until then, it had been an excellent day. Khiruev had figured out how to catch bees with your fingers. You could crush them, too, but that wasn't the point. The trick was to ease up behind them and apply polite, firm pressure to trap them between your thumb and forefinger. They rarely took offense as long as you released them gently. She wanted to tell her mothers about the trick. Her father wouldn't have been interested; he couldn't stand bugs.

Khiruev came home earlier than usual to show them. When she stepped inside, she heard Mother Ekesra and her father arguing in the common room. Mother Allu, who hated shouting when she wasn't the one doing it, was hunched in her favorite chair with her face averted.

Her father, Kthero, was a teacher, and Mother Allu worked with the ecoscrubber maintenance team. But Mother Ekesra was Vidona Ekesra, and she reprogrammed heretics. The Vidona faction had to educate heretics to comply with the hexarchate's calendrical norms so that everyone could rely on the corresponding exotic technologies.

Mother Allu spoke first, without looking at her. "Go to your room, Khiruev." Her voice was muffled. "You're an inventive child. I'm sure you can entertain yourself until bedtime. I'll send a servitor with dinner."

This alarmed Khiruev. Mother Allu often went on about the importance of eating together instead of, for instance, straggling in late because you'd been taking apart an old game controller. But this looked like a bad time to needle her about it, so she obediently traipsed toward her room.

"No," Mother Ekesra said when she was almost to the hallway. "She deserves to know that her father's a heretic."

Khiruev stopped so suddenly that she almost tripped over the floor. You didn't joke about heresy. Everyone knew that. Was Mother Ekesra being funny? It wasn't true what they said that the Vidona had no sense of humor, but an accusation of *heresy*—

"Leave the child out of this," Khiruev's father said. He had a quiet voice, but people tended to listen when he spoke.

Mother Ekesra wasn't in a listening mood. "If you didn't want her involved," she said in that Inescapable Logic tone that Khiruev especially dreaded, "you shouldn't have taken up with calendrical deviants or 'reenactors' or whatever they call themselves. What were you *thinking*?"

"At least I *was* thinking," Khiruev's father replied, "unlike certain members of the household."

Khiruev edged toward the hallway in spite of herself. This argument wasn't going to end well. She should have stayed outside.

"Don't *you* start," Mother Ekesra said. She yanked Khiruev's arm around until she faced her father. "Look at her, Kthero." Her voice was flat, deadly. "Our *daughter*. You've exposed her to heresy. It's a contamination. Don't you pay attention to the monthly Doctrine briefings at all?"

"Quit dragging this out, Ekesra," Khiruev's father said. "If you're going to hand me over to the authorities, just get it over with."

"I can do better than that," Mother Ekesra said.

Khiruev missed what she said next because Khiruev finally noticed that, despite Mother Ekesra's mechanical voice, tears were trickling down her cheeks. This embarrassed Khiruev, although she couldn't say why.

"—summary judgment," Mother Ekesra was saying. Whatever that meant.

Mother Allu raised her head, but didn't speak. All she did was scrub at her eyes.

"Have mercy on the child," Khiruev's father said at last. "She's only eleven."

Mother Ekesra's eyes blazed with such loathing that Khiruev wanted to shrivel up and roll under a chair. "Then she's old enough to learn that heresy is a real threat with real consequences," she said. "Don't make any more mistakes, Kthero. I'll never forgive you."

"A bit late for that, I should say." Kthero's face was set. "She won't forget this, you know."

"That's the point," Mother Ekesra said, still in that deadly voice. "It was too late for me to save you when you got it into your head to research deprecated calendricals. But it's not too late to stop Khiruev from ending up like you."

*I don't want to be saved, I want everyone to stop fighting,* Khiruev thought, but she wouldn't have dreamed of contradicting her.

Khiruev's father didn't flinch when Mother Ekesra laid a hand on each of his shoulders. At first nothing happened. Khiruev dared to hope a reconciliation might be possible after all.

Then they heard the gears.

Maddeningly, the sound came from everywhere and nowhere, clanking and clattering out of step with itself, rhythms abandoned mid-stride, unnerving crystalline chimes that decayed into static. As the clamor grew louder, Khiruev's father wavered. His outline turned the color of tarnished silver, and his flesh flattened to a translucent sheet through which disordered diagrams and untidy numbers could be seen, bones and blood vessels reduced to dry traceries. Vidona deathtouch.

Mother Ekesra let go. The corpse-paper remnant of her husband drifted to the floor with a horrible crackling noise. But she wasn't done; she believed in neatness. She knelt to pick up the sheet and began folding it. Paper-folding was an art specific to the Vidona. It was also one of the few arts that the Andan faction, who otherwise prided themselves on their dominance of the hexarchate's culture, disdained.

When Mother Ekesra was done folding the two entangled swans—remarkable work, worthy of admiration if you didn't realize who it had once been—she put the horrible thing down, went into Mother Allu's arms, and began to cry in earnest.

Khiruev stood there for the better part of an hour, trying not to look at the swans out of the corner of her eye and failing. Her hands felt clammy. She would rather have hidden in her room, but that couldn't be the right thing to do. So she stayed.

During those terrible minutes (seventy-eight of them; she kept track), Khiruev promised she wouldn't ever make either of her mothers cry like that. All the same, she couldn't stand the thought of joining the Vidona, even to prove her loyalty to the hexarchate. For years her dreams were filled with folded paper shapes that crumpled into the wet, massy shapes of people's hearts, or flayed themselves of folds until nothing remained but a string-tangle of forbidden numbers.

Instead, Khiruev ran toward the Kel, where there would always be someone to tell her what to do and what was right. Unfortunately, she had a significant aptitude for the military and the ability to interpret orders creatively when creativity was called for. She hadn't accounted for what she'd do if promoted too high.

As it turned out, 341 years of seniority rendered the matter moot.

KHIRUEV WAS IN her quarters, leaning against the wall and trying to concentrate on her boxes of gadgets. Her vision swam in and out of focus. All the blacks had shifted gray, and colors were desaturated. With her luck, her hearing would go next. She felt feverish, as though someone was using her bones for fuel. None of this came as a surprise, but it was still a rotten inconvenience.

After quizzing everyone about the cindermoth, the swarm, and the swarm's original assignment, and making Khiruev relay his latest orders to the swarm, Jedao had retired to quarters. This had occasioned a certain amount of shuffling, since Jedao was now the ranking officer. Khiruev didn't mind. The servitors had done their usual excellent job on short notice. But Commander Janaia, who liked her luxuries and hated disruptions, had looked quietly annoyed.

Five hours and sixty-one minutes remained until high table. Jedao had scheduled a staff meeting directly after that. Khiruev had that time in which to devise a way to assassinate her general without resorting to the Vrae Tala clause. Vrae Tala was more certain, but she thought she could get the job done without it. She wasn't eager to commit suicide.

If she hadn't been a Kel, Khiruev would have taken the direct route and shot Jedao in the back. But then, if she hadn't been a Kel, Jedao wouldn't have been able to take over so easily. Presumably Kel Command had no idea that Jedao was walking around in Captain Cheris's body, or they would have issued a warning in response to Khiruev's earlier inquiries.

As it was, it would be difficult to get into position to shoot Jedao without formation instinct asserting itself. Contemplating the assassination was already agonizing, and Jedao wasn't anywhere in sight. And Khiruev was a general, nearest in rank. She was the only one with a chance of resisting formation instinct. The effect would strengthen with more exposure. If she was going to pull this off, she had to make her attempt soon.

Khiruev had always liked tinkering with machines, a pastime her parents had tolerated rather than encouraged. When on leave, she poked around disreputable little shops in search of devices that didn't work anymore so she could rehabilitate them. Some of her projects came together better than others, and furthermore she was never sure what to do with the ones she did succeed in fixing. Currently her collection contained a frightening number of items in various stages of disassembly. Janaia had remarked that the servitors scared baby servitors by telling them that this was where they'd end up if they misbehaved.

The important point was that she had access to components without having to put in a request to Engineering. She had considered doing so anyway, since dubious military equipment was two steps up from dubious equipment she had bought from shopkeepers who beamed when paid for shiny pieces of junk. Still, she couldn't risk arousing the suspicions of some soldier in Engineering who would report her to Jedao.

Khiruev nerved herself up, wishing she didn't feel so dreadful, then gathered the components she needed. Small was good; small was best. It took her an unconscionably long time to lay everything out on the workbench because she kept dropping things. Once a nine-coil rolled away behind the desk and it took her three tries to retrieve it, convinced all the while she was going to break it even though it was made of a perfectly sturdy alloy.

The tools were worse. She could halfway convince her traitorous brain that she was only rearranging her bagatelles. Self-deception about the tools was harder.

She had to finish this before high table, and to make matters worse, she also had to allow for recovery time. She wasn't confident that Jedao wouldn't see through her anyway. But the alternative was doing nothing. She owed her swarm better than that. If only Brezan had—but that opportunity had passed.

Khiruev reminded herself that if she had survived that biological attack during the Hjong Mu campaign, the one where she'd hallucinated that worms were chewing their way out of her eyes, a minor physical reaction shouldn't slow her down. The physical effects weren't even the issue. It was the recurrent stabbing knowledge that she was betraying a superior.

Her palm hurt. Khiruev discovered that she had been jabbing herself with a screwdriver and stopped. Briefly, she considered removing her weapons so that formation instinct didn't compel her to commit suicide rather than put her plan in motion, but that wouldn't work. It would raise suspicions at high table. Her glove had a small tear in it, which knit itself back together as she watched.

The best way to proceed, it turned out, was to break down the task of assembly into the smallest imaginable subtasks so that she didn't have to think about the end product. (She tried not to think about who she'd learned that from.) She had to scratch out some of the intermediate computations for the correct numerical resonances on a corner of her workbench, an endeavor complicated by the bench's tendency to heal itself after a few moments. At least it got rid of the immediate evidence. It wasn't hard to read the marks out of the material's memory—she could do it herself with the right kind of scanner—but you had to know to do it in the first place.

Khiruev's chest hurt, and she paused. Her hand ached from how tightly she was gripping the screwdriver. She brought it up so the blade pointed at her lower eyelid. It wouldn't take much force to drive it into her eye.

She was a traitor no matter what she did. There was no way to be loyal both to Kel Command and to her general. She angled the screwdriver so it—

*I have to kill him,* Khiruev thought desperately. She couldn't leave the swarm in the madman's hands, not when it was needed to defend the hexarchate against the Hafn. Khiruev forced herself to lower the screwdriver. Then she dropped it with a clatter and put her head in her hands, breathing hard. She had to complete the assassination drone no matter what.

The drone, when she finished it, wasn't one of her better efforts. It looked like nothing so much as a sickly cockroach. She rigged the needler unit using seven- and nineteen-circuits scavenged from a music box, of all things, instead of the preferred semiprime circuit, but it couldn't be helped.

The next step was programming the drone to recognize its target. Triggering it manually would have been better, but if she'd had the ability to do that, she would have been able to shoot Jedao in the back in the first place. The drone had a basic optic system. She'd cribbed from the mothgrid for the leanest pattern recognition routine she could load into its processor and given it the videos from Captain Cheris's profile. She had a bad moment when her own vision shorted out while she was feeding the drone the data. Luckily, the process didn't require much more intervention on her part. By the time it was done, she was drenched in sweat, but her vision had mostly returned.

No wonder the Shuos had never gone in for formation instinct. Not being able to assassinate their own hexarchs, historically a popular Shuos pastime, would have driven them up the wall.

Khiruev gritted her teeth and shoved the drone into her boot. With any luck it wouldn't shoot her foot by accident. Only forty-nine minutes until high table. Had it really taken her that long? But she knew the answer to that question. She spent fourteen of those minutes taking a shower, which did not relax her at all, and twenty-nine minutes putting everything away. The shelves looked like a war zone, but that was normal.

Her left boot felt disproportionately heavy all the way to the high hall, even though she knew the drone's mass to an improbable number of significant figures. She arrived six minutes early, no more and no less. It didn't reassure her that she arrived within sixteen seconds of General Jedao. Commander Janaia showed up two minutes after that, but she had always been slightly lackadaisical.

"Good to see you, General," Jedao said, as though a normal working relationship was possible. "Shall we?"

Jedao took his seat at the head table. Khiruev sat at his right hand, Janaia at his left, Stsan at the other end of the table. The senior staff officers arranged themselves after a moment's hesitation.

Servitors were bringing out the food in trays. Janaia wasn't paying any attention to them, instead casting surreptitious glances at the cup Jedao had brought to high table, even though one had been provided for him, after modern tradition. The fact that Jedao had remembered the tradition was more important than the cup itself, a plain metal affair. Morbidly, Khiruev wondered if the cup had belonged to Captain Cheris.

Jedao inclined his head to the servitor that delivered his chopsticks and spoon. Curious: Khiruev had never seen an officer do that before. Or anyone, for that matter. The servitor, a birdform with extra limbs, made a cautious quizzical sound. It probably knew as much about Hellspin Fortress as any of the humans, although it had never before occurred to Khiruev to wonder how much machine sentiences cared about history. Jedao cocked an eyebrow at it. The servitor chirred thoughtfully and went on with its work.

"All right," Jedao said in a voice that was clearly audible without being too loud, "this didn't matter aboard the needlemoth, but I'd be much obliged if someone would tell me if there are any crashingly important rules for how to eat this stuff. Especially the rolled-up seaweed things. Do I use my fingers or what?"

Janaia was startled into a laugh. "We're not Andan, sir. Getting it into your mouth without dropping it is the important part."

"The 'rolled-up seaweed things' are mostly vegetables and fish inside," Khiruev felt obliged to add, "unless the servitors are feeling experimental."

"Good to know," Jedao said. "At least you can't do creative experimental things to chopsticks. I recognize those." He took the water pitcher, filled his cup, and sipped. All the Kel watched him intently. He had to be aware of it, but his expression was serene.

Khiruev had the urge to fish the drone out of her boot and confess everything. Jedao, however, was passing the cup her way. The cup felt like an ordinary object in her hand, and the water was the same clear, sweet water she was used to drinking. In a just world it would burn out her throat—*Stop that,* she told herself. She passed the cup to her right, her fingers numb.

Janaia persisted in trying to make small talk. "I don't suppose military food was any better in your day."

Jedao's mouth quirked. "You were made a moth Kel directly, weren't you, Commander?"

"That's correct, sir," Janaia said. "I got lucky. Don't care for dirtside all that much. Flowers are nice, but you don't need a whole planet to grow them."

Khiruev couldn't fault Janaia. The Kel in the high hall were terrified. Hardly anyone was talking, and everyone was fixated on

Jedao's table. Janaia knew as well as anyone what kind of threat Jedao posed. She was also doing her best, by acting as if nothing was out of the ordinary, to keep people from panicking entirely. Khiruev should have been doing the same, no matter how rattled she was.

"I ate some awful things when I started in the infantry," Jedao said. "When I was a lieutenant, we were once trapped behind enemy lines. Eventually I had to shoot two people for fighting over who got to eat the maggots."

"We don't have maggots that we know of," Stsan said, "but some of the servitors enjoy hunting. Captain-engineer Miugo tells me that they sometimes leave their kills at her door, like a cat might. Thankfully Miugo has a strong stomach."

"Point them out to me?" Jedao said.

"Rakish-looking man over there," Janaia said, waving her spoon, "hair pinned up in braids."

"Ah, I see him." Jedao turned to the rest of the table and invited the staff to introduce the rest of themselves more fully. He learned that Lieutenant Colonel Najjad of Logistics had three children, and either found it genuinely interesting that the middle child was a researcher in comparative linguistics, or was faking it very well. The acting head of Intelligence, Major Lyu, was drawn into a friendly debate on some opening gambit in an obscure Shuos board game. Only Operations remained uncommunicative, but Jedao seemed amused rather than offended.

For her part, Khiruev wondered how the history lessons that had gone into such loving detail on the tactics that had won the Battle of Candle Arc could have failed to mention how *chatty* Jedao was, to say nothing of the astonishingly filthy Andan jokes he knew. Upon reflection, Khiruev realized she had only the haziest notion of how the black cradle provided immortality. It had always been rumored that the device acted more as a prison than anything else. Maybe Jedao was starved for conversation after centuries.

The high hall became, if anything, more tense over the course of the meal. The Kel were waiting to find out just how Jedao meant to massacre them. *I'm going to fight the Hafn,* Jedao had said. How serious was he? Even if he had good intentions, an unlikely proposition, he had to know that Kel Command was unlikely to allow him to run around unmolested.

Jedao had only eaten half his rice by the end of high table. He set his chopsticks down and said, "We may as well head straight to the meeting. I trust you all know what to do." He drained his cup, stood, and nodded to the officers at the table before heading out of the high hall with the cup hooked to his belt.

The Kel watched him go in silence. "Commander," Khiruev said politely to Janaia before filing out of the hall with the staff heads. She had to admit she had no idea what Jedao intended for her specifically. It hadn't escaped her attention that Jedao had fished for little of her personal history, although there had been no other sign of disfavor, and Khiruev didn't like talking about her family anyway. Even so, she ached with the desire to make herself useful to her superior.

She couldn't afford to think about what she was going to do next. Her vision was faltering around the edges again. And her left foot cramped. She clenched her jaw and walked on.

The designated conference room wasn't far from the high hall. Khiruev caught up to Jedao mainly because Jedao kept pausing to admire the art on the walls: ashhawks rising from devastated cities, ashhawks nesting on improbable spires, ashhawks tearing through storm clouds. Khiruev had come to take Kel decor for granted years ago, but now that she looked at it anew, she admitted it was on the gaudy side, with flourishes in couched gold thread and beads of amber. For that matter, she had no idea how the Kel had decorated their moths during Jedao's lifetime, but given how many times he had allegedly been revived, surely the hangings couldn't be that much of a shock?

"I should stop gawking or I'm going to be late to my own damn meeting," Jedao said to Khiruev as she fell into step half a pace behind him. "Did you know I used to wear a watch? I haven't seen one of those in a couple centuries. Er, you probably have no idea what I'm—"

This was getting into uncomfortable territory. "I've seen a few," Khiruev said. "Antique stores, with the guts removed so they'll be in no condition to do anything heretical to the calendar."

Jedao snorted. "Why am I not surprised."

The conference room's door slid open at Jedao's approach. Irrationally, Khiruev was surprised that the far wall was still imaging the last thing she'd set it to, an ink painting of a gingko tree. The original was attributed to General Andan Zhe Navo, although it was anyone's guess as to whether she had really painted it.

Jedao took his seat at the table, which was made of black stone with faint gold whorls in it, like spectral fingerprints. He had produced a deck of jeng-zai cards out of nowhere and was shuffling them with the ease of long practice. Then he caught the way Stsan was staring at the cards, grinned unsettlingly at her, and put the cards down.

Khiruev told herself that this was going to be an ordinary meeting, wishing she was better at lying to herself, and sat to Jedao's right. The other staff heads took their seats in glum silence. Major Lyu looked as though he wished the Shuos analyst who had headed his section hadn't been booted. Strategy's Lieutenant Colonel Riozu, on the other hand, kept eyeing Jedao with that *I'm going to pick your brains clean* expression she got when she met someone new and exciting.

"All right," Jedao said, "they didn't exactly provide me with a library while I was busy being undead, but I did attempt to do my homework. If I'm understanding this correctly, the Fortress of Spinshot Coins had its defenses upgraded seventy-six years ago?"

*My leg itches,* Khiruev thought deliberately. This self-deception business wasn't getting any easier. How did the Shuos manage it? Ironically, formation instinct prevented her from blurting out her plan. She was seized by the conviction that she mustn't interrupt the senior general.

Trying not to wince too obviously, Khiruev reached down under the table. Her hand spasmed. She almost hissed, more in surprise than pain. Which was ridiculous, because she had known this would happen. *Just an itch.* Her fingers found the drone, switched it on after a mercifully brief moment of fumbling, and released it. If she hadn't heard it scuttling into position, surely no one else had. Of course, there was the possibility the thing had failed to activate, but best not to dwell on that.

"—phantom terrain," Riozu was saying. She tapped something into her slate. "Here's a summary of the Fortress's guns. I imagine you'll find only a few details have changed. Phantom terrain is the bit you might not be familiar with."

Jedao glanced over his own slate for the figures. "Yes, I see. How about you explain in your own words what you think I ought to know. The operational details, not the dry lists of numbers they put in the grid database. Pretend I'm a cadet." He smiled at their palpable dismay. "I mean it. I assume it's an exotic—weapon? A defense?"

"Exotic defense," Riozu said. "Effectiveness falls off as inverse radius squared and it blows through the power cores like nobody's business. But it does exactly what its name suggests. It generates temporary terrain in space."

Where was the drone? Under other circumstances, Khiruev would have provided a better explanation. Riozu always thought she was more clear than she was. Sweat trickled down Khiruev's back. She didn't dare drop her pretense of attentiveness to look, and if she thought about it anymore, the debilitating physical effects would resume.

Jedao had taken up his cards again. He fanned them out and flipped over the first six. Ace of Gears, Ace of Roses, Ace of Eyes, Ace of Doors, the Burning Banner, and the Drowned General. A very unlucky hand, if you were superstitious.

"Terrain can refer to all sorts of things," Jedao said, very mildly. "Especially when it comes to exotics. Are we talking impedance of motion like swimming through mud, actual physical barriers, force walls—"

Everyone became aware of a curious thready melody, high-pitched, coming from the side of the room. The drone had crept out from under a cabinet. Khiruev knew instantly what part of the wiring she had gotten wrong. She also had a moment to curse herself for using that wretched music box for parts. She clearly hadn't thought through the resonance activations carefully enough.

The drone's needler fired four times in lockstep with the horrible skewed melody. Everyone was already moving. Khiruev had reflexively lunged out of her chair to shield Jedao, as had Lyu, Riozu, and Operations' Kel Meriki. Jedao had his gun out, but hadn't fired into the tangle because he had no clear shot.

The needler jammed. The music hiccupped, caught on a two-note figure whining out of tune. The drone skittered back and forth for a moment. Meriki fired anyway. The bullet ricocheted. Khiruev's knees buckled. More gunshots, she could feel them, but she couldn't hear a thing even though people's mouths were moving.

The drone came apart as two bullets finally hit it. Khiruev hadn't built it to last. Fragments scattered across the room in several directions. One hit the table's leg and bounced off, but Khiruev didn't see where it went. A moment after that, Khiruev realized she hadn't noticed all the blood, even though she could smell it, because she'd lost most of that side of the spectrum. Everything in her vision was blue-shifted, wintry. She tried to get to her feet, but her muscles wouldn't cooperate.

Kel Lyu was sprawled on the floor. Meriki was slumped across the table.

"—Medical," Jedao was saying from far away, his voice hard and crisp. "Two dead, don't know about injuries. And I'm going to need a word with Doctrine about stepping up security if Hafn agents planted something on the fucking command moth. I heard about General Cherkad's assassination."

A team of servitors arrived first and confirmed that Lyu and Meriki were dead. Lyu had taken three needles. The fourth was buried in the wall next to the gingko image. One of the drone fragments had nailed Meriki in the eye.

"All right," Jedao said, still in that clipped voice. "Notify Major Arvikoi that they're the new acting head of Intelligence, the same for Major Berimay and Operations. We're going to try this meeting again after Doctrine assures me there aren't any other traps. Out, all of you." He thought for a moment. "Except you, General Khiruev. Come with me."

There was no way Jedao didn't know, despite the flimsy cover story he had fed Medical. "Sir," Khiruev said, or thought she said. She hauled herself to her feet. The surviving staff heads saluted them as they passed out of the room.

"All right," Jedao said when no one else was in earshot, "your place or mine?"

His hand wasn't anywhere near his gun, but then, it hadn't been when he had fired on Brezan, either.

"I'm certain my quarters will be safe, sir," Khiruev said, with no particular emphasis on 'safe.' When Jedao saw the boxes of dismembered gadgets, he'd have all the evidence he needed. Might as well get it over with.

Khiruev's quarters were down the hall from Jedao's. Jedao let her enter first. The door slid shut behind them.

"You weren't kidding about watches, General," Jedao said, inspecting the shelves where Khiruev kept her favorite trinkets. "That rose gold one would be nice if you fixed it up, but never mind. You were probably shocky when I called Engineering asking if anyone had recently requisitioned gewgaws. But then, you wouldn't have needed their help. Engineering subspecialty as a cadet, isn't that right?"

Khiruev wasn't sure what she wanted more, a bullet in her head or a cane. Standing up without collapsing was taking all the concentration she could spare. "Come again?" she said.

Jedao eyed her, then brought over a chair "Sit down, for love of fox and hound. I'd rather not be talking to the floor."

She sat.

Jedao crossed his arms. "I'm not unaware of the effect that formation instinct is having on you right now, General, but I need you to pay attention to what I'm saying with your actual brain and not the part of your brain that's going to 'sir' me to death. If you'll pardon the expression."

Khiruev stared at Jedao's holstered gun. "I've betrayed you, sir," she rasped. "My death is yours."

"That's not the salient point, General."

Khiruev tried to make sense of the statement. For that matter, Jedao was being awfully conscientious about addressing her by her rank. What was going on?

Jedao's eyes were very cold. "You fucked up, General. You got two of ours killed. If that's the standard needler unit, then it holds twelve rounds and we're lucky it jammed so more people didn't die."

Khiruev shook at the contempt in Jedao's voice.

"I'm not unaware of my reputation. I really did slaughter a Kel army. So I'm not unaware that the Kel have a million reasons to want me dead.

"But I meant it when I said I was going to fight the Hafn." Jedao's mouth twisted. "Shooting people is one of the few things I'm good at. It's the only way I can make amends. And to do that, I need soldiers, not corpses."

"Sir," Khiruev whispered, and couldn't think of what to say after that.

"I used to be a Shuos agent," Jedao said in a more normal tone of voice, which made Khiruev's heart freeze. "Didn't stay at it long before transferring to the Kel, but you'd be surprised how many assassinations you can pull off in eight months if your heptarch insists. There were Kel between me and the drone, including yourself. Given formation instinct, you needed to get me alone. You could have sent the drone after me on the way to the conference room, assuming you had it available then. You were half a step behind me, but you might have been able to submerge formation instinct long enough to keep from tackling me or some damn thing while it went to work. I assume you didn't build in a weapon with better penetration for lack of appropriate parts. Anyway, it would have had a clear shot at my back. If you'd done this in a semi-competent fashion, you'd have your swarm back and those officers would still be alive."

Khiruev's first thought was that of all the things she had expected of this conversation, a critique of her assassination attempt had not been one of them. The second was that she should have known that even a four-hundred-year-old Shuos who had spent his adult life in Kel service would display the Shuos obsession with competence. "That option didn't occur to me," Khiruev said simply.

"Obviously."

"My death is yours, sir."

Jedao gave her a cockeyed look. "How do you tell the difference between a violin and a Kel?"

She knew the answer to that one. "The Kel burns longer."

"Listen," Jedao said, "I'm only good at speaking the language of guns, so maybe I haven't made myself clear yet. I don't want your fucking *death*, General. Killing people is so easy, but it's usually irreversible. Kel Command clearly thinks you're good. They've been mulling over promoting you someday, if I'm understanding the notations in your profile correctly."

Khiruev stiffened in spite of herself, but Jedao went on.

"I want your *life*, General. I want your help fighting the Hafn. But you need to promise me you're not going to get more people killed through this kind of carelessness. Because if you pull that again, I'm going to show you a damned nasty way of killing someone with a playing card." Jedao pulled a card out of his sleeve: the Deuce of Gears. His personal emblem.

"You have my service, sir," Khiruev said, "as long as you require it."

Jedao smiled brilliantly at her, and Khiruev knew then how completely she'd been defeated.

# CHAPTER THREE

WHEN RHEZNY BREZAN was a third-year cadet at Kel Academy Secondary, he learned why Exercise Purple 53 was listed as Purple Paranoia. His class had known that the exercise was coming, although not how bad it would be. A few years back, one class had drawn the one that involved lots of orbital bombardment. The consensus was that no one else would get as lucky so soon. Besides, two years ago, a new commandant had been appointed, and she had a reputation for designing no-win scenarios over breakfast.

The usual instructor was a stocky, graying man who never smiled. Brezan, sitting in the classroom with the other cadets, noticed the gleam in his eyes. Not a good sign. Next to him, Onuen Wei was taking slow, deep breaths, which meant she had noticed, too.

A slim manform entered the room. Brezan recognized the alt, who had worn any number of faces, all of them cheerfully ugly. The sight of their naked hands made Brezan's stomach knot with revulsion. None of the cadets wore Kel gloves; they'd only earn that right upon graduation. But the newcomer's unostentatious bearing gave the impression of great experience. The manform wore no faction or rank insignia. They didn't have to. No one here dared cross them.

The room went dead silent.

"For this exercise," the instructor said, "I'm handing you over to a guest instructor. Shuos Zehun is on loan to us from the Shuos hexarch." Zehun was Hexarch Shuos Mikodez's personal assistant, one of the few Shuos scarier than the hexarch himself. Zehun had switched to this face several months ago; it had been impossible to escape the news. "I expect you to accord Zehun the same respect and obedience you would myself or any Kel superior." The instructor's not-smile turned fiendish. "There's every possibility that they know more ways of dismembering annoying cadets than I do."

The threat wasn't necessary. Everyone had heard about how Mikodez had assassinated two of his own cadets on a lark shortly after he rose to power.

"Pleased to meet you all," Shuos Zehun said. Their voice was quiet but not soft.

The regular instructor nodded to them and walked out, whistling pointedly.

"All right," Zehun said. "Come with me."

They filed out after Zehun, walking down a long hall and through several passageways until they reached the variable-layout sections of Citadel 9. From that point on, Brezan concentrated on not looking too closely at the walls, whose angles seemed to be on the verge of shattering apart, or the floor, which put him in mind of great and restless snakes. Brezan's bunkmate, an engineering candidate, liked to read trashy adventures set in the bowels of the campus. They inevitably involved rogue killer robots, the occasional talking ferret, and plucky cadets who never ran out of ammunition. Brezan had tried some and found them unnaturally compulsive reading. Of course, most of the adventures had happy endings. Nothing involving a Shuos could possibly have a happy ending.

At last they reached a door. Brezan's eyes refused to focus on it, so instead he looked at the Shuos. The fact that Zehun's right hand never strayed from their side was unreassuring. Brezan couldn't spot a weapon, but that didn't mean anything.

"You're wondering why you're having a fox lobbed at you," Zehun said. "I'll be frank. Your commandant lost a bet with my hexarch. For reasons beyond my understanding, my hexarch is letting her off light."

This didn't make Brezan feel better, either.

"That being said, we might as well make the most of the situation. When I give you leave, you'll enter the door single-file. Inside, you'll arrive at a desk with an envelope on it and a pen to write with. I advise opening the envelope straightaway, because while this scenario is turn-based, the turns are timed. Six minutes per tick, to be exact."

Brezan thought for a moment. "Sir, a question."

"Your name, fledge."

Aggravating to be addressed thus by a non-Kel, but as a guest instructor, Zehun was within their rights. Not to mention that it would be suicidal to cry insult against a hexarch's assistant. "Cadet Rhezny Brezan, sir."

"Your question."

"Is there a clock in the room?" He'd noticed that his augment was being uncommunicative.

Zehun smiled suddenly. "No."

Wonderful. Brezan decided that he could wait to find out more rather than sticking his neck out any further. He tried not to think about what his Kel sister Miuzan would have said. Her "I'm going to be more Kel than *everyone*" taunt had been the bane of his existence when he was little.

"Most of the instructions will be in the paperwork," Zehun said, "but the scenario is basically this. You're part of a Kel task force sent to deal with an insurrection at an isolated city. You've been given information that one of you is a crashhawk working with the insurrectionists, but the informant died before being able to finger the traitor. Good luck figuring out the situation."

A crashhawk: one of those rare Kel for whom the injection of formation instinct failed. Brezan's lip curled in distaste. He was looking forward to a chance to smash the traitor.

Wei wanted to ask a question, and received permission. "Sir, what is the win condition?"

"Let me put it this way," Zehun said. "You'll know immediately if you lose."

No one else had a question

"All right," Zehun said, "in you go."

The door opened. It was impossible to see what lay beyond it. Brezan saw in the shimmer-haze his signifier, the Ashhawk Sundered, with the headachy sensation that meant that everyone was seeing something different, probably their own signifiers. He was reminded that his older sister Miuzan had fetched up with a much more respectable Ashhawk Vigilant, although the last time they'd both been home, their oldest father had told Miuzan to shut up about a stupid personality test done up in pictures and go clean the family's staggering collection of antique guns. In retrospect, he should have gone into sound engineering like his oldest sister. Then he wouldn't be here sweating over a Shuos's sense of humor, which was bound to have teeth in it.

The line was moving. Brezan clenched his jaw in spite of himself when his turn came. Astonishingly, it didn't hurt to cross the threshold, although he had braced for it. For a scrabbling moment he couldn't tell where his hands and feet were in relation to the rest of his body. He knew better than to freeze, though. Who knew what happened to people who got stuck in the door. Then he rediscovered which way was up and which was down, and he was standing alone in the room.

The room had walls of glassy black brick, if anyone made bricks that gave the impression of great unfolding wings when you looked at them out of the corners of your eyes. Brezan shook himself out of gaping at the walls—careless, he ought to know better—and approached the desk. The desk and its accompanying chair were, to his relief, ordinary. He took up the envelope, which was of pale, creamy paper. The moment he touched it, he knew something was off. Who the hell wasted mulberry paper of this quality on a training exercise? On the occasions that the academy used actual paper instead of gridpaper, it favored the slightly waxy stuff made to be used with grease pencils.

The first item in the envelope was a map of the city and its garrison, both undoubtedly fictional. Of course, there were a lot of lonely cities on isolated moons in the hexarchate, so who knew.

The map had been copied out by hand by someone with an artist's sensitivity. The envelope also contained two more maps, thankfully just printouts, giving estimated dispositions and a terse rundown of critical installations. Any moment now he was going to blink and they would turn into treasure maps written in ghost ichor, like in his bunkmate's adventure stories.

The next set of papers talked unhelpfully about the insurrectionists—dubbed the Purples, for obscure reasons—and the Purples' first move. They had assassinated a visiting Andan potentate. He was probably not the only one thinking good riddance, although the Andan in question had to be fictitious, too. Kel-Andan relations had been strained for the past decade.

After that came the rules, including a reminder that a turn lasted six minutes. He was to keep the maps and other materials. There was a single sheet of blank paper. He could address his move to a single unit or to a fellow cadet, and it all had to fit on the sheet. The rules said nothing about how legible your handwriting had to be. Moves had to be stuffed back into the envelope before turn's end. The envelope would scan and convey the sheet's contents to the instructor. A bell would tell him when to open the envelope for the next move.

Then he reached the final instruction. It was on a smaller sheet, on even nicer paper, and it had been calligraphed beautifully. Brezan had taken the obligatory calligraphy lessons and was only passable with a brush, but he knew beauty when he saw it. For a moment the aesthetics distracted him from what the instruction said.

*You are the crashhawk,* the sheet informed him. It gave the rules by which he could give orders to Purple units and what he was allowed to do to the Kel. The rules were succinct, elegant, and brutal. He had no idea what roles had been assigned to the other cadets, but he could already see ways to maneuver to find out.

"Fuck you," Brezan said out loud, although it was certain that he was being monitored. He wasn't going to be a traitor.

He had gone through First Formation like all the other cadets after the initial injection of formation instinct, but he had barely passed. Not a' crashhawk, a formation-breaker, but the next best thing to one. Had Shuos fucking Zehun assigned him the role on purpose, as a test?

*I am going to beat you,* Brezan thought. But he had to do it by the rules. He wouldn't cheat the way a Shuos might. Tempting as it was.

Six minutes couldn't have elapsed already, assuming Zehun had told the truth about that. Brezan's hands were sweating. He knew what he needed to do. No sense in delaying.

If he was the crashhawk, then technically he was a Purple unit.

He picked up the pen and wrote, *Order for Rhezny Brezan, Purple unit. Assist any Kel unit that contacts you to the best of your ability.*

Brezan stuffed the paper in the envelope. There were ink stains on his thumb and forefinger. He had a fit of anxiety over whether he'd written neatly enough, but he refrained from reopening the envelope.

*There,* he thought savagely, and waited to be booted from the exercise.

It wasn't long in coming. Five moves in, a slip of paper informed him that he'd died in a Purple bombing of a university while directing a Kel squad working as riot police during a demonstration. Vidona work, except in the exercise there were not enough Vidona to be had.

There was a knock at the door. "Come out if you're done reading your fate," a voice said. It was Zehun. "You can bring the materials or leave them, your choice."

Some choice. Brezan gathered up the materials and exited through the door into a conference room. Shuos Zehun sat alone, peering at a terminal showing what looked like a cross between an inkblot and a traffic accident.

"I suppose I died first, sir?" Brezan said, regarding the room sullenly.

"No, a few got offed after the second move," Zehun said. "There's always somebody. You must be wondering why you're here."

Brezan stiffened, wishing for body armor.

The corners of Zehun's mouth lifted. "What, no guesses?"

"It's un-Kel to use a loophole the way I did," Brezan said. He couldn't wait until this conversation ended. "I expect to be reprimanded."

"Oh, we Shuos don't do anything like that," Zehun said. "If anyone botches a training scenario, we make them design the next one under supervision. Then we run it, and we make sure every cadet in the exercise knows who the scenario's author is."

Brezan was grateful that Kel Academy was run by Kel, who did things according to rulebooks, and not ferrets, ghosts, or Shuos. He looked at Zehun with their calm, dark face, wondering what response was expected of him.

"You're here because your solution caught my attention," Zehun said. "Kel spirit, un-Kel method. You remained loyal to your people by finessing the rules."

"It still got me killed, sir," Brezan said, although it wasn't in his best interests to remind Zehun.

"Because it's so surprising when a Kel fetches up dead?"

"I'm not a Kel yet, sir."

"Details, details," Zehun said. "Anyway, want to see how everyone is doing?" They tapped a command into the terminal.

The terminal's display flattened, then reappeared in three dimensions over the conference table. It didn't take any genius to realize that the Purples were slaughtering the cadets. Granted, the opponent was being run by a senior Shuos who hadn't played fair since they were six, but Brezan had hoped for a less one-sided showing. A couple of his classmates usually excelled at tactics. What had gone wrong?

"I have information you don't," Zehun said. "These are the roles I assigned." They tapped again.

Calligraphy in the same rhythmic hand imaged itself next to the purple-blotched map.

*You are the crashhawk.*

"Everyone got that," Zehun said.

Brezan started, then gripped the edge of the table. "I asked about the wrong rule," he said flatly. "If I'd asked about the right one, would you have answered, sir?"

"Doubtful," Zehun said, eyes crinkling. "I'm an excellent liar."

"I'm surprised we're not destroying ourselves faster." No one had thought to question the orders, typical Kel pathology. Since the cadets were isolated from each other, they had fallen easy prey to the trick.

Zehun zoomed in on a particularly disastrous part of the map. "Useful lesson, don't you think? I'll tell you something, though. Years ago at Shuos Academy Prime, we ran a similar training exercise. Infiltrators instead of Kel units doing counterinsurgency work they weren't trained for, but same basic idea. The cadets won that round."

"I'm sure it was a clever solution, sir," Brezan said in his most neutral voice. What had it involved? Invisible ink? Trained messenger squirrels? Poisoning the instructor?

"Don't look so unhappy," Zehun said, almost kindly. "They won because one of the cadets came up with the same solution you did. The difference was, he had figured out which scenario was being run ahead of time. We have different rules about cheating, after all. He briefed the other cadets. Everyone used the solution as their first move, and from that point on they worked as a team to defeat the instructor."

Given that the Shuos were notorious for backstabbing each other out of sheer reflex, Brezan was impressed in spite of himself.

"You didn't have that opportunity, exactly, not just because of Kel prejudices but because my security was going to be better than any hypothetical hacking attempts. But it does raise a question I've been asking myself. Why did you decide to become a Kel?"

"My family, sir," Brezan said after a damning pause.

"That's not an explanation. I have no doubt you'll do well, but frankly, you'll do well if you allow yourself *not* to be a typical Kel. Which is going to be tough in, sorry, a society of rigorous conformists."

Brezan fought down the urge to glare at Zehun, which probably wasn't helping his case.

"I wouldn't mind recruiting you for the Shuos," Zehun said with the air of someone who knew just how terrifying their words were. "We'd be able to use you better, to say nothing of training you to hide your reactions. I hope you stay out of jeng-zai games or you're going to lose a fortune. But I expect you're determined to do things your own way."

Moves were flashing at Zehun on a subdisplay. Zehun ignored them. Their voice became brisk. "Incidentally, you might be interested to know who that Shuos cadet was. His name was Vauhan Mikodez."

Hexarch Shuos fucking Mikodez. Cadet-killer Mikodez, the most brilliant Shuos who wasn't also a mass murderer. This was the last thing Brezan wanted to hear.

Zehun turned then to their slate. Brezan stared at those ungloved hands and swore to himself that he was going to be a boring, ordinary, unimaginative Kel like the ones in all the Kel jokes.

After Jedao's takeover, then, it was blackly hilarious to regain consciousness to an argument over whether or not he was a Kel.

"—anyone can put on black gloves and a uniform if they're willing to get shot over it," a high-pitched voice was saying. "Look, just wait until we figure out where the hell a working gene scanner is. I don't know what possessed Hachej to take the good one apart just because it made that weird intermittent gleeping noise."

Brezan attempted to blink or open his eyes. His eyelids might as well have been chained down. He had some understanding that he was still in the sleeper unit that they had stuffed him into on Jedao's orders. The prep had been rushed, not that he remembered much besides fragmentary cold and the sense that someone was playing music out of reach. Experimentally, he tried to move his hands. That didn't work either.

The darkness behind his eyelids was suffocating, and he almost missed what the second, much deeper voice was saying. "—rotten luck. A mutiny, really?"

"Or maybe it was Kel Command with some convoluted new plan. You know how it goes," said the first voice.

This reminded Brezan that he had a warning to convey to Kel Command, except his head was swimming and he couldn't seem to stop hyperventilating.

"—this one here. Honestly, if they were going to do prep this shoddy, why not just shoot the lot?"

Brezan wouldn't have minded the answer to that question himself. He screwed his eyelids open. Light filtered dimly into the sleeper, and he could see one of the medics as a reticulated blur. He attempted to knock, although he wasn't sure he succeeded in moving his arm.

After an interminable interval, the medic opened the sleeper. Brezan would have cringed from the sudden brightness if he'd had any coordination. Speaking was equally hopeless.

"Look at the insignia," the man said. "That's some kind of officer, isn't it?"

Whoever the medics were, they clearly weren't Kel.

"That's a lieutenant colonel, you dimwit." The owner of the first voice sounded like they wished their companion were something smarter, like a slime mold. "But any bored kid these days can steal and hack a Kel uniform."

Brezan opened his mouth to object to this. Instead, he went into a painful coughing fit. His mouth tasted like copper. After that, he couldn't tell whether he was breathing, which was so distracting that he didn't notice the servitors extracting him to a pallet.

"—clearly what happened," the first voice said. "I mean, there's no way they'd simply dump a crashhawk. The Kel shoot crashhawks who get caught at it. He's got to be some kind of impostor. Although I'm not sure why they wouldn't shoot an impostor, either. I get why they have to return the Nirai and so on to their own people, but this one's a mystery. The whole thing is so random. It must have been one hell of a mutiny. I would have bought tickets."

"It wasn't a fucking mutiny," Brezan said before he realized he had his voice back. It sounded as though someone had taken a rasp to it, but it was better than nothing.

The two medics peered down at him with great interest. The first speaker was small and pale and had deeply cynical eyes. The second was fidgeting with his stylus. "Yeah?" he said. "What did happen? No one so far has a coherent story."

Brezan regrouped enough to register that neither medic was dressed in faction colors of any sort. He couldn't blurt the truth out to civilians. Another coughing fit prevented him from answering in any case.

"He's going to be just as hysterical as the others," the first medic said. "Sedate him and let the servitors sort it out."

Between wheezes, Brezan said, "I'm Lieutenant Colonel Kel Brezan. I need to get to a secured terminal."

"He sounds like he means it," the second medic said as though Brezan weren't right there.

"What's he going to do to us, pull rank? I mean, doesn't it strike you as bizarre that we're 73% through decanting these losers and this is the only hawk—I don't mean officer, I mean any Kel at all—in the whole lot? Damned suspicious if you ask me."

Brezan was ready to throttle them both, but in his current condition that was a wretched idea. Fine. If the first medic had some conspiracy theory—not all that unreasonable, given the evidence—he might as well play to it.

"All right, you have me," he said, trying not to sound as irritated as he felt. "They booted me because I'm working for the Shuos. I suggest you let me report before I kill you with my belt buckle." Stupid threat, but he couldn't think of a better one.

The medics exchanged glances. "I told you it had to be something like that," the first medic said to the second, eyes alight. To Brezan: "You're in bad shape. I'll have to monitor you while you make the call."

They were fishing for gossip. Shit. If he tried to tell the truth to Kel Command, besides the security leak, the medic might jab him full of sedatives for being delusional.

It was hard to think clearly, and when he tried to examine things too closely, he started seeing double. But he had to convey his warning. "Send a message to Shuos Zehun with as much priority as you can pile on the thing, from Rhezny Brezan of the Swanknot swarm," he said. Zehun must ignore half the junk addressed to them, but there was a chance they might remember him from that cadet exercise years ago. How much was safe to reveal, though? Over a channel whose security he couldn't guarantee? "Say I came across someone else who knows how to beat Exercise Purple 53 and that I'd like to discuss it with them."

That might be too oblique, but Brezan had a desperate need to sink into sleep so the world would stop looking like someone had drowned it in undulant water.

Of all things, the first medic looked enthusiastic. The wretched message had to be an exciting change from their daily routine. "You rest, Shuos agent," the medic said. "I'll see to it that your message gets out."

The conversation continued after that, but Brezan was too busy slamming into unconsciousness to hear it.

# CHAPTER FOUR

HEXARCH SHUOS MIKODEZ'S latest hobby was container gardening. At the moment he was admiring the spectacularly ugly flower his green onion, which he had given a prominent place on his desk, had produced. He was also having tea with his younger brother, Vauhan Istradez. Istradez was less than thrilled by this development. It meant one more detail about Mikodez to memorize, to say nothing about all the notes on potting soils and drainage.

Mikodez was blessed with the Vauhan line's good looks, which had hardly required genetic tinkering. He was tall, and a little too thin from the drugs he took, with flawless dark skin, glossy black hair, and smiling eyes. He had once joked that he had joined the Shuos because the faction's red-and-gold uniform complemented his coloration. At that point his youngest parent threatened to hold Mikodez down and dye his hair turquoise.

Istradez looked identical to his brother, which was not a coincidence. Today, along with the duplicate of the hexarch's uniform, he also wore the same topaz earrings. While he'd been born Mikodez's younger sister, he had undergone modding to serve as Mikodez's double on the grounds that this was almost as good as Mikodez being able to be in two places at once, and the benefits were almost as good as the downsides.

"Thank you for picking such an ugly plant, by the way," Istradez was saying. He spoke effortlessly with his brother's inflections. "Couldn't you have chosen something nice to look at, like forsythias? Even Zehun agrees with me that that thing is an eyesore."

"Yes," Mikodez said, knowing that Istradez was carping not because he cared about the scenery but because he'd been cooped up in the Citadel of Eyes—the star fortress that served as Shuos Headquarters—for a month and twelve days. "But it made a nice garnish for the chicken ginseng soup, don't you agree?"

Istradez eyed the hapless green onion's snipped-off leaves. "I don't see how you can tell, since you hardly touched the soup." He tapped the cookie tray, which Mikodez had demolished.

"It's the price I pay for never sleeping," Mikodez said blandly. His assistant Zehun regularly tried, and failed, to get him to follow a healthier diet. Mikodez's usual retort was that the sweets hadn't killed him yet, so why mess with what was working?

"At least you're in a good mood today," Istradez said, and smiled Mikodez's own smile at him.

In his more honest moments, Mikodez admitted that he couldn't tell the difference, but then, that was the point. *You don't have to do that in here,* he sometimes thought of saying, except it wasn't true. Even in the Citadel of Eyes, even in this fucking room where they sat across each other like twins, he didn't dare. Sad truth: paranoia was his trade. He wouldn't have survived forty-two years as hexarch otherwise.

"I thought the chicken soup would be to your taste," Mikodez said. Kel fare, which Mikodez found dreadfully plain. But after long assignments eating the things that Mikodez himself was known to fancy, Istradez went through periods bingeing on bland fare. It was hardly something Mikodez would deny his favorite sibling.

Istradez fluttered his eyelashes at Mikodez. "It was. I'm just being difficult."

"Foxes preserve us."

"As if foxes have ever been known for their constructiveness."

"You wound me," Mikodez said. "Foxes are capable of being useful if you train them appropriately."

"But then they're not foxes anymore, only hounds."

It was a distinction peculiar to the Shuos. Most people outside the faction called all Shuos foxes. The Shuos themselves distinguished between foxes and hounds. The former were the flashy 'secret' agents you saw on the dramas; the latter were the bureaucrats, technicians, and analysts who got the real work done. (Mikodez, who had trained as an administrator with a side of analysis, had his own biases.)

"You say 'only' like it's a bad thing," Mikodez said. He reached for one of the candies in the bowl on the table between them, and bit through the hard, sugar-dusted shell into the even more sugary plum-flavored center. "One fox is smarter than one hound; a pack of hounds is another beast entirely. And I have always believed that a properly guided bureaucracy is deadlier than any bomb."

"I'll avoid making all the obvious jokes about paperwork." Istradez was avoiding the more obvious jokes about Shuos Jedao. "I'm so glad I don't have your job. It's bad enough being shot at without also being in charge of policy."

This wasn't strictly true. By necessity, Istradez sometimes had to make policy calls while in his role. But Mikodez always made sure that he was fully briefed and that he had a team of advisers to rely on, the way Mikodez himself relied on Zehun and his staff.

"Speaking of which, do you have another assignment for me *yet*?"

"It's not yet time," Mikodez said. "Getting bored of your surroundings? I swear, your attention span is almost as bad as mine these days. You should meet with Recreation and give them some suggestions."

"Sorry, you're only paying me to be you, not to also do Medical's job for them."

"Worth a—"

An alert gleeped at Mikodez. "High priority to the hexarch, Shuos Zehun," the grid said. "Zehun requests an immediate meeting with you, alone."

Istradez smiled ruefully at his brother. "I'll leave you to the latest national emergency," he said. "You know where I'll be if you break your mirror." He leaned in and embraced Mikodez, kissing him on the mouth. They were lovers on and off, something the rest of the family had regarded with bemusement. *At least they keep each other occupied,* had been their older mother's opinion. As the two had been crèche-born exactly a year apart, family superstition considered it inevitable that the two would be particularly close. Mikodez didn't have any particular interest in bedroom gyrations for their own sake, but he liked keeping Istradez happy.

Mikodez waved his brother off. "Yes, yes," he said, "enjoy your date, and feel free to put the gory details in an appendix so I can skip it at my leisure."

"I'll tell you *all* about it in person," Istradez said sweetly. "I'll look in on our nephew for you while we're at it."

"Appreciate it."

Istradez sauntered out with a very un-Mikodez-like gait.

Minutes after Istradez departed, Zehun requested entry into Mikodez's office. Mikodez let Zehun in. He was always surprised that they were just a bit shorter than he was, as if he was still that cadet who had been called out for a surprise evaluation. (Late growth spurt.) Zehun had wrapped themselves in a shawl of maroon wool. They were getting on in years, and claimed that Mikodez kept his workspaces too cold.

A cat wriggled in Zehun's arms: the orange tabby Jienji, who, like all of Zehun's cats, was named after a notorious Shuos assassin. Even someone who liked cats as much as Zehun did was unlikely to run out of names anytime soon. At the first opportunity, Jienji squirmed free and leapt up onto Mikodez's desk.

"Oh, no you don't," Mikodez said, scooping up the cat and depositing her back on the floor. He wasn't about to lose his green onion to a feline nuisance. "So, Zehun, what's so urgent that you had to interrupt my family time?" Ordinarily, after chatting with Istradez, the two of them would have gone to see their nephew afterward.

Zehun didn't smile in response to his cajoling tone. He immediately went alert. "You're going to love this," they said. "Hexarch Nirai Kujen is confirmed missing."

Mikodez didn't waste time gaping. He turned to his terminal and said, "Details."

Zehun gave him a file code. He brought it up. The report's contents were, if anything, worse than he expected.

In theory, six factions shared rule of the hexarchate. Three high factions: Rahal, which governed the high calendar and set the law; Andan, with their financiers, diplomats, and artisans; and Shuos, which specialized either in information operations or backstabbing, depending on whom you asked. Three low factions: Kel, known best for their military; Vidona, which handled education and the ceremonial torture that was fundamental to the calendar's remembrances; and Nirai, which consisted of the technicians and researchers.

'High' and 'low' were old designations, more a matter of tradition than actual power, which fluctuated according to resources, infighting, and the interplay between the current hexarchs. The Nirai were irregular in that their true hexarch, Kujen, was immortal. Or, more accurately, undead, a revenant who anchored himself to a living marionette to wield continued influence.

The Nirai's public face was False Hexarch Faian. Kujen had selected her for a combination of administrative ability and a certain narrow genius in calendrical mechanics. Mikodez had always suspected that Kujen had known from the outset that Faian would develop a mind of her own.

Mikodez had also suspected that Kujen figured it out very quickly when Faian and the Rahal hexarch conspired to develop an alternate immortality device, one less inimical to its users' sanity. Kujen called his the black cradle, and seemed perfectly happy with it, but Kujen was also psychotic. Most people who knew how the black cradle functioned considered it a glorified torture device.

Kujen had stood at an impasse with the other hexarchs for centuries. He would have disposed of the rest of them long ago if not for the fact that they did the tedious work of government so that he could focus on the research that was his passion. The hexarchs, especially Kel Tsoro, put up with this arrangement because Kujen offered ever-better mothdrives to convey people between the stars and ever deadlier weapons for Kel warmoths.

Now Kujen was gone, with no indication of his destination. This from a man who preferred to hole up with his projects for years at a time, allowing the false hexarch to attend official functions in his stead. Faian was apparently driving herself to distraction trying to determine what had become of Kujen and whether she should seize the opportunity to oust the man who had put her in power. Mikodez wished her luck. If he could find out as much, he would be surprised if Kujen didn't know and have countermeasures in place. It was unlikely that Kujen had survived nine centuries of parasitism without picking up some basic survival skills.

Jienji had gotten bored of the desk and was busy shedding orange hairs on Mikodez's carpet. Oh well, the carpet was largely self-cleaning, and the servitors would take care of anything the carpet didn't eat. In point of fact, one had already swooped in and was methodically following the cat's trail.

"You were right to bring this to me," Mikodez said to Zehun, "although I'm not sure what we can do beyond monitoring the situation. The part that bothers me the most is the timing. It can't be a coincidence."

"When is anything a coincidence?" Zehun said. "I can only assume that Kujen insisted on the new, especially excessive retrieval protocols for General Jedao and his anchor to make us think that he was especially invested in sticking around to look at the test results."

"He must have taken exception to the fact that Iruja and Faian are almost ready to seize immortality for themselves," Mikodez said. For all the hexarchs. He planned on opting out—as much as he enjoyed chatting with Kujen about everything from Kel-shopping to budget management, he wasn't convinced that immortality *improved* anyone's psyche—but they didn't need to know that.

"Even if he hasn't hacked your contingency files," Zehun said, "he has to have guessed that you're the one responsible for offing him on the others' behalf."

"Well, yes," Mikodez said. "It makes our conversations all the more entertaining. Still, he hates leaving his home station, and I don't like the thought that he's out of sight. Iruja will expect me to drag him back, if only to make sure that he won't drop some crazy new superweapon before she can have her shot at immortality." Never mind that Faian claimed that she could prevent aging, but a well-placed bullet would still kill you dead. Mikodez had long ago stopped expecting Iruja to be rational on the topic.

He frowned at the report. "Schedule a meeting with the relevant analysts in half an hour. That damn thing with the financial irregularities will have to wait until tomorrow morning."

"I was hoping you'd seen this coming."

"Since when do I anticipate things that you don't?"

Zehun gave him that *don't play innocent cadet* look he remembered so vividly from academy.

Mikodez grimaced. "I will be disappointed if you haven't adequately pillaged my worst-case scenario files on the matter. The question is, will Faian break the news to the other hexarchs first, or should I preempt her? I almost wish it were a bomb. Kujen might be a splendid weapons designer, but I'm pretty sure he doesn't have the requisite experience launching surprise attacks without getting caught."

"No, you have him confused with the other, much less dangerous sociopath in the hexarchate's arsenal," Zehun said, with the merest trace of sarcasm.

"Please," Mikodez said. "Which do you think is more dangerous, the mathematician our entire way of life is chained to, or a mere general with a gift for self-destruction?"

"As if 'dangerous' is something you can measure on a single axis," Zehun returned, then leaned down. The cat, with perfect foresight, sprang for a table, missed, and landed ungracefully on the nearby chair. Zehun was forced to hunt Jienji around the office until they cornered her by a shelf. (It was the same shelf every time. Jienji was stupid even for a cat. Mikodez had asked Zehun if this was a comment on the intelligence of Shuos assassins—a matter of particular interest, considering how they had met—and Zehun had smiled unhelpfully.)

"At least Jedao's out of the way," Mikodez said. "If Kujen has left the picture too, maybe I have a chance of convincing Kel Command to stop fielding Jedao. And then you'll be free to name that adorable black kitten after him."

"Not on your life," Zehun said. "Superstition is irrational, but a little irrationality is perfectly justified where that man is concerned."

Mikodez would have plenty of opportunity to reflect on those words in the days to come.

# CHAPTER FIVE

Khiruev could think of good reasons why General Jedao might not want to corral her after the latest staff meeting, none of which implied any trust on the general's part. Eleven days had elapsed since Jedao had claimed the swarm. Jedao had divided that time between meetings and drilling the swarm on unusual formations. For the past four days—lucky unlucky four, she couldn't help thinking, Kel superstition—Jedao had been inviting staff officers singly to his quarters for meetings that averaged an hour and thirty-seven minutes. Khiruev was reminded of the bedtime stories of ravenous fox spirits that Mother Allu had liked to tell. And it couldn't be a coincidence that Jedao had ordered composite wiring shut down. Khiruev's best guess was that he didn't want to risk the Kel conspiring against him over a channel he couldn't monitor, since Jedao's body was not wired for composite work. She couldn't blame Jedao for not wanting to risk the necessary operation.

But all the staff came out intact. Major Arvikoi, who looked terribly young even in a society where most people chose to look young, emerged with a disconcertingly pleased expression. Lieutenant Colonel Riozu's smile was downright predatory. And Colonel Stsan, who had been Khiruev's chief of staff, went around politely blank. She almost certainly knew that Khiruev had authored the assassination attempt.

Khiruev could trust no one, having helped get rid of the lone Kel who had stood up to Jedao. She reflected on this fact daily.

"Here we are," Jedao said as they approached his quarters, as if nothing was wrong. Two servitors awaited them inside, sleek metal and blinking lights, a birdform and a spiderform. If Khiruev hadn't known better, she would have said they looked sheepish. "Don't suppose you mind playing jeng-zai with a couple servitors, General?"

"I don't see why I should, sir," Khiruev said. She hadn't realized servitors had any interest in card games, but who knew what they did in their spare time?

Khiruev's eyes were caught by a painting imaged over the table. To be fair, it was hard to miss. Jedao took one look at her face and burst out laughing. "All right, General," he said. "Let's hear it."

Since she had been asked for candor—"It looks like a rainbow vomited over a fragmentation grenade."

"I like colors," Jedao said, and the soft yearning in his voice made Khiruev shudder inside. "There are so many of them. But I won't torture you with this any longer." He waved a hand and the visual flicked out. "Anyway, the servitors are very firm that they don't want me to give them money for proper betting, which is good because I'm flat broke." He smiled suddenly. "Imagine how Kel Command would react if I asked for my back pay."

Khiruev took the seat indicated, across from Jedao. The servitors blinked their lights at her, a friendly yellow-orange. She nodded at each in turn, feeling odd—but why not.

The spiderform passed out tokens. "Standard rules, sir?" Khiruev said. She knew better than to ask why they were wasting time on a card game. Jedao was sure to have some twisty Shuos lesson to convey. Khiruev sometimes thought that Kel-Shuos relations would improve if someone sat the Shuos down and taught them to make presentations with easy-to-read captions like normal people.

"Standard suits me fine," Jedao said. He looked at the servitors. "You two know the rules?"

Both servitors made subdued acquiescent noises.

"If I may ask, sir," Khiruev said, "why servitors?"

(Much later it occurred to her to wonder what the servitors themselves had made of the entire business.)

Jedao blinked. "Well, why not? We didn't have machine sentiences when I was alive. I asked them if they had pressing duties elsewhere, and they said no."

Servitors might not be human, but after centuries among the Kel, they must recognize commanding officer for 'or else' as well as anyone else. They turned out to be well-behaved jeng-zai opponents. The spiderform made no attempt to bluff. Khiruev couldn't tell for certain, but the birdform seemed to be using a pseudorandom generator to guide its raises. Jedao, on the other hand—

Khiruev shook her head as Jedao flipped over the latest card to reveal a Four of Roses. It was just as well that they were playing with tokens. "Sir," she said, "the odds of you drawing to an inner Splendor of Flowers *three times in a row* are—"

"—some number so tiny you can't inscribe it with a needle, yes," Jedao said, leaning back and smiling crookedly.

The birdform made a small cheeping sound. The spiderform drew its legs in.

"I'm glad somebody finally called me on it," Jedao said. "I was starting to wonder what the hell I'd have to do to get a Kel to crack. Anyway, bad form to cheat when no real money's involved. Not that that stopped some of my classmates. You have my apologies."

"That's not necessary, sir."

"Of course it's necessary."

"Then why do it?"

"Because," Jedao said, gathering all the cards up and squaring them in his hands, "we're not fighting Kel. We're fighting people whose only interest in Kel rules of engagement is to tie us in knots with them. They're going to cheat. Which means we have to cheat better."

Jedao laid the deck down. "I have a certain personal interest that you may not be aware of," he added. "It was long ago and no one has any reason to remember it, but my world-of-birth was conquered by the Hafn a long time ago, and it passed out of the heptarchate's control."

"I don't think I ever knew that," Khiruev said.

"As I said, no reason you should." Jedao's voice held no sentiment, but Khiruev wondered. "Anyway, if the records aren't lying about your victory at Wicker's End, you don't need me to explain the value of unconventional warfare to you."

"Surely you didn't miss the part where they reprimanded me for my actions," Khiruev said. She had taken a reduction to half-pay for four years, and had barely escaped a demotion.

"You won."

"My methods didn't sufficiently conform to Doctrine. Kel Command had every right to—"

Jedao laughed shortly. "Kel Command would rather pin medals on corpses than on people who survived by doing the sensible thing. Still, I'm crazy, so who am I to talk?"

"There's no point in saving the hexarchate's citizens if they're going to fall prey to heresy," Khiruev said carefully.

"Where in Doctrine does it say that it's wrong to teach people to organize themselves against an insurrection instead of waiting for the people in pretty uniforms to show up and do the hard work?"

"The isolation of Wicker's End made it an unusual case, sir. If there had been another way—"

"As they used to say at Shuos Academy, 'Counterfactuals never feed the children'. Which is hilarious coming from us, but never mind." Jedao slammed his hand on the table, causing some of the cards to slide down from the pile, and got up. "I've poked about the mothgrid and I've quizzed your staff heads and I've been putting in calls to the moth commanders and driving them to distraction, and now I'm asking you. Where the fuck is our intelligence on the Hafn?"

"Sir," Khiruev said, bracing herself, "we're telling you very little because very little is all we know."

"That's remarkably unfunny."

"It's the truth." She would have liked to produce a file for Jedao's delectation, if only to have Jedao's attention on an actual enemy. "All we have are old scraps of history—" She remembered what Jedao had revealed, but Jedao only shrugged. "—and a few notes that the Andan deigned to share from a cultural exchange several years back. If you read between the lines, the Andan are pretty baffled themselves."

"I saw those fascinating treatises on the Hafn reverence for the agrarian lifestyle, not to mention all the pastoral poetry. Fucking peculiar for spacefarers, not to mention their descriptions of milking machines are bizarre—who writes poetry about *milking machines?*—but I agree that the Andan are no help. Which is a shame, because they're the ones with the contact specialists and if they're stuck, we're not likely to do much better."

Khiruev tried to remember if she'd read anything about milking machines.

Her question must have been evident, because Jedao said deprecatingly, "The descriptions can't be anything else. My mother made me learn to milk cows the old-fashioned way even though the research facility had perfectly good machines for it. You would be surprised how many ridiculous footnotes there are in my life."

*This is not the strangest thing I have ever heard,* Khiruev told herself, not with a whole deal of conviction.

Jedao was grinning at her. "I should tell you more about my mother sometime. She was something of an eccentric. She liked to watch those dramas where giant things with tentacles invade from gate-space and the only survivors are stalwart country people with big guns and loyal, delicious farm animals. I'm hoping the Hafn aren't like my mother. That would be disturbing."

Too bad the servitors seemed disinclined to rescue them from this line of thought. "Sir," Khiruev said, "if you think any of us are withholding vital information from you, then you may as well shoot us all. We've told you all we know."

"You've got to get over that Kel thing where you offer to commit suicide just to make a point," Jedao said, but he wasn't looking at Khiruev. "The Hafn are technically human, so I wish I could assume some basic motivations, but 'human' covers a lot of ground. What I do know is that their attack on the Fortress of Scattered Needles almost succeeded. We want to blow them up before they unleash the next awful thing, but to do that we need more information. Which means getting them to talk to us."

"Crescendo 2," Khiruev said flatly. "Crescendo 3. Knifer."

Khiruev had seen a great deal of war in her career. It wasn't a secret that the hexarchate was perennially one rebellion away from sputtering into pieces. Even heretics' weapons, however, tended to fall into well-understood classifications. Between Rahal regulations and the work of the Vidona, heresies rarely had the opportunity to metastasize into truly degenerate forms.

The Hafn had an entire society based on an alien calendar, and their worlds must be likewise alien. The Andan had spoken of delegates who cared a great deal about etiquette, but the delegates had been aristocrats, and who knew what the rest of the culture looked like.

The first time Khiruev had seen the videos of the attack on Crescendo 3, she had thought they must have been concocted by a dramatist. Towers upon towers of crystal, great jagged spires and spiraling steps held up only by glittering webs. Vast singing storms and rains that left charred spatter marks on rocks. Red-blue trees that writhed upright, then collapsed, crawling into frenzies with their fellows. The analysts had concluded that the tree-things with their ugly chambered hearts had once been people. Which begged the question: did non-aristocratic Hafn resemble people as they existed in the hexarchate? While the Shuos and Andan went in for body-modding, even they acknowledged certain boundaries.

"I watched everything I could drag out of the mothgrid, yes," Jedao said.

"People who launch unprovoked attacks without making any attempt to communicate are unlikely to be interested in negotiation."

Jedao was pacing. There was an odd hitch in his stride, as though he hadn't gotten used to the length of his legs. Entirely possible, given the circumstances. "I agree with you there. But guns talk. Moths talk. Everything has something to say if you know how to—"

"Command center to General Jedao," Communications' voice said from the terminal. "Hafn contact. Commander Janaia requests your presence."

"General Khiruev and I are on our way," Jedao said. "You two," he said to the servitors, "thanks for humoring me. See you some other time if we all live?"

It must be nice not to have to respond to jokes like that. Khiruev followed Jedao out. The servitors blinked respectfully, then began cleaning up the cards that had been spilled.

The cindermoth had rearranged its corridors so their route to the command center was short and direct. Khiruev disliked the accompanying sense of vertigo. In her dreams she was always convinced that the floors would gnash open to reveal the teeth of eager gears, but Jedao gave no sign of discomfort.

Commander Janaia saluted them on behalf of the command center's crew. "Hafn outriders of some sort, sir. Scoutmoth 7 is staying at maximum scan. Formants are a mess. Hard to tell whether they've spotted us."

"All moths on combat alert," Jedao said. Red light washed from all the terminal boundaries. He took the command chair and studied the scan readings while the webbing secured him. Khiruev took her place to the general's right, feeling redundant.

"Oh, don't look like that," Jedao murmured. "I have every intention of making use of you."

How serious was he? "If you want information from the Hafn," Khiruev said, "now's the time. It's not any secret to them that they have an enemy swarm incoming. Assume they've spotted us and probe them for their capabilities."

"Agreed," Jedao said, half-smiling. "Communications, get me Commander Kavinte."

That was the commander of *Singe the Hour*, lead bannermoth of Tactical Group Five. "I should warn you that she's argumentative, sir," Khiruev said.

"Yes, I saw that in her profile."

"*Singe the Hour* responding, sir," Communications said, and forwarded the call to Jedao's terminal.

Commander Kavinte had an overly pretty face, all symmetry and graceful nuance, until you got to her eyes. The intimation of casual ruthlessness in her eyes reminded Khiruev of Jedao, now that she thought about it. "General," Kavinte said.

"We have no idea how many Hafn are out there because their mothdrives fuck up our readings," Jedao said with cheerful bluntness, "and for that matter who knows the range on their scan, either. Want to help me figure it out?"

"Sir," Kavinte said crushingly, "you're our general. You don't have to put it to a vote. Just give the order already before the Hafn notice we're dithering and call their friends."

"Oh, I never put anything to votes," Jedao said, "but your brain is a resource and I intend to use it as one. You want to prove to me how good Tactical Five is at Lexicon Secondary?"

Lexicon Primary referred to the formations that the Kel were benchmarked against in drill, and which they used in battle. Lexicon Secondary mostly contained formations that were of historical interest, or that were trotted out for colorful effects in parades and during celebrations. Kavinte had a standing interest in obscure formations. Khiruev had been guessing that that was why Jedao had singled her out.

"We're Kel, sir," Kavinte said. "We'll execute whatever you have in mind." There was more than a hint of challenge in her words.

"Good to know." Jedao adjusted some figures on his tactical subdisplay, considered them, then looked up. "Tactical Five, assume formation Swallow Braves the Thorns. Once you're in formation, approach the long axis of the outrider spindle exactly head-on until you're at extreme scan range. Scoutmoth 7 will withdraw to—" He named the coordinates. "All other tactical groups, assume grand formation Harrower Hawk with forward central null and the command moth as primary pivot. Moth commanders acknowledge."

The terminal lit up with acknowledgments in neat amber columns corresponding to the tactical groups and scoutmoth flights. Commander Janaia's eyes were alight. She turned to her executive officer and began giving orders.

Khiruev wished she felt as sanguine. She was certain that Swallow Braves the Thorns was a test for the Hafn. It was a flashy parade formation from Lexicon Secondary, but if you didn't see the disposition of the rear elements, it could be mistaken for Wave-Breaker from Lexicon Primary.

Tactical Five reported that it had reached extreme scan range and that the Hafn moths' formants didn't look any clearer, but the Hafn didn't seem to be reacting, either.

Jedao tapped out a calculation. "General Jedao to Tactical Five. I want you to maintain formation and advance at 19% of your secondary drive. Alert me the moment you get a reaction, and also report your distance from their leading elements at that time." To Khiruev, he said, "Odd that they're just maintaining their distance. Can they not see Tactical Five, or is it a trap?"

Khiruev had her mind on something else. She had a clear view of Jedao's calculation. One of the systems of modulo congruences that Jedao had asked the grid to solve for him was something that any first-year cadet should have been able to do in his head, by inspection. The general couldn't—but now wasn't the time to ask. Khiruev looked away and told herself that her unease was baseless, but she was honestly surprised that Jedao was weak in abstract algebra.

"Commander Janaia," Jedao was saying, "I've forwarded you a series of waypoints. Advance, but keep Tactical Five within eighteen minutes of the swarm at current acceleration at all times."

"Sir," Janaia said, and gave the necessary orders to Navigation.

"Incoming from Commander Kavinte," Communications said.

"Put her on," Jedao said.

"General," Kavinte said, "we got a reaction when our leading element tripped past forty-nine Hafn ayyan." She gave the hexarchate distance conversion. A databurst accompanied the transmission with further details. "No attack still, but look at this—"

The close-up scan data showed the Hafn outrider positions relative to each other, stretched into the shape of a curving dish with Tactical Five's axis of advance pointed straight at its center. Khiruev wasn't a scan specialist, but she could tell that the formants were better defined than before, giving them a better idea of the individual outriders' locations. Just as interestingly, Tactical Five had intercepted signals from a number of outriders. It didn't take much triangulation to deduce the region of space those signals were aimed at.

"Forward transmissions to Intelligence," Jedao said, "although I don't expect fast results. Commander Kavinte, I have another formation for you. Try Every Mirror Is a Flatterer and approach the outrider dish's focal point."

"Sir," Khiruev said, "that will allow the Hafn units to focus fire on Tactical Five. If they have real guns"—Hafn units had respectable invariant weaponry, last she'd checked—"it could get ugly."

"I understand the concern," Jedao said, "but here's the thing. You notice how they've been moving?" He played back some of the observations. "I don't think those outriders are human. I think they're geese."

Khiruev caught Janaia's eye when Jedao returned his attention to the scan record. *Is he out of his mind?* Janaia mouthed. Khiruev could only shrug.

"You have your orders, Commander Kavinte," Jedao said. "If I'm right, the geese will let down their guard when they see the configuration. You'll have ample opportunity to blast holes in them. I'm as much for that as the next soldier, but capture a few intact if you can. Give our engineers something to take apart."

"Acknowledged, sir," Kavinte said in a tone of dour resignation.

Jedao cocked his head at Khiruev. "You're convinced I've lost it."

Or getting rid of a commander who annoyed him, but Khiruev couldn't express that out loud. "If it's not a trap, then I don't know what it is," Khiruev said. "Although it's possible that their scan has short range because it's operating in hostile calendrical terrain." The Hafn weapons were all fired at short range in previous engagements, but they'd discussed this before and she didn't need to remind Jedao of it now. "Perhaps they're attempting to deceive us as to their capabilities." She kept an eye on Tactical Five's movements in the subdisplay. "No one with two brain cells is going to fall for Every Mirror."

YOON HA LEE

Every Mirror Was a Flatterer was an illusion generator specifically affecting the swarm's scan formants rather than direct visuals, which meant it wasn't even useful for impressing civilians. The Kel never bothered with it in battle because the illusion only was visible from such a short distance that any enemy with halfway decent scan would already have spotted you first. No one would mistake them for Hafn at this point.

"Didn't say the outriders were stupid," Jedao said. "I said they were geese. Excellent sentries, geese, for what they are. Oh, don't look at me like that. You've clearly never had to beat off an offended gander with a stick." He leaned forward. "There we go, that's the last pivot moving into place."

The Hafn outriders, faced with what were apparently more Hafn outriders, began adjusting themselves to form a greater—Khiruev couldn't help thinking of it as a flock.

"It makes no sense, sir," Janaia said. "Why use rather stupid drones for your advance warning system?"

Tactical Five knew an advantageous situation when it met one. The subdisplays were suddenly crowded with reports of fire. Impossible to tell whether Jedao's request for captive outriders would be honored amid that mess of hellfire and kinetics.

"The Andan made no mention of Hafn servitors," Khiruev said, "only pre-sentients. Maybe the Hafn lag in that area of technology."

"If they could get into the Fortress of Scattered Needles," Jedao said, "stealing some invariant technology wouldn't have been difficult." His mouth curled sardonically. "For all we know, there's some peculiar cultural prejudice at work."

Commander Kavinte issued terse periodic reports. Janaia's eyes had a decidedly longing look at being left out of the shooting. Her executive officer's expression was unreadable, but that was Muris for you. He could be counted on to be businesslike about everything. The operation had so overwhelmed the outriders that Khiruev expected something with long, serrated teeth to materialize behind her shoulder as a way of ensuring cosmic justice.

69

Eventually Kavinte said, "Sir, most of the outriders blew themselves up rather than be captured. We'll send you our reports when we have a better analysis. But the scoutmoths managed to retrieve one of them in the confusion before they figured out what was up."

"Good work," Jedao said. "My compliments to your people. Crack the thing open, but use every precaution. For all we know, there are death spores or haunts inside."

Kavinte laughed at that. "All the more fun for us."

"Pull back Tactical Five and fill our null for us while you're at it. Just in case the Hafn main swarm is much faster or nearer than we reckoned on."

"Of course, sir."

Three hours and twelve minutes passed before the next call. "General Jedao," Communications said, "a message from Commander Kavinte. Your eyes only."

"This can't be good," Jedao said, although his tone was more annoyed than worried. "I'll hear it in my quarters. General Khiruev, let me know if anything exciting happens."

"Sir," Khiruev said.

Exactly one hour after that, Jedao called Khiruev in the command center. "Come see me," Jedao said. That was all.

"I hope it's not death spores," Janaia remarked.

"I don't think anyone could keep death spores secret from the whole swarm," Khiruev said. "I'd better see what the issue is."

"Better you than me," Janaia said. They shared a chuckle. Muris exuded disapproval, ever so faintly.

The door to Jedao's quarters opened at Khiruev's approach. Jedao stood with his hands clasped behind his back, staring at something angled so Khiruev couldn't yet see it in any detail. Khiruev saluted and waited.

"At ease," Jedao said. "You know, I always hated it when my commanding officers told me to be frank. But hell, I'm going to ask you to be frank.

"I have spent most of an unnaturally long life doing horrible things to people. Assassination. Torture. Treason. Mass murder. It doesn't sound like anything when you pare it down to such a short list, but those were real people. It was—I did real harm. Which is the long way of saying that my personal metric for horrible things is not calibrated right. I need you to tell me how bad this thing is that I'm going to show you."

Khiruev considered this, then decided that honesty wouldn't cost her anything. "Sir," she said, "I'm a high officer. I got to my present rank by doing many of the same things you did."

"Just humor me, General. I'd like to believe that someone in this damn swarm is a better human being than I am."

"Then show me whatever it is."

Jedao gestured for Khiruev to come around and stand next to him. The video had been taken by the engineering team on *Singe the Hour*. Jedao fast-forwarded past the decontamination precautions to the part where the team breached the casket. There wasn't a better word for the object. On the lid of the casket shone a golden plaque. It was engraved with an archaic form of the Hafn script, which Khiruev recognized but couldn't read. The border featured an elaborate design of unfamiliar flowers, fruit, and feathers entwined in knotwork. When she looked more closely, she could see odd cavorting insects worked into the design, and what looked suspiciously like cat's cradle figures.

The technicians in their suits had worked out how to remove the lid from the casket. It came off with a whisper of blue-violet vapor. Someone had appended a note saying that they were still studying the gas, but preliminary results said it was not toxic. It took Khiruev a long moment to understand what she saw within the casket. Jedao kept silent.

The first thing Khiruev noticed was the care with which the components—she struggled for a better term—had been laid out. Beautiful long-necked birds of a type she had never seen before, their curling crests arranged just so. Flowers whose petals moved as though they were breathing. Filaments of gold and crystal threading in and out of flesh and stem, eventually winding their way to the circuit-inscribed walls of the casket.

In the center of the casket was a boy, or a very young man. At various junctures, his flesh was pale and translucent. A complicated circulatory system grew out of the translucent regions and joined him to the birds, the flowers, the filaments. The veins were also translucent, and an endless procession of small red spiders crawled through them.

In one hand he clutched a faded purple cord tied into a loop. It was exactly the right length for cat's cradle, and it was the only item in the casket that didn't look expensively contrived.

Jedao paused playback. "They got medics in there," he said, almost in a normal voice, "but the boy—the whole whatever-it-is—went into cardiac arrest or the equivalent. They shoved him into a jury-rigged sleeper unit, but I don't think there's any hope."

Khiruev had vaguely assumed that Jedao was one of those people who disliked children since she'd never heard any mention in the histories that Jedao had fathered any. The shadow of anguish in Jedao's eyes made her reconsider.

Jedao was looking into the distance. "Tell me, General, what the fuck are we fighting? What's so wrong with the Hafn calendar that this is their best way of making masses of scouts?"

"If they're like us," Khiruev said, "they're locked into their existing calendar for exotic technologies they can't bear to give up, and that means they're stuck with some bloody awful options in other areas."

"Tell me you didn't know about this," Jedao said.

"I didn't know about this," Khiruev said. "It must be a new development permitting this invasion, or an old one they were hiding from us as a trump card. But it wouldn't have made a difference. We're Kel. We fight where we're told. I understood that you already wanted to fight the Hafn."

Jedao turned the video off. "Khiruev—"

The sudden use of her name made her wary.

"—if I ever think it's all right to do that to someone, shoot me. I don't care how rational I make it sound. I have a history of sounding very rational, and we all know where that ends."

Astonishing: Jedao sounded sincere. "I hope the boy's death was quick, sir," Khiruev said.

"Someday I would like to live in a world where people can aspire to something better than caskets and being sewn up with birds and quick deaths."

"If you want to fight for that, the swarm is yours."

"I'd say that I'll try not to abuse the privilege," Jedao said, "but we're past that point."

Khiruev stood with him after that, wondering when she had started to see Jedao as a human being and not a death sentence.

# CHAPTER SIX

TWENTY-TWO DAYS LATER, after the third flock of Hafn outriders, everyone figured out that they weren't just geese, as Jedao insisted on calling them. They were expendable geese. The Hafn had scattered them strategically in the region surrounding the Fortress of Spinshot Coins, specifically screening the approaches where the high calendar's terrain gradient was strongest. The numbers were staggering. Jedao ordered more of them retrieved. There were more caskets, which came in different flavors. The children in each set had their own sewn-up symbionts, everything from vines to mosses, scorpions to pale salamanders. No one knew what the variation symbolized.

The most troubling aspect, beyond the caskets' contents, was the matter of logistics. Engineering was banging their heads against the problem of the outriders' propulsion systems. As far as anyone could tell, they only possessed invariant drives, suitable solely for in-system maneuvering. This implied that they had been launched from some sort of carrier. Yet as far as the Kel could determine, the Hafn swarm didn't possess nearly the capacity for this many geese—and who knew how many more in reserve—unless they had developed a form of variable layout an order of magnitude better than what the hexarchate employed.

Khiruev recommended leaving most of the flocks intact. "Kel Command would want them cleared," she said to Jedao as they reviewed the scoutmoths' latest updates from the command center, "but you are in the enviable position of not having to care what Kel Command wants."

"Well, that's not true," Jedao said, "since Kel Command understandably wants my head on a pointy stick. But yes. How would you like to fuck up the Hafn, General?"

There were only a few reasons why a man who always won his battles would be soliciting Khiruev's input. Given that Jedao was a Shuos, Khiruev could guess which one applied. After all, she was already a game piece in a contest whose stakes she saw but dimly, through a veil of gunsmoke and fractures.

"Detach a single tactical group," Khiruev said. "Commander Gherion of *Stormlash Glory* with Two." Gherion was good at autonomous action, and Jedao's nod suggested that he approved the choice. "Set them loose to shoot up some geese—" She plotted locations: a listening post, a Nirai research facility, a habitat with a significant Andan presence. "So far the evidence is that the Hafn especially dislike planets, but we don't know when that will change." Naturally, there were no systems near enough the Fortress's nexus to use as bait.

Jedao passed on the orders unaltered to Commander Gherion. Khiruev could tell that Commander Janaia didn't like this development, but she had no pretext for an objection, and in these matters she was a very proper Kel. Gherion, for his part, was torn between enthusiasm at getting into action sooner rather than later, and the conviction that Jedao was sending him off to die. But he acknowledged his orders promptly.

"Six remaining tactical groups for maximum flexibility in grand formations, is that it?" Jedao said. "What else do you see?"

Khiruev felt like a cadet all over again, disconcerting at the age of seventy-two, and reminded herself that Jedao had to have been a cadet himself at some point in his existence. "The outrider concentrations nearer the Fortress are spaced inconveniently for some of the larger grand formations," Khiruev said, "most notably the ones that invoke area effects. But it would be a small matter to clear the flocks at need."

"If that's what you recommend—"

"What I recommend, sir, is travel formation River Snake." Janaia was giving Khiruev an irritated look. She ignored Janaia. River Snake had negligible combat effects, and moth commanders naturally hated it. It was best for getting efficiently from one place to another in situations like this: a glorified column.

"River Snake it is," Jedao said, and gave the very movement orders that Khiruev had suggested on the map. "I don't care how good Hafn manufacturing capacity is, if you can call it that. They can't have an infinite supply of geese, whatever their method of transporting them here, or we'd be neck-deep in them."

Khiruev had reservations about the reliability of intuition when it came to people so alien that they made scouts out of child-bird-insect-flower composites. The thought must have shown on her face. Jedao raised an eyebrow, but didn't comment.

The long hours of their circuitous approach to the Fortress passed by like trickling water. Jedao occasionally asked for Khiruev's opinions and implemented them directly as orders. The Kel in the command center had noticed what was going on. They sneaked glances at Khiruev with the same deadened anxiety that they had formerly reserved for Jedao. They knew, even if they hadn't guessed the true story behind the assassination attempt, that Khiruev could not offer them any protection from the traitor.

The Hafn were expecting to fight Khiruev, so they would fight Khiruev. Right up until the point when Jedao intervened. Too much to hope that Hafn intelligence was inept, after all.

When Jedao didn't require her presence, Khiruev distracted herself by organizing her boxes of gadgets. Surprisingly, Jedao hadn't ordered the lot vaporized. On the other hand, Khiruev was hung up on whether gears should be sorted by radius or number of teeth instead of manufacturing more assassination drones, so maybe Jedao was on to something.

Khiruev had given up sorting and was reading the rambling memoirs of a courtesan when the advance scouts made scan contact with the main Hafn swarm. The courtesan's escapades evaporated out of her head on the way to the command center. Red lights everywhere, low voices. Jedao was already seated, posture perfect, looking damnably relaxed.

After taking her place next to Jedao, Khiruev saw that they would reach combat distance in about four hours if everyone continued moving along the projected trajectories, which was unlikely.

"All right, General," Jedao said, very clearly. "For your purposes, I'm not here. Deal with the Hafn."

Khiruev shivered, but an order was an order.

"Communications," she said. "Message for Commandant Mazeret of the Fortress of Spinshot Coins. Inform her that we're about to engage the Hafn swarm and that she may see some fireworks." She hesitated over how much detail to give her, then left it at that. Best not to risk fouling up Jedao's plans. Still, no reason not to take advantage of the Fortress's defenses if they could convince the Hafn to get within range during the encounter.

"Fortress acknowledges," Communications said after a while. And after that: "Commander Gherion reports that Tactical Two is in formation to minimize scan shadow and is headed for the rendezvous point as ordered."

Not that anyone was positive that Hafn scan worked like the hexarchate's, but the precaution couldn't hurt. Khiruev adjusted the scale on the tactical display, then rotated it while she considered the available geometries. Jedao watched, his face tranquil.

"Order for the swarm," Khiruev said. "All units assume formation Thunder of Horses." She tapped out the pivot assignments. "Tactical Three and Four, you'll be tripping the nearby outriders." She had almost said 'geese.' "Destroy them at your discretion." No sense chancing that these outriders had defenses the earlier ones hadn't employed.

The moths, represented on the tactical display by flattened gold wedges, began moving into position relative to each other. She could hear Janaia giving orders to Navigation: it was customary for the command moth to hold the formation's primary pivot. Muris was speaking tersely to Doctrine.

The Hafn showed up as smudges, location probability clouds. Scan reported that the scouts, which had pulled back, still had trouble getting coherent formant readings from the foreign mothdrives. Reports from the Eyespike swarm, which had been destroyed delaying the Hafn, had put the enemy at eighty Lilacs, roughly equivalent to bannermoths in size and armament, and ten Magnolias, larger than the Lilacs although not as formidable as cindermoths. Forty-eight years ago, Kel Command had switched to flowers for designating enemy moth types after a spat with the Andan. Sometimes Khiruev wondered about Kel Command's priorities.

Even after a few decades of doing this, Khiruev found the apparent slowness of the moths' motion aggravating. It made her want to reach through the display to the moths themselves and yank them into place. She recognized the ugliness of this impulse. No doubt something like it was how Kel Command had come up with formation instinct in the first place.

She missed, too, the thrumming ease of working as part of a composite. Being the general in charge of a composite was not quite as thrummingly easeful, but it had afforded her the illusion of subsuming herself in a single will, which was the point. Jedao would have seen even that illusion as threatening. Besides, if the calendricals tilted in the Hafn's favor suddenly, composite technology would fail. Every Kel with half a brain knew that compositing was required mainly for reasons of internal discipline between missions, rather than being a useful coordinating tool in battle against heretics.

"Doctrine," Khiruev said, "what do you have for calendrical fluctuations?"

To the side, Jedao was looking at Doctrine measurements of calendrical values and laboriously putting together a query for the grid. Was this some issue of getting accustomed to a modern interface? Khiruev itched to show him how, but she had other matters to attend to, and it would cause Jedao to lose face. A puzzle for later.

"Effects must be localized, sir," Doctrine said in a subdued voice. "We should be seeing the effects of the heretic calendar's intrusion and there's still nothing."

This was consistent with earlier reports, but worrying nonetheless. Khiruev would have felt better if they had some idea how the Hafn could use their exotics in hexarchate space without skewing calendrical terrain. The fact that they had an interest in the Fortress suggested that this ability came at a price and that they'd rather be on home terrain, or at least, flipping the Fortress would enable them to project their native calendar in the surrounding space and deny the hexarchate that advantage. A pity that Jedao had ditched all their Nirai, who would have had the best shot at cracking the mystery.

The Hafn had spotted the Kel. Their moths wheeled to form what looked like a three-petaled flower. Each petal elongated in its approach to the Kel's Thunder of Horses.

"All units banner the Swanknot," Khiruev said flatly.

"Sir—" Janaia protested.

Khiruev narrowed her eyes at Janaia. Jedao had moved on to some other system of congruences and was ignoring the two of them. "The order stands," Khiruev said.

She wasn't the swarm's ranking officer anymore. Jedao was. The banner defied Kel protocol. But Jedao had said that he wasn't here. Khiruev's emblem was the only one available, and it would have been worse not to banner.

The Hafn seemed to understand what bannering meant now. In the first engagement, according to the records, they hadn't responded, and the Kel had—disastrously—taken it as an insult. Here, the Magnolias transmitted the Hafn government's emblem. It was an antiquated-looking shield with a plain gold band across the top and a hectic tangled mass of vines, fruits, and insects beneath the band, overlaid for good measure by gold curlicues. Atrocious graphic design if it had originated anywhere in the hexarchate, but looking at the tangles, Khiruev thought of the boy with the cat's cradle string whom they had retrieved from the outrider. Her hands clenched.

"The Hafn are twenty-one minutes out of dire cannon range," Weapons said.

"We're about to find out about their long-range weapons," Khiruev said.

The Hafn approach slowed. The three petals had become three concave dishes facing the Kel. The dishes had to be their equivalent of formations. The geese had used it, and the Hafn swarm had used it against General Kel Chrenka's Four-Eyed Shrike swarm. Unlike a formation, however, it seemed to have no consistent set of effects.

Khiruev made the mistake of glancing over to check what Jedao was up to. Jedao was smiling sardonically as he played jeng-zai against a grid opponent. He didn't meet Khiruev's eyes, but this was clearly mad tactical prodigy for 'pay attention to your job, fledge.'

"Hafn maintaining distance, sir," Scan said.

At this point, a few things were clear. First, the Hafn were staying almost exactly sixty-four of their minutes out of range of the formation's kinetic lances, which were currently inactive and which were controlled by modulating three component formations. Second, the fact that the Hafn general could read Kel formations meant they could potentially be manipulated that way. Third, said general had read the particular placements of the component formations, suggesting that the main swarm might have longer-range scan than the geese, whose virtue must be in their numbers and expendability.

The problem with the kinetic lances was that they telegraphed themselves. Their sideways raking motion could only be hurried along so much by precise execution of the subformations. Certainly the lances would maul what they hit, and they had better range than anything the Hafn had yet to reveal, or the Kel swarm would have seen incoming fire already. But Khiruev looked at those waiting dish-shapes and sensed that the other side wasn't worried yet. She also remembered that the Hafn had annihilated Kel swarms already, by means yet unclear, and they had successfully infiltrated a nexus fortress before. It wouldn't do to get overconfident.

Time to test how well the Hafn had studied up on the Kel. "General Khiruev to all units, maneuvers on my mark," she said, setting up trajectories on the subdisplays. "Give me Wildfire Over the Aerie with Pivots One, Two, and Three refused as shown." She passed the

Pivot One parameters to Janaia separately. "Do not, repeat, do not fill Pivots Two or Three without my direct order. Mark."

Janaia blanched, but she only gave Khiruev one questioning look before she executed her part of the order. Communications reported that four moth commanders wished to speak to Khiruev. She turned them all down.

Wildfire Over the Aerie was both a grand formation and a suicide formation, a rare combination. It had only been tested once in battle. Two hundred ninety-eight years ago, General Kel Dessenet had used it to blow up an invading swarm. Kel Command had put it on the proscribed list because, as a side-effect, it filled the affected region of space with long-lasting calendrical dead zones, some of which still existed today. In any case, the question was, how well did the Hafn know formation mechanics?

Out of the corner of her eye, she glimpsed Jedao pausing at his card game to note the development. Nice that he was paying attention.

As it turned out, the Hafn didn't do research by halves. Partway into the Kel's formation modulation—messier than she would have liked, but it wasn't as if they'd had any reason to drill this—the Hafn reacted by peeling away. They headed straight for the Fortress.

"They think we're serious," Janaia said, blackly amused. "Terrible trade just based on the numbers, don't you think?"

"Not like they haven't figured out that we're Kel," Khiruev said. "For all they know, we haven't met our daily suicide quota. Communications, advise Commandant Mazeret of the situation. All units maintain formation in present state and pursue."

She knew what the Hafn were thinking. If they retreated to the Fortress's environs, the Kel wouldn't dare activate Wildfire because it would take out the Fortress as well. This was true as far as it went. None of the Fortress's defenses would protect it from that particular conflagration.

The scoutmoths alerted her that unfamiliar formants were showing up in the Hafn swarm's wake, small and rapid.

"Change course," Khiruev said, and indicated the correction. It would slow them down reaching the Fortress, which was a problem, but getting obliterated would also be a problem. There were too many of the things to sweep with the scatterguns in a reasonable amount of time. Best to go around.

"Sir," Communications said. "Six bannermoths in Tactical Three are taking some kind of corrosion damage."

Khiruev frowned at the display and put in another course correction.

Communications spoke again: "Tactical reports that bannermoths *Scratching Shadows*, *Beyond the Ocean*, *Two Books Bound Together*, and *Snakeskin Drum* have been lost, sir." After a few moments, she added the other two.

"General Khiruev to Commander Nazhan," Khiruev said. Tactical Three's commander. "What the hell happened out there?"

"Those spiderfucking web-looking Hafn things *effloresced* at us, sir," Nazhan said thinly. "One moment." Voices in the background; red washing over his face. "Engineering thinks their weapon did something to cause the moths' biotech innards to rupture. Best readings suggest that everything's messed up with parasites or an infection of some kind"—he didn't mention Kel fungal canisters, although everyone was thinking of them—"but we can't very well send a decontamination team in there right now."

The swarm detoured farther. The Hafn were well ahead of them now. Jedao still gave no sign that he was about to take over.

"The Fortress has activated phantom terrain," Scan said.

The terrain manifested as dizzying blue swirls on the tactical displays, with inclusions that resembled waving strands of kelp, like a captive mantle of ocean. The Fortress's defenses were beginning to fire on the Hafn, with shifts in the terrain coordinated to permit the guns to speak through momentary windows.

"Forty-six minutes until we're in dire cannon range," Weapons said.

Muris looked up. "Telescoping formation to bring them into range, sir?" he asked.

"Not yet," Khiruev said. For someone otherwise so conservative, Muris was fixated on that class of formation. Most of the telescoping formations had serious drawbacks. "They'll see the formation and zip out of range anyway."

The Hafn had to have some way of dealing with phantom terrain. Its existence was no secret. While certain details of the technology were classified, that wouldn't necessarily have stopped Hafn intelligence. And whatever they did know might not bother people who had alien weapons to begin with.

Khiruev considered sacrificing an arm to make the swarm go faster. It was just as well that that wouldn't work. She would have run out of arms as a much younger woman.

Jedao had thrashed the grid opponent at jeng-zai and had moved on to pattern-stones. Khiruev almost felt sorry for the grid. It looked like Jedao was using a subdisplay to write up a tactical critique at the same time. Wonderful.

Twenty-six minutes out of dire cannon range, Scan gave Khiruev the bad news. "Sir," she said, "look at this."

The Hafn were now arrayed in a rough dumbbell shape, except each end was an outward-facing concave dish. One dish faced the Fortress. The other was swinging around toward the Kel. The bar was bending so the dishes stayed connected. Khiruev doubted it meant anything good for them.

Sensors had sent her the forward scouts' close-range readings of the terrain gradient, along with Doctrine's notes on what it should have looked like under normal operating conditions. Phantom terrain behaved like a dense but manipulable fluid. As a moth commander, Khiruev had participated in a couple training exercises that demonstrated its properties. Her tactical group commander had described it as 'space mud that's out to get you.' (All right, she had been a little coarser than that.) Khiruev remembered how aggravating it had been to have her moth's motion slowed to a crawl, to be unable to rely on scan to behave properly.

The Hafn weren't afraid of phantom terrain because, incredibly, their weapons had some way of degrading it in a fashion that the hexarchate's own exotics couldn't. Scan showed the terrain developing further inclusions in the shapes of fantastic trees, ferns, vines all tangled together. Something tickled at the back of Khiruev's mind, a warning, but she couldn't figure out how the threat worked—

The Hafn attack hit the entirety of Tactical Four as they swung around. They were still too far away for the dire cannons to respond. Khiruev's display hemorrhaged red and orange light. "All units withdraw out of range now!" she said sharply. "That's a direct order."

The dying moths sent databursts almost as one. Crystal fibers. A cavalcade of pale-lipped flowers. The cries of flightless birds pecking their way up through the floors. Walls grown over with mouths breathing wetly.

Jedao was still jotting something down in that critique.

*We're doomed,* Khiruev thought.

Flowers and birds. The plant-like shapes growing in the fluid. The Hafn were degrading the phantom terrain. That bizarre not-formation of theirs looked like they were *funneling* something from one dish to the other. And then she knew.

"Communications," Khiruev said, "urgent order for Commandant fucking Mazeret. Tell her to turn off the fucking terrain. All of it. Now."

The Kel were in disarray due to the retreat, although at least they weren't losing moths in all directions anymore, and they were attempting to form up again.

"Call request from Commandant Mazeret," Communications said, very neutrally.

"What part of 'order' doesn't she understand?" Khiruev snapped, although in her position Khiruev would have done the same thing. "Tell her that the Hafn can draw power for long-range attacks *from the phantom terrain itself*. Her Doctrine analysts should get on the problem. That's all she needs to know."

From a Kel standpoint, phantom terrain was just another exotic technology. But they had every indication that the Hafn had a peculiar reverence for worlds—for planets and their ecosystems. Enough that their scouts were sewn to the representations of faraway homeworlds. From a Hafn standpoint, phantom terrain was an unclaimed world, and they had some way of linking themselves to it, sourcing power from it the way the Kel sourced power from formations and loyalty. Khiruev scrawled this observation down and passed it on to Doctrine.

The tactical display's blue swirls and ripples went black as the phantom terrain shut off.

"Good," Jedao said, "you figured it out with a couple minutes to spare."

Jedao had passed a document over to Khiruev's terminal with the READ IMMEDIATELY indicator. Thankfully, it was short. Jedao had figured out the Hafn trick three minutes before Khiruev had. The timestamp was unmistakable.

He hadn't said a word.

Khiruev contemplated shooting Jedao.

Jedao wasn't paying any attention to Khiruev, which was just as well, because Khiruev's vision was shorting out, predictable effect of formation instinct. "This is General Jedao," he said. "All units continue to reform by tactical group. Banner the Deuce of Gears. Engineering, I understand we're carrying twelve threshold winnowers. Lob the lot at the Hafn and put them into dispersed orbits around the Fortress at the conventional 90% limit of phantom terrain, will you?"

Captain-engineer Miugo called the command center. "General," he said, "we don't have enough personnel to safely crew all the winnowers." *Because we ditched the Nirai,* he didn't say. "Recommend we step down to eight."

"Yes, I should have figured," Jedao said. "My apologies for being unclear. Launch all twelve uncrewed. I understand they're fitted with remote triggers for emergencies?"

The temperature in the command center plummeted.

Threshold winnowers were indiscriminately destructive of lives, although they did not damage nonliving objects. They were also finicky to operate, hence Miugo's concern. Jedao had notoriously used them at the massacre at Hellspin Fortress.

"We'll waste time if we disable them first," Jedao said, as if he hadn't picked up on the sudden tension. "But if the Hafn are any good, they'll spot the winnowers on scan, and they'll know about the remote option. They'll even know that I'm willing to pull the trigger, even if Kel Command wouldn't be." The corner of his mouth pulled up. "And this will go much better if they believe it's me, not some cocked-up desperate impostor."

The command center fell horribly quiet as they waited for Engineering to comply. Khiruev recognized, from the clipped tone of Miugo's status reports and their frequency, that he was upset, and was hoping that Jedao would change his mind. She couldn't imagine that Jedao himself was unaware of Miugo's reaction. But Jedao did not seem inclined to change his mind.

The *Hierarchy of Feasts* launched the winnowers. Khiruev could tell to the second when the Hafn figured out what they were. The Hafn abandoned their funnel and began a rapid, well-organized withdrawal.

Jedao had put together movement orders for Tactical One, which had been the first to regain a semblance of its assigned formation. "Ah, there you are," he said to himself.

Commander Gherion had arrived with Tactical Two. "Commander," Jedao said, "do me a favor and bite the Hafn's heels, will you?" He accompanied this with a transmission of more specific instructions, which Khiruev studied to calm herself. "You should be safe from that really nasty attack you just saw." He didn't elaborate. "Modulate formation as you deem fit."

"We're on it, sir," Gherion said. The tactical group narrowed and reshaped into Black Lens, which telescoped distance. Its effects were short-lived and it damaged the moths' drives, which made it risky, but the dire cannon barrage swooped out and raked a cluster of fleeing Hafn. Tactical Two slowed immediately afterward and modulated into a shield formation.

More orders. Jedao was giving them in a steady stream, with brief pauses to adjust to the situation as it developed. Tactical One joined the pursuit. The Hafn continued to retreat. They left shattered moths behind them, and more of the web-mines, but not so many as before.

When the final Hafn units were out of the effective range of phantom terrain, not to mention the Fortress's guns, the Fortress switched the terrain back on. Khiruev stiffened. She could guess what was going through Commandant Mazeret's mind. Tactical Two and most of Tactical One were clear, but the rest of Jedao's swarm was suddenly mired.

"Tactical Three through Seven, get your asses out of there," Jedao said. "Abandon formation if necessary. That's a direct order. You don't want to be stuck here if the Hafn rally. I'd better have a chat with the commandant. Communications, raise her for me."

The cindermoth, with its more powerful drive, was having reasonable luck getting clear of the terrain. Khiruev noted with relief that the plant-growths had dissipated. However, the other, smaller moths were less fortunate. Their tactical groups had dissolved out of formation, and probably would have even without Jedao's permission.

Commandant Mazeret was a sturdy, pasty-skinned woman who held her shoulders stiffly. Khiruev could see the image from where she was sitting. Her expression was obstinate. "I don't recognize you," she said curtly, "but I assume from the Deuce of Gears that you're claiming to be General Jedao." Insultingly, she used the inanimate form of the second person pronoun. The high language had two, inanimate and animate, although it might be argued that the former applied to a general who was listed as a part of the Kel Arsenal—a weapon—rather than as a human officer.

"That's me," Jedao said, smiling his tilted smile at her, "had to take the first body available." He couldn't be unaware of the effect that this statement had on the crew, even if it wasn't anything that they didn't already know. "Commandant, I appreciate that the Fortress feels naked without any clothes on, but would you mind terribly switching the terrain off again, or clearing us a path? You're interfering with our pursuit of the enemy."

"Damn straight I mind," Mazeret said, biting every word off. "This is General Khiruev's swarm, not yours." Touching that she was using the high language's present/future tense. "Kel Command would have informed me if you'd been deployed."

"Commandant," Jedao said, no longer genial, "snuff the fucking defenses already. We can kill the Hafn, but not if we can't catch the snakefuckers."

"Then let General Khiruev do it."

Jedao drummed his fingers, then said to Communications, "Recall Tactical One and Two. I don't want them to get into trouble ahead of the main swarm." To Mazeret: "I'm awaiting an explanation, fledge."

Mazeret's eyes slitted. "I see two threats here. One of them is already in flight. I'm dealing with the bigger predator."

Jedao glowered at her, then laughed. "All right," he said, "I suppose I deserved that. Hell of a way to let an enemy slink off, though. I don't envy you the paperwork you're going to have to submit to Kel Command."

Khiruev looked at him in astonishment, although Mazeret's obstinacy should have surprised her more.

"I advise you to surrender the swarm to its appointed general before you dig yourself in any further," Mazeret said.

"Seriously, you're not afraid of standing in my way?"

"You might be able to sieve the Fortress," Mazeret said, not sounding any less hostile, "but I guarantee we will make you work for it. I know my duty."

"You could be a crashhawk," Jedao said, scrutinizing her, "but I don't think that's it. Tell me, Commandant, how long have you had Kel Command fooled?"

"Still digging," Mazeret said icily.

"I'm going to have to send the Shuos hexarch an apology with candies for making one of his operatives blow their cover," Jedao said. "What do you suppose his favorite flavor is?"

It was a preposterous accusation, but Khiruev had to wonder. Some Shuos infiltrators, especially the ones who could change their signifiers at will, were supposedly that good. Mazeret's subordinates might be wondering, too. If she wasn't a Shuos who had faked her way through a Kel career, or replaced the real Mazeret, the fact that she was defying Jedao meant that she was a crashhawk. Kel

Command would never tolerate a crashhawk in charge of a nexus fortress.

Crashhawks weren't automatically disloyal. Take Lieutenant Colonel Brezan, for instance. (Khiruev was almost certain that Brezan hadn't known himself until Jedao showed up.) The only difference between an obedient crashhawk and an ordinary Kel was that the crashhawk had a choice, and Kel Command had better things to do than test the levels of formation instinct in personnel all the time, mostly for reasons of cost. Even so, crashhawks rarely survived to any position of prominence.

The *Hierarchy of Feasts* had worked free of the phantom terrain and was now orbiting the Fortress at a respectful distance from its guns' effective range. The other Kel moths straggled after it, resuming formation as they came clear. The Fortress hadn't opened fire on the bannermoths and scoutmoths. Probably even a crashhawk Shuos agent had second thoughts about a contest of guns with the Immolation Fox. Besides, it must have occurred to her that Jedao could have rigged the winnowers to go off if something happened to him.

"Are we going to fight about this?" Mazeret said.

"No," Jedao said after a telling pause. "I came to fight the Hafn. You're in the way, but you're not my target."

"Kel Command should have destroyed you after Hellspin Fortress."

Khiruev had to admire the commandant for speaking so bluntly to somebody with Jedao's kill count.

"It's not an uncommon opinion," Jedao said.

The Hafn were now out of scan range.

"I'll have to get them another way," Jedao said. "Good luck with Kel Command." He signed off before Mazeret could answer.

Khiruev looked at him and couldn't help thinking that for someone who had lost an opportunity to smash nails into the enemy, Jedao's smile was worryingly pleased.

# CHAPTER SEVEN

ACCORDING TO HIS augment, Mikodez had two minutes before the conference started. He had watered his green onion in the morning, just when his schedule said to, and was resisting the temptation to do so again because he didn't want to kill it. He was also resisting the temptation, in advance, to suggest container gardening as a hobby for the Kel hexarch, even if it would be a good idea for Tsoro to learn to relax. Even—especially—given the latest news.

Forty-two years ago, Mikodez had become the youngest Shuos hexarch in almost three centuries. No one had taken him seriously then. Shuos hexarchs regularly backstabbed their way to the top. As a result, few of them lasted longer than a decade, if that. Two decades if they were particularly good. People took Mikodez more seriously now, but they still disregarded his advice on the salutary effects of a few well-chosen hobbies. Their loss, really.

"Incoming call on Line 6, top priority," the grid informed him.

Mikodez leaned back and smiled. "Put it through."

The other five hexarchs' faces appeared in the subdisplays with their emblems below them, as if he hadn't learned those as a toddler. Rahal with its scrywolf above Nirai's voidmoth, Andan's kniferose above Vidona's stingray, Shuos's ninefox with its staring tails above Kel's ashhawk.

Rahal Iruja spoke first, her right by tradition. She was a dark woman with coiled gray hair cropped short, and would have been beautiful if not for the severity of her eyes, the absolute lack of humor. He liked that about her. "We all know what this is about," she said. "General Shuos Jedao survived an assassination attempt that Andan, Vidona, and I were assured he couldn't escape."

"I can't believe you let him run off with a swarm," Vidona Psa, a large, pale man with incongruous hunched shoulders, said to Kel Tsoro. Psa wasn't bothering to conceal his scorn. "Jedao walked right in and your general let him pull rank."

Tsoro's scarred face was impassive. The scars were an affectation, but no more so than the face: Tsoro spoke for the entire hivemind that formed Kel Command. "We don't make a practice of stripping the dead of rank, Vidona," she said. "He served after his own fashion. We had no reason to believe that he could survive the carrion bomb."

Psa harrumphed. "Well, he clearly did."

"Jedao has been discharged, but it's anyone's guess as to whether any of the Kel in that swarm will be allowed to receive the bulletin we've been transmitting. We tend to doubt it."

"What I don't understand is how he got off the *Unspoken Law*," Nirai Faian said. She had been promoted from false hexarch to actual hexarch in an emergency meeting after convincing everyone that Nirai Kujen had, in fact, vanished, but she had trouble getting the others to give her the respect due her rank. She was a quiet woman with wavy shoulder-length hair framing a face like fine ivory, usually mild. There was no mildness in it now. "It's unfortunate that he convinced Cheris to let him possess her. We should have had the cindermoth destroyed with invariant explosives as well to get rid of her."

"Yes," Andan Shandal Yeng said sourly. She was fidgeting with her sapphire rings, all of which were the exact sultry blue of her satin dress with its embroidered seed pearls and smoke-colored diamonds. "Except we only have so many cindermoths, and the Kel keep complaining they can't afford to build another six." Not least because of certain Andan monopolies; Tsoro's face remained impassive. "I'm honestly surprised that Kujen was lying about wanting to retrieve that anchor for dissection or mathematical foreplay or whatever it is that he does."

Faian wasn't interested in discussing Kujen's extracurricular activities. "All the hoppers and transports on the *Unspoken Law* were accounted for, so how—?"

"I checked the analysis," Mikodez said. "Wasn't there that suggestion that one might have gone astray? Looked like it was hard to piece everything together, given all the damage."

"That's a dissent among my analysts," Faian said. "And even so, either Cheris or Jedao would have had to repair the hopper and fly it all the way to the Swanknot swarm, or rendezvous with a conspirator. Neither is known for being an engineer. Too much doesn't add up."

"We can figure that out later," Shandal Yeng said. "We have to deal with the reality that we have a vengeful madman loose with a Kel swarm at his disposal."

"Jedao won't have taken the *assassination attempt* personally," Mikodez said. "Appeals to his extravagant death wish and all that. He'll be pissed that we blew up his *soldiers*. Delicious, really."

About 8,000 soldiers, in point of fact. Nirai Kujen had wanted to be sure of catching Jedao with one of the few weapons that could kill him, and had insisted on blowing up the swarm, too, for good measure. Mikodez hadn't pushed back too hard because by then he had acknowledged that Jedao's victory at the Fortress of Scattered Needles had dangerous repercussions. You had to admire Jedao for coming out ahead. Upgrading to a bigger swarm, even.

Psa scowled. Like many drawn to the Vidona, he was obsessed with rules and as flexible as a pane of glass. Most people in the hexarchate feared the Vidona, who served as a police force against low-level heresy, but Mikodez found it boringly easy to finesse his way around Psa. "I'm sorry, Mikodez," Psa said, "but you do remember Hellspin Fortress?"

Mikodez suppressed a sigh. At least Kujen, who did remember, wasn't around to make snide remarks. Actually, Mikodez wouldn't have minded the snide remarks. It was just bad form to show it.

"Let's not retread ancient history," Shandal Yeng said. "We still have to decide what to do about Jedao and his submissive army of

Kel." She must be rattled. No matter how much she disliked Tsoro, she was generally better at tact than this. Unless—hmm. Maybe that wasn't Shandal Yeng after all. Mikodez paid closer attention to her face.

"We have to concede that he put a good scare into the main Hafn force," Tsoro said dryly.

"If your agent hadn't intervened, Mikodez," Iruja said, "we'd have one less threat operating in hexarchate space."

"I stand by Mazeret's decision," Mikodez said. "She had her choice of targets and she knows as well as everyone how dangerous Jedao is. For love of fox and hound, he had threshold winnowers *in orbit* around the Fortress with who knows what modifications. We're lucky we didn't have a replay of Hellspin."

"We need to discuss why you felt the need to plant a spy in our fortress," Tsoro said, her tone wintry. "As the *commandant*. What were you trying to prove, Shuos?"

Mikodez gave her an equally chilly smile. "Yes, about that," he said. "Let's talk extradition."

"Need I remind you that we're facing a madman who has the unsavory habit of winning all his battles?" Shandal Yeng said. "This is hardly the time—"

"This is exactly the time," Mikodez said. "I'm not in the habit of letting loyal agents rot in detention. Talk to me, Tsoro."

"We can deal with this later," Tsoro said.

"We're hashing this out now. You're going to have a fun time chasing Jedao and the Hafn when your listening posts start going deaf."

"*Shuos*—"

"Look, I get that individual Kel are as expendable as tinder and you can use formation instinct to yank them in whatever direction your strategy requires, but I don't have that option. If I operated that way, no one would want to work for me anymore. Mazeret belongs to me, Tsoro. Your quarrel's with me, not the agent. Give."

Iruja looked faintly irritated by the exchange. "Is it worth throwing a tantrum over one agent, Mikodez? Unless you're planning on mass-assassinating the Hafn all by yourself."

"Oh, I don't intend to try anything of the sort," Mikodez said respectfully. "But I can take down a scary number of Kel listening posts in an amount of time you're happier not knowing, and the agent is important to me."

"Tsoro," Iruja said after a considering moment, "I realize that, like everyone here at some point, you're fantasizing about running Mikodez through with a bamboo pole for his latest caprice. But let him have the agent as a favor to me. The Rahal will reckon with him later."

"As you desire, Rahal," Tsoro said, inclining her head.

Mikodez decided it would be better not to smirk at Tsoro. Why couldn't one of the Kel with a sense of humor be hexarch? "Tsoro's earlier remark brings up an interesting possibility," he said. "If Jedao's so hell-bent on exchanging bullets with the Hafn, why not let him wear himself out that way?"

"What an intriguing proposal from someone who recently agreed to have the man offed," Psa said.

"I'm adaptable?" Mikodez suggested.

"We could get lucky," Shandal Yeng said. "Maybe the Hafn will kill him for us."

Tsoro coughed. When Shandal Yeng raised her eyebrows, Tsoro said, "We'd be left trying to defeat the general who defeated Jedao. This is unlikely to be a strategic improvement."

"If there's no way of retrieving the swarm," Iruja said, "we may be stuck with that."

"This is the curious part," Faian said. "If General Khiruev's stray staff officer is to be believed, the Kel on the command moth authenticated off the wrong thing, to the extent authentication's even possible with a revenant. All of Jedao's anchors inherited his movement patterns and, eventually, his accent, thanks to bleed-through. Of course, the Kel are used to reading each other that way." As part of formation instinct, a certain baseline body language was imprinted on cadets. "Neither of those proves anything, however. A sufficiently good actor or infiltrator could fake them. It's the apparent inheritance of Jedao's skills, too, that's more worrisome."

"Nobody's ever scrounged up any evidence that Captain Cheris had the least scrap of acting ability," Tsoro said. "We made some inquiries with former instructors and classmates. She couldn't even shed her low language accent until she was a second-year cadet."

"I wish I knew why anyone would capitulate to Jedao to the point of giving up her own existence," Faian said.

Tsoro shrugged. "No one else could hear what he said to her, so we'll never know for sure. The fact that she responded to being nudged toward Jedao in the first place is suggestive, but for all that, she was determined to be a good Kel. She joined up despite family resistance."

"No ties there, then," Psa said, thoughtful.

"Not entirely true," Tsoro said. "She wrote to her parents regularly, and exchanged the occasional letter with some of her old classmates."

"Well, then," Psa said. "We could apply pressure from that direction. We already have Cheris's parents under surveillance, as a precautionary measure. We could detain them and let Jedao know, see if we get a reaction."

"That isn't a good idea," Faian said, her brow creasing. "If any part of Cheris is alive in there, she's not remotely psychologically stable."

"Faian," Iruja said, "that may give us the opening we need."

"It may drive her even crazier."

Tsoro was thinking about something else. "If we're applying pressure anyway," she said, "we might as well turn it up all the way. Cheris used to write to her parents in Mwen-dal, which is only spoken by her mother's people, the Mwennin. There are scattered communities of them on the second-largest continent of Bonepyre, and there are so few of them that they're extinct by any reasonable standard. We could round them up and threaten to wipe them out if the swarm isn't restored to Kel control. Vidona, you'll find a use for them sooner or later, won't you? It's too bad they're so obscure that a massacre of them would be no use as a calendrical attack. In any case, if Cheris is indeed alive in there, it might give her the incentive she needs to resist Jedao's influence."

"I don't see that anything's lost by trying it," Shandal Yeng said. "I for one would feel better if we didn't have a rogue swarm rampaging through the hexarchate." How many times had she said that already? Or, more accurately, had her protocol program said that to cover for the side conversation she was having, and which Mikodez was recording for review after the meeting now that he'd picked it up? "If this works, then fine."

Iruja turned a hand palm-up. "I have no objections either."

"I'll make it a priority," Psa said.

Nirai Faian looked intensely frustrated, but said nothing. She knew when she'd lost, and she was the least powerful hexarch.

"No," Mikodez said. "That's as in absolutely not, we're not doing this."

Shandal Yeng pulled off one of her rings and slammed it down out of sight. "I wasn't expecting you to be the one with the sudden attack of humanitarianism."

"This is me, remember?" Mikodez said. "I could care less about that. I don't object to atrocities because of ethics, which we've never taught at Shuos Academy anyway." She rolled her eyes at the old joke. "I object to atrocities because they're terrible policy. It may be the case that no one cares about the Mwennin or whatever they call themselves, but if we had so tight a hold over the populace as we like to advertise, we wouldn't perennially be dealing with heretic brushfires. Make threats against Cheris's own parents, fine. But it's unwise to be indiscriminate about these things. We'll just be creating a new group of heretics, however small."

Iruja steepled her hands and sighed. For a moment Mikodez was reminded of her age: 126 years, old enough to feel every clock's ticking heart. "Are you going to throw a fit over this, too?"

As if that would work. Iruja had intervened earlier because she wanted to get the meeting moving and the agent had already been exposed. (Mikodez bet that there would be a lot of extra personnel screening in the next months, though.) On this issue, however, only Faian agreed with Mikodez, and she wasn't a credible ally. "It's not worth it to me," he said.

She laughed without humor. "Good to know. Not that I'm interested in putting this to some kind of vote, but this endeavor will go better if we coordinate."

"I do appreciate that, Iruja."

"Well." Iruja exhaled slowly. "We're going to send Jedao an ultimatum. The important thing is recovering the swarm. The precedent can't be allowed to stand. What do you suppose the odds are that General Khiruev is still alive?"

"It doesn't matter," Tsoro said. "Khiruev's already been compromised even if she survived. We don't want her in charge of that swarm after Jedao's had a chance to mess with her mind."

"I assume you have an alternate."

"We've recalled General Kel Inesser from the High Glass border. If Jedao can be persuaded to turn himself in, she's more than capable of handling the Hafn."

Inesser, the Kel's senior general, and one of their most respected. Mikodez snorted. "Isn't that the woman you've been holding at arm's length for the last two decades?" He'd met her a few times at official functions: a woman vainglorious about her hair, with a disarming fondness for talking about her cross-stitch projects. It hadn't escaped him how adroit she was at manipulating conversations while pretending to be a typical blunt Kel. "I peeked at some of the evaluations. I'm surprised you wouldn't rather assimilate her already."

Tsoro gave him a look. "Inesser may be one of the best strategists we've seen in two hundred years, and she's an excellent logistician, but we'd prefer that she not end as another Jedao." She didn't elaborate on the evaluation, which she'd discussed with Mikodez, reluctantly, in the past. The textbook Kel opinion of Jedao was that Jedao's battlefield successes added up to him never thinking far into the future, since he always assumed he could fight his way out of whatever fix he landed in, instead of asking whether the battle was worth fighting in the first place. Mikodez had preferred the much more succinct words of a Kel instructor who had spoken off the record: "Brilliant tactician, shit strategist." Presumably Kel Command was supposed to think about the big picture for him.

"I realize that you're saddled with almost four centuries of condensed prejudices," Mikodez said, "but don't you think it's time to stop letting Jedao dictate everything you do? You'll turn Inesser into an entirely different kind of enemy at this rate."

"Shuos," Tsoro said, "when you feel the need to pull stunts like assassinating your own cadets, we don't send you memos telling you how to run your faction."

Mikodez fiddled with one of the leaves of his green onion. "Fine," he said, "but never say I didn't give you good advice."

"If you two are quite finished," Iruja said without raising her voice. "Mikodez, I'll need you to monitor the situation. Don't intervene as long as Jedao makes no play against us, and especially leave him alone if he's fighting the Hafn."

"I have a useful number of shadowmoths moving into position," Mikodez said. "Trust me, their commanders have as little interest in getting into a firefight with Jedao as I do."

Psa grunted. "I've seen you at the firing range, Mikodez. I'd give you even odds."

"Very flattering," Mikodez said demurely, "but while Jedao has demonstrated that his solution to a man with a gun is shoot it out of his hand—the kind of idiot stunt I tell my operatives to avoid attempting— *my* solution is not to be in the same damn room to begin with."

Andan Shandal Yeng was smiling. "I'm glad we have a course of action, regardless."

Mikodez kept his expression noncommittal. He'd caught Kel Tsoro's eyes flickering several times. She and Shandal Yeng had definitely been holding that side conversation. Both used kinesics and protocol programs to smooth things like that, but Mikodez had bypassed them ages ago. Both hexarchs would have been better served lying the old-fashioned way, not that he was about to inform them.

"One last thing," Iruja said. "Faian, how's progress on the immortality process?"

"Kujen's notes are a mess," Faian said. She meant the ones she had stolen from him, on the grounds that she would rather not accidentally recreate something as unappetizing as the black cradle that had once caged Jedao. It wasn't so much that Kujen was disorganized—quite the contrary. The man was meticulous about everything. The reports that he sent to the other hexarchs, before he'd vanished, were flawlessly organized and proofread, models of clarity. But his private notes, on projects that he didn't mean to share with anyone else, took a great deal of decoding because he recorded them in a personal shorthand and his genius made it difficult (so Faian had explained once) to follow the odd jagged leaps of intuition.

Faian went over some of the recent technical difficulties, addressing herself mostly to Iruja, who had the background necessary to follow her. Mikodez simply recorded the details to run by his staff later. Watching everyone else tie themselves up in knots about the prospect of living forever had its entertainment value, not that he meant to let on.

The conference wrapped up after that. Soon Mikodez was left alone with his green onion. It was clear that the other hexarchs were going to make hash of their attempts to control Jedao. Mikodez supposed that no one had been thinking clearly after Hellspin Fortress, but the long-dead Kel and Shuos heptarchs had a lot to answer for. In what universe was keeping an insane undead general as an attack dog a good idea?

On the other hand, wrangling hexarchs had grown tedious. The fact that Jedao had slipped his leash gave Mikodez a new challenge. While he went over the transcript of Tsoro and Shandal Yeng's conversation, he called up a set of files he had poached from Nirai Kujen, back when. He'd be reviewing those next.

# CHAPTER EIGHT

BREZAN CAME AWAKE in snatches, like a puzzle assembling itself out of a junk heap. "What?" he said, then grimaced at the furry, sour, metallic taste of his mouth. Gradually, he took in his surroundings. Walls of warm gray, with a single abstract painting where he could see it without lifting his head. After that, it occurred to him that he was lying on a pallet, hooked up to a standard medical unit. Spider restraints held him fast.

All right, this was an improvement over the fucking sleeper unit that Jedao had had him stuffed in. "Hello?" Brezan called out. It emerged as a croak. He tried again, without much better results.

Around this time he discovered that someone had shut down his augment, which either implied a very good technician or someone with the overrides or both. Bad news, either way. He assumed there was a local grid, but even if it wouldn't talk to him, it would have been nice to be able to access his internal chronometer and basic diagnostics. How long had he been out of it? And where the hell was he, anyway?

Brezan waited some more. Infuriatingly, despite the lingering pain when he breathed, he developed an itch behind his left knee. Which he couldn't reach to scratch.

Just when he decided to have a go at the spider restraints anyway, a very pale, smiling woman with an elaborate shimmering tattoo over her right cheek came in. She wore a purple half-jacket over lavender clothes liberally decorated with aquamarine tassels, and silver jewelry chimed from her throat and wrists. The fluttering slits at her neck suggested that she had gills. The only useful hint as to her identity was the clashing gold pin over her left breast: the Shuos eye.

"Hello there," she said. "Give me a moment and I'll get you out of those."

"I need to talk to Kel Command, please," Brezan said, remembering his mission.

"We need to process you first."

There it was: the hint of Shuos obdurateness despite the flowery getup. Still, as a staff officer, Brezan had his share of experience bowing to bureaucratic prerequisites. Shuos procedures tended to be well enforced. Best to go along.

After she'd unhooked him from the medical unit, a process that hurt more than he wanted to admit, the woman said, "Glass of water?"

"Water closet is more like it."

"One moment. I still have to unspider you." She didn't do anything visible, but he bet *she* had a working augment. "You can move now." She pointed to a door. "Don't take too long if you can help it?" Her smile again, winsome. "Someone wants to talk to you."

Both her friendly demeanor and her vagueness about 'someone' made Brezan suspicious. Unfortunately, there wasn't much he could do but comply. He braced himself and sat up. Pain, yes, but not the slicing pain associated with spider restraints, which he'd experienced years ago as a cadet, in a demonstration.

"Thank you," Brezan said, and managed not to stumble on the way.

After he emerged, appalled anew at the shakiness of his legs, the woman held out a glass of water. Wordlessly, he accepted it and drained it in several desperate gulps. It didn't taste of anything in particular, but if they'd wanted to drug or poison him, they could have done so at any point before he regained consciousness.

"All right," the woman said when he had finished. "Just set that down, a servitor will clear it later. Ready?"

Brezan nodded.

"Even if you are a hawk," she said, so amiably that he couldn't take offense, "you're awfully incurious."

He smiled unconvincingly back at her.

This didn't seem to bother her. "Oh well," she said with a cheer that he was certain was unaffected, "none of my business. Shall we?"

If she didn't mind his reticence, all the better. They took a lift to another level. Brezan still couldn't tell whether they were on a moth or a moon or a station, or something else entirely. They didn't pass any obvious viewports, and the doors were singularly inexpressive. Nine levels down, a walk through corridors barren of other human presence, and finally, an office with its door standing open to receive them.

"Brought the hawk," the woman said loudly. Brezan almost jumped. "You busy in there, Sfenni, or shall I send him up, or what?"

"Please tell me he's cleaned up," a man's rumbling voice said from within.

"Medical took care of that. I don't think he'll expire messily during the interview."

"Excellent," Sfenni said in a tone implying the opposite.

"In you go," the woman said, and pivoted on her heel without waiting for Brezan to walk into Sfenni's office. Granted, there had to be a hidden security team scrutinizing his every move, but Brezan couldn't help feeling offended at being counted so small a threat, even if the Kel and Shuos were nominally allies.

Brezan squared his shoulders, wondered if he should adjust his uniform, then decided that medium formal was good enough. He stepped in.

The first thing Brezan noticed about the office was the shelves. It wasn't so much that they were finely made, although he couldn't help wondering if that was genuine cloudwood, all shimmering gray with subtle pearly swirls, or one of the better facsimiles. The shelves were crammed with books. Not just books, either. They looked hand-bound, and the smells of aged paper and glue almost overwhelmed him.

Shuos Sfenni sat at a much less expensive-looking desk overshadowed by all those shelves. He had an incongruously round, soft face atop a boxer's blockish frame. For all Brezan knew, he whiled away his time between alphabetizing tomes and dealing with inconvenient Kel by pummeling unlucky bears. At least, unlike the tasseled woman, Sfenni wore a proper Shuos uniform.

"Have a seat," Sfenni said, indicating the chair on the other side of the desk. "So. Colonel Brezan, is it?"

"Yes," Brezan said, and waited.

"I'm substituting for Shuos Oyan, who would ordinarily be processing you," Sfenni said, "so you'll have to forgive me if I'm a little slow. We intercepted your, ah, request to talk to the hexarch's personal assistant."

"Yes," Brezan said, more cautiously this time. Granted, he hadn't expected it to be *easy* to get to a secured terminal, but he didn't like where this was going.

Sfenni not-smiled at him. "Let me summarize what we fished out of that pile of reports."

The high language didn't inflect for number, but 'pile' was pretty unambiguous. Just how many hand-offs was Brezan dealing with? His stomach clenched.

Sfenni's summation was, thankfully, accurate as far as it went. After he had finished, he scrutinized Brezan and sighed. "Enough games, Colonel. Tell me why you're really here."

*What does he mean,* 'really'—"I don't know how to verify my identity or rank if you haven't been able to get the necessary information from the Kel," Brezan said, "but I assure you that my need to contact my superiors is urgent and then I'll be out of your hair. I apologize for involving the Shuos. Circumstances made that seem like the best way forward." More like he had been muzzy from sleeper-sickness, but no need to spell that out. He didn't know how much more was safe to say, no way of telling what Sfenni's security clearance was. For that matter, even if Sfenni let him access a terminal, there was no guarantee it would be secured. Still, one problem at a time.

Sfenni reached into a drawer. Brezan tensed, but all Sfenni did was retrieve a pill dispenser and dry-swallow one of the bright green capsules. "All right, look," Sfenni said after a painful-sounding coughing fit. "Can we level with each other, Colonel? You're in holding on Minner Station"—*Where?* Brezan wondered—"and this is the most boring place in the march, for all that it's become very exciting lately. The thing is, some of us *appreciate* boredom."

Brezan knew where this was heading.

"So here's the thing, Colonel. I understand that you hit the ceiling of your career"—Brezan bristled, but Sfenni didn't pause—"and you'd like to be seconded to the Shuos or retire to some nice planetary city and dabble in energy market intelligence or whatever the fuck. But Shuos Zehun is known for being unforgiving when people waste their time. Things around here could get very uncomfortable, and some of us like our comforts."

If Sfenni said 'some of us' with that particular greasy inflection again, Brezan was going to throttle him. "I don't care about your philosophy of life," he said, and Sfenni's eyes became moistly reproachful. "Would you get to the fucking point already?"

"Well," Sfenni said, "inconveniences are inconveniences, you know."

Then, to Brezan's massive irritation (that note in his profile about anger management was never going away at this rate, but this one time surely he was justified?), Sfenni got up and trundled over to a decorous cloudwood-or-next-best-thing cabinet. "What's your poison?" he said.

Oh, for—Brezan bit down on what he'd been about to say. Sure, he shouldn't be randomly getting drunk, but if it got this loser to get him to that fucking terminal, why not. It couldn't make the inside of his mouth taste any worse than it did anyway. "Peach brandy," he said. He despised peach brandy, but it was the most expensive drink he could see from where he was sitting.

Sfenni pulled out a decanter, then two snifters. "Sorry, my collection of brandies is atrocious," he said, as if Brezan cared, "but my supply has dried up of late." With fussy courtesy, he poured for them both.

Brezan took the tiniest sip that could still be construed as polite and forced himself to smile. Overpriced brandy or not, he couldn't tell, and anyway it didn't matter. He needed this despicable man. Sfenni would come to the point in his own time.

"I'm not an unpatriotic citizen," Sfenni said. It had been so long since Brezan had heard 'unpatriotic' without an expletive attached to it (or 'patriotic,' for that matter) that he almost burst into laughter, and he only just caught himself in time. "But the administration of Minner facilities requires more funding than we're usually able to wheedle out of regional headquarters." He let the statement hang there.

'Administration of Minner facilities,' his ass. More like every ill-gotten mark that Sfenni received in bribes went into cultivating that garden of books. Brezan didn't know whether to laugh, cry, or lunge across the desk. Kel Command wouldn't care that much about a transgression like bribery, under the circumstances, especially if he reported it before they uncovered it independently. And especially if he had a good excuse, which he did. Brezan cared fuck-all about *Shuos* opinions on the matter. But Brezan did very much care about having to compromise his principles like this, even when the need was so great.

*Get over yourself,* Brezan told himself. *No one cares about your petty irrelevant scruples.*

But sometimes—sometimes he wished someone did.

In the meantime, his higher duty had not changed.

"Since we're being so delightfully candid," Brezan said, "I have funds, yes." Unlike General Khiruev, he didn't go on leave and shop for staggeringly overpriced antique trinkets. Brezan's vices were simpler and less expensive: alcohol (just not peach brandy), the obligatory spot of dueling, and the occasional cooking class, because sometimes the best way to understand people was through their food. All this meant that he was reasonably well-off.

"Then an accommodation is possible—?" Sfenni said.

"I know how to make a transfer," Brezan said. "I don't know how to keep the transaction from being traced." Not completely true. He'd learned odd tricks from the people he talked to. He just thought those tricks wouldn't fool a full-on audit.

"I can instruct you," Sfenni said. "But an honest man like myself—"

At the end of this whole unreal interlude, Brezan was either going to emerge as the hexarchate's best actor, or he was going to spontaneously self-combust.

"—needs to take precautions." Sfenni's eyes crinkled suddenly. "And in case you're thinking that an honest Kel would rather take precautions of his own, I assure you that this will go more smoothly if we come to our agreement peaceably."

"I wouldn't have imagined otherwise," Brezan said.

Sfenni passed a tablet to him. He named a sum.

Brezan didn't bother to hide his contempt. "Fine."

As promised, Sfenni's instructions were easy to follow. Brezan made note of the fancy accounting tricks. They weren't far off what he'd already known.

"Excellent," Sfenni said. "We'll get you settled while that goes through. For our mutual protection, you understand. Do you want me to have more brandy sent up to you while you wait?"

Tempting to make Sfenni waste the stuff, but... "That won't be necessary," Brezan said as diplomatically as he could manage. His parents would have been proud of him.

Sfenni tapped out a summons on his terminal. After an agonizing wait, the tasseled woman appeared again. "Hi there," she said with no sign of diminished cheer. "What do you have for me now, Sfenni?"

"Take our guest somewhere comfortable to wait," Sfenni said. "Make sure he's fed, hydrated, the usual. I absolutely must deal with that damnable Vidona envoy now."

"Sure thing," the woman said, and dimpled at Brezan.

Fuck, he hoped she wasn't flirting with him. Not because she didn't attract him, but because she did, and right now he desperately needed fewer distractions in his life. Thankfully, the woman left it at that.

They took the lift again, to an entirely different level. To distract himself from his misgivings, he cataloged the decor. Whoever had decorated this level liked monochromatic paintings of ice planets bordered by dizzying fractal swirls. Nice work: Brezan wasn't artistic himself, but his youngest father was a children's illustrator with a chronic inability to look at artwork without vivisecting it.

By the time they arrived at the waiting room, it had already been set up with a tray of little dishes, everything from a bowl of noodles topped with half a boiled egg to platters of sliced fruit. Even a shelf of books that Brezan had no intention of touching. The room was overwhelmingly blue-and-cream, so soothing that Brezan's shoulder blades itched.

"And that's that," the woman said. "Anything I can provide to make this less aggravating?" She dimpled again, hopefully.

Tempting, but—"No, I'm fine," Brezan said. His dilemma wasn't her fault.

"All right, then. I'll fetch you later."

Brezan had just enough time to sag into a damnably comfortable chair and wonder what it would be like to go through life so blithely. Then, appallingly, he fell asleep. He woke up an indeterminate amount of time later with a horrible crick in his neck. The remnants of the peach brandy tasted foul, although he had scarcely touched it. And the tasseled woman was nowhere in sight.

Deliberately, Brezan hauled himself up, stalked over to the wall, and began writing on it with his finger:

FOXES ARE COMPLETELY TRUSTWORTHY

over and over again, like a children's writing lesson. Could handwriting be sarcastic?

The waiting room opened into a compact but complete bathroom. He knew what this implied about how long they planned to stash him here. He demanded to talk to someone in charge. This didn't work, but he hadn't expected it to.

Resigned, he ate the food. Pure military practicality. Besides, that milk-and-carrot pudding was tasty. He'd have to try to duplicate it if he ever got out of here, which was looking increasingly unlikely.

More waiting. More food trays, always deposited through a slit that looked like it would guillotine his hands if he put one in. More sleeping in chairs, in spite of his resolution to do better. His sergeant back in academy would have been ashamed of him. The next time he saw General Khiruev, he swore he would apologize for ever thinking of watch repair as a frivolous hobby and ask for engineering lessons.

Finally, scant moments before he tried ramming the door with his shoulder, the kind of stupid stunt even a Kel would only do in a Kel joke when trapped in a Shuos building, the tasseled woman showed up.

"There you are," she said, as if she hadn't been the one to deposit him here. "Let's go!"

She might have made small talk on the way to Sfenni's office. Brezan responded with distracted grunts. Still, he envied her the ability to be unoffended by his terrible manners.

"Sfenni," the woman said once they'd made it to the office with its menagerie of books. "Here he is. Enjoy!"

Her teasing voice would have made Brezan smile grudgingly at her on another day, but not today.

"There's been a complication," Sfenni said as soon as the door shut behind Brezan.

Brezan's heart sank. Sfenni wanted another bribe, the wormfucker. Which could be managed. That wasn't an issue in itself, since at this rate he was going to die of exasperation before retirement became pressing. But what guarantee did he have that Sfenni wouldn't string this out until Brezan was broke, and all without ever delivering the promised terminal access?

FOXES ARE COMPLETELY TRUSTWORTHY, indeed.

"It's your turn to listen," Brezan said coldly, without bothering to sit, no matter how much his legs would have appreciated it. Out of habit, he stuck to the polite forms of verbs, and the more-or-less polite pronouns. "I bet you know to the hundredth how much I have left in my primary account, and my obligatory health and retirement accounts, and my independent investments, and everybloodything else. Just clean it all out and buy yourself a few libraries, or hell, hire yourself a planet of bookbinders. I need to get that warning out. Name your price. The real one this time."

Sfenni didn't blink at this outburst. But then, who knew how many just like it he had weathered? Instead, matter-of-fact, he slid his tablet across the desk. "I know you hawks are used to the big, wallopingly fancy terminals that look like ancient shrines from back when people sacrificed chickens to fox spirits," he said, "but this is a Shuos model, and it *is* secured."

The hexarchate's six-spoked wheel with its faction emblems sheened gold-silver-bronze against the black of the tablet's display. Sfenni said, "I'll leave the room so you can make your call. You'll be monitored in the sense that alarms will go off if you try to set anything on fire—which I don't recommend, by the way, I'm positive some of that paper is made of weird toxic shit—but otherwise you'll be left alone. Believe me, don't believe me, it's all one to me."

"Then what do you mean, 'complication'?" Brezan said, because he couldn't let well enough alone. What he should have done was snatch up the tablet, although admittedly he expected it to be rigged to zap him. Shuos Sfenni, collector of bribes, gardener of books. What had changed? "I don't understand."

"We received word that the Swanknot swarm had been subverted about a month ago," Sfenni said. "You've been out of it for a few weeks."

Brezan hissed in despair.

"We only found out about your outlandish claim to be a personal agent of Shuos Zehun's because an analyst was double-checking the usual torrent of nonsense messages to find something especially funny to tell their teammates about. Your story was sufficiently odd that we looked into the matter. We figured we'd better evaluate your motives before dumping you back on the Kel, because it was clear that you'd had some kind of breakdown. Let's not kid ourselves, Kel Medical's solution to broken birds is usually to throw them in the stewpot."

"And—?" Brezan said, flabbergasted.

"Let me guess," Sfenni said. "You couldn't get anyone to believe a crashhawk"—Brezan didn't bother correcting him—"so you played up a glancing connection to Shuos Zehun back in academy in the hopes of getting your warning out. It's the Immolation Fox, isn't it?"

The world shuddered dark. "General Jedao," Brezan said. "Jedao's made his move and I'm too late."

"Don't be like that," Sfenni said kindly. "Any information you have might yet be useful in putting down the hawkfucker for good. Now, go ahead and make that report. And don't bother looking for the green pills in the desk unless you're into foul-tasting rubbish. They're not real anxiety medications, and something tells me that placebos don't do you a whit of good."

# CHAPTER NINE

THE DAY AFTER the hexarchs' council, Mikodez skimmed through a pile of reports examining Jedao's responses to Hafn movements and making educated guesses about what he'd do next. The best one came from an analyst whom Zehun kept trying to fire. Zehun was correct, but the analyst in question came up with the best scenarios. Her latest suggested that Jedao had induced an army of ghosts to possess the swarm and that an assault on the laws of entropy was next. The woman was wasted in intelligence. She should be writing dramas, but Mikodez was too selfish to let her go.

None of the reports had suggested what Mikodez considered to be the obvious next step. Zehun had remarked that he was going to do as he pleased so no one was bothering to dissuade him. In the meantime, Line 3 was blinking bewitchingly at him. He'd instructed Zehun and Istradez not to interrupt him unless the interruption promised first-rate entertainment. Zehun had given him a very tolerant look. Istradez had laughed at him and threatened to pop in partway through to confuse matters.

"All right, I'm ready," Mikodez told the grid. "Put the call through."

A woman's face, framed by a neat bob, appeared on the terminal. Mikodez wasn't fooled. It looked like Jedao's body had lost weight since Brevet General Cheris had reported in from her final assignment, not surprising given the circumstances. He considered telling Jedao to feed his stolen body better, although Zehun and

Istradez would both have laughed at the thought of him, of all people, lecturing anyone on eating properly. Jedao's uniform was in full formal, unnecessary but touching.

"Fair day, Jedao," Mikodez said in a deprecated language. He hoped he was pronouncing it right. It had been a while.

Jedao blinked. "I haven't heard Shparoi spoken in a very long time, Shuos-zho." He was speaking the high language with the same Shparoi drawl he'd had when they first met, decades ago, at the black cradle facility.

Mikodez had always suspected that Jedao could shed the accent any time he cared to, based on his language evaluations from academy, but there was no need to press. For that matter, the use of -zho, an archaic honorific reserved for hexarchs (or heptarchs, back when), was pure affectation, a reminder of Jedao's age. "I thought it would only be polite," Mikodez said.

"That's considerate of you, Shuos-zho, but I'm not sure I could speak Shparoi myself anymore. I'll make the attempt if it pleases you, though."

"Speak whatever suits you. I'll figure it out. I make a point of keeping on hand interpreters who speak everything you ever did, even Tlen-Gwa."

"I have to admit," Jedao said, "I'm not entirely sure why you requested to speak to me. You've got to reckon that I'm not surrendering the swarm to Kel Command. It's the only leverage I have left."

Everything up to 'I'm not surrendering the swarm' was a nearly verbatim replay of an exchange that Mikodez had had with Jedao thirty-five years ago. If Nirai Kujen had told the truth then, Jedao himself no longer remembered the exchange. Jedao had only used a different word for 'considerate,' one less ironic than his original choice: remarkably little drift. For once Mikodez was inclined to believe Kujen, who had had an unhealthy obsession with controlling the contents of a dead man's memory. There was a chance that Kujen had messed up and Jedao had found time to coach Cheris about the old exchange, or that Jedao himself was messing with him, but Mikodez doubted it.

"No," Mikodez said, thinking that if he had been shoved into a black box with no one to talk to (but maybe Kujen) for the better part of four centuries, he wouldn't be eager to go back in, either. "I didn't expect any such thing."

"You're lucky I'm not in the Citadel of Eyes with you," Jedao said icily. "If you wanted to shoot me, fine. There was no need to massacre my swarm to get at me. Soldiers, technicians, medics—they didn't deserve to die."

"Are you trying to make me feel guilty?" Mikodez said incredulously. "That only works on people with consciences, so both of us are immune."

Jedao started to speak. Mikodez raised a hand, and Jedao subsided. "I realize you're insane," Mikodez said, "but look at the situation rationally. There isn't a schoolchild anywhere who doesn't know what you did at Hellspin Fortress. Not to mention your perfect battle record."

"Not perfect anymore."

"Stop being modest, my dear. The Hafn were routed, even if they failed to be obliterated. Anyway, we had some indication that you were slipping Kel Command's control. The thought of you running off and randomly slaughtering another million people—more, if you put your mind to it—bothered me. In that context, sacrificing 8,000 people to be sure of putting down a ruthless and effective killer was a bargain."

"Then why not leave me to rot in the black cradle?"

"Because we had to win back the Fortress of Scattered Needles, and—don't tell Kel Tsoro about this bit, she dislikes me enough already." True as far as it went. "Only one of the available Kel generals was deemed good enough to crack invariant ice and handle the situation, Kel Inesser. But Kel Command didn't want to hand her that victory because she's too popular with her own troops, and they think she's a potential threat to them."

Jedao's mouth twisted. "Not that we're on the same side, Shuos-zho, but has Kel Command ever in the past four centuries considered that it might be better not to field generals it doesn't trust?"

"I'm not a soldier, so I don't feel qualified to comment," Mikodez lied. "It wasn't a good solution, but it was a damn sight better than ceding the Fortress of Scattered Needles to Hafn control. It was also better than letting you charm your way out of captivity afterward. I admit we didn't see your solution coming, even if everyone realizes that the Kel are expendable."

Jedao didn't fall for the bait. But then, his control had been moderately good during the previous conversation, and Mikodez was working his way up to the harder questions. "What do you seek to gain from this chat, Shuos-zho?" Jedao asked.

"I'm not going to tell you that I have your best interests at heart, because I don't, and no one should believe a Shuos making facile remarks anyway." He could tell that Jedao was refraining from making a sarcastic rejoinder. "But the fact remains that you're a Shuos, even if Kel Command thinks you're pretty in that uniform. That means you're one of mine. Every time you hare off course, I'm responsible."

"Shuos-zho, you don't need to break it down into words of one syllable for me. They were teaching this stuff four centuries ago, you know."

Mikodez quirked an eyebrow. "We'll just agree that we both speak fluent Shuos and go from there."

Jedao leaned back. "Are you looking for assurances? You'll notice that I've aimed my guns consistently at the Hafn and not your moths or cities. That Shuos commandant of yours should have told you that I offloaded all my threshold winnowers. I know people are, shall we say, sensitive about them. Although maybe it's a bit much to expect forthrightness from someone who spent her career under deep cover." He smiled briefly, ironically.

"No, she was frank about that," Mikodez said. He had instructed Zehun to find Mazeret the posting of her choice in return for her extraordinary service. "But Jedao, it can't have escaped your notice that the only people who will ever 'trust' you are people who have no choice in the matter. You can't expect to convince *me* of your sincerity. I'm not a Kel, and we were both trained to be paranoid."

"I know," Jedao said, very quietly. "But it doesn't matter. I refuse to return to the cradle. There's no light in there. If I have to run out of the hexarchate and turn mercenary, then fine. That's what I'll do."

"You'll kill a lot more people that way. You have a talent for it."

"I know."

"You didn't ask for this assessment," Mikodez said, "but I'll give it to you anyway. Did it never occur to you that if you'd been a standard-issue happy-go-lucky sociopath like the rest of us foxes, instead of a Crowned with Eyes visionary, a lot more people would be alive and a lot less evil would have been done?"

Ninefox Crowned with Eyes was Jedao's signifier. During his lifetime it had been interpreted as an indication of his brilliance. But visionaries and the mad sometimes turned up with it, and they all knew how that story ended.

"If you were a 'standard-issue happy-go-lucky sociopath' yourself," Jedao retorted, "you wouldn't give a fuck about lives saved or lost." His gaze shifted sideways. "Fox and hound, Shuos-zho, are you growing a vegetable on your desk? Is there a food shortage in the Citadel? I would have recommended something that offered a little more sustenance, personally."

Transparent change of topic, which Mikodez had expected. Besides, it was nice to see Jedao taking an interest in something that wasn't ordnance. Maybe he should send the swarm some cuttings? "That's what my assistant said. Every so often I snip some leaves to put in my soup. Speaking of which, how are you enjoying Kel food? Is it very different from what you used to eat?"

"Don't recognize what they've done to the pickles," Jedao said drily, "and I'm afraid to ask about some of the fish. If they're fish at all. So how many hexarchs has your assistant served?"

At least Jedao still recognized Shuos power structures. The Shuos who made a play for the hexarch's seat were almost always foxes. Even then, only the vainglorious, the rabidly ambitious, or the terminally bored bothered with the exercise. (Mikodez thought of himself as a category three.) No: if you wanted to wield lasting influence, you skipped the dramatics, became a bureaucrat, and made yourself too indispensable to purge.

"I'm Zehun's third hexarch," Mikodez said matter-of-factly. "Of course, my predecessor only lasted three years before I happened to him."

"Bullet? Poison? Point-blank knitting needle?"

Jedao had never had much imagination, even for Shuos infantry. "He was having a nervous breakdown," Mikodez said. "He wanted to retire somewhere quiet and change his face and sex and, I'm not making this up, breed cockatiels. I visited her once afterward, to make sure she was doing all right. Lovely birds, cockatiels. I often think she got the better end of the deal, especially when I have to deal with budget allocations and my agents whine about not getting all the latest toys. Anyway, my assistant had to talk me out of bringing one of the birds home as a pet. Zehun's such a killjoy sometimes."

Jedao looked bewildered. "I realize it's impertinent of me to ask, Shuos-zho, but why did you decide to become hexarch? Instead of taking up landscape architecture or tiger-taming or anesthesiology?"

Mikodez grinned at him. "Because I'm good at it and it's fun. Not necessarily in that order. Honestly, even some of the Kel figure out that duty can be fun. You have some peculiar knot in your psyche that says everything has to be about suffering. But then, considering that you're practically half-Kel, it's not surprising you react like a hawk."

Pointedly, Jedao held up his left hand and inspected his half-glove. "It's just a uniform, Shuos-zho. You do have my transcripts from Shuos Academy, don't you?"

"Yes, and I also happen to know how hard you had to work not to fail out of those math classes. But I'm not joking. At one point you had formation instinct." Mikodez studied Jedao's face intently. Thirty-five years later and they were winding back to the part of the conversation that Nirai Kujen had so disapproved of. They'd quarreled afterward, and then Zehun had yelled at Mikodez for getting into a fight with the Nirai hexarch on his home station. Worth it, though.

Jedao scoffed. "That's preposterous. I'd know if they'd made me into a counterfeit Kel. Even outprocessing can't suppress a memory that—" He fell silent, eyes going opaque as the uncertainty hit.

He didn't remember this time, either. "Not a counterfeit," Mikodez said. "You were the prototype. Where do you think they got the idea?"

Jedao met Mikodez's eyes. His face had cleared of all expression, an obvious tell. He was silent for a long time. "You're not lying to me."

"My dear," Mikodez said, "I shouldn't have to remind you that sometimes the truth serves better than a lie."

A longer silence. "Why would they get rid of formation instinct if they'd managed to inject me with it? I would have assumed that they'd want to leash me as tightly as possible." Brief pause. "At least now I understand why they didn't—didn't just kill me. If they thought they could do this. If they *did*." Jedao drew a shuddering breath, regrouped.

"I don't know why they uninjected you," Mikodez said. Also true, although Jedao was unlikely to believe him. "But it should be obvious to you who would have that information, if you can track him down."

There was a chance that Kel Command's hive memory, never entirely reliable, had degraded over time. Mikodez and Jedao both knew that Nirai Kujen had perfect recall, however. Getting Jedao to retrieve Kujen was a long shot, but Mikodez had nothing to lose.

"At a guess," Mikodez said, "they gave up on it because the results were unreliable. You'd be a lousy Kel candidate to begin with, so even with modern techniques a standard injection wouldn't take. Who knows how long they spent getting a psych surgeon"— meaning Kujen—"to do a custom job."

"It's redundant for you to give me more reasons to avoid Kel Command," Jedao said.

"That wasn't why I told you." Mostly true.

"Then—?"

"Because you deserve to know."

Jedao's eyes widened. Then he laughed.

"You're one of mine," Mikodez said. "I despise seeing my people mishandled, but until very recently you've been under Kel jurisdiction, so there was only so much I could do."

"Yes," Jedao said, growing distant. "I remember when they told me that Khiaz-zho had signed me over to the Kel Arsenal. I don't know why it came as such a shock. But I deserved no less." More silence.

"Whatever's on your mind, you might as well ask."

"Is it true that you assassinate Shuos cadets?"

Interesting. Jedao was trying to gauge his moral fiber. Kel Command would have been singularly unamused. Or possibly gone out to get collectively drunk. (Did they ever do that? Intelligence was unclear on that point.) "My dear," Mikodez said, "I'm happy to tell you the dirt, but you're not good enough to determine whether I'm lying or not."

"Try me anyway," Jedao said.

"The answer is yes. I specifically targeted two cadets, whom my agents successfully terminated. There were no secondary casualties. The cadets were part of a heretic plot to blow up Shuos Academy Tertiary. The details are messy. I didn't have a lot of time. Since I didn't fancy a panic, I had my agents shoot them while they were playing some drinking game. The plot came much closer to succeeding than I generally like to admit."

"Why not release the truth after the matter had been handled? Your academy commandant should have been able to keep the lid on a little panic."

"You didn't ask when the incident happened." Mikodez grimaced. "I was twenty-seven. It was my second year as hexarch, and I didn't have a lot of credibility. I felt it was more useful for people to be afraid of what I might do to top that."

Jedao laughed wryly. "I can't say I envy you your job, Shuos-zho. I was never tempted to try for it."

Mikodez believed him, which was just as well. The prospect of someone with Jedao's psychological problems in charge of the Shuos appalled him. Jedao's solution to people who disagreed with him was to shoot them. While even Jedao couldn't shoot everyone in the hexarchate, the evidence to date suggested that he'd do a fantastic amount of damage on the way out.

Jedao did have a swarm—Shandal Yeng's anxiety wasn't entirely unfounded—but Mikodez hoped that the Hafn would keep him occupied with something familiar and soothing until he could be stabilized. In any case, it was Mikodez's turn. "Tell me something so I can settle a few bets around the Citadel," he said idly. "How is Khiruev in bed?"

Jedao went ice-white.

Damn. That meant he'd been thinking about it. The taboo had not been as strong during Jedao's lifetime. However, after the institution of formation instinct, due to the potential for abuse, Kel who had sex with other Kel were executed. Even Kel Command recognized the morale problems that would result. And Jedao, who had spent almost his entire adult career, and several lifetimes besides, in Kel service, thought of himself as a hawk.

"You wouldn't entirely be to blame for gravitating toward hawks after the way Khiaz worked you over," Mikodez said. As a matter of fact, her notes on all her victims were in his archives. (Heptarch Khiaz had been a very well-organized predator.) In Jedao's case, she'd taken the extra step of allowing him to transfer out of her office when he was a young man, so that he thought he'd escaped being harassed by her. She'd waited until his promotion to brigadier general to strike.

"Shuos-zho," Jedao said, in a voice so pleasant it was poisonous, "it's no secret that I'm one of the hexarchate's greatest monsters, but I draw the line at rape."

"That's fucking hilarious considering whose body you're walking around in," Mikodez observed.

Jedao's face was recovering some of its color. "Kel Cheris had already died," he said. "I didn't see any harm in wringing some final use out of her carcass. The dead aren't around to care."

"You're one of us, all right."

"I'm so glad I have your approval, Shuos-zho, but feel free to get to the point."

Jedao's sexual hang-ups hadn't been a concern while he was a revenant, but the fact that he had a body now complicated matters. "Never mind Khiruev, then," Mikodez said. "At some point when you're done walloping the Hafn, you ought to take some time off and try sex with someone who isn't a Kel. I hear some people find it fulfilling." Istradez always laughed whenever he heard of Mikodez giving this particular advice. But Jedao's discomfited expression made the whole conversation worth it. "Unless you have some archaic problem with being a womanform?"

"Shuos-zho," Jedao said patiently, "I haven't had a dick in four hundred years. I got over it fast, promise."

"It's still frustrating that I can't send over a licensed courtesan, although I'm not sure I can afford one good enough to work through your particular problems."

"You say this like I'm going to have time for extracurricular activities. This fucking swarm doesn't run itself, you know."

"Tell me," Mikodez said in exasperation, "what the hell would you do if there weren't a war on?"

Jedao faltered. For a moment his eyes were wrenchingly young. "I don't know," he said. "I don't know how to do anything else."

Which meant, although there was no way that Jedao was ready to admit it to himself, that he'd start a war just to have something to do.

"I've kept you long enough," Mikodez said, "but one last thing." The most important thing. "Does the term Mwen-denerra mean anything to you?"

Home of the Mwennin. The scatter-home, the braid of all the small communities bound by blood and custom.

Jedao cocked his head. "I can't even tell you what language that's from, Shuos-zho. Foreign? Hexarchate?"

"The hexarchs want to destroy it," Mikodez said.

He had thought there might be a reaction this time, but still nothing. "Is it a weapon?" Jedao said. "A sculpture? A really terrible snack food?"

"Never mind, then," Mikodez said. "I just thought you might be able to tell me about it."

"I failed the test, didn't I," Jedao said ruefully. "In my defense, it's hard to read up on things when there's no light."

"It genuinely isn't important," Mikodez said. It looked like Cheris was dead, or unavailable, or whatever happened to possessed people. Besides, it wasn't as if Jedao, or Cheris for that matter, could do anything useful about the planned genocide. Mikodez himself certainly didn't need Jedao's permission to do as he pleased about the situation. "Try not to kill more people than necessary."

"I'll keep that in mind," Jedao said. "Goodbye, Shuos-zho." His image flicked out and left the Deuce of Gears in its place, gold on a field of livid red. Then that, too, vanished.

"That could have gone better," Mikodez said to his green onion. But he hadn't hoped to fix four centuries of mismanagement in one conversation. It would have to do for a start.

# CHAPTER TEN

KHIRUEV HAD GOTTEN accustomed to the fact that Jedao was, as commanding officers went, conscientious about details. She couldn't imagine that someone with Jedao's battle record had achieved what he had by dashing around without paying attention to logistics. And logistics were going to be an issue since they were renegades. So far their supplies had held up, but who knew how long a campaign Jedao had planned?

Jedao was also conscientious about getting to know his staff as individuals, and holding regular conferences with the leaders of the tactical groups and the scoutmoths, and even walking through the *Hierarchy of Feasts'* levels and chatting with the crew. No one would ever forget who Jedao was or what he had done, and no one would ever feel at ease around him, despite his pleasantness. But then, this was a very old game to Jedao.

Sixteen days after the engagement at Spinshot Coins, as the swarm continued its pursuit of the Hafn, Jedao and Khiruev had returned from one such walk and ended at Khiruev's quarters, which was odd. The walk itself had been nothing remarkable. Indeed, it wasn't unusual for a swarm's general to inspect their command moth with the high officers aboard. Khiruev remembered such walks as a brigadier general under Lieutenant General Myoga, who, while excellent at training large swarms, had possessed an unfortunate soft, droning voice that resisted everyone's augments' attempts to decipher it when she inevitably trailed off at the end of a sentence.

This didn't matter when you were composited and the pickups transmitted everything from subvocals, but it became embarrassing when you were fumbling for a response to whatever she had just said while poking around the engine room. At least Jedao spoke loudly enough to be heard, and his drawl, while unusual, was paradoxically comprehensible.

Jedao's divide-and-conquer tactics, which involved talking to individuals rather than groups whenever this made sense, were transparent. Yet no one could do anything about it. Khiruev made a point of reminding herself every time she woke up that the swarm had been stolen from her, not as a matter of personal pride (although, if she was honest with herself, there was an element of that too). It didn't make a damn bit of difference. Jedao might be a manipulative bastard, but he was the manipulative bastard that Khiruev was bound to serve.

So it came as no especial surprise when, having gotten Khiruev alone, Jedao asked her a personal question. It didn't matter that Khiruev's own quarters should have been friendly terrain. Ever since that scathing critique of her assassination attempt, Khiruev would always be slicingly aware of Jedao's dominance whenever they met here.

Khiruev was shuffling a deck of jeng-zai cards, not because they were going to play (she hoped; Jedao was unnaturally good), but because it gave her hands something to do. One servitor, a scuffed lizardform, was making the usual doomed attempt to clear debris from under Khiruev's workbench. Another, a deltaform, had accompanied them during the walk and into the sitting room. Perhaps it thought Jedao might call for refreshments.

Jedao wasn't looking directly at Khiruev when he said, "General, how do you feel about children?"

Any question of Jedao's was bound to have teeth hidden in it, but this one baffled Khiruev. "I haven't got any, if that's what you mean," she said, setting the cards down and squaring them neatly. Surely Jedao could have looked that up?

"Let me rephrase that," Jedao said. "You don't have any children in the Tieneved—excuse me, in the legal, high-language sense. But did you ever become a mother?"

It took Khiruev a while to work out what Jedao was getting at. Jedao was Shparoi, from a culture that no longer existed in the hexarchate. Khiruev was accustomed to people entering marriage contracts for mutually agreeable periods of time to form a shared household or, if children would be involved, a lineage. Said contracts laid out whether those children would be natural-born or crèche-born. (Outdated terminology: most people were crèche-born, and had been for some time. The language had not caught up to contemporary practice.)

Jedao was asking about being a non-custodial parent, a paradox in the high language. Children might be adopted, or might be formed from some combination of genetic material from the household's parents, or from a donor or donors if that was desirable. But the marriage contract would spell out clearly who had birth-custody of the children, and only that person or persons were the parents. Apparently, Jedao was conflating being a genetic contributor and being a parent, even if the donor was not part of the contracted household.

"Sir," Khiruev said, wishing she hadn't been put in the position of deciphering Jedao's real question, "did *you* have genetic spawn?" Horrible circumlocution. The high language term she'd used referred to animals. It was offensive to use it to refer to humans. But in the absence of an adequate word, she had to get the idea across somehow. Khiruev did speak two low languages, but both came from the same language family as the high language and suffered the same deficiency of lexicon.

To her relief, Jedao snorted. "No, that wouldn't have happened," he said. "I saw to that medically and I didn't sleep with many womanforms to begin with. But I've always wondered if other"— he used a word Khiruev didn't recognize, sibilants and an oddly pinched vowel. Shparoi, presumably. "If I had other siblings. Ones that survived."

Jedao's hand dangled over the arm of the chair. He gazed at a world folded up into myth and mystery and footnotes no one read anymore but historians with high security clearances. "Once in a while, when Kel Command took me out of my pickle jar, I'd ask one of my anchors and they'd know about my mother, my sister, my brother and his family." Assassinated; vanished; murder-suicide on Hellspin's anniversary. "But no one had heard anything about any other siblings.

"I had a father, in the Shparoi sense," Jedao resumed after a long pause, "but not in the hexarchate one. He died before Hellspin, flitter accident. We'd met only twice years before that. He was a violist, very handsome. My mother was forever complaining that she'd gone to the trouble of picking a particularly nice one and I didn't have the decency to inherit either his musicality or his looks." The note of affection when Jedao mentioned his mother sounded disquietingly genuine. "Anyway, I never asked him if he'd sired others, in arrangements like the one he'd had with my mother. I didn't investigate, either. It would have been extremely improper. Now he's over four centuries dead and I'll never know if anyone in my lineage survived."

"Would you feel better if you did?" Khiruev asked.

"I doubt it, but I wonder all the same."

"I was never tempted to contract for children," Khiruev said. "I don't feel strongly about them one way or another. They're loud and messy"—she'd never forget the expression on Mother Ekesra's face that time she'd shorted out one of her pastry machines—"but if they weren't like that there'd be something wrong with them."

She also remembered Mother Allu complaining once to Mother Ekesra, *She's so* quiet, and Ekesra's reply that at least she wasn't getting into trouble.

"The hardest thing Kel Command ever made me do was shoot children." Jedao's voice was soft.

Khiruev hadn't known about this, but then, her interest in historical generals had been confined to their strategies and tactics rather than biographies. "Secondary casualties are always difficult," she said neutrally.

"I'm not a linguist, but do you ever think there's something wrong with the things we do and don't have words for?"

So this was what Jedao had been leading up to. "Sir," Khiruev said, with a hint of a bite, "they didn't *have* formation instinct in your day." Jedao's mouth twisted as though that had brought something to mind, but if so, he kept it to himself. "And you're a Shuos, anyway. Why didn't *you* do something?"

"You know what?" Jedao said. "The Kel called me the fox general, although there was a Shuos brigadier general who overlapped my service, a staffer posted somewhere obscure. But the Shuos called me a hawk."

Khiruev waited for an answer, or some moral, some further revelation. Instead, Jedao called up a digest of news reports and a regional map hazed with annotations. "Sometimes it amazes me how big we've gotten," Jedao said, and smiled with predatory benevolence. "Tell me, what do you know about that system?" He struggled with the map before getting it to focus on Weraio 5.

"It's one of a thousand conflagrations," Khiruev said wryly. She had paid it more attention than most not because it was noteworthy in itself—sporadic outbursts of calendrical warfare and student demonstrations on the subtropical archipelago, yes, but many planets suffered similar incidents—but because she'd visited it twice. If you avoided the hotspot archipelago, it could be a perfectly reasonable vacation. She hated warm weather, which reminded her of home, and had instead gone for a tour of the city of Miifau, famed, if you followed that sort of thing, for its orchestra. Every time the Weraio system came up in the digests, she'd scanned them for any mention that Miifau's orchestra had gotten bombed. It was a stupid thing to care about, especially when so many people died everywhere, in every passing moment. Yet the fractal nature of the hexarchate's fight against heresy made it impossible to care about those blotted numbers.

Khiruev doubted Jedao cared particularly about Weraio 5, other than having zeroed in on Khiruev's own interest in it, even if it was theoretically possible that he had caught word of a nasty development from that direction. But Weraio wasn't located anywhere strategic and was yet some distance from the Hafn incursions. Instead, Khiruev said, "Sir, we"—*I*—"will be of more use to you if we have some indication of the next objective."

So far Jedao had maneuvered them past the Fortress of Spinshot Coins and toward the Hafn while keeping them from engaging any Kel, either by luck, an intelligence system he had yet to reveal to Khiruev, or intimidating Kel Command from a distance. Khiruev didn't expect Jedao to level with her about his grand strategy. At the same time, Jedao couldn't expect anyone to take his motives at face value, either.

"What, thrashing the Hafn isn't good enough for you?" Jedao said.

Khiruev suppressed a shiver. She had long practice hiding her reactions, dubious benefit of growing up in a household with a mother who terrified her. Still, taken literally, a question was a question.

"If all you cared about was the defeat of the Hafn," Khiruev said, "you could have left that to the Kel after whatever happened at Scattered Needles. Flitting around the hexarchate with a renegade swarm merely advertises our weakness to the enemy, especially since they've already engaged us."

"All right, then," Jedao said, "what is it you think I do care about? And why bring it up now, General, and not earlier?"

"Does every card player you encounter give away everything after the first hand?" Khiruev said. Brezan, for instance, had a terminal inability to bluff. Not coincidentally, he stayed out of high-stakes jeng-zai.

Jedao's smile flickered at her like a candle flame. Khiruev caught herself wishing it had lasted longer. Nevertheless, for all that the argument was transparently designed to appeal to a gambler, Jedao didn't draw it out. "Fair enough," Jedao said. He fell silent, and Khiruev was reminded that Jedao hadn't answered the first question.

Khiruev, no longer young, had not dueled except casually in years. But she had a counter ready. "Why is it," she said, "that you're so determined to teach me how to think autonomously? What would that give you that simple obedience wouldn't?"

Jedao leaned back, began to put his feet up on the table between them, caught himself. The whole sequence looked so natural.

Khiruev wasn't fooled. "Simple obedience won't suffice for what I have in mind," Jedao said. "Never mind that for now. Tell me what I'm really up to, since I've apparently lost my ability to bluff."

Highly unlikely. But then, Jedao's arched eyebrow suggested that he hadn't meant the remark seriously. At any rate, Khiruev was stuck in the role of pupil. She didn't care to dispute Jedao's superior experience anyway.

"I can only assume that you're at war with the hexarchs," Khiruev said, "and that the Hafn are only useful insofar as you can use them against the hexarchs, or to gain influence with the mass of citizens." Anyone could have come to the same conclusion. But Khiruev had the nagging sense that she shouldn't have approved of this goal as much as she did, considering how long she had served the Kel loyally.

"The great difficulty of a Kel army," Jedao said with surprising bitterness, "is that there's no one to tell me when I'm wrong."

"You can't possibly hope to prevail."

Jedao's grin had just a glint of teeth. "Funny, that's what Commander Chau said going into Candle Arc."

The only reason Jedao wasn't best-remembered for Candle Arc—a space battle in which he'd been outnumbered eight to one and still smashed the enemy—was the massacre. "You said yourself that the hexarchate is a big place," Khiruev said. "Eight to one is nothing compared to what you face now. 'Outnumbered' doesn't begin to describe it."

"That's what everyone says. And so the hexarchs keep their stranglehold on the populace."

The stirring of hope that rose in Khiruev was ridiculous. How could Jedao hope to coordinate a rebellion across the entire hexarchate? As the heretics proved, over and over, rebelling was easy. The coalescence of a viable successor government was another matter. And yet, she wanted to warm herself by that hope: proof that she was a suicide hawk.

Jedao rose all at once, not graceful so much as efficient, and stood before Khiruev. No wonder he'd been a fabled duelist in his first life, that flawless balanced poise. He looked down at Khiruev, intent, unsmiling. "Tell me what you want me to do," he said, as if he hadn't lined up all the advantages on his side of the conversation.

Khiruev's heart contracted. "Sir," she said, as steadily as ever, "I wouldn't presume."

"Don't tell me you never tire of the endless wheel of failed heresies." His words spoke of one thing. His eyes, as sweet and merciless as ashes, spoke of another. He reached out, hand pausing just short of Khiruev's jaw.

Khiruev knew where this was leading. Her disappointment in Jedao was almost as great as her desire. Even so, Jedao's phrasing was sufficiently ambiguous that Khiruev could construe it as a simple remark. And so she had the defense permitted even a fledge-null. She stared mutely at Jedao and waited to see if he would force the issue.

Over her lifetime, Khiruev had failed at all her relationships. She hadn't dated until she was in her thirties; had only managed a single short-lived, dismal marriage. Or maybe it had started earlier, with the mawkish tone poem she had composed for an alt when she was fourteen, only to think better of ever playing it for anyone. (She still remembered every note.)

Upon reflection, the marriage had been a disaster from the beginning. She had been thirty-seven, awestruck by the beautiful, elegant singer, Dosveissen Moressa, and her ability to come up with double entendres for engineering jargon, to say nothing of her dazzling smile when she brought her gifts. Moressa's favorite had been the music box Khiruev had restored for her, exquisite decoupage tigers on the outside and, once opened, an endless hunt of clockwork figures.

Moressa and Khiruev had contracted for a year after dating for several months. A year was a pitiable length of time for a marriage contract. The relationship cooled off after five months. Khiruev had been so convinced at the outset that they were being rational about building something lasting. Who would have guessed that a conservative approach to romance would end so badly? But the fact that they had rarely discussed long-term plans, even after they'd known each other intimately, should have warned her that they would founder on fundamental points.

The funny thing was, years later, Khiruev couldn't remember the topic of the quarrel that had finally driven a spike into the relationship, in part because the topic was sideways to the emotional undercurrents. Moressa had spoken in a voice that was never anything but calm, yet at the end her face twisted with frustration. *Even when you laugh you never smile,* she'd finally burst out.

*I have no idea what you're talking about,* Khiruev said, just as calmly. The lie knifed between them. Moressa stalked out of the apartment after an icy pause rather than continue looking at her. Khiruev stared at the sudden meaningless detritus of figurines and jewelry scattered around the apartment for the rest of the night. Moressa never returned. Indeed, they communicated only once for the rest of the marriage (the rest of their lives), to negotiate over some fine point of mutual finance that neither of them cared about. Even then they didn't meet in person.

Khiruev hadn't told either of her mothers about the whole debacle, which had taken a great deal of finessing. They would have been unbearably understanding or, worse, inclined to blame Moressa. In fact, Moressa's only transgression had been telling the truth.

After that, Khiruev made a point of consciously sabotaging all her relationships by choosing unsuitable partners on the grounds that this beat doing it unconsciously. Khiruev was most ashamed of the time she'd picked out a man who'd been a refugee and who begged her over and over to leave the Kel and do something safe. Khiruev had never contemplated abandoning her career, least of all for a lover who grated on her almost from the beginning. It wasn't anything the man did so much as the constant reminder that Khiruev was in the business of creating refugees when she wasn't creating orphans and corpses.

She had thought she had her heart under control, by which she meant that she had memorized the usual trajectories and had well-established protocols for dealing with the inevitable recriminations and breakups. It served her right to be confronted by a man who could demand her devotion in more than the usual sense, who had a dark history with the Kel, and who had no reason to fear the execution that would ordinarily await a soldier who slept with a soldier; who might well miss even the cold facsimile of companionship.

Jedao's hand shook visibly. "It would be so easy," he said to himself. His thumb grazed Khiruev's chin. Khiruev froze. It was as though her heart had crystallized inside her.

Then Jedao sighed and stepped backwards, and sank back down into the chair. "There are things I will do and things I will not do," he said simply. "But I don't blame you for believing the worst." He didn't look all that convinced himself.

Khiruev knew better than to pretend that she had been thinking about something else. "It doesn't matter one way or another."

"But it does," Jedao said, hot and cold and sharp at once. "This is exactly what matters. The difference between what should and should not be done. This is what the fight's about."

"Someday I will understand you, sir," Khiruev said, meaning it.

"I hope so," Jedao said. This time the smile lasted longer.

# CHAPTER ELEVEN

EVERY MORNING, MIKODEZ had a Kel infantry ration bar for breakfast. According to the Kel, consuming them voluntarily suggested interesting things about your mental health. Mikodez ate them in the hopes that they would immunize him to any poisons, and because they seemed to make his medications more effective. He knew poisons didn't work that way, and that the latter effect was illusory, but it was a nice thought. Besides, he had to do something to atone for all the candy he put in his system.

He'd opted to get to the conference room forty-eight minutes early and eat there, on the grounds that he was getting bored of the decor in his offices. All his offices. There was more than one of them, for reasons that were not entirely clear. The architects who had designed the Citadel had included Shuos, with Shuos habits of thought. His favorite hadn't originally *been* an office, but had been converted to one as a test of variable layout, which Mikodez considered very brave of that long-vanished heptarch. (Said heptarch had died shortly after, not because of variable layout, or the Citadel's security. She'd attended a meeting on some distant planet and caught what might or might not have been a bioengineered disease.)

"You have the stupidest eating habits of anyone in the entire Citadel," Istradez said. "If anyone else did that, they'd get dinged on all the medical evaluations." He had already finished his own breakfast, consisting of seaweed soup, rice, a modest scallion pancake, and Kel pickles.

"So how's your latest girlfriend?" Mikodez was frowning at his tablet, which he had set at a comfortable angle in its holder so he wouldn't get a crick in his neck staring down at it. "I hope you're not bored with her already. I can only hand out security clearances so fast."

"Just how much detail did you want me to go into?"

"Kind of not."

Istradez smirked at him. "You want me to clear out so you can have your meeting?"

Mikodez's senior staff knew about his doubles, including Istradez, and even the general populace had some idea that he used them from time to time. Not all of Mikodez's advisers approved of him using a non-Shuos for the role, but he'd pointed out that no one else knew him as well as the younger sibling he'd grown up with. Istradez was only one year younger than he was. Their parents joked that they'd been meant to be twins, except they had realized that two of them at once would have been overkill.

"No, come take my seat," Mikodez said. They'd done this before and he was certain that Intelligence and Accounting's division heads could tell them apart, but it was good to keep them guessing. "Run the meeting. I'll take notes. Also, I have some other things to keep my eyes on, so I won't be able to give my full concentration to the meeting."

"Why show up at all?" Istradez wondered.

"Because if we're both here they'll figure there's a higher chance one of us is real." Mikodez had two other doubles, one of whom was still in physical therapy after narrowly surviving an assassination attempt during his last assignment. The man had so far refused to retire, but Mikodez thought it was only a matter of time. The other one was attending a conference.

"You could hole up in your bedroom and sip plum wine before taking a—" Istradez's eyes narrowed. "When's the last time you slept, Mikodez? I bet you missed chatting with our nephew, too. If I'd known, I'd have gone to see Niath myself so he doesn't get lonely."

Mikodez had to ask the augment how long it had been. "Two days and three hours and change."

Istradez moaned and put his head in his hands. "I am the worst little sibling ever. Go to *bed*."

"I can sleep after the meeting."

"Are you out of your fucking mind, Miki? You *know* that Shenner"—that was the head of Intelligence—"always makes the meetings run over by an hour. If not more."

The problem with Shuos heads of Intelligence was that they, with some cause, conceived of themselves as occupying the high rung on the ladder. Certain Shuos heads of Intelligence took this as license to go into threat analyses in exhaustive detail even when theoretically confined to twenty minutes.

"Yes," Mikodez said, looking wistfully at the cookies that he shouldn't eat because he should leave them for Istradez so he could get into the role. "My hints to Shenner get less and less subtle, but for someone who's ordinarily so astute at picking up on cues, she's proved remarkably oblivious."

"Oblivious my ass. Shenner likes the sound of her own voice. It's going to take a direct reprimand to get her to shape up. You should let me give it if you're squeamish. And it's not like you to be squeamish."

"Well, then her voice will make an excellent lullaby. No one will be surprised to see you sleeping in the corner after last night's excesses."

"They weren't *that* excessive."

"Besides," Mikodez said, "Shenner has a very touchy ego. Which makes it difficult to suggest that she get some more therapy for it. The problem is, she's obsessive, paranoid, and loyal, all of which make her excellent at her job—and all of which mean that I have to handle her very delicately. Best to leave things as they are."

"If you say so," Istradez said, sounding unconvinced. He jerked his thumb in the direction of the corner seat. Mikodez took it, and Istradez lowered himself into the customary hexarch's seat. "Dare I ask what you're working on, anyway?"

"Best if you don't know."

"I was afraid you'd say that."

"Then why did you ask?"

Istradez looked pensive. "Because someone has to." Then, with an effort, he straightened and eyed the cookies. "Couldn't you do something to reduce the size of these damn platters? It's getting harder and harder to choke all this stuff down without getting fat."

"Your metabolism's even faster than mine is," Mikodez said unsympathetically, "it's just that you put less junk in your system."

"And whose fault is that?"

"Oh, look, it's almost time for the meeting," Mikodez said, just to annoy Istradez, although they had a good fourteen minutes left and no one ever arrived more than six minutes early.

"If you don't spend part of Shenner's inevitable rant about the inadequacy of our data-processing throughput catching up on sleep," Istradez said, "I shall ruin your reputation by flirting with Accounting." Accounting was run by a married individual who got a body mod every three months like clockwork, according to whatever was in fashion with the Andan. Some of the fashions were extremely distracting, like the thankfully brief period when the high diplomats had gone around sporting neck-frills. Otherwise, Accounting was staid and conservative, and entirely modest about what went on in the bedroom. "I bet I could get them to stray."

Mikodez yawned pointedly and curled up in his chair, slate tucked under his arm.

Eight minutes later, the door opened, but it was only a servitor come to clear Mikodez's tray. Mikodez had only eaten half the ration bar, but he only ever ate half, so it knew to take the dish away. As for other food, the conference table was already home to two lavish plates of cookies and pastries (mostly for Mikodez, who had never met a sweet he didn't like), seasoned rare meats cut up into slivers and stuck with absurdly decorative gold-toned toothpicks, spring rolls, slices of crisp fruit. Mikodez believed that no one thought well on an empty stomach, so while people were certainly welcome to eat before they came to meetings, he made sure they could fill up during them if they chose to.

A minute after that, the division heads filed in one by one. Mikodez's eyes were closed, but he listened to the exchange of greetings. Istradez would be smiling at each person individually because that was what Mikodez himself did.

For a while Mikodez followed the threads of his people's interactions. Shenner's voice was more shrill than usual. She despised the Hafn not because she'd lost family to them but because she had once met a Hafn aristocrat and he had commented disparagingly about her accent speaking in his language. Shenner was vain about her language skills. Fortunately, Accounting interrupted what could have been a lengthy diatribe. In the early days, Mikodez would debrief with Istradez after meetings, pointing out things he would have done differently. These days that was rarely necessary.

While he didn't feel drowsy in the slightest, Mikodez's mind felt fuzzy. The medications hadn't kicked in yet. Medical didn't like the number of drugs he was abusing. He could tell because instead of lecturing him about it (ineffectual), every single one of the courtesans he saw was painstakingly and consistently polite about how he needed artificial assistance to do his job (also ineffectual, but at least it saved everyone the arguments). While sex didn't interest Mikodez, he believed firmly that all of his people should talk to trained conversationalists/therapists on a regular basis. He did not exclude himself from this requirement.

Idly, Mikodez brought up a puzzle on his slate and began playing it. It wasn't a cover for anything. A cadet had designed it during the academy's games competition several years ago, and it had been one of the top entries in its category. Mikodez liked the game not for its originality but for its ability to numb his brain. It involved pattern-matching, music (piped in through his augment, although this made it difficult to follow the meeting at the same time), and just enough randomness to make it a challenge. Right now Mikodez couldn't score points to save his life, which confirmed his decision to hand off the meeting to Istradez. He hadn't asked Medical whether the game was a reasonable test of his cognitive function, but he didn't need to.

Partway through an impassioned speech by Propaganda on how the Andan were botching the media fallout by allowing the broadcast of dramas about Jedao portraying him in a favorable light, the drug hit Mikodez. It was as though all the lights in the room had sparked brighter. Istradez glanced at him very briefly. He knew. Instead of drawing attention to Mikodez, Istradez instead pointed out that they were going to have to offer the Andan incentives to step on the dramas. Unfortunately, the Andan liked profit as much as anyone else. The dramas had to be making them a lot of money just now.

Mikodez dismissed the game, wondering in passing how that cadet was doing, then opened one of the files on Jedao's history. Opened another one on Kujen. Four centuries in one case, nine in another. Both of them contained frustrating lacunae. Or rather, Jedao's profile existed in as much detail as you'd expect, minus the usual slow rot of history. No one had anticipated that he'd prove to be a time bomb. Kujen, on the other hand, had actively obfuscated his profile for so long that Mikodez didn't trust everything in the files. But he had to start somewhere.

Jedao had responded to Mikodez's second attempt to contact him not with a direct communication but a simple message: *Make you a deal, Shuos-zho. You stay out of my way, I'll stay out of yours. We can hash out the rest after the Hafn are gone.*

Not a bad offer, as such things went. Even if Mikodez and his staff had good reason to believe that ensuring the Hafn's trickling survival was Jedao's primary plan. After all, Jedao couldn't claim to be defending the hexarchate without the invader. Admittedly, getting rid of the Hafn wouldn't help much, as the hexarchate had plenty of other enemies, but it might trip Jedao up. Mikodez had not said anything in response to the message. Jedao wouldn't expect assurances in any case.

His attention turned to Kujen, whose disappearance had left such an odd hole in Mikodez's life. They were not friends. Kujen might understand friendship as an abstraction, but he was no more *friends* with another human being than a shark was with a fish.

They were, however, colleagues, and they had consulted with each other on many occasions since Mikodez took the seat. Mikodez had grown dangerously fond of him, even if he hadn't become aware of it until now. But he liked challenges, and there was no denying that dealings with Kujen, however cordial, were never *safe*.

Mikodez had visited Kujen's home station twice. Kujen preferred to let his false hexarchs administer the faction, or so he said, although Mikodez had good evidence that he kept a close eye on what was being done on his behalf. Faian had ascended to false hexarch twelve years after Mikodez himself took the seat, under circumstances that strongly suggested that Kujen objected personally to Faian's predecessor skimming off parts of the budget. The man in question had later turned up as a technician on Kujen's personal staff—"No sense wasting talent," Kujen had said blithely. He was much prettier, and much more docile, after Kujen got through with him.

Kujen's taste for the beautiful was not limited to men (and the rare woman or alt). He surrounded himself with luxuries from the hexarchate's bounty of worlds. Even if Mikodez hadn't known from the threadbare records that Hajerct Kujen had spent his childhood as a refugee on a world whose name had changed twice in the past nine centuries, he would have guessed it from Kujen's particular obsession with everything from hand-woven carpets to blown-glass figurines of flowers to cabinets inlaid with abalone and slivers of moonstone. He collected these objects but took no notice of them once he owned them. Mikodez had given up trying to bribe him with such mundanities long ago. When he really needed a favor, he instead offered ancient sextants and finely made orreries, artifacts that appealed to the scientist in Kujen.

Faian had stopped waffling and her people had taken control of Kujen's old base. Mikodez expected that she'd be turning it upside-down for clues for the next decade without much luck. He'd offer help, except she was unlikely to take kindly to the suggestion that she needed it. That, and she didn't trust him. Which, fair enough. Since he spent all that time cultivating his reputation, he couldn't blame people for taking it to heart.

"...Miki."

The use of his childhood nickname made Mikodez look up. Istradez wouldn't have used it if any of the division heads remained anywhere near the room. "Yes?" he said, and rubbed his eyes. His stomach rumbled. When was the last time he had eaten?

"Fine, cookies," Istradez said. He was standing over Mikodez with his hands on his hips. "If I can't get you to eat anything better. And then you are going to bed."

"Don't be absurd," Mikodez said. "You haven't debriefed me on what the hell went on in the meeting."

Istradez eyed him incredulously. "Are you kidding? You've been asleep all this time? Or sleeping with your eyes open, whatever. You're ordinarily better about managing than this."

"I can't have been asleep that—" Mikodez checked the augment. Yes, he had, apparently.

Istradez's voice softened. "Well, it's not all bad. You missed the spectacular pissing match between Intelligence and Propaganda. I'll fill you in later, promise. Just, you can sleep in my room, and I'll cover for you until you're fit for duty again."

"Fine," Mikodez said, since he was clearly losing this round. "Fine."

"I'll escort you," Istradez said.

"No, that won't be necessary."

Istradez visibly wavered, then nodded. He stalked back to the table, snatched up a cold spring roll, then pressed it into Mikodez's hand. "I don't care if you're going to look like a kid purloining this from the appetizer tray. Eat it." And he stood over Mikodez until he did, in fact, eat it. Then he had to drink half a glass of water to wash it down because it'd gone dry. He made a note to himself to have a word with the kitchens about that.

Mikodez took the long way to Istradez's apartment, on the grounds that he had no reason to hurry. He amused himself by affecting Istradez's so-what-if-I-have-my-brother's-face slouch and cynical smile. Istradez was the better actor, since his livelihood depended on it, but Mikodez liked keeping his hand in.

He trailed his hand along the green walls, livened up from time to time by paintings of cavorting foxes or, for variety, the occasional coy moon-rabbit. Sometimes he thought about taking a vacation. The sad fact was that he rarely left the Citadel, when the highest ceremonies dictated his presence. Otherwise, he did the most good here, in the never-sleeping Shuos headquarters.

When he entered Istradez's apartment, he almost called for security. There was someone in the room already. But then she rose up from the couch in a whisper of languid silks, bronze pearls rattling around her neck and wrists and ankles, and he relaxed.

"Spirel," Mikodez said as the door shut behind them both.

She floated up to him in a haze of perfumes and embraced him, not entirely with platonic intent. Spirel and Mikodez and Istradez had slept together once, because Spirel had expressed an interest, Istradez was drunk out of his mind and thought the idea was really funny, and Mikodez hadn't cared one way or the other so why not. Curiosity allegedly satisfied, she hadn't asked again, but Mikodez occasionally wondered.

"It's you, isn't it," she said with that particular wry tone.

"I hate how you can always tell," Mikodez said into her ear.

Spirel disengaged as neatly as a voidmoth pilot and smiled at him. "That's why I get paid so much, yes?" In academy she had been tracked not as a courtesan but as Shuos infantry. He knew from experience not to get into an arm-wrestling match with her. Technically he was stronger, but she never played by the rules. (He had no idea why, that first time, he had expected a fellow Shuos to play by the rules, even a fellow Shuos who was his sibling's long-time lover.)

She then gave him a critical look that was so similar to the one that Istradez had given him back in the conference room that

Mikodez sighed and traipsed obediently to the couch. He began to arrange himself. Spirel cleared her throat. Meekly, he took off his shoes. Spirel had very strong opinions about shoes on her couch. It might be Istradez's apartment, but Mikodez was sure that even in Security's room roster the couch was listed as Spirel's particular possession.

"I'm tired," Mikodez said without meaning to, and was additionally horrified by how blurry his voice sounded. He'd better visit Medical again. They were always fiddling with the cocktail he had to take, but the meds hadn't failed him this badly in a while.

"Sleep, then," Spirel said with the brisk practicality he liked about her. "Scoot over."

He did, even though it was taking an increasing amount of effort to get his muscles to respond. Spirel climbed in next to him and pulled the blankets over them both. Her heat radiated from her like a living thing in its own right, and she smelled of mint and citrus and an odd twist of lavender. She burrowed against him until he let her pillow her head on his shoulder. *Great,* was the last thought he had before falling asleep, *I'm going to wake up with no circulation in that arm.*

When he woke, though, his arm wasn't numb at all. Spirel had already gotten up and was sketching at the window that opened up onto a view of one of the Citadel's gardens. She liked drawing dragonflies. This particular garden had an abundance of them.

"Good afternoon," Mikodez said. "Where's Istra?"

"Right here," Istradez said, emerging from the bathroom. He was still toweling himself off. He grimaced at the hexarch's uniform that Spirel had laid out for him, then shook his head and stomped off to the closet. "No, no, no, no—hmm. I haven't worn that one in a while."

"You mean you haven't worn that one ever," said Spirel, who had nearly infallible skills of observation when it came to clothing and jewelry.

"How would you know?" Istradez demanded.

"Because I bought it for you two weeks ago, remember?"

Mikodez translated that into fourteen days. Spirel insisted on using the seven-day week even though it was, if not technically illegal, considered unlucky through most of the hexarchate. It came from her people's traditions. She had remarked once that she had no idea what the rest of their old calendar had looked like before her people looked around and decided to join the hexarchate before getting wiped out as heretics. Mikodez had asked her why she had chosen this particular bit of calendrical minutiae to preserve, and she had shrugged.

Istradez changed his mind yet again and put on a set of robes in pink and yellow, a deliberately attenuated variation on Shuos colors. He was swearing as he tried to put on jewelry that went with it, rose quartz and heliotrope and the startling, contrasting pale flashes of aquamarine in glittering facets. Spirel pulled a face at Mikodez behind Istradez's back and matter-of-factly went to help Istradez with the clasps.

"Thank you," Istradez said.

"I could have sworn I paid you enough to afford real gems and not synthetics," Mikodez said. He knew everything Istradez kept in his collection, all the careless strands of rose gold, the music boxes, the emergency hairpins. Mikodez and Istradez both wore their hair short in back, despite the long forelock, but Spirel was forever losing her hairpins.

Istradez shrugged with one shoulder. "Not like I wear these anywhere that anyone is going to find out and care."

Mikodez hoisted himself off the couch and strode across the room to grab Istradez by the shoulders and force him to face him. "You are the vainest person I know," he said, snatching up a comb and some mousse from the nearby dresser and beginning to fix Istradez's hair. "Honestly, one of these days the details will get you."

"*Excuse* me," Spirel said. "Are you saying that he's vainer than I am on account of a few bits of glitter? I'm clearly not trying hard enough." She had laid her charcoal down. Her hands and sleeves were smudged black all over.

Istradez's pupils had grown large, swallowing the amber-brown irises. "I like shiny things, all right? It's not a crime to like shiny things. At least I don't assassinate children with them."

Spirel made a frantic shushing motion.

"All right," Mikodez said, remembering what he'd jotted down in the notes to his own procedures for dealing with aggravated employees—except Istradez was also family. *Deescalate.* "What did I do this time?"

"Nothing," Istradez said.

"No one ever says 'nothing' and means it." Mikodez set down the comb before Istradez grabbed it and stuck it in his eye. Istradez had always had a bit of a temper. "Are you ever going to debrief me on that damn meeting?"

Istradez growled low in his throat, then leaned forward and kissed him, nipping his lower lip. "Leaned" wasn't entirely the word for it. Istradez was pressing his full body into Mikodez's. *We're not twins,* Mikodez thought ironically, clothes aside. Istradez's cock was hard where his was only half-roused, for reasons that had nothing to do with sex.

"Brother-sweet," Mikodez said, unemotional, "you know you only have ever to ask."

"That's what I tried to tell him," Spirel remarked with a distinct lack of sympathy, over the splashing of water. She had gone to the bathroom to wash the charcoal dust from her fingers, an endeavor that never went well. She often wore gloves to hide the dust beneath her fingernails.

Istradez raised a hand to slap his brother. Mikodez caught it and brought it to his mouth, kissed the knuckles above the cheap rings. A sob choked its way out of Istradez's throat. "It's easy for *you*," he said. "Good, bad, right, wrong, you don't *care*. It's only ever about efficiency for you."

"I do my job," Mikodez said, "because after all the trouble I went to get it, it would be irresponsible not to." He continued kissing as he bore Istradez toward the couch and pushed him down. Istradez was resisting very little.

Mikodez knelt before the couch and laid his hand on the inside of Istradez's thigh. Yes: that got a reaction. "I will always do my job. I am the will of the Shuos. But don't ever, ever doubt that I love you."

Spirel came out of the bathroom then, and he nodded at her. She smiled at him, a little sadly, before taking his hand and helping him up so he could drape himself over Istradez. For her part, she sat on the floor, as curled and comfortable as a cat, and kissed her way up the side of Istradez's neck. With one hand she reached up to massage Mikodez's back, unnecessary but welcome. He wondered if she had gotten all the charcoal out. Istradez's eyes were wide and glazed, and he said something in a half-gasp, half-moan.

"Shh," Mikodez said. "Shh." And he set himself to the task of pleasing Istradez, making a note in the back of his head to check Istradez's most recent evaluations.

# CHAPTER TWELVE

BREZAN HAD NO reason to expect anything to change when he heard footsteps beyond the door to the cell's antechamber. Hunger was a familiar sharp ache, and his mouth was always dry. The past weeks, which he had lost count of after his captors disabled his augment, had been predictable. Too bad there was singularly little pleasure, under the circumstances, to be had from telling himself 'I told you so.'

All he remembered about his transfer from the Shuos to the Kel was a blur of untalkative people in the faction's garish red-and-gold uniforms. What had become of the two irritating medics he would never find out, which was just as well. As for Sfenni and his tasseled minion, he imagined that they were doing just fine.

The Kel had lost no time in verifying his identity. Then they put him in this cell. After two interminable days, during which he resisted the urge to shout at the walls, a colonel showed up. "Kel Brezan," she had said, "you are excused from standing, given your condition. Do you understand me?"

He would have risen to salute her anyway. She shook her head. He settled for the least half-assed sitting salute he could manage.

"Kel Brezan," she said, "until the circumstances that led to the dismissal of yourself and the Swanknot swarm's seconded personnel are understood, it is necessary for your rank to be suspended."

Standard procedure. He had divined as much from the mode of address. The Kel interrogators would speak to him next. Formation instinct would get them the best results if his rank didn't get in the way. "Understood, sir," he rasped.

"Tell me something, soldier. Why seek rescue from the Shuos?"

He had known this was going to be a sticking point. This wouldn't win him any friends, but he had accepted that when he decided on his course of action. He summarized his line of reasoning.

"In other words," the colonel said, "General Jedao offloaded personnel he couldn't control with formation instinct, and you were one of them."

"Yes, sir," Brezan said. The words cut his throat like glass. "I was the only Kel eyewitness to the takeover to get out." He had heard nothing of the Doctrine officer. It was possible that they had died of medical complications.

The colonel's eyes were frosty. "You have just become someone else's problem, soldier. Enjoy the rest you get now. You won't be getting much more of it."

"Sir," Brezan said dully. He knew what the Kel did to crashhawks. At best they would revoke his commission and outprocess him. At worst they would execute him. But he had seen no other way to fulfill his duty.

Brezan spent a long time alone after that, observing remembrances with meditations whenever the dead-sounding voice over the announcement system reminded him to. Presumably they were sending for Rahal or Vidona, since Kel interrogators hated dealing with crashhawks, as if they were contagious. A servitor brought him food at intervals, never more than a little tepid rice and water. He was starting to wish he'd taken more advantage of Shuos Sfenni's hospitality while he'd had the chance. Brezan made a game of trying to tell the servitors apart. Either it was a different servitor each time, or they modified themselves for the hell of it.

In spite of himself, Brezan wished for a Vidona. He didn't like the Vidona any more than any sensible person did, but he had endured the straightforward application of pain before. Heretic terrorists had captured a transport when he was a captain. They hadn't held the captives long before the Kel freed them, but to this day Brezan remembered the hot filaments of pain in his feet and face, the recuperation afterward. They'd had to regrow one of his eyes. The Vidona could only torture you. The Rahal could scry your signifier, including signifier reactions to specific questions. Not as direct as lie detection, or anywhere near mindreading (although there were rumors), but a skilled practitioner could trick the truth out of you.

When the hex of Rahal inquisitors arrived thirteen days after he was taken into custody, he knew they were taking his warning seriously. He'd started to wonder. He was pacing at the time, if you could call it that when he was moving agonizingly slowly both due to his lingering sleeper-recovery and the spider restraints, even on a relaxed setting. It took him a moment to register the hex's presence. The plain robes, gray with bronze hems, were impossible to mistake, the wolf equivalent of full formal. The Rahal did their uniforms backwards, wearing more ornate clothing on more casual occasions.

The head inquisitor was a woman with curly hair and an imperturbable expression. All six wolves' eyes sheened bronze, indicating that they had activated scrying. They murmured a greeting in an archaic form of the high language.

Brezan fought down the lump of fear that threatened to choke him and gave them a formal bow as best as the restraints permitted, which wasn't very. The Rahal had a reputation for being fussy about protocol, but they also prided themselves on rationality. They wouldn't blame him for something that wasn't under his control.

The head inquisitor acknowledged the bow with a nod, which meant she had decided not to take offense. "Kel," she said, "I am Inquisitor Rahal Hwan. We are here to determine the truth of your claims." She spoke a very pure form of the high language.

"I'll do my best not to get in your way, Inquisitor," Brezan said, as if he could withstand a full hex.

"You may as well be seated," Hwan said. "This will take a while."

Brezan dragged himself to the bench and sat. His legs wobbled, but damned if he was going to show it. He looked up, determined to meet Hwan's eyes even if it wasn't strictly necessary, and fell sideways through a fissure in his head.

Part of him was sitting on the bench. The rest of him was in his parents' apartment on Irissa Station, in the dreamspace triggered by Hwan's first question. He wondered fleetingly what it had been before his attention was caught by the walls. They looked like they'd been redone in gun components caulked in something that gleamed viscously. Why had his three fathers done that?

Brezan checked for his oldest sister Keryezan at her favorite reading spot by the lamp with the painting of the grasshoppers. She wasn't there, nor were her two children. Keryezan was the only one of his sisters he got along with, and he enjoyed cooking indulgent dishes for the kids.

He turned around and his other sisters, the twins Miuzan and Ganazan, sat playing pattern-stones with their youngest father's set. Ganazan, who wore her hair pinned back from her face, had somehow talked Miuzan into giving her a three-stone handicap. Miuzan categorically hated giving people handicaps. Brezan had never gotten her to give him one growing up despite the fact that she was six years older than he was.

Both the twins were in uniform. Ganazan served as a clerk on a boxmoth, which she considered superior to running around in a combat moth. Logistics had always appealed to her. Miuzan was a colonel on General Inesser's staff and couldn't be made to shut up about it.

Brezan opened his mouth and said something, he wasn't sure what. It didn't matter. Both his sisters gave no sign of having heard him. He inspected his hands. No black gloves. No uniform, either, just sober brown civilian's clothing.

Another fissure opened, and he fell through again. He and Miuzan stood in a dueling hall that stretched out so far to either side that the ends curved away. Miuzan's calendrical sword was bright in her hand, numbers glowing red with white sparks. She had always been good at dueling. As a child, Brezan had loved to watch her practice her forms, admiring the ferocity of her discipline.

Brezan activated his own sword to salute her. The blade wasn't its usual sullen blue, but red shading to yellow. *Foxes,* he thought in aggravation. It was tempting to blame Shuos Zehun. In all fairness, however, Zehun hadn't hanged him. They had merely tossed him a nice long rope.

"You're going to lose, little brother," Miuzan said with her usual superiority. "But you're getting better, I'll give you that."

Brezan frequently had fantasies of shoving Miuzan in a cloisonné box and sending her to the Andan so they could teach her to be less condescending or, at least, less obvious about it. The hell of it was, she seemed to be unaware of how much she made his teeth ache. He had long ago given up on ever having her approve of him; he'd settle for getting her to shut up.

"I'm a better shot than you are," Brezan said, although it was a mistake to make any rejoinder at all.

She eyed him critically. "Yes, that will come in handy if you want to be stuck in the infantry for the rest of your life."

There came a count of four, and Miuzan lunged. Brezan parried too late. It would have made no difference anyway. Miuzan's sword flared up and the flames became dark-bright wings. The blade itself stretched out into an ashhawk's head and sinuous neck.

Brezan swore and ducked. The ashhawk with its vicious raptor's beak passed harmlessly through him. The flames roared up around him, heatless despite the stench of roasting flesh.

Miuzan was burning red and gold. Her hair had come loose from its braid and was whipping around her head. Blackened sheets of skin were already peeling loose from her face, making a dry crackling sound. Bone showed white at her skull and knuckles. "Oh Brezan," she said, her voice entirely normal in spite of all this, "you'll never be formation fuel at this rate."

"Who the everliving fuck joins the Kel with the *intent* of becoming formation fuel?" Brezan shouted at her. Miuzan might be infuriating, but she was still his older sister. She had taught him pattern-stones and swordplay and how to take apart and reassemble every single one of the family's guns, not to mention how to bake amazing honey-ginger cookies. He didn't want her to die in a suicide formation or to an enemy bullet or, for that matter, by tripping down the stairs.

He just wanted her to stop treating him like he was still the gawky eight-year-old who kept following her and Ganazan around hoping they would play forts with him.

Miuzan might have responded, but Brezan couldn't hear her over the roaring of the fire. He developed a crazed notion that if he burned himself too, he would be able to follow her so he could shake some answers out of her. Try as he might, however, the flames took no notice of him. He was wearing his black gloves now—funny how that had happened. Unfortunately, it made no difference.

The scrying continued in this vein for quite some time. Back on the bench, Brezan hunched over and shook with hunger. The Rahal might be used to fasting, but he still hadn't recovered from whatever they had botched putting him in the sleeper. A servitor brought him water. He choked it down. It tasted like it was heavy with soot.

The Rahal took their sweet time working their way to the topic of Jedao. In the interrogation, Jedao didn't appear as a womanform, like Brezan himself, but as he had in the archival videos, a lean, slightly short man. His uniform was in full formal with the old-fashioned red-and-gold braid of a seconded Shuos officer, making Brezan feel underdressed. Jedao had the same tilted smile, however. He was playing pattern-stones with Brezan. In the back of his mind, Brezan resolved never to play another board game unless someone ordered him to. The stones shifted position each time Brezan blinked. Behind him, although he didn't dare glance over his shoulder, he heard distant shrieks and sobs.

Jedao had a revolver in his left hand. He wore no gloves, fingerless or otherwise, which Brezan took to mean that he was playing for keeps. Each time Brezan placed a black stone—naturally he was the weaker player—Jedao shot one of his fingers off. The bullets didn't do any damage to the board or its shifting array of stones, neat trick, although Brezan flinched at the ricochets.

Even though this was a scrying and not the real thing, the pain was riotous. The real thing might have been preferable. Then he'd have had a chance of passing out.

Brezan tried to breathe steadily. *Pretend this is a remembrance,* he told himself. Did that ever console heretics? He had to defeat the fucking ninefox general, but he only had four fingers left. He placed a stone. Jedao reloaded and fired without looking. His aim was impeccable.

Three fingers left. Then two. Then one, with which Brezan managed by scooping the stone between his remaining finger and left palm. At last Brezan had no fingers at all, just a set of bleeding stumps.

Jedao cocked an eyebrow at him. "What now?" he said.

"I am going to stop you if it kills me," Brezan said, wishing he had a better gift for futile last words, especially since, with the Rahal, he had an audience.

He bent over to pick up one last stone with his teeth—

Everything after that hurt even worse, which he hadn't thought possible. Eventually the Rahal hex went away. For a while he didn't realize it. He forced down more water when they offered it. The gnawing pain at the pit of his stomach wouldn't go away, but it felt like it was happening to someone else. Being someone else sounded like an excellent career move right now.

"I am Kel," Brezan whispered to the wall when he was sure no one was around. He couldn't hear his own voice. The words scraped his throat raw.

Time passed. The taste of ashes receded. He shivered constantly. But he had to endure. The Kel might require more information from him. He needed to be in a fit state to give it to them. With any luck, they wouldn't ask too late for it to stop Jedao.

Brezan thought of the Kel who had been in the command center when Jedao took over, training their weapons on him. He thought of General Khiruev, and the first time they had met. Brezan had been surprised to be tapped for Khiruev's staff after his predecessor developed a rare medical condition, and not sure he liked what it implied. The general had a reputation for unconventional thinking, not to mention flouting Kel Command's wishes, which could be good or bad, depending.

During the first meeting, the general had asked him how he was settling in, to which Brezan made the only possible tactful response. (He did occasionally find his way to tact.) Khiruev had then said, unexpectedly, *I hope you help me never to forget that it's people that we send out to die.* She was looking at a casualty list from the recent battle. It wasn't the sort of confidence you'd expect as a newcomer, but he'd seen the bleakness in the general's eyes and resolved to do what he could.

A sane person might be forgiven for not feeling a whole lot of affection for Kel Command at this point, but the fate of Khiruev and his swarm might depend on Brezan's information, and Kel Command wasn't why Brezan had become a hawk anyway. Indeed, Kel Command was a great argument for avoiding the Kel. Family wasn't the reason, despite what Brezan had told Shuos Zehun in academy, although family had something to do with it. No: it was that the hexarchate was a terrible place to live, but it would be an even worse one if no one with a conscience consented to serve it.

You couldn't pull the hexarchate apart and exchange it for something better. The fact that the heretics always lost was proof of that. So you had to do the next best thing, the only thing left: serve, and hope that serving honorably made some small difference.

Now, as the door to the antechamber slid open, Brezan staggered to his feet and prepared to bow. The person standing there was a rattled-looking Kel corporal. "Sir," Brezan said, saluting instead.

The corporal opened the cell's door and shut off the restraints. "Come with me, soldier," he said.

Brezan wished he could ask what was going on, but he might as well enjoy blissful ignorance while it lasted, not to mention the odd sensation of being able to move freely. It was a minor miracle that he could walk fast enough to keep up.

They didn't have far to go. The corporal brought him to an oversized conference room with a secured terminal, the Kel kind that had a nook of its own in the wall. "I'll be right outside, soldier," the corporal said. "Come out when they're done with you."

The light on the terminal indicated that someone wanted to talk, and the subdisplay had a summons with his name on it. Well, he couldn't get more presentable, so he might as well approach the terminal. He saw his signifier like a dark, broken ghost in the golden metal. "Kel Brezan reporting as ordered," he said, saluting preemptively. It only occurred to him too late to wonder if he should have changed his uniform into full formal.

The terminal brightened. "Kel Brezan," said a woman's voice, measured, precise. The broad, unsmiling face on the main display belonged to Hexarch Kel Tsoro.

Brezan had no idea what the hexarch required of him. He doubted she was going to personally order him to get a hot meal and a good night's rest. "Hexarch," he said.

"At ease," Tsoro said. "Your information on Shuos Jedao has been verified. We have a new assignment for you."

Brezan said nothing. According to his augment, seventy-seven days had elapsed since Jedao booted him from the Swanknot swarm. How much bureaucracy had prevented him from getting his warning through earlier, and how much damage had the Immolation Fox done in that time?

"Assignment" meant he wasn't being dismissed from Kel service. On the other hand, the list of atrocious assignments filled up whole planets. He tamped down the flare spark of hope.

"You seem to be confused on a certain point," Tsoro added, with an instructor's dryness, "so let us clarify this for you, because it's important. You're a crashhawk, Kel Brezan."

He flinched. "Sir—"

"The test results are clear. Your formation instinct has decayed even from the low levels it displayed when you were in academy. It's rare but not unheard of. But really, you should have figured it out during your confrontation with Jedao."

"I wish to serve, sir," Brezan said hoarsely. "It's all I know."

"Happily, there are precedents for crashhawks being permitted to remain among the Kel," Tsoro said. "But you understand, it will be more difficult for you. Your actions will be scrutinized. You will have to choose, over and over, to be loyal. You won't have formation instinct to guide you, especially when your orders give you pause and the habits of obedience wear thin. We are offering you this opportunity because you risked a great deal to bring us your warning, and because we approve of your conduct."

"Then let me be a Kel, sir," Brezan said, his heart thumping too rapidly.

"The assignment, then. This is to be a joint Kel-Andan operation. You will be assigned to Agent Andan Tseya of the silkmoth *Beneath the Orchid*."

An Andan? For that matter, a silkmoth? They were small, swift courier vessels. He'd heard that you could build half a cindermoth for the price of one of the things. "Our objective, sir?" Brezan asked. He hadn't realized that the Kel were now on friendly terms with the Andan, but he'd been too busy worrying about Jedao and the Hafn to pay attention to faction politics.

"Agent Tseya is to assassinate Jedao on his command moth," Tsoro said, and smiled. "You will facilitate this as she directs."

Assassinating Jedao as a single target, as opposed to blowing the whole moth up, would take either an Andan or a Shuos for preference, so that much made sense. Still, Brezan felt a stab of revulsion. The Kel had formation instinct, the Rahal had scrying, and the Andan could enthrall you if you were in range, assuming they knew you well enough. There were undoubtedly lots of records on Jedao's personality structure to help Tseya out. He didn't imagine that Jedao was long for this world once Tseya made him her pet.

"Your job, Kel Brezan," Tsoro was saying, "is to wrest back control of the swarm once the agent is done."

There was a problem with this scenario. "Sir," Brezan said, "wouldn't we be better off returning the swarm to General Khiruev or whichever senior officer is still alive?" He hoped Khiruev had survived, something he hadn't permitted himself to contemplate earlier. As for himself, as much as he wished otherwise, he was no strategist. The swarm needed a line officer's leadership in case the Hafn struck at an inconvenient time.

"If Jedao has some trick in store and eludes the agent," Tsoro said, "we need someone to break his hold over the Kel. Khiruev won't do. She's already buckled once to Jedao's authority. We've revoked Jedao's commission, but by now Jedao has had a lot of time to talk to Khiruev, and the ninefox has a history of being extraordinarily persuasive when cornered. No, a general is no good to us. We need to send a high general."

It took Brezan a moment to piece together the implications. "I believe you've coined a brand-new Kel joke, sir," he said, too wrung-out and angry to care who he was talking to. "It's quite unfunny."

Tsoro smiled thinly. "Don't be absurd," she said. "The Kel never joke. You'd be surprised how hard it is to come up with a new one, besides."

For a few muddled seconds, Brezan tried to work out if there was any non-insubordinate way to say that he would rather kill himself with a wooden spoon than join the Kel hivemind. He had always been secure in the knowledge that he'd never succeed to command. Clearly the universe was punishing him for making sensible assumptions about his career.

Tsoro's eyes crinkled with amusement. "Don't worry," she said, "there would hardly be time to integrate you, and you'd need to be on site with the rest of Kel Command for it. In any case, historically speaking, not all high generals have been part of Kel Command, although Kel Command has always been composed of high generals." The change in practice had taken place after the establishment of the hivemind.

"Brevet rank," Brezan suggested.

"We prefer to limit the use of brevets because not all Kel respond to them satisfactorily."

There went that.

"You can still decline the mission."

He drew a shuddering breath. "I accept, sir."

"Good," Tsoro said. "Consider yourself promoted, High General Brezan. We'll expedite the paperwork. There have been enough delays already. Don't fail us, and don't forget to adjust your insignia. Your first stop should be Medical. After that, may we suggest that you use your first order to scare up some real food?"

Brezan opened his mouth to make a retort. Thankfully, the hexarch saved him from making an ass of himself by cutting the connection.

It looked like the universe was giving him another chance at Jedao. All he had to do was not fuck it up.

# CHAPTER THIRTEEN

KHIRUEV WAS HAVING an energetic argument with Colonel Kel Najjad in one of the conference rooms when the ultimatum arrived. They'd been having variations of this argument ever since Najjad joined Khiruev's staff. At this point, Khiruev would have felt disoriented if they discussed logistics without also sniping at each other about completely irrelevant points of musicology.

"—that flute concerto by Yeri Chejio," Najjad was saying as he jabbed the map. The interface couldn't make up its mind about what Najjad wanted it to do about the jabs. Add a waypoint? Assign the waypoint to Tactical One? Change the color of the marker? Create an inset centered at the site of the jab?

"Colonel," Khiruev said, "would you please stop doing that? I'll even concede that the seven-movement suite is a valid form on the grounds that the early post-Liozh composers can't be put into proper historical context without it. Just stop doing whatever it is you're doing."

Najjad grinned at her. "I'll show you the trick if you like, sir." He had a positive gift for breaking interfaces, or causing the grid to hang. Sometimes Khiruev thought she should loan the man to the Shuos the next time she needed a favor. "It's all about confusing the—"

Khiruev looked at Najjad's latest map and winced. "I don't want to know how to duplicate the feat. I just want to stop getting a headache every time I try to figure out who in this radius is still talking to us that has the setup to do repairs on this many bannermoths."

"If we still had any Nirai," Najjad said, "I could torture one of them with the inadequacy of the interface controls. But our beloved general sent them packing, so I'm afraid you're stuck."

"I'll be sure to put it on the list of grievances I have against him," Khiruev said, "so I can present it to him the next time I'm feeling suicidal."

Najjad stopped making the terminal have fits, thank goodness. "At least he hasn't stuck knives in us yet. I'm actually rather—"

The grid said, "Message for General Khiruev from Communications."

Khiruev checked the headers and hid her surprise. She had a hunch that Communications was trying to tell her something that should properly go first to the ranking officer. There were a number of reasons Communications might choose such a course of action. None of them had pleasant implications. "Clear out, Colonel," she said. "I'll get back to you when I can."

Najjad thumped a salute, gave the interface one last jab to make Khiruev twitch, and left the room.

"Secure the room until I say otherwise," Khiruev told the mothgrid. "Get me Communications."

Communications forwarded Khiruev not one but two messages from Kel Command. She saw immediately why Communications had hesitated to bring either to Jedao's attention directly. It was clear which message was more important, but Khiruev knew the order in which she ought to deal with them.

She requested, and got, a link with Communications. "Make sure Commander Janaia gets these orders," she said. Janaia was off-shift at the moment, but she knew Janaia slept lightly. "General Khiruev to all units. I am aware that you may have gotten word from Kel Command. All units are to hold formation. Formation breaks will be met with the usual consequences."

"It's gone out, sir," Communications said after a moment.

"Good," Khiruev said. It wouldn't buy much time, but with any luck, she could get this sorted out before the swarm began to panic.

She asked the mothgrid where she could find Jedao and flagged the query as urgent. After an unusual stutter, the grid replied that Khiruev should meet Jedao in the latter's quarters. Strictly speaking, Jedao could choose to be as inaccessible as he pleased. There could be some mundane reason for it. Still, there was nothing to do but show up and trust that the general was willing to talk to her.

Khiruev departed the conference room and headed straight for Jedao's quarters. The door admitted her. Jedao was standing with his hands folded behind him, contemplating several large paintings projected at various points against the far wall. At a guess, he was trying to figure out how colors harmonized with each other and mostly failing, one of his favorite pastimes.

"Have you heard the news, sir?" Khiruev asked as she entered.

"What news?"

Communications hadn't wanted to be the messenger. Khiruev couldn't blame her, although she had taken one hell of a risk routing the messages so Jedao didn't catch wind. "Two things," Khiruev said. Time to take a risk herself. "We've received an ultimatum from the hexarchs."

"There must be some reason it went straight to you," Jedao said, fixing her with an interested stare. He dismissed the paintings with a wave. "Care to enlighten me?"

"May I?" At Jedao's nod, Khiruev played back the message from the primary terminal. The old familiar chill ran through Khiruev when she saw the Vidona stingray. Jedao's expression was politely curious. A woman's affectless voice said, in clear, pure high language, "Shuos Jedao. You are to release the Swanknot swarm to the nearest Kel facility by the twenty-seventh day of the Month of Pyres, and turn yourself over to hexarchate authorities. The Mwennin are in Vidona custody. If you fail to comply, we will annihilate them. In case you need the reminder—"

Her voice went on, giving a summary of who the Mwennin were, their numbers, where they lived. There were an estimated 58,000 of them, concentrated on the world of Bonepyre. The only reason Khiruev had heard of them earlier was that Lieutenant Colonel

Brezan had brought that part of Cheris's profile to her attention. The hexarchate was home to a staggering number of ethnic groups, but the Mwennin were unusual for avoiding faction service and predominantly practicing natural birth, among other cultural quirks. She and Brezan had wondered what had driven Cheris to the Kel. Cheris's profile had suggested a need to fit into the hexarchate's broader culture. The assessment had approved of this, but Khiruev bet Cheris had had second thoughts.

"I'm not certain what they're hoping to accomplish," Jedao said, his voice revealing little concern. "It's taken, what, two and a half months for them to come up with this threat? I wonder how much paperwork they had to do first. But then, I've never had a high opinion of Vidona proceduralism."

Khiruev counted to six. The gamble was going badly already. When she could trust her voice not to shake, she said, "Sir, don't you care at all? They're about to die because of the body you choose to wear." Had she misjudged Jedao after all? "There must be something you can—"

In her head she saw Mother Ekesra laying her hands on Kthero's shoulders, the crinkling corpse-paper, the folded swans. Swanknot.

"I can what, General?" Jedao said coolly. "Let's find out where Bonepyre is." He tapped out the query. A map of the hexarchate swirled into focus. The swarm's location was highlighted in gold. Bonepyre's location was highlighted in blue. "I trust you studied logistics at some point? Guess what, Bonepyre's in the Ausser March, on the other fucking side of the hexarchate. That's one hell of a detour, and we don't know, because the Kel rather reasonably aren't talking to me about their operations, if a decent swarm is available nearby to hold the Severed March in our absence. Are you saying that I should give the invaders a free hand here on the behalf of 60,000 people I have no agents in place to help?"

"I was hoping you might devise some plan," Khiruev snapped. "One of my mothers was a Vidona. Do you know how they carry out purges? I do. She'd come home and talk about it because it was just a job to her. Every little thing was compartmentalized into subtasks, like pieces of a jigsaw puzzle. Rescind the target population's jobs. Issue them special identification. Refuel the processing facilities. Make sure there were enough bullets or knives or poison canisters or whatever the flavor of the month was. Send out extra patrols to deal with any that try to go terrorist or rouse the rest of the population. If you focused on the little jigsaw pieces, you never had to notice that the whole puzzle added up to people dying."

"I'm aware of your family history, General," Jedao said. "I appreciate that your father's death must have affected you greatly. But you've got to stop reacting and start thinking. I don't have supernatural powers, and neither do you. Neither of us has any pull with the authorities on Bonepyre, and even if someone in this swarm did, it would already be too late for a useful intervention. And where exactly would we evacuate 60,000 people to? Our swarm doesn't have the capacity to handle that kind of influx."

"I'm so glad you're girding yourself with reasons not to try," Khiruev said. Distantly, she was impressed with herself for losing her temper this badly. What was wrong with her? And more importantly, why had she expected better from a mass murderer?

"Still with the reacting," Jedao said. "Does it not occur to you that the Vidona could be lying? While 60,000 people is too many to conveniently haul away to an imaginary refuge, by the hexarchate's standards it's a trivial number to wipe out. And I imagine you can tell me all about how the Vidona pride themselves on their thoroughness. For all we know, those people are already dead."

Khiruev looked at him in frustration. She was serving someone walking around in a Kel's body. She was complicit in the threat to that Kel's people.

"It's not entirely bad that you're so rattled," Jedao said quietly. "It gives me hope for the Kel." Khiruev startled. "But General, you can do better than this. Think it through. Suppose that some miracle is possible after all. We teleport across the hexarchate with a flotilla of just-add-water habitats and get the Mwennin out. What then?"

Khiruev began pacing because she couldn't think of anything else to do with her nervous energy. Jedao had left the door to the first inner room open, the way he usually did. As Khiruev passed the doorway, she spotted a polished rock with a bird engraving that had been left on a table. *How odd,* she thought, uncomfortably aware that she was prying. Other than the ubiquitous jeng-zai cards and the metal cup, it was the first indication Khiruev had had of Jedao's personal effects.

When she reached the wall, Khiruev pivoted on her heel—and stopped dead. She had been about to say something, but it went clean out of her head when she saw that Jedao had unholstered his gun. Jedao was looking abstractedly at the wall as he ran the gun's muzzle along his jaw. Khiruev's heart stuttered.

"Sir," Khiruev said unsteadily, "do you require a refresher course in firearms safety?"

Jedao frowned at him. "What? Oh, sorry. Bad habit."

Khiruev refrained from mentioning what she'd do to any soldier of hers with such a 'bad habit.' To her relief, Jedao set the gun down on a table next to a jeng-zai deck. He shifted his weight, then settled there momentarily, tapping the table with an erratic rhythm.

*He's not as unaffected as he would have me believe,* Khiruev realized. She had rarely observed Jedao fidgeting before, even if Jedao's face revealed only exasperation with the situation. It made Khiruev feel better, paradoxically.

"Anyway," Jedao said as he began meandering around the room, taking the jeng-zai deck with him and scattering cards on every available surface like a constellation of thwarted gambles, "think it through. Fine. We magically save the Mwennin. Tell me what the hexarchs' next move is."

Khiruev paused by one of the cards. The Chained Tower. She couldn't stop herself from looking for the Deuce of Gears, but had no luck spotting it. Jedao had, however, left the Ace of Gears peeking from beneath a face-down card.

"Two of my parents came from the Khaigar community on Denozin 4," Khiruev said slowly. "There are more Khaigars scattered throughout the system. Then there's Commander Janaia. She's a mix of things, but she's always identified most strongly with the Moionna because of her favorite grandmother. Muris has Moionna in him, too, far back. Colonel Riozu's four parents were part of a wave of immigration from Anxiao to Eng-Nang during a civil uprising. I could go on." Brezan would have known more of this without having to look everyone up, but mentioning him in front of Jedao was a rotten idea. "There are a lot of people in the swarm, and a lot of peoples represented."

Jedao's mouth curved into a not-smile. He was waiting for Khiruev to follow through the logic.

"The Vidona will be able to obtain the personnel records through Kel Command," Khiruev said, "assuming they don't have them already. They could easily pick out the most expendable peoples and target them as well to put pressure on the swarm's crew." She wasn't proud of how steady her voice was when she said 'expendable.' "It would touch off massive uprisings, but they might be desperate enough to try it anyway."

"Unfortunately," Jedao said, "even if we show no sign of giving a damn about a people as obscure as the Mwennin, there's no guarantee they won't try what you described anyway. I'm hoping the Kel will argue against for the reason you mentioned, but I can't say I have a lot of faith in Kel Command."

"Sir," Khiruev said, "I ask again: what are your intentions toward the swarm? You must have had some form of long-term objective."

*You must have known that something like this would happen eventually.*

"I have no reason to be fond of what the hexarchate has become," Jedao said. "But people won't fight their own government unless they think they have a way to win. We're going to provide them with a way to win."

"My Vidona mother used to come home with bulletins about heretics who thought they could outfight the Kel and Shuos with some new secret weapon," Khiruev said. "None of them ever succeeded."

"That's exactly their problem," Jedao said. "You think I haven't put down my share of heretics at Kel Command's orders? They always think it's about the fucking tech. It's not. It's about people."

Khiruev studied Jedao's face. "Exotic technology is already about belief systems, so you must be referring to something else." They were discussing treason.

She had spent a long career doing Kel Command's will because she had chosen to be a Kel. Once she became Kel, she had very constricted choices. Nevertheless, she wondered if she should have contemplated treason earlier. She would never have done so if she hadn't encountered Jedao. She knew herself that well, at least.

Jedao made an abortive gesture. "General," he said, "you may have noticed that math isn't my strongest subject, so any plan of mine wouldn't rely on it. I use grid assistance a lot when we're in battle."

"I assumed you had some way of compensating," Khiruev said without concealing her curiosity. Someone with the mathematical difficulties she suspected Jedao of having would never have been accepted as a Kel officer candidate. However, Jedao had come in sideways, through the Shuos, and it was hard to argue with his performance.

"I have a form of dyscalculia," Jedao said. He glanced away. "They didn't even catch it until I was partway through Shuos Academy because I—I just worked harder. But it did mean that while my classmates were doing fancy calculations, I was busy figuring out how to trick them so those fancy calculations didn't come into play. And anyway, I thought I was going into a career that wouldn't require me to be fast with numbers, so for a while it didn't matter.

"But this is the thing about heretics. They're typically fixated on the numbers, whether it's manipulating atmospherics or spiking calendars so their new variety of gun will work when the Kel pop up. People are obsessed with guns"—his mouth compressed briefly—"but they're missing the point. It's about standing together against the hexarchs, not shooting them down. It's possible. I learned propaganda from a master of the art." His voice hitched on 'art,' settled. "You'll see."

Khiruev considered this. "Was the hex—heptarchate very different in your day?"

"Some things were bad," Jedao said. "Some of the same things, even. But it wasn't as all-around awful as it's gotten." The fractures in his eyes were unbearable. "Some of the things that got worse—they got worse because of me. I have to set it right."

There was no tactful way to ask when Jedao had figured this out. The Kel historians had skirted the issue, but it didn't take much perspicacity to figure out that half the problems with Kel Command could be traced to the early hivemind's fear of Jedao. That fear had not diminished over time. The undead general and the hivemind had circled each other like dancers for four centuries; they might continue circling for centuries yet.

"I am done serving the hexarchs," Jedao said. "Think what you will, but I couldn't endure the black cradle any longer and I couldn't keep butchering people for Kel Command. Maybe it's too late to develop a conscience. Still, I'd be remiss if I didn't stay on for one last round of cards." His smile had a hard edge. "You haven't had a choice, any of you. I'm no better than they are. But I needed a swarm, and here we are."

"Your plan—"

"No. I can't tell you details because I can't tell anyone. I am asking for your trust. I have done nothing to earn it."

"You've won battles. A war is not beyond you."

"If there were a way to save the Mwennin, we'd be doing it right now," Jedao said. "Doubt everything else if you want, but that one's true."

Khiruev gave him a long look, remembering what Jedao had said about killing children, then nodded. "There's one more thing you ought to hear, sir."

"I think I can guess." Jedao quirked an eyebrow at her and leaned against the wall.

At least he had a sense of humor about it. Khiruev triggered playback of the second message. It opened with Kel Command's ashhawk-and-sword emblem. Hexarch Kel Tsoro appeared after the emblem faded out. She was wearing full formal.

"Bulletin to all Kel personnel," Tsoro said in a flat voice. "Owing to circumstances, Shuos Jedao's commission with the Kel has been revoked effective immediately. His movements are to be reported to hexarchate authorities. Kel Command out."

There was something anticlimactic about the bulletin, as though it ought to burst into fire at the end.

"There you have it," Jedao said. He dragged a chair over, sat, and put his chin in his hands with his elbows on the chair's back. "You're free."

That wasn't the response Khiruev had been expecting.

Jedao's smile almost warmed his face. "You showed me the other message first so you could sound me out, didn't you? I should give you more credit for deviousness. You know, Kel Command seems to think that I can enchant people into doing whatever I want them to, as if I were some kind of super-Andan. They should have more faith in their own people."

"I am holding the swarm for you, sir," Khiruev said, wondering if Jedao fully appreciated the gravity of the situation, "but they're going to want a more definite understanding of their position shortly."

"You're choosing this instead of redeeming yourself in the eyes of Kel Command. Surely it wouldn't be hard for you to deliver them my hole-ridden corpse."

Khiruev grimaced. "I'm not the marksman you are."

"Missing the point. There are a lot more of you than there are of me. Unless you really think I'd try to massacre my way off a fucking cindermoth."

"It would mean betraying you, sir."

"Have you forgotten who I am, General?" Jedao's smile widened. He picked up the gun, neatly emptied it of ammunition, tossed the gun into a far corner. Khiruev winced, thinking, *Do the Shuos not teach firearms safety* at all? "Make it easy for you," Jedao said. "No resistance."

*Yes,* Khiruev thought bleakly, *because I like to shoot helpless targets.* Never mind that a four-hundred-year-old Shuos was anything but helpless. "Why are you so determined to have me turn on you?"

"You're a hard woman to figure out," Jedao said, meaning the opposite. "This whole conversation. You apparently don't want to be welcomed back by Kel Command. They'd be delighted to hear you'd dealt with me for keeps."

Khiruev glared at him.

Jedao's voice softened. "You could have your career back. That's the problem, isn't it? The moment they started piling on the commendations, you applied to be an instructor. The notation in your profile says that you had a temporary loss of nerve, but I don't see that there's anything temporary about it."

Khiruev said icily, "If you wish to accuse me of cowardice, you are well within—"

She wasn't arguing because she wanted to, except the part where she wanted to because she had a general who expected it of her.

Jedao was speaking over her. "It can't be that you hate the thought of composite work. This body isn't wired for it, and it didn't exist back when I was alive, so I have no idea what it feels like, but you've been composited plenty of times and you did fine. You could even be using composite work against the Hafn, given the odd way calendrical disturbances have been so localized, but I got in the way. No—it's because you hate the thought of joining Kel Command, isn't it? Or perhaps it's more accurate to say that you're afraid."

"By this point," Khiruev said, "it shouldn't be any surprise to you that I harbor no great fondness for my superiors. But I am hardly unique among Kel in that regard, even high officers."

"I get the part where you're determined to throw away your career once an ally, albeit a dangerous one, comes along. What I don't get is why you became a hawk to begin with."

"I expected to die in service when I was young," Khiruev said. "The hexarchate was in considerable turmoil then as now. I've heard you might know a thing or two about death-wishes yourself."

"In four hundred years," Jedao said, "I've learned that some fates make death look like a stroll. I told you before that I want your life, not your death. It's still true. But I need to know how it is that you're defying orders direct from Kel Command."

"You're right here," Khiruev said, wondering how Jedao could have no idea, "and Kel Command is in a secret fortress far away."

"A touching rationalization, but it doesn't work. If you were suffering formation break effects so badly when you were trying to assassinate me, you ought to be having some kind of reaction at the prospect of selling Kel Command out for someone who's just been kicked out of the service."

"Who says I'm not reacting?" Khiruev said. Her knees felt watery. She selected a chair and sat.

"You look terrible, at that," Jedao said. "What's it like, having formation instinct?"

"It's been sufficiently long that I don't remember what it was like before I was injected," Khiruev said. She wanted to close her eyes and await the inevitable bullet. By now she was old enough to realize that not all bullets were made of metal, or fired from guns. "Sir, I ought to warn you. I said I'd hold the swarm for you, and I will, but I'll only be useful to you for so long." Coming out and saying it was proving to be remarkably difficult. "The timer has already begun."

"Timer?" Jedao said sharply.

He didn't know after all. That was genuinely funny.

"General, if there's something I need to know, you'd better be the one to tell me. Now."

"Sir," Khiruev said, "are you aware of the Vrae Tala clause?"

"Never heard of it in my life."

"Then you don't know about Lieutenant General Vrae Tala, either."

"I assume you're winding around to some kind of point."

Khiruev smiled grimly. Her heartbeat felt sluggish, but this early it was only her imagination. "The general was assigned to the Fire Grasses campaign 281 years ago. Due to a breakdown in communications, she was left with orders for a full frontal assault on a heavily defended enemy stronghold, with the arrival of enemy reinforcements imminent, and none of her own support in sight due to logistical failures. You should take a look at the official account sometime. The Kel historians are unusually scathing."

"What, did Vrae Tala fail in the face of terrible odds? That's not a new story in the history of warfare."

"Vrae Tala was a good general. I've looked at the account. She did her best with those orders. The real issue is that Kel Command would never have stuck her with them if they'd had current information about what was going on."

Jedao's mouth pressed thin. "By 'timer' do you mean what I think you mean?"

"It only applies to general officers," Khiruev said, "and we don't discuss it much, but yes. If I think my orders have put me in an untenable situation, I can suspend formation instinct to get the job done. There's a price, of course. They wouldn't have relinquished control that easily, or allowed the clause to be abused, so invoking the clause is invariably fatal. I have one hundred days. We have a saying: every general is a clock. Well."

"You ratfucking idiot," Jedao said. "You had no call to—"

"It was inevitable that Kel Command would hear you were still alive," Khiruev said, squaring her shoulders. "At that point, they were obviously going to shred your commission into little pixels. But they weren't going to denude the swarm of all its officers because that would get ridiculous, especially if they wanted the swarm to remain functional on short notice. They must have someone on the way to take over, but until that person gets here, I haven't been discharged and I can give orders on your behalf. You'll have to figure out what to do once I drop dead. Then again, you're a fox. I imagine you'll work something out."

For once Jedao was speechless.

"You asked for my life, sir," Khiruev said. "This is the best I can give you."

"This does beg the question of why you didn't invoke this earlier. Your assassination attempt might have gone better."

Khiruev met his eyes. "I wasn't willing to commit suicide for Kel Command," she said. "Not even to stop you."

"I didn't want this for you," Jedao said after a moment.

"I know," Khiruev said. "That's why I did it."

They lingered in silence for a while. Then Jedao dismissed Khiruev, looking troubled. Khiruev headed out. She noted in passing that Jedao must have palmed the mysterious polished rock while pacing earlier, but she didn't think about it again until much later.

# CHAPTER FOURTEEN

BREZAN WASN'T SURE what he had expected from a silkmoth, but 'dainty' wasn't it, even if the Andan went in for that sort of thing. Currently he was on a transport set to rendezvous with the silkmoth *Beneath the Orchid*. Kel Command had offered him an honor guard. At first he had thought they were joking. Then he argued them out of it. The composite he had dealt with had seemed baffled by his insistence, but damned if he was going to let a promotion they'd cooked up for a one-off special mission get to his head.

"Almost there, sir," the pilot's voice said from the wall. "I'll get you a good view of it."

"Thank you," Brezan said automatically.

The confounding thing about the silkmoth was that it didn't share the wedge profile common to Kel warmoths, but it also didn't resemble the other Andan moths he had seen, with their scrolled finials and etched flower motifs, close-up details no one had any practical use for. Instead, *Beneath the Orchid* looked like a stellate glory of silver-blue lace suspended in the void. He had to squint to reassure himself that the starfield wasn't visible in the holes of the lace.

"We're cleared for a shuttle to ferry you over, sir," the pilot said after a while. Brezan had been so busy gawking at the silkmoth that he had forgotten to keep track of passing time. "Follow the gold markers and you'll be right there."

Brezan unwebbed himself, then his duffel bag. "I appreciate it," he said.

The shuttle hop was uneventful. He had expected landing on a silkmoth to feel different, and he laughed at himself. Stepping off the shuttle was another story. When the hatch opened, he had the unshakable impression that he had disembarked into a garden, if gardens came hung around with lights like floating crests and falling petals and—was that a miniature waterfall? While he'd previously encountered a couple of Andan moths, none of them had been this extravagant. He should have remembered that the Andan often entertained guests, sometimes from outside the hexarchate. Presenting the appearance of power and luxury would be important.

Andan Tseya was standing atop a sculpted hill, flanked by three birdform servitors on each side. Trust an Andan to seize the high ground. It was one of those tactical principles you could count on even very unmilitary Andan to have internalized.

Tseya was a tall woman, almost as tall as he was. Long black hair rippled down to her waist. Her skin was porcelain-pale, and she had the kind of face that was calculated to stop hearts if you forgot what she was, which Brezan had no intention of doing. Her eyes were currently brown—he checked—although he looked away as soon as he could, just in case.

Her blue silk blouse had been tailored very precisely. On someone less poised it would have looked stiff and uncomfortable. Her slacks were a darker blue, and her shoes had been dyed dark. A blue gem glittered from the brooch at her throat. He assumed it was a sapphire.

Brezan bowed deeply to her, remembering his etiquette class. "Agent," he said, using a very polite honorific. Andan hierarchies confused him, but you couldn't go wrong by erring on the side of flattery. "I am at your service by order of Kel Command."

"I honestly didn't think they'd send me my very own high general," Tseya said. She had a warm, wry voice, an alto, and it made him want to trust her. "I'm Andan Tseya, as you already know. I have to be frank, General. Your people and mine haven't been notable for playing nicely with each other in recent years. Is this mission going to be a problem for you?"

What was she reading in his body language? General Khiruev had once told him, with an amused glint in her eye, that he looked perpetually irascible. "Look," Brezan said, "the Kel may be strong, loyal, and stupid, but none of those is synonymous with 'bigoted.'"

"Or 'tactful,'" Tseya said, her smile sudden and merry. "I can tell you don't approve of the decor, so why don't we get you settled in? One of the servitors can take your duffel bag."

Brezan would have preferred to hold on to it, but he had no polite way to demur. He handed the bag over. The servitor said, "It is our honor to serve." He almost jumped, having forgotten that Andan servitors sometimes spoke.

The silkmoth's hallways weren't straight, or even curved in a sensible way. Rather, they meandered. Brezan was convinced that Tseya was taking the scenic route. It stood to reason that even a moth this small could have variable layout if it had a state-of-the-art power core, but why would you make the interior less efficient on purpose?

"We'll be consolidating the gardens for the trip to conserve power," Tseya said, confirming his suspicion. "Not one for flowers and calligraphy scrolls, are you?" She had paused next to a scroll that was artfully draped over a tree's low-hanging branch. Brezan was afraid it would blow away, even though there was no wind.

If this had been a glancing encounter at some official function, he could have entertained her by trying to lie his way out of this, but as it stood... "It's good calligraphy," Brezan said. "If you expect me to be able to identify the style, though, you're looking at the wrong Kel."

"At least you know there are different styles," Tseya said, smiling. "I daresay a lot of my people can't tell a dagger from a toothpick."

"No, that's us," Brezan said, deadpan. "I'm fairly sure I've never heard of toothpicks."

"I think we're going to get along, General."

They rounded a bend that featured, among other things, a clear, bright pond with the biggest carp Brezan had ever seen. He hoped like fuck that the carp were an illusion because what did they eat? What if they got hungry? Could they leap out of the pond and attack passers-by?

A tiny, tidy arch bridge with the factions' emblems carved into the rails spanned the pond. Tseya stepped onto the bridge without any sign that the scene bothered her. After a moment, Brezan followed, giving the carp a last nervous look.

Tseya had noticed, not that he had made any effort to hide his reaction. "You think this is extravagant, don't you? Personally, I find the meditations for the remembrances much more pleasant when I can do them in beautiful surroundings." Moth personnel were exempt from observing the remembrances while in transit, but some people insisted anyway.

Brezan considered this. "I suppose I could get the grid to image me something pretty," he said, "but I can't see why I would want to. It would be too distracting."

"And blank walls aren't distracting?"

Had they just passed a waterbird with wise eyes? "I'm used to them," Brezan said. He'd been raised on a station that didn't believe in pretending to be a miniature planet. It had had parks, but none as lavish as this garden.

"Suit yourself."

Thankfully, they soon arrived at his assigned quarters. Small potted trees stood to either side of the door. Brezan had expected to be deposited in some small, soothing, out-of-the-way room. He hadn't reckoned on Andan notions of 'small' or 'out-of-the-way.'

The room was a suite like the one General Khiruev had had on the *Hierarchy of Feasts*, and which that prick Jedao would have kicked her out of. Brezan hoped this suite wasn't bigger, but it sure as hell looked like it. For guests of state, he assumed. Thoughtfully, Tseya had decorated the receiving room with an ink painting of an ashhawk clutching arrows in its talons. General Andan Zhe Navo, who had served with such distinction among the Kel, was supposed to have been an archer as well as everything else. Not a subtle reminder, but it didn't bother him.

The servitor discreetly set his duffel bag down, then withdrew. Tseya paid it no heed. "I'll give you an hour to settle in," Tseya said, as if the walk had been strenuous. "Join me for lunch when you're ready. One of the servitors will be on call in case. Failing that, you can't go wrong by following the yellow flowers."

"I'll keep that in mind," he said. He'd noticed the flowers and their different colors, but he hadn't realized that they were functional as well as decorative. A neat alternative to hanging signs, unless you had one of those rare incurable allergies.

"Oh, and we have every sort of tea you might want to relax with. I mean it. The grid will tell you. Get me to talk you through the alcohol if that's what you're after, though. One of my cousins stocked the *Orchid* and their taste in wines is a little abstruse."

"I'll keep that in mind, too," Brezan said, although his taste in alcohol ran to the stuff you drank primarily to get drunk, and which could hardly be described as 'abstruse.'

Tseya regarded him questioningly, then murmured an excuse and left. When the door closed, Brezan slumped in relief for all of six seconds. Then he looked around at the wasteful expanse of the receiving room, at the beautifully executed painting. The brushstrokes were neither too loose nor too controlled, which he had found out during calligraphy lessons was harder than it looked. He had a quiet few moments of panic. Any second now a real general was going to show up and kick him out.

*Shut up,* Brezan told his brain. Kel Command was unpredictable, but they didn't pull this kind of stunt for laughs. Besides, he couldn't afford to lose his head. He had to help rescue General Khiruev and the swarm from Jedao.

He spent about twelve minutes unpacking and arranging his belongings. What was he supposed to fill all this space with? Some officers hauled lots of personal items around with them. General Khiruev's collection of gewgaws. Commander Janaia's octopus figurines. (She refused to explain why octopuses.) Major-analyst Shuos Igradna's flutes, most of which weren't in tune with each other, or possibly anything. For his part, Brezan had left most of his belongings with his parents. He wasn't sure why he had wanted to split his life in two. The partition had seemed very important when he was young, and then he had never grown out of the habit.

Ruefully, Brezan looked at the one item he had put on the largest table in a vain attempt to make it look less empty. His twin sisters Miuzan and Ganazan had given it to him when he graduated Kel Academy: a miniature orrery. A beautiful piece of work, he had to admit—silver-gold circles and gleaming gears and spinning jeweled planets. When he watched it too long, he could almost hear it singing. All the moons exhibited a shadowfall of feathers, an endless ashen drift. The orrery didn't correspond to any system any mothgrid he had accessed would admit to. The twins professed ignorance of the matter; he tended to believe them. In his gloomier moments, Brezan thought that the orrery represented some quiet procession of worlds and moons untouched by the hexarchate's rot—except there was that endless shadowfall, the touch of ashhawk conquest.

He reached for the orrery, then decided to leave it alone. In the meantime, if he was going to rattle around here, he might as well distract himself by considering clothing options. He had taken a protocol class in academy like everyone else, but he'd forgotten most of it. The refresher had been more confusing than anything else.

Brezan sorted through his civilian clothes several times, then shook his head. Fuck it, he'd stick to the uniform. It was, if not necessarily the best option, at least not incorrect. So what if she thought it was boring? If she disdained his attire, he could console himself that he hadn't designed the damn thing. On impulse, however, he put on two of his rings so that he didn't feel so damn stiff.

He sat and kicked at the floor, wishing he didn't feel so intimidated. Dealing with another Kel officer would have been one thing. There he knew what to do. But here? Tseya was running the operation, and she wouldn't consider him reliable if he was scared off by a show of (say) fancy cutlery.

*Be fair,* he told himself. So far Tseya had been perfectly civil. As long as they had to work together, he owed her the same.

Brezan asked the grid how long it would take him to reach wherever it was that Tseya wanted to meet for lunch. He added eighteen minutes to the answer just in case. Then he fidgeted until it was time to set out. He wondered how hard it would be to get lost. Too bad he hadn't brought anything to draw a map on, not that maps helped with variable layout on a potential hostile—*Stop that.*

As it turned out, the yellow flowers helpfully leaned over on their thornless stems to point the way whenever he approached. Brezan supposed some Nirai lab had received a great deal of money to get them to do that. He passed some more long-necked birds, usually but not always white, some with fanciful colored crests. They seemed unconcerned about his presence. He could only assume that no one had told them how many Kel enjoyed hunting. Brezan had never tried it, mainly due to squeamishness. Maybe the birds sensed they had nothing to fear from him.

*I am such a stationer,* Brezan thought, and hurried on, ignoring the sudden unsettling trill of frogs. He even managed to hurry past the carp. He was almost but not entirely certain it was the same pond that Tseya had led him past earlier.

The bewildering garden path and its accommodating yellow flowers led to a more normal corridor and an open archway hung about with curtains. "Come in," Tseya called out.

Eleven minutes early, not too bad. Brezan had to keep himself from glancing back at the last yellow flower to see if it now pointed in a different direction. Bracing himself, he stepped into the room. To his surprise, the decor was restrained. Of note was a single vase in the corner half as tall as he was, some kind of celadon. Food awaited them on a low table. Tseya was already seated on the floor. Across from her was a blue cushion for him. And, interesting touch, at the center of the table was a container full of toothpicks. Andan humor?

"You look like you think the food's rigged to blow," Tseya remarked. "Alas, I'm only mediocre at demolitions, which was a great disappointment to my instructors. Do sit down, there's no sense going hungry while we size each other up."

"Of course, Agent."

"You needn't be so formal. I do have a name." She smiled with her eyes.

He stopped himself from protesting just in time, and sat down. "I assume you've been warned not to play jeng-zai."

It wasn't as though he'd be admitting to a weakness she hadn't already guessed. "I avoid it, yes," Brezan said. "I once joined General Khiruev and some of the other staff officers for a game. She cleaned us all out despite drawing consistently terrible hands."

Tseya poured tea first for him, then for herself. She didn't make a ceremony of the act. In response to his blink of surprise, she made a moue. "Has it never occurred to you, General—"

His turn. "Just Brezan, please."

"—Brezan, then. Has it never occurred to you that not all Andan are equally enamored of the rules of etiquette? Sometimes I just want to drink the damn tea."

If this was a ploy to gain sympathy, it was working admirably. "I'm afraid the only significant contact I've had with your people has been during official functions," Brezan said.

"And I'm sure you found those occasions charming," Tseya murmured. She picked up a piece of something in dark sauce with her chopsticks, chewed, swallowed. "Shall I taste everything to prove there's no poison?"

"That won't be necessary," Brezan said, besides which it wouldn't prove anything anyway. He began eating. The dark sauce was mildly sweet, with a hint of lemongrass and maybe fish sauce. As for the meat, he couldn't identify it. But it was likable enough. He'd have to ask for the recipe later.

"You're awfully quiet," Tseya said after a while. Brezan had finished most of his rice and she was only a quarter of the way through her bowl. "I can't imagine it was easy for you to be separated from your comrades this way."

Explaining to her what he thought of Kel Command's decision to make Jedao immortal was tempting, but a bad idea. "I ought to be grateful," he said, feeling anything but. Sitting here with an Andan only reminded him how much he missed high table. "I'm given to understand that Jedao hasn't blown up the swarm, at least." He'd had some time to catch up on reports before the rendezvous.

"He's a Shuos," Tseya said, "which means he's like an Andan, except with worse public relations."

Brezan nearly choked on a vegetable. Old joke, except the context.

"If he hasn't destroyed the swarm, it's because he has some use for it. And unfortunately, there's only one use for swarms." She sighed. "If he were blowing up our stations indiscriminately, I would be less worried. But no, he's fighting off an invasion. This can't be anything other than a ploy for the populace's sympathy."

"He's a mass murderer," Brezan protested.

"You're a Kel," Tseya said, "so you'd see it from a Kel point of view. The Shuos have it in for him too, not unsurprisingly. To everyone else, especially the masses who have no faction affiliation and are busy trying to avoid being noticed by people like us, he's more like a storybook figure come to life than a threat. Hellspin Fortress was several generations ago. A lot of people simply don't care anymore, or anyway, they don't care enough. I mean, think about the bombing that took out Hexarch Nirai Havrekaz 373 years ago. Even if you knew about it"—Brezan shook his head—"would you get worked up about it?"

Brezan thought it over. "I was happier before you made that point," he said finally, "but you're right." It made their mission all the more important. They had to stop Jedao. They had to stop the Hafn. And, as a bonus, they had to stop Jedao from stopping the Hafn and making a hero of himself.

They ate in silence again. Brezan made himself slow down. He wasn't used to taking meals at leisure. His oldest father, once Kel, hadn't believed in lingering over meals. By the time Brezan was old enough to have memories, said father had retired from active service, but Kel habits died hard.

"I know why Kel Command sent you," Tseya said as a servitor brought small cakes to the table. The slices were festooned with slices of fruit, pale green and orange and luscious red, arranged in the shapes of flowers. "So it appears I have you at a disadvantage. I don't believe you know anything about me. Of course, there are a lot of people in the hexarchate."

Brezan tried a small bite of one of the cakes. Its sweetness was balanced by the tartness of the fruits. He hoped he didn't grow too fond of it because sooner or later he would have to go back to eating sensible Kel food. Maybe he could ask for the recipe to this one too, assuming it wasn't a faction secret. "If you're concerned with my ability to carry out my orders—"

"What I'm trying to say is that we'll work better together if you know what my stake is, and why they picked me instead of someone else." An undercurrent shadowed Tseya's voice, not exactly bitterness, but close.

"Tseya," Brezan said, wondering where this was heading, "you don't owe me an explanation."

She caught his eye before he understood what was going on, and smiled. It was an impersonal smile, not a warm or pretty one, and it made him afraid. He couldn't look away. But then, he had already known that Andan enthrallment worked like that. He just hadn't expected her to blow the ability, whose effectiveness diminished with repeated use against a given target, so soon. Naive of him. Her eyes were still brown, not dark blue, rose-blue. Once they changed, he would be hers for as long as she could sustain the enthrallment.

Then Tseya broke eye contact. Brezan breathed again. He shoved his hands under the table so he could clench them to stop their shaking. She might know, but she wouldn't see. That would have to do.

"Perhaps I don't owe you explanations," Tseya said, "but we're going to have to rely on each other. You need to know that I won't compel you into doing anything that's contrary to your duty. I need to know that a crashhawk will follow orders. I've got it easier, frankly. Kel Command aside, I think you really are loyal."

Brezan wasn't sure he liked being summed up so neatly. Now that the shock had worn off, he was starting to be angry.

"It was an empty threat." Tseya's hand closed on the teacup, paused there.

"Do tell," Brezan said.

"I can't enthrall you."

Her mouth was all straight lines. She didn't like admitting this to him. But why send a defective Andan? He knew they existed, the way crashhawks existed. He had heard that they lasted about as long.

"It's not what you're thinking," Tseya said. "The issue isn't the faction ability as such. It's operating fine. But my name used to be Andan Nezhe. The issue is that I'm disgraced and you're not."

It didn't take Brezan long to work out what she meant, even if the name meant nothing to him. "Never heard of you."

Her eyes lit with some private cynical amusement. "Well, that's refreshing. You'll have to take it on faith that I made some powerful enemies among the Andan."

"So Jedao won't pose any problems for you."

"That's right."

Formation instinct triggered on rank. Enthrallment triggered instead on social status. Or, as Brezan's middle father had explained to him when he was little, "This is how they keep baby Andan from running around forcing their social superiors to hand over critical investments." An Andan could only enthrall someone lower in the pecking order.

Tseya's mouth pulled into a moue. "I mean, think about it. Jedao no longer has any rank, even if he controls that swarm. He's running on pure notoriety. Imagine how much trouble it'd be inviting him to dinner. You could give one of my people nightmares by putting them in charge of the seating chart."

Brezan was unamused. "So you're here because you're expendable, too."

"I'm here because I am particularly motivated to redeem myself in the eyes of my superiors," she returned. "I've had some violent differences of opinion with them on policy matters. They didn't take them well."

"I suppose I'm not in a position to judge," Brezan said. He finished the slice of cake in the silence that followed, and still couldn't decide whether he liked it or not.

# CHAPTER FIFTEEN

KHIRUEV HAD NEVER expected her intimate, if eccentric, acquaintance with curio stores to come in handy during swarm operations. In particular, she had learned more about the art of dickering than she had realized. She missed high table when Station Tankut Primary responded to her suggestion that they negotiate over repairs and supplies, and she was currently in the command center examining their latest offer.

Colonel Najjad of Logistics was shooting her looks of dismay. Najjad had obviously hoped to get their own raw materials so they could print their own components rather than relying on the station to do it for them at exorbitant rates. Khiruev and the crew's conventional assets had been frozen by the Andan, but they were still able to sell combat data on the Hafn to the black market and, of all things, independent dramatists and historians. However, there was only so far Khiruev could push the station chief, who was not a Kel. Indeed, the fact that the station chief had no faction affiliation, plus Tankut's reputation for black market dealings, was what had led Jedao and Khiruev to pick it.

The station chief, a woman with excellent teeth and a smile she used with needle precision, was awaiting Khiruev's response. Khiruev made a few adjustments to the list and sent it back. "Final offer," she said. "Otherwise we'll take our chances selling Hafn trophies to private collectors directly." That was not entirely an idle threat. She was getting curious as to what some of those odd engine components would bring. Someone had mentioned the caskets, but she had quashed that notion the moment it was brought to her attention.

"Pleasure doing business," the stationer said, sounding sincere. "I've sent over local regulations. Ensure that your people stick to them while we get working on this."

The grid ran through the document and found only a few sections that deviated from common practice, none of which Khiruev expected to cause trouble. Jedao had agreed with her that contact with the locals be kept to the minimum necessary to ensure resupply. "The pleasure is mine," Khiruev said dryly. "I'll keep this place in mind in case I ever decide my real calling is to be a smuggler."

The station chief grinned before signing off.

"What," Khiruev said in response to Najjad's glum expression, "you never used to fantasize about running off and becoming a pirate? This is what it'd be like."

"In the dramas they're never short on matter printers as much as we are," Najjad muttered. "But I guess there's no help for it."

Khiruev paused in the middle of composing a report for Jedao. "Look at it from the station's point of view. They're risking excommunication by dealing with us."

"I doubt it's anything that altruistic. More like they're being paid by the local Shuos authorities to plant some bugs. Or currying favor with whoever is closest so we'll be inclined to protect them from the Hafn. Or, possibly, planning to sell us out to the foreigners."

"Above my pay grade," Khiruev said deliberately.

Najjad stiffened. It was subtle, but Khiruev had been watching for it. By this point, everyone in the swarm knew that she had invoked Vrae Tala. She wouldn't be surprised if there were betting pools as to whether she'd make it to the end of her hundred days. Najjad was civil about it, but he clearly didn't approve.

They exchanged a few more words on the workarounds they'd needed to institute due to the absence of their Nirai and Shuos personnel. Then Jedao interrupted with a summons for Khiruev, atypically laconic: "Come now."

Khiruev looked at Commander Janaia, who had spent the last hour meeting her eyes only when she had to. "Let me know if the stationers take us up on the offer of tacky souvenirs," Khiruev said.

"Naturally, sir," Janaia said, quite formally.

Khiruev sighed to herself. She couldn't blame Janaia. Khiruev had damned the swarm. Assuming they survived the whole tangled mess, even if Janaia hadn't had any say in Khiruev's decision, Kel Command was unlikely to regard her charitably. Khiruev's threadbare consolation was the knowledge that Janaia would carry out every order faultlessly, even if she found a loophole somewhere. She was that kind of Kel.

When Khiruev reported in, Jedao was playing an unfamiliar board game with three servitors. Khiruev saluted, bemused by how much more lively the receiving room felt with the servitors' presence, even though it was hardly cramped by any reasonable standard and the rooms had seen their share of past servitor traffic on more usual chores. Besides the servitors—a mothform and two lizardforms—the terminal was surrounded by paperwork pertaining to the swarm's provisioning, documents neatly arranged in a grid and casting a faint pale light over the walls and floor. Curiously, a mathematical paper was imaged over to the side.

Khiruev waited. Jedao was pondering a game token stamped with a trefoil knot. "At ease," Jedao said without looking at her. "Damnation," he said to the mothform, "you weren't kidding about that gambit. Teach me to run off my mouth about odds around people better at math than I am."

The servitor responded with an amused flurry of pink-and-yellow lights.

"Anyway," Jedao said, "you'll have to pardon me for a—" Jedao's terminal flashed a code that Khiruev didn't recognize. "Another one? I'd better see to this." Khiruev jerked her chin toward the door, wondering whether she should withdraw, but Jedao said, "No, stay."

The message started with a confusing snowfall of static and gradually coalesced into a woman with long hair and a habit of gnawing on the end of her stylus. Eventually they found out that she was Researcher Nirai Maholarion of Station Anner 56-5. More interestingly, the recording wasn't an official report, but a compilation of notes she had made while debating whether to recommend to her superiors that her data be forwarded to the Kel, even if the Kel had loftier matters on their mind.

Jedao had her preliminary abstract image itself so Khiruev could get a good look at it. "We've had a few of these come in from various stations," he said. "I can read basic scan, but these don't look like any formants I've seen in 400 years. You got anything?"

The scan data weren't Khiruev's immediate concern. She had gotten distracted by the last part of the video, which showed Maholarion absently handing off a stack of data solids to a mothform servitor. She had thought that Mevru solids were obsolete, but maybe the Nirai used them for reasons of backwards compatibility.

"Just how reliable are your sources, sir?" Khiruev said. She was betting that, over in the command center, Communications had no knowledge of these notes, or the other reports Jedao had alluded to. And how had he suborned these people to begin with?

"They're reliable enough to satisfy me," Jedao said.

She could take the hint. Khiruev considered the scan readings, then paged through the accompanying analysis. "I'm impressed they detected this at all, even with state-of-the-art noise cancellation." She highlighted the relevant portions of the paper.

Jedao looked politely blank. "I can't read most of that notation." He jabbed at an example.

Khiruev had been afraid of that. "It shows up in that paper you were looking at," she said. "See?" She highlighted it in gold. As a point of fact, the treatise looked more difficult by orders of magnitude.

Jedao grimaced. "That wasn't me. The servitors were having a side-argument about some theorem. I thought it meant they would be too distracted to pay attention to the ambush I was so cleverly setting in the game, so I let them have at it. No such luck, oh well."

The mothform blinked in blue and purple this time, with a suspiciously smug flash of red.

"It *could* be some stray new astronomical phenomenon," Khiruev said, "but the researcher seemed to think it might be a side-effect of the Hafn tearing around our space."

"I hope it's a scan glitch," Jedao said, "but multiple reports from independent observers? We're not going to get so lucky. Anyway, I'm going to pass that on to Scan and Doctrine and see what they make of it. This wasn't what I wanted to talk to you about, however. Tell me, General, what do you know about Devenay Ragath?"

Devenay—suddenly Khiruev was concerned. "You don't mean Colonel Kel Ragath?" she said. "I had heard that he was assigned to your campaign at the Fortress of Scattered Needles."

"That's correct," Jedao said, "but I didn't ask you what *I* know. I'm hoping you can tell me what's in *your* brain."

"He has training as a historian and he's very well-regarded," Khiruev said, "although I have never had the honor of working with him myself."

"Hmm," was all Jedao said to that. "Well, listen to this."

It seemed to be a day for listening to things. In response to Jedao's gesture, a video blazed up, displacing a summary of casualties in Tactical Group Four. The man in the video was definitely Ragath, with his long jaw, narrow eyes, and cynical slash of a mouth, but he wasn't in uniform. Instead, he wore a dark brown jacket over a taupe shirt. Khiruev's disquiet increased.

"This message is addressed to General Cheris," Ragath said, "by a communications channel I trust she will find satisfactory."

Khiruev was jolted into studying Jedao anew. That body had never belonged to Jedao to begin with. It had belonged to a Kel woman, who had probably never imagined that she'd end up hosting a traitor's ghost.

The message was still playing. Jedao had trained his regard on Khiruev's face, his expression coolly considering. Khiruev made herself go blank and returned her attention to the message.

"If the fox general has taught you anything," Ragath was saying, "you're wondering how I survived and where the trap is in this. I regret to say I owe the former to a couple of chance fuck-ups. I was supposed to be on the *Badger's Stripes* when the bomb hit the swarm, but thanks to a riot on the Fortress I was delayed getting to my shuttle."

Khiruev paused the message without Jedao's permission. Jedao's eyebrows rose. "Sir," Khiruev said, "he must be a deserter." She didn't say *crashhawk*. "I don't understand how—"

"Keep listening," Jedao said, and unpaused playback.

"I left the Fortress at the earliest opportunity," Ragath said. "It so happens that Kel Command frequently neglects to issue orders to the dead, something I imagine we both found handy. At this point, you're wondering what I have to offer you. I wasn't sure of that myself, once I learned that you'd survived. But if you're doing what I think you're doing, some of this information will help you. I will attempt to report in again if I find anything else you should know, but I don't expect to live long. Devenay Ragath out."

"He appended an exhaustive strategic overview of the local marches and their surrounds," Jedao said. Maybe this was the source of Jedao's mysterious intelligence network. "I have a feeling that's not what's on your mind, though."

Khiruev decided that this was an invitation to broach the subject. "Sir, Ragath appears to be under the impression that you're Brevet General Cheris." Was that why Ragath had broken formation? Loyalty to a dead woman?

"His mistake," Jedao said, "but I plan to use it. If you know anything about Kel Cheris"—the offhanded way he said her name was chilling—"then you know she was an expendable infantry captain. I regretted it when the bomb killed her, but it gave me the opportunity to escape the black cradle. I was in there for a very long time, General. I would do it again in a heartbeat."

"She can't have been as expendable as all that if she earned the colonel's trust," Khiruev said. "I've seen the list of Ragath's decorations. He wouldn't have done this lightly."

"Was it trust, or the presumption of a shared grudge? Don't answer that."

"What exactly is it that Ragath thinks you're up to?"

Jedao eased himself back against one of the pillows on the couch and motioned Khiruev to sit, which she did. It amazed her every time she came in here that these rooms, which she had inhabited so recently, had completely changed character with Jedao in them. The servitors were almost done clearing the game. Jedao grabbed a token stamped with a hexagon and flipped it in the air, catching it neatly.

"I imagine Ragath thinks I'm going to conquer the galaxy and make it into a place where your superiors don't randomly bomb an entire swarm just to off one person," Jedao said. He tapped the token against the edge of the table. "I wish I could say this was a low bar for reform. However, our regime's history argues otherwise. Given his background, Ragath has to be aware of that."

He flipped the game token a few more times, then set it down with a click. "We're going to start offering people some choices." The humor in his smile had an edge. "Our location is no one's secret, partly because it's hard to pretend cows are chickens, but partly because I want us to be seen."

Khiruev didn't remark on this. It was the kind of thing Shuos liked to do, but no field commander lasted long without doing similar. As much as the Kel hated admitting it.

"We are shortly going to send out a transmission in the clear in all directions," Jedao went on. "I don't plan on going on at length. People's nerves are already shot and I imagine their attention spans aren't doing much better. Yes, I can see that you doubt that I'm capable of brevity, but I can manage it when I put my mind to it."

Khiruev didn't trust herself to respond to that.

Jedao drummed his fingers on the couch's arm, then examined his glove. "I plan on sending an account of our engagements to date, highlighting in particular what happened at the Fortress of Spinshot Coins. We could have had the Hafn swarm there, General. It's only thanks to hexarchate interference that we haven't blasted the Hafn into little glowing pieces. Even now, we're being treated as though we instigated the fireworks." His eyes hardened. "I want it to be excruciatingly clear that we could be dealing with the invasion a lot more effectively if not for the hexarchs."

"Sir," Khiruev said, "the Hafn aren't stupid. What you're proposing—if you send out a message *in the clear*, you'll make it obvious that the hexarchate is easy meat. Is this your intent?"

Jedao smiled at her. "You're reckoning this backwards."

She'd been afraid of that. Why alienate the populace by opening fire on them when Jedao could get the invaders to do it for him?

"It would be inconvenient for them to go home after getting their noses bloodied," Jedao said. "They need an incentive to stay in the game. I'm giving them one. Moreover, if the Hafn are still hanging around making a nuisance of themselves, the hexarchate's citizens will have a bright blazing excuse to think about just what protection the existing regime is offering them, and what the alternatives might be."

Khiruev wasn't fooled by Jedao's casual tone. He was gambling a lot on this. "It's my turn to be the pragmatic one," she said. "You have only the one swarm. There are Vidona in every settlement of any size. Unless you can magically disappear all the Vidona?"

"The Vidona aren't the biggest problem. When you get right down to it, the Vidona have a lot of toys"—Jedao's voice dipped sardonically—"but they hardly outnumber the mass of citizens. Sufficiently motivated cadres of insurrectionists could maneuver around them, as I'm sure you realize. The biggest problem is that everyone's too afraid to try."

Khiruev's mouth went dry. She had no rejoinder to the charge of cowardice because it was true.

Jedao's tilted smile flicked at her: he was waiting for the response. Khiruev said, after a pause of several seconds, "A lot of people will die if it works. But I imagine you have it all calculated out."

She hadn't meant it as a dig at Jedao's math difficulties. But Jedao turned his hand palm-up to acknowledge the hit.

Kel Command had reprimanded Khiruev for organizing guerrilla warfare during the Wicker's End campaign. They didn't like the possibility of citizens getting it into their heads that techniques that bought time against entrenched heretics could be turned against their legitimate masters. Of course, at some point you had to ask yourself how much legitimacy any government had that feared dissension within more than invasion from without, but if you had any desire for a quiet life, you kept those thoughts inside your skull where the Vidona couldn't see them.

"As much as I usually lament people's obsession with numbers," Jedao said, "in this instance you're correct. But is it better to let people die at random because we flinch from anticipating the casualties, or to go into battle knowing exactly how many people we're putting into harm's way?"

"I don't contest this," Khiruev said. "I can't figure out your angle, though."

Jedao laughed suddenly. "The fact that a Kel general is hoping that I have a *reasonable* plan is cause for optimism, in its way."

"Am I mistaken, sir?"

"The plan isn't reasonable," Jedao said, entirely too cavalierly. "But it has good odds. As Devenay would tell you, history forgives the winner a lot of things."

Khiruev thought hard before she asked the next question. "Do you expect forgiveness?"

Next to the wall, the mothform and one of the lizardforms, speaking to each other in flashes of light, paused. Khiruev paid them no heed.

A shadow passed through Jedao's eyes. "No," he said. "I lie to myself about a lot of things, but that's not one of them. We're long past that point."

# CHAPTER SIXTEEN

Moroish Nija was hot beneath her coat and knitted dress. The coat was slightly tight at the shoulders. Ordinarily she preferred more vivid shades of rose, but she hadn't had time to be picky. Right now she was stuck inside a store full of shawls she couldn't have afforded if she wanted to, although that pale green one with the tassels would complement the coat nicely.

Nija had spent her entire life on the world of Bonepyre, and even then she had never before left the City of Hollow Processions, where she had been born, except on a couple of school trips. Terrible irony: she was supposed to have caught a shuttle off-planet, an adventure she'd longed for all her life, and instead she'd fled back home. If anyone recognized her, they wouldn't send her to school, where her classmates were sitting that exam in discrete mathematics she hadn't pretended to study for, or to her parents, who were probably dead. They'd send her straight to the Vidona, as they'd done with all the other Mwennin.

She had ducked into the store when the remembrance was about to begin, the Meditation of Needle Tongues. She didn't know how she had forgotten it, when all her life her elders had emphasized the importance of adhering to the high calendar's external forms. Even better, a Vidona stood in the store, a man with a disconcerting resemblance to her kindly history teacher. He wasn't wearing full faction uniform, but the green-and-bronze sash said all that needed saying.

Mostly Nija could hear people's breathing and the rapid thudding of her own heart. It seemed impossible that the Vidona couldn't hear it, too, despite being on the other side of the room looking bored with the proceedings. It seemed equally impossible to concentrate on the official litany being read in the unquiet silence. Nija settled instead on composing mental critiques of the shawls. The one right in front of her was a dead loss, she'd never cared for that style of lace, but the one beside it had promise. She wouldn't mind wearing something with that touch of sparkle on a date. Not that she'd ever owned anything nice enough to go with it.

Finally the remembrance ended. Nija lingered in the store a little longer, then headed out into the street with its mingled smell of spice and damp earth and expensive perfumes. Trees were planted at precise intervals. Servitors were busy clearing away leaves and twigs from the walkways. The air was humid, the sky overcast, but she didn't think it would rain again so soon. Still, maybe she should pick up an umbrella. She clenched her jaw thinking of her grandfather's absurd oversized umbrella, the blue one with the stripes. The Vidona had probably tossed it in the recycler with everything else.

Nija's attention was brought unpleasantly back to the present when she realized a brown woman in cream robes and an unflattering profusion of pearls was following her. She was wondering what to do about it when the woman lengthened her stride, then stooped and cleared her throat. "Excuse me," the woman called out to Nija. The woman straightened, holding out a handkerchief. "Did you drop this?"

Nija's demurral died in her throat when she looked at the handkerchief, an elegant affair in matching cream silk. For a second, words appeared in red light upon the handkerchief. Words in Mwen-dal, her native tongue: *Come with me.* Beneath the words was the Shuos eye in yellow.

She almost bolted, but it was too late already. Although the street was by no means crowded, there were enough shoppers and people sipping tea outdoors or taking strolls that someone would notice and alert the authorities, assuming the authorities weren't already paying attention. Besides, if the woman was a genuine Shuos, she could drop Nija unconscious with a flick of her fingers.

"Thank you," Nija said, accepting the handkerchief with a forced smile.

"I'm Trenthe Unara," the woman said. She fell in beside Nija. "Do you know where's a good place to get flowers around here?"

Why couldn't she look it up the way normal people did? Still, Nija had passed an extravagant florist earlier today. She tried not to wonder what a Shuos needed with flowers. "I'll show you the nearest one I know," she said, feeling hopelessly stilted.

Unara smiled. "I'd like that."

Nija wanted to demand an explanation. Why the charade? Why not arrest her? A Shuos agent didn't need a pretext to detain her. Nija had no faction affiliation or friends in high places to protect her.

She lost the ability to notice anyone but Unara, as though they walked about hedged by walls. Even the sight of the extravagant florist only increased her anxiety. Maybe some of the flower arrangements were used for assassinating people, or drugging them.

The curl to Unara's mouth suggested that she had divined Nija's worries, but she didn't say anything. Instead, she forced Nija to stand there with a burgeoning headache as she picked out a bouquet of fantastic proportions. If not for the headache, Nija would have enjoyed watching the florist put it together. Some of those flowers, with their wildly disparate shapes and colors, shouldn't have harmonized, yet the florist made it work. Nija's favorite touch was the lace-spray of drooping cloud-bells.

A hoverer awaited them when Unara declared herself satisfied with the bouquet. The driver, in front, was hidden behind a shaded partition. Meekly, Nija climbed in the back. She had given up trying to understand the situation. Unara sat across from her. The bouquet, held up by stabilizers, took up an impressive chunk of the back. The mingled fragrances, stronger in the enclosed space, aggravated Nija's headache.

As the hoverer took off, Unara said, no longer bland, "I'm Agent Shuos Feiyed. You know, if it were up to me, I'd fucking recruit you. I put three of my people on report because you slipped out from under their noses earlier."

"I'm sorry," Nija lied, although she did remember to use an appropriate humble verb form now that they weren't pretending to be chance-met strangers.

"I'm not saying the Shuos are infallible," Feiyed said, "because we're clearly not, but as one of them, I have to ask. Where'd you pick up that trick for vanishing into crowds? Your school records looked completely unremarkable. Perfect attendance, glowing conduct reports, all of that."

Nija flushed and stared out the hoverer's window. Below, the city with its streets appeared to be calm and orderly, with flashes of silver or gold as other hoverers swooped by. No sign that an entire people had been scrubbed out of it. The parks were patches of cloudy green. Sunlight glinted faintly off the snaking river. "Iusedtoshoplift," Nija mumbled.

"What?"

"I said, I used to shoplift," Nija repeated, blushing. The shopkeepers hadn't caught her, mainly because she had been too smart to go after the pricier items and, like any number of her classmates, she knew the tricks by which you could fool the more common security systems. She had only stopped when her grandmother took sick and she felt irrationally guilty, as though purloined baubles attracted germs.

Nija's mortification grew when Feiyed started making alarming wheezing sounds. "Oh, that's priceless," Feiyed said when she was done. "Like my aunt's always telling me, never underestimate teenagers."

Nija glowered at Feiyed in spite of herself.

"You're very stupid for being so clever," Feiyed said without any trace of kindness. "Headed straight back to your hometown, of all places, instead of some quiet city where they don't know your face. Do you *want* to end up in a detention camp? The only reason your people aren't already extinct is that the Vidona get slowed up by petty paperwork almost as much as the Rahal do."

"I've been watching the news reports," Nija said, trying to hide her renewed terror. Mostly she'd had useless fantasies of sneaking onto Shuos Jedao's command moth and kicking him naked into vacuum for what he'd done to her people. "I—I watched some of the executions."

"Well, it's a good thing I caught up to you," Feiyed said. "As I said, it's a pity I can't recruit you. Knock some of the dumb ideas out of your head and you might be good for something, but it'd be a pain to arrange on such short notice. We're headed to a nice, boring, remote campground where we'll get you to the shuttle that will take you to a nice, boring moth to get you out of the system."

Nija crossed her arms and glowered some more. This had no effect on Feiyed. Finally, Nija burst out, "You're a *fox*, what could any of this matter to you? What are you getting out of this?" Especially since the measure was supposed to punish Jedao, or pressure him, for all its blatant ineffectiveness. There was a Shuos game going on, but she couldn't imagine what it was.

She had the dangerous tickling thought that the Shuos weren't supposed to be rescuing randomly selected Mwennin. Unfortunately, she couldn't leverage this knowledge. What was she going to do, turn Feiyed in to the Vidona? That was supposing Feiyed hadn't selected her for some extra-gruesome form of execution.

Feiyed's answer didn't reassure Nija. "We've been holding a betting pool asking that very question ourselves," she said. "Not like your lot have much to offer us. But our hexarch, well, he's *whimsical*. He gets these notions in his head, so we carry them out."

Nija could have done without the reminder of the assassinated Shuos cadets.

"Anyway," Feiyed said, her eyes canny, "are you registering a complaint?"

Nija was aware that she'd slipped up on the formality level of her speech. She resolved to speak more carefully. "The Vidona took away Boherem Roni's family," she said. "I went to school with the son." The Boherem boy had had the annoying tendency to drone on and on about his collection of inkstones, but that wasn't a good enough reason to wish him dead. "Why me and not one of them?"

There had to be others, lots of others, but the initial evacuation, the one she had slipped free of, had been hushed and hurried and full of rumors. When she thought of it, it came back in snatches: the brusque Shuos agents, the carefully regulated lines, the transports. It had been pure chance that she had heard about the Boherem family from two adults whispering to each other before they were separated. Most of the Mwennin had been convinced that the Shuos were taking them to face firing squads. The general sentiment had been that Shuos bullets beat Vidona torture any day.

"You want to know the truth, Nija?" Feiyed smiled. "I can't speak for my hexarch, but I don't care about your people one way or the other. It's just orders, as arbitrary as"—her smile turned cutting—"fashion. If I wanted to be in the business of rescuing people, I'd be a firefighter."

The Shuos's frank callousness reassured Nija. She didn't have to pretend to like her.

"Logistically speaking, my superiors picked people based first on ease of extraction, then ran a lottery because we couldn't get more of you out without attracting attention."

"You shouldn't have bothered," Nija said, too upset to be careful about formality levels all over again. "The Mwen-denerra"—she stopped, rephrased. "There won't be enough of us left. Our traditions will die. Considering that we're supposed to be tidy piles of ash, it's not as if we can teach them to anyone else."

Nija considered herself to be an indifferent Mwennin, as Mwennin went. She had memorized the list of Mwennin calendar-saints not out of any great faith but because her family had always looked so happy whenever she faked interest in the old ways, the forbidden ways. She only mouthed the prayers with their invocations of raven prophets and heron oracles, the queen of birds in the wood-with-no-boundaries. Admittedly she liked traditional food, especially lamb with yogurt sauce, but that was a low bar.

She was certain that the Shuos would profess indifference to this matter as well. But Feiyed said, "You would have to be careful, it's true. However, I don't think it's impossible. The question is, how much are you willing to compromise? I mean, it's not like anyone in the hexarchate knows or cares about your customs. They wouldn't recognize them, and that works in your favor. You could lie low for a dozen years—forever at your age, I realize—and start introducing your customs to the receptive. You *do* accept adoptive Mwennin, don't you?"

Nija stared at her. She hadn't expected Feiyed to know about that point of Mwennin practice. It was the only reason the Mwennin hadn't died out entirely, according to—she clamped down on the thought. Her grandfather was dead.

Feiyed chuckled softly. "I was adopted myself, so I keep track of these things. Besides, I have an ulterior motive. You'd make an entertaining Shuos if you put your mind to it. Fight from within and all that."

Nija's first instinct was to say something her father would have chided her for. After all, the destruction of the Mwennin was that bitch Cheris's fault for being stupid enough to enter faction service in the first place. But Cheris had already paid for her mistake, and Feiyed was making a disturbing amount of sense. "I'll think about it," Nija said.

Feiyed leaned back and smiled.

AJEWEN DZERA WISHED she could lose track of how long she had been sitting in the cell, under spider restraints that tightened painfully whenever she moved too suddenly. The walls were a white just gray enough to look oppressive. The door, only four paces away, might have been on another planet. Whenever she approached it, she was wracked by a burning sensation that started at her skin and needled inward. Incongruously, the cell smelled of a persistent, pleasant fragrance, with notes of lilac and starbloom. One of her Vidona handlers liked perfume.

There was a clock display on the wall. Dzera hated looking at it, but it was impossible not to let her eyes rest on it periodically. In two days there would be another remembrance. She imagined the Vidona would execute her before then. In the meantime, the illicit prayers that had comforted her all her life stuck in her throat like hot stones.

They had taken away her partner of twenty-nine years almost from the start, rousing them in the middle of the night. Harsh bright lights everywhere, enforcers in Vidona green-and-bronze tramping through the small garden where their daughter Cheris had liked to watch the birds as a child. Derow hadn't been born Mwennin, he had married in and learned their traditions, but this distinction hadn't mattered to the Vidona.

Another minute ticked past. Dzera caught herself watching the clock, and slowly and carefully averted her face. Her bangs fell in her eyes. Slowly and carefully, she reached up to brush them away. If she had known this would happen, she would have picked a different hairstyle. A haircutter had come in once to trim her hair. She had prayed to fall dead then, but they hadn't killed her afterward.

Dzera often thought of Cheris, who had left the City of Ravens Feasting for the Kel. Cheris had left them long before then, if the truth were told. Dzera hadn't been able to admit it to herself, however, until the day Cheris came to them, pale, shoulders squared, to inform them that she had been admitted to Kel Academy Prime.

There were so many of the old stories she had not told her daughter, although she had made a scrabbling effort to pass on the language, the prayers, the poetry. The story of the one-eyed saint who kept a casket with no lock, and what became of her lovers who found a way to open it. The story of the half-tailed cat who lived in the world's oldest library. The story of the raven general who sacrificed a thousand thousand of his soldiers to build a spirit-bridge of birds to assault the heavens.

Sometimes Dzera thought that if she had found the right stories to tell Cheris, Cheris wouldn't have needed to run away from her own people. But as much as Dzera agonized over it, she'd never figured out which stories those would have been.

Without warning, a video came to life right where she had been looking, an unremarkable patch of wall. She jumped, although she knew better, then choked back a sob at the restraints tightening around her. No matter how often this happened, she never got used to the experience.

It took her a few seconds to understand what the video was showing her, partly because of the bite of pain, partly because she didn't want to. A man in dust-colored clothes like the ones they had put her in held still in a chair very like her own. Next to the chair was a table with a bronze tray. The chair explained everything. It was of a dark green material, glossy, with bronze striations.

Next the video showed a Vidona officer entering. Her uniform was a slightly lighter green, the bronze piping and buttons brighter. In her hand she held an instrument that resembled a spoon, if a spoon had incandescently sharp edges.

Dzera guessed what was coming, but not in time to look away. The image tracked the movements of her eyes. It was suddenly impossible to squeeze her eyes shut. The spoon flashed. The man screamed. His eye was a lump with red flesh clinging to it. Blood and fluid dripped from it, and tracked viscous lines down the man's face. The Vidona tossed the eye onto the tray. The tray was much larger than the eye was. Dzera could guess what that meant, too.

The Vidona were unlikely to go through this with every single Mwennin in custody. Too inefficient. But Dzera couldn't look forward to an efficient death because she was Cheris's mother.

*I can't do this,* she thought.

She looked sideways, seeking to escape the video even though she knew it was hopeless. The next one had already begun playing where her gaze had fallen. This one showed a young woman who might have been Cheris's age, although Cheris had never worn her hair that long. Dzera liked to think that Cheris would never have cringed like that.

When the spoon flashed again, Dzera felt a sudden sting in her right ear. She tensed up, breath scraping against her throat.

"Don't react," a tiny crystalline voice said right in her ear at the young woman's next scream. The voice spoke flawless Mwen-dal. The timing was just as well, because Dzera flinched anyway. "It will be painless. We tried to find a way to free you, but this is all we can do."

The stinging sensation intensified, and then there came a subtle flash of heat. A hundred questions crowded in her mind, then ebbed away. The last thought she had before her benefactor's drugs scoured everything to static was that there would be no one to restore the garden.

# CHAPTER SEVENTEEN

BREZAN WISHED HE could claim that he had no idea how he and Tseya had started sleeping together, but he knew very well how it had happened. Nothing in the Kel code of conduct forbade it, and their pursuit of Jedao took enough time that they both welcomed the diversion. He wasn't under any illusions that either of them saw it as anything more than that.

Right now Tseya was sitting at the edge of her bed combing out her hair. She had an astonishing variety of outfits. Today's involved a blue-gray chemise beneath a vest that seemed to be more lace than substance, and darker pants. Her bare feet looked weirdly incongruous. She had a grudge against socks when she wasn't wearing shoes.

"I should make you help me with this," Tseya said, amused, when she caught Brezan admiring her hair. He appreciated the aesthetics when it was someone else's problem. "There are days the stuff tangles if I so much as breathe."

Brezan located a spare comb on her dresser, half-hidden under some pearl necklaces, and weighed it dubiously in his hand. He couldn't tell what it was made of, possibly wood. Would it snap if he tried to use it? What if it was an heirloom?

Tseya chuckled. "I bought that cheap in some souvenir shop in a city whose name I can't remember," she said. "My mother did always say I had abysmal taste. Anyway, it won't bite you, and I won't cry if it breaks."

He eased himself down behind her and began combing, careful to work through the tangles without yanking, a skill he'd learned from his sisters as a child. Tseya's perfume wafted back to him: citrus-sweet, no roses at all. He resisted the urge to inhale more deeply.

She hummed contentedly. "You must think Andan are terribly indolent."

"No, just you," he said. It had taken him a while to adjust to life on a silkmoth. It felt as though he ought to spend longer shifts in the command center, or else that he should be constantly embroiled in paperwork. But Tseya had pointed out that a moth ordinarily intended for a single pilot couldn't have that single pilot on duty continually. The *Orchid* relied on a lot more automation than Brezan was accustomed to.

Tseya reached over to stroke the inside of his thigh. Brezan made a noncommittal noise, although his hand trembled. He kept combing. "Have you ever considered that wigs would be easier to manage?" he asked. "You could swap them out at whim, or program one to change colors to harmonize with your outfit."

She snorted.

"Just a suggestion."

After a little while, she said, "I'm clearly not distracting enough."

Brezan paused. "You're not even facing me. How can you tell?"

"People talk with their hands as much as they do with their tongues, Brezan." She never used endearments, even when they fucked, which he liked about her. "Shall I try harder?"

"I'd have to start over with your hair," he said in dismay, as much as he liked running his hands through the glossy-dark mass.

Tseya twisted around and kissed the side of his face, then his chin. "I could let it hang in tangles and go around as a ghost."

"Why do ghosts in the stories always have long, tangled hair?"

She pushed him down with one hand, which he didn't resist, and regarded him with a slow smile. "Do all Kel get sidetracked that easily, or are crashhawks special?"

It almost didn't hurt when she said that, especially considering what she was doing with her other hand. He slitted his eyes at her and said, "Are you ordering me to answer?"

"What, you won't volunteer the information?"

"Kel never volunteer if we can help it. I thought you'd heard."

Her hair brushed over his face. It tickled, but if he laughed it'd get in his mouth, which Tseya found hilarious. He craned his head up, and she dipped her head so they could kiss.

He woke alone some time afterward. Tseya never stuck around, although hot tea always awaited him on a side table. The other thing Tseya liked to do was leave his clothes folded over a chair. Brezan couldn't help wondering if this was something they taught in Introduction to Seduction at Andan Academy, or if this was some personal quirk. Kel speculation was divided on just what was in that course's curriculum. He was almost tempted to ask. Brezan got dressed and drank the tea quickly, since Tseya wasn't there to watch.

Then he went to the silkmoth's command center. By now he had almost developed the knack of ignoring the aquarium in the command center, which took the shape of a fluted column. It was filled with seahorses and striped colorful fish with comical eyes and snails and green-dark kelp. Once he would have thought the Andan were frivolous. Now he suspected advanced psychological warfare. Tseya refused to say which.

Tseya was already there. It had been evident from early on that she had a lot of specialized training, especially with the moth's scan suite, some of whose functions were more advanced than what they'd had on the *Hierarchy of Feasts*. Tseya had grimaced when he remarked on it, and confirmed what he'd heard about silkmoths: "There are trade-offs. We can sneak, run, or see things far away, but we're only good at two of the three at any given time. Right now we're running and sneaking so we can catch up to Jedao without getting caught, so the scan suffers a lot."

"Anything interesting?" Brezan said as he took his seat.

Tseya nodded at him, all business. "Take a look at the chatter," she said.

Brezan picked through the backlog of communications, which the mothgrid had sorted according to their criteria. An alert flashed red just as he got through the second of the digests. He groaned. "Jedao again?"

"More propaganda, I expect," Tseya said, leaning forward. "I want to see what he has for us this time." She played the message.

The piece opened with the Deuce of Gears, which Brezan wouldn't have minded burning up or melting down, then went into a two-dimensional animation, brushstrokes applied to elegant spline curves, unrelieved black and white. Swarms of moths as stylized as paper airplanes flew and wheeled and fought against a backdrop of—

Those weren't stars, although it only became evident when the camera zoomed in on one moth colliding with another. Those were lanterns. The battle dissolved into ashes. The ashes became ink; the brushstrokes condensed into a single column of calligraphy: *penance*. And that was just the introduction, in a few seconds.

"Fuck you," Brezan said as the propaganda continued to play, as though Jedao stood in the command center with them smiling his tilted smile.

"I admit this wasn't the angle I expected him to take," Tseya said after the rest of the piece had finished. The earlier propaganda pieces had included maddeningly irrefutable documentation of how the commandant of the Fortress of Spinshot Coins had prevented Jedao from mauling the Hafn. Said commandant had been removed, but no one knew the full story. You would expect the Shuos to have broadcast a rebuttal; no such luck. Jedao had also made straightforward requests for specific systems not to interfere with swarm operations, which they tended to honor, mainly because his requests were sensible.

"It's infuriating that people are retransmitting his broadcasts," Brezan said, "but I suppose people will be people. What I want to know is, why would he *want* to remind his nervous but gossipy listeners about Hellspin Fortress? How does that help him?"

Tseya's smile had a curious sour quality. "Brezan, he's rewriting the story. It's one thing to have it out of the archives, or some drama no one expects to be historically accurate, and another to hear it told by someone who was there."

Brezan bit off what he'd been about to say and busied himself with a map depicting Jedao's movements over the last two weeks in red. Hafn movements appeared in a ghost-cloud of gray. The latter had speared past the Fortress of Scattered Needles in the Entangled March and into the adjacent Severed March. Ever since the battle at Spinshot Coins, Jedao and the Hafn had been feinting at each other without engaging. The two swarms were now approaching Minang System, home to a wolf tower. The tower acted as a calendrical beacon, facilitating navigation, and contained one of the great clocks by which the hexarchate reckoned time.

Tseya was going through more of the chatter. "Here's another one," she said. This time it concerned the Vidona extermination of the Mwennin. Very little text on this one, either.

"Hold on," Brezan said when the video got to an appalling clip of a screaming boy and an instrument made of hot curved wires. He paused it. "Who the hell is passing Jedao these?" A quick check confirmed that this particular clip hadn't been released by the official news services, but he wasn't sure he bought that Jedao had faked it, either. The video displayed the Vidona seal in the corner. The mothgrid believed the seal was authentic.

Tseya pursed her lips. "An excellent question, although there's not a lot we can do to find out. All the histories go on and on about Jedao as a tactician, but he did graduate from the Shuos before running off to play soldier. I presume he learned *something* about setting up intelligence networks while he was there. No, what I want to know is, why has the hexarchs' response been so tepid?"

"What response?" Brezan retorted. "Other than the occasional bulletin, they haven't done anything to counter the damage he's doing to public morale." Not that that was ever good to begin with.

"Yes, exactly," Tseya said. She had pulled out her hairstick and was fiddling with it, her hair in disarray. "Managing information fallout is what the Shuos are for. Is Mikodez asleep or something?"

Brezan noted, with sharp alarm, the odd familiarity with which she mentioned Mikodez. She didn't use an honorific, just the personal name, as though they were equals. Just how high a position had she occupied before her disgrace?

Tseya tapped the hairstick against the base of her palm, looking for all the world like she wished she could pin Mikodez and make him get to work. "It just figures," she said. "We finally have a Shuos hexarch capable of hanging on to the seat longer than a hiccup, and the man has the attention span of a ferret. He probably got bored of the invasion in the first week and is off learning to bake custards instead."

Ever since Exercise Purple Paranoia, Brezan had belonged to the category of people who thought about Shuos Mikodez as little as possible, in the belief that this would keep him from coming to Mikodez's attention. But Brezan always remembered what Shuos Zehun had told him about Mikodez. He couldn't help thinking that Tseya was missing part of the picture. Shuos cadets were not known for being willing to cooperate with each other. The fact that Mikodez had persuaded his classmates to do so for the exercise, put together with his forty-two years in power, suggested that he was dangerously charismatic, ferret or no ferret.

"Well, we can't prod Hexarch Mikodez from here, either," Brezan said, "unless you plan on calling him up."

"Absolutely not," Tseya said.

"Well, then. Anything else I should pay attention to in current events?"

He wasn't sure whether he hoped the answer was a no or a yes. They knew, for instance, that Jedao had resupplied at Tankut Primary thirteen days ago, although Brezan couldn't hope that the stationers had indulged in some sabotage. The idea was to take out Jedao with minimal damage to the swarm, after all. Elsewhere, several systems in the general vicinity were experiencing civil disruptions. Lensmoths had been dispatched, which meant the Rahal suspected that full-fledged heresy was around the corner.

Tseya scanned the digests. "Nothing out of the ordinary."

They passed the next two hours and seventy-three minutes with a minimum of conversation. Guiltily, Brezan was starting to wish that something would implode, just for variety, when Tseya swore under her breath. "What is it?" he asked.

"This isn't going to end well," she said, and passed the message over to his terminal.

"Please let it not be a surprise."

"You won't find it surprising, but it's regrettable all the same."

A moon-city and an orbital station had transmitted the Deuce of Gears when the Hafn veered close to their system. It had to be Brezan's imagination that the red field was even bloodier than the one Jedao used. He smashed his fist against the terminal, then swore at the pain. Tseya frowned at him.

"Idiots," Brezan said bitterly. "They didn't need to do that. The Immolation Fox would have rescued them for some grandstanding purpose of his own if they'd been in real danger." Aside from terrorizing the population, Brezan couldn't see any good reason for the Hafn to bother. Neither city nor station had significant military value. "Now they're going to be scoured."

"Look at it from their point of view," Tseya said. "The only Kel force in a position to chase off the foreigners is under Jedao's control. They probably thought it was worth a try." She put the hairstick down and fixed Brezan with a speculative stare. "Speaking of emblems, did you ever have a chance to register one?"

"My what?" Brezan said before he worked out what she meant. He blushed and averted his eyes, looking at the aquarium, then at the hairstick, anywhere but at her face. "You can't be serious."

"What, are you going with the temporary emblem?" she said, referring to the sword-and-feather.

Brezan made himself return her stare. "I don't see why this is important all of a sudden," he said. Was this some Andan thing about projecting the right image? "Jedao can't have killed everyone in the swarm if it's still functioning. There'll be someone able to—"

"—take charge?"

He disliked the mocking edge to her tone, but maybe he had imagined it. "Look," he said, "it's inconsequential."

Tseya leaned over and laid her palm on his chest right over the wings-and-flame insignia.

He froze.

"Are you telling me this is an illusion?" she said. "I thought the point of this exercise was for you to pull rank on Jedao the way he pulled rank on General Khiruev."

Brezan wished desperately that he could pull away and stalk out of the command center, but Kel Command had assigned him to Tseya. Damned if he was going to slink away because of a few words. "It's not an illusion," he said. "It's just—it's just temporary." How had the conversation turned hostile so suddenly?

"You're not going to convince your own people if that's all the conviction you can scare up."

He glared at her, not trusting himself to speak.

"Look, you're from a Kel family, yes?"

Brezan didn't like where this was going.

Tseya waited. Her hand didn't move.

"Yes," he said stiffly, "although I don't know why you're asking me questions you know the answers to."

"Two Kel sisters. One of whom is on General Inesser's staff."

"Go on," Brezan said after counting to six, "tell me about my childhood."

Her smile had no teeth in it. The teeth would have been friendlier. "You must be so disappointed that you can't tell them about your spectacular new promotion."

He couldn't suppress his wince in time.

"Is there a proper way to tell your family that you're a crashhawk?"

Thinking clearly was impossible. He had a flash of memory: the heat of her mouth, the curve of her neck, the delicious creamy skin of her thigh. "You know there isn't," he said. It was usually outprocessing or execution.

"It must be nice to be a special case," she added before Brezan could devise a suitable retort. "I feel for you. I can't imagine what they have planned for you once the mission's over."

Brezan clenched his teeth. The Andan were supposed to be the diplomatic ones. "I am Kel," he said, although it felt as though he had to drag each word through fire and thorns. "I do what my orders tell me to. By choice if I must."

Tseya's eyes were pits of shadow. "You're young yet," she said, reminding him that he had only a vague idea of her age. "You're going to be faced with orders for a long time. It doesn't matter how perfectly you execute them, however many times. They'll never accept you as a real Kel."

Shuos Zehun's words came back to Brezan with unhappy clarity: *I wouldn't have minded seeing you in the Shuos.* Not that he could imagine why, given his inability to prevail in this conversation. Just because he was a failure as a Kel didn't mean he'd make a good Shuos. He looked at Tseya, having given up on witty rejoinders, and waited for her next sally.

Tseya lowered her hand.

Brezan set his jaw and tried not to shudder with premature relief. He didn't want to keep looking at Tseya. He made himself do so anyway.

"General," Tseya said quietly, with none of the mockery from earlier.

He didn't understand.

"General," she said again, "have you figured out what the point of this exercise is?"

"I'm not a Shuos," Brezan said, "and I'm not properly a Kel, either. Why don't you explain it to me in one-syllable words and stick figures so I have a chance of following you."

Tseya ignored his tone, which was just as well. "We have to be ready to fight Jedao," she said. "If we're unlucky, the matter might not be settled by a well-aimed bullet, or by enthrallment. He's not just a soldier, Brezan. Ex-soldier, if you prefer. He's the oldest Shuos, and while he's crazy, he's not stupid. Just because you're a crashhawk doesn't mean he can't get you to do exactly as he wants. The records say he's very good at persuasion, at needling people until they capitulate—or join him. You have got to be prepared."

Brezan couldn't contest any of this, but that didn't make him feel any better. "You've made your point."

"In case you're wondering," Tseya said, "I'm going to have to be careful myself."

He didn't trust himself to ask about her vulnerabilities.

"It was a long time ago," Tseya said. Her hands opened and closed. "My mother is also an Andan, but we've spent most of our lives arguing. This last argument—it wasn't a good one."

"I'm sorry," Brezan said then, because he ought to say something.

"As I said, it was a long time ago. I mostly don't miss her." She smiled oddly at him. "It will be very satisfying to dispatch the Immolation Fox, regardless. Especially since my mother doesn't believe I can do it."

# CHAPTER EIGHTEEN

"So what kept you this time?" Zehun asked as Mikodez entered their office suite with its cheerful mix of cat toys and ink paintings by various grandchildren and other young relatives. "You're fourteen minutes late."

Mikodez gave Zehun a pained look. On his way to the most comfortable couch, he knelt to pet the friendlier of Zehun's two cats, Fenez. The other one was hiding, as usual. Fenez still bore a scary resemblance to a knitting project gone horribly awry. Mikodez had learned the hard way to beg off brushing her coat.

After paying homage to the cat, Mikodez sat across from Zehun. On the table between the two of them rested a pot of tea painted with roses stabbed through their hearts, which he had given Zehun after an Andan assassin almost killed them. There was also a tray of cookies and candied flowers. Today Zehun wasn't even trying to coax him out of his beloved sweets. They knew talking to his nephew always made him moody. Niath, who had trained as an Andan contact specialist, had been the only survivor of a border encounter. The incident had left him unstable. Mikodez had accepted him as a ward when Niath's own parents, who had no faction affiliation, were too afraid to take him back in; an Andan without full control of enthrallment was liable to fry people's brains. As hexarch, Mikodez had nothing to fear from Niath's ability, and Istradez was good enough at fooling Niath that he was willing to take the risk. Their nephew's loneliness was palpable, and family was family, after all.

Mikodez helped himself to one of the flowers, more crunch than flavor, then said, "Sorry about the delay. Niath is doing as well as he ever does. On the way here I got tied up with a shadowmoth commander calling about an urgent matter of etiquette."

"Normal etiquette or Shuos etiquette?" Zehun asked as they poured him tea. It smelled of citron and rose hips. "By the way, I should warn you that everyone in the office thinks those almond cookies are unbearably sweet. If you don't like them either, I'm going to dump them on Niath and see if he can enthrall anyone into eating them."

"Very funny." Mikodez didn't like discussing his nephew's condition with anyone but Istradez and Medical. The cookies must be extraordinarily bad for Zehun to bring Niath up like this. That, or Zehun was in a mood. The current situation had *everyone* in a mood. To be polite, he tried one of the cookies and grimaced. "Just toss these. They're no good."

Zehun scowled at the cookies. "Oh well, it was worth a try."

"Anyway, the issue was Shuos etiquette." This meant things like whether circumstances made it proper to unstealth and blow an unsuspecting target to smithereens. Rahal Iruja hated it when he did that without submitting paperwork in advance, which killed the point. "I handled it." He sipped the tea, smiled a little at the taste of honey, and tapped the edge of the cookie tray. "I presume you have your scenario all figured out, so you might as well go ahead."

In order to keep from locking into interpretations of events prematurely, Mikodez and Zehun ran through counterfactual scenarios periodically. With both Jedao and Kujen at large, he felt it particularly important to continue the exercise, although the subject of today's was the former and not the latter. He would have liked to run through the scenario with some other members of his senior staff, but scheduling was proving more difficult than usual.

"All right," Zehun said. They called up two jeng-zai images. Mikodez suppressed a groan. He could hold his own at the game, but he had gotten sick of it as a cadet and had never recovered.

The first image was a gruesome portrayal of the Drowned General. Most artists didn't go in for curved ice spikes or dissevered silver-green light or pale, frenetic eyes peering out of cracked flesh. Mikodez bet the artist had taken inspiration from some remembrance.

The second image was the Deuce of Gears, but done up in the traditional colors, silver on black. Like every other card in the suit, it had been associated with the Nirai before Jedao happened to it. Spirel had explained to him that most jeng-zai artists drove themselves crazy trying to do *something* to the card to compensate for the connotations that Jedao had stapled to it. It had originally meant 'cog in the machine,' a show of submission to Kel Command, although Mikodez doubted Kel Command had been fooled even before Hellspin. This particular interpretation had etched the character for *one million* into the gears' degenerating surfaces.

"Are we too old to bother with subtlety anymore?" Mikodez inquired.

"Forget old. I'm too cranky to sit around thinking of creative ways to present a fictional scenario when the real situation is so bad," Zehun said. "All right, here it is. Shuos Jedao has persuaded key Shuos officials in the Crescendo March to declare for him." The Crescendo March overlapped both the Severed March and the Stabglass March, putting it uncomfortably close to the Fortress of Spinshot Coins on the one hand and the Citadel of Eyes on the other. "He hasn't made an attempt on your seat, precisely—"

If Zehun meant to get his attention, they already had it. He knew where this was going anyway.

"—but he's seceded from the hexarchate," Zehun said. Fenez mewed and hopped up into Zehun's lap, then began purring loudly. Mikodez had always known that cats were more treacherous than his own people. For their part, Zehun buried their hands in that mess of calico coat, expression content. "The other hexarchs are pushing for you to resolve this rapidly. The Kel have offered their compliance, mainly as a way of rubbing it in, but you will lose considerable prestige by taking them up on it. What went wrong, and how did the Shuos get to this point?"

Fenez yawned hugely. Light from the two jeng-zai images sheened yellow-green in her eyes. "Just one question about the scenario," Mikodez said. "Has Jedao set himself up as some kind of dictator?" The thought was almost funny enough that he wanted to see it happen, except for the implications.

Zehun laughed at him. "In the interests of watching you struggle, I'm going to say no. He's put someone else in charge and is running around as their pet general and all-around enforcer."

"Well," Mikodez said, "I suppose that even my favorite suicidal revenant might have enough of a sense of self-preservation to know that it's better not to be the primary target. Plus, this way he can deny that he wants power for its own sake."

"Quit stalling and get started, Mikodez."

Mikodez considered what he'd been given. "I posit this: we're too lackadaisical about responding to Jedao's propaganda campaign. Ordinarily it's a mistake to draw attention to whatever chatter is being distributed, but that's when you have a better chance of monitoring the sources. We apparently never manage to track down the distribution channels. Even now there's circumstantial evidence that he's doing something unusual there. Istradez tells me it's driving Intelligence wild, as if I couldn't tell." He eyed Fenez, who was clearly unimpressed. "Scenario aside, it's infuriating that traffic analysis hasn't yielded anything illuminating. If our agent on the *Hierarchy of Feasts* had run across anything, she'd have passed on word, but that's assuming she hasn't been killed or subverted or turned into a paperweight."

"That's just distribution, though," Zehun said. "You haven't accounted for the effectiveness of the propaganda. Yes, we've seen a few system-level successes on Jedao's part, but they can be attributed to locals reacting to the Hafn breathing down their necks. So go back to the scenario. Jedao can't have kept on broadcasting bulletins that suggest that he's as nicely leashed as someone's dog. What changes?"

"Jedao buys a brainwashing ray off the black market?" Mikodez said, remembering some of Kujen's caustic remarks. You couldn't find more of an expert on brainwashing than Kujen. Too bad they still had no idea where he'd gotten off to.

Zehun gave him the flat stare that had earned them a reputation for eating slow-witted cadets back when they'd been an instructor.

"All right," Mikodez said, sobering, "I'll stop being a pest."

Zehun muttered something that might have been "No danger of that."

"Jedao isn't a propagandist," Mikodez said, "although he picked up the basics and absorbed some stylistic quirks from Khiaz. He's very good at talking people into things, but with his anchors he had the advantage that no one else could monitor what he was saying once they left Kujen's presence, and with the Kel he could use formation instinct as a crutch. Anchoring no longer applies, and the Shuos are not conformist enough to be manipulated in the same ways that modern Kel can be.

"Given all that, I'm proposing a few things. First, he recruits a propagandist or six. I doubt anyone with the necessary imagination was lurking in General Khiruev's swarm. It simply wasn't what they were assembled for. Still, Jedao can always recruit someone on some station. Face it, the man has raging ego problems the way most Shuos do, myself not excepted, but he didn't become a general without learning to delegate."

"What about Jedao's motivations?" Zehun said.

"The other hexarchs default to thinking that he's out for old-fashioned vengeance and let it go at that," Mikodez said. "I don't buy it. He's at war because it's the world he knows, but he tells himself he's putting something right in the process because he needs a reason for the butchery.

"If he successfully creates a splinter state, it's either because that was his goal all along, it's a stepping stone to some other goal, or it's a feint and he's after something else entirely. I assume we fuck up our assessment for him to get as far as he does. He doesn't issue some kind of manifesto, does he?"

"Nice try," Zehun said, "but no."

"What, you don't think it'd be fun to draw up a mock document in Jedao's style?" Mikodez started making a fort of the cookies. Zehun, used to such behavior, sighed. "The other logical possibility is that Jedao wants something else but was stuck with secession as a consolation prize. Since the point of the exercise is a disaster scenario, I have to assume that's not the case and he's out to stick it to us."

"It would be one hell of a consolation prize, yes." Zehun lowered their cat to the floor. Instead of darting off, Fenez rolled over on her back and began writhing comically.

"As of right now in the real world," Mikodez said, "Jedao has intimated that he'd like to ingratiate himself back into the hexarchs' favor. Granted, everyone remembers that he looked sane from his childhood until Hellspin Fortress, so a couple months of ostentatious good behavior isn't much of an indication, but he always did like playing long odds. In the scenario, we misread the threat that he represents. Say he takes a left turn and obtains more threshold winnowers, which puts everyone on high alert. We're occupied making sure he doesn't sprint somewhere to blow up another million people because with a mass murderer you can't afford to ignore the threat. In the meantime, he's busy negotiating with a number of senior Shuos." He fell silent.

Zehun said, "Ah," very softly, and waited, hands resting on their knees.

All but two of the cookies had joined the fort. "You know," Mikodez said, "Jedao's record as an assassin has always puzzled me, as though I should be able to diagnose whatever the hell went wrong twenty years down the line. He wasn't enthusiastic about torture or seduction, but he'd follow his handlers' orders. And then his service with the Kel. Superficially gregarious, but no close friends or lovers. For the longest time, people just figured he lived for his job, like any number of soldiers, and then. It's vexing that I can't solve the puzzle when there's so much on file."

Zehun shook their head. "I know you like to think that there was some cunning pattern back then we ought to have picked up on, but face it, we make a point of recruiting people who are comfortable getting friendly with others only to stab them in the kidneys. Some of them are even decent, helpful human beings who just want to rescue kittens in distress and the occasional hostage. With Jedao we got unlucky. It's not like he's the only Shuos to prove unstable, given the personality traits we select for, even if he happens to be one of the more destructive of the bunch."

"Short of dragging Jedao in here and scaring up some ace interrogators," Mikodez said, "we can't resolve that question. But the point is that we assess Jedao as a military threat rather than a political one. It's the curse of being a Shuos, or a Kel, for that matter. All we see is a general in a box, when the general might have other ideas now that he's free." He picked up a candied violet and crushed it over the cookie fort. "What I hate about my own logic is that this is exactly what we're doing right now, whether or not it's wrong."

"How does he know which Shuos to target?" Zehun said. "I don't trust a number of things Kujen claimed, but I do believe him when he says revenants are blind and deaf when locked up in the black cradle. On the occasions it came up, he seemed far too pleased about it for it not to be true. Anyway, that's something you have to explain. I'll accept that a few entrepreneurs might have contacted Jedao on their own, but that wouldn't account for a full scale secession."

Too bad Mikodez couldn't use the terrible cookies to bribe some possibilities out of someone else. He liked making use of other people's brains, to say nothing of other people's cookies. And why did Zehun think that this many cookies was remotely appropriate for two people anyway? Did they think the cats would develop a taste for them?

"Mikodez," Zehun said, "you're getting distracted."

He smiled brightly at Zehun, but he knew they weren't taken in. "Freedom of choice," he said. "Jedao never had any choice about his anchors. But recruiting Shuos? The hexarchate is a large place. He just needs to keep trying until he hits on enough people who find his offer attractive, and he'd target people who have reasons not to report the contact to higher authorities. Whatever we do, corruption never dies. He's hampered by not starting out with a network of agents, but whenever he talks to a station or a system of any size, he can pump the locals for information. Since he had basic analyst training, he'd know what to look for, and—"

"And?" Zehun said when he broke off.

"The succession problem crops up everywhere, doesn't it?" Mikodez said. "I could come up with alternate paths to the end scenario. Irritatingly, it always winds back to the fact that this entire faction is held together by spit and fraying thread. The moment someone offs me, it's back to the usual chaos, as you like to remind me. So the issue is that I can't foster enough faction cohesion to stop people high up the food chain from finding Jedao's offer attractive. Since you mention that he's going around as an enforcer, I'm guessing he'd install someone with both ambition and the arrogance to think that they could control him. There's a lot of that going on—yes, Zehun, I can see what you think of my efforts in that direction."

"I didn't say anything." Zehun shrugged. "I don't even disagree with your attempts to give Jedao long-distance therapy. It's doomed, but it's not *more* doomed than everything everyone else has tried already."

"He hasn't been answering my calls anyway," Mikodez said. "You know, let me amend what I said. Now that I think about it, Jedao doesn't target people who are keen on power. That'd be too obvious, and they'd end up quarreling down the line. Not that he'd be reluctant to shoot obstacles in the head."

Mikodez met Zehun's pitiless eyes and drew a long breath. "He goes after the idealists. The ones who dream about fixing our government. A few always slip through academy, although the dangerous ones are those who develop the notion during their careers. As a bonus, he finds one who not only thinks that a sufficiently big gun will get rid of all the impediments, but that they can reform him. At that point, all Jedao has to do is play into the fantasy."

"All right," Zehun said, "that's good enough for our purposes."

"Jedao hasn't tried to subvert *you* recently, has he?"

"What, as if he'd tell me anything useful I could pass on to you? You should be so lucky." Zehun removed a cookie from the top of the fort and nibbled at it, then winced. "Anyway, based on this, what should we be doing differently?"

"Too bad we can't find some creative ways to divert more funds from the damn Andan. We're going broke as it is." Mikodez drummed his fingers on his knee. "It can't hurt to order additional checks on the regions Jedao's passed through. Although I can't imagine he'd have the time to be up to much, even if he can ditch tons of the paperwork that Kel Command would make a general do. Speaking of which, I'm tempted to play hooky from mine."

"Don't be ridiculous," Zehun said. Their gaze became hooded for a moment. It caught his attention because Zehun was normally more composed than that. "Mikodez. You do know you're staring right at a long-term solution to the succession problem."

"We're not discussing this now," he said, very pleasantly.

Zehun's expression flickered, but they acceded.

Mikodez wasn't looking forward to the conversation when it resurfaced. This would do for now. Instead, he asked, "I know we've had similar fiascoes, but how many out-and-out secessions?"

"Three big ones. The first was that Andan-Rahal revolt during Heptarch Liozh Honenda's reign, which the Liozh put down in an impressively short period of time. Then there was that one Kel general whose name I can never pronounce. She allied with some foreign powers that we gnawed into pieces after. The last was another Kel general." Zehun smiled cynically. "People forget formation instinct hasn't always been around."

"Do you think secession is Jedao's play?"

"I doubt it," Zehun said. "He's one of us, Mikodez. Both assassins and soldiers like to operate from ambush. Whatever he's doing, he's working hard to make sure it'll blindside us. We're going to have to get ahead of him somehow."

"I'd say that we have numbers on our side," Mikodez said, "except for Hellspin Fortress. Alas, leaning harder on the Kel is unlikely to accomplish anything but make them crankier. Still, we need *someone* to rout the Hafn so the shadowmoths can make their strike without leaving us open to unsavory foreigners. In the meantime, we're going to train one eye on the political realm and see what that gets us."

Zehun rubbed their eyes, and then he realized how tired they must be. "I still feel like he's toying with us," Zehun said.

"Yes, that's the point," Mikodez said ruefully. "Now I know how everyone else feels."

"Don't flatter yourself," Zehun said, but they were smiling.

# CHAPTER NINETEEN

KHIRUEV RECEIVED COMMANDER Janaia's request after the third time the Hafn refused battle. They were eight days out from Minang System with its wolf tower. Khiruev was painfully aware that she had turned up her terminal's displays brighter than anyone else in the command center. Everything around her looked as though someone had painted it over with shadows.

Irritatingly, Jedao was playing jeng-zai against the mothgrid again. Khiruev, who could see the score, wished he would lose just once. Jedao appeared to be absorbed contemplating his hand.

Janaia prodded her terminal for the twelfth time in as many minutes, then muttered under her breath. She wasn't the only one frustrated with the Hafn's continued flight. The Kel wanted battle.

"They'd better make a stand somewhere, sir," Janaia said, her annoyance at the situation overcoming her desire to speak to Jedao and Khiruev as little as possible. "Do you suppose the master clock in the tower will be a sufficiently inviting target?"

"They've certainly arrowed straight toward it," Jedao said. "Aside from the Rahal billing us for any damage to it, the calendrical destabilization if the Hafn wrecked it wouldn't do us any favors. Even if their objective is elsewhere, they might bomb it in passing."

Khiruev was scrutinizing a map. It didn't take much military acumen to determine that something was amiss, but she couldn't undermine Jedao in front of the crew. After being driven away from the Fortress of Spinshot Coins, the Hafn swarm might have been forgiven for withdrawing toward the border. Instead, they had persistently zigzagged farther into the hexarchate.

Khiruev could only think of two compelling reasons for this behavior. One, this swarm was a decoy for a second invasion force, in which case Jedao was leaving the Fortress open to a second attack. True, the Hafn ability to turn phantom terrain against hexarchate forces was no longer a secret, but that didn't mean they hadn't prepared other tricks. The other explanation, which she kept returning to although she wished she could scrub it out of her brain, was that Jedao wasn't just herding the Hafn, he was colluding with them. Hafn movements were too convenient, considering the plans that Jedao had already confessed to.

As the Hafn neared the Kel military outpost at Tercel 81-7178, Khiruev waited tensely for any indication that they were slowing or circling around. Nothing.

Afterward, Khiruev went to contemplate her shelves of disassembled machines. She picked up the watch Jedao had admired, trying not to think about the gnawing sensation inside her, as though her bones were shuddering apart. When she was around other people she could set it aside, but here it nagged at her. She put on music, a plaintive zither piece. That didn't help either.

When Commander Janaia requested to see her, Khiruev was grateful for the distraction, even if it was likely bad news. The wording of her request was both correct and unrevealing. Khiruev put the broken watch back on the shelf, then indicated that Janaia should see her in twelve minutes.

Janaia came by almost exactly on time, unusual for her. It filled Khiruev with foreboding. Khiruev had set the door to admit Janaia automatically. "At ease," Khiruev said, emerging to greet her.

There were faint lines around Janaia's eyes. "Permission to speak freely, sir," she said.

"Granted," Khiruev said. "You may sit, if you like." She nodded toward a chair.

After a significant look at the chairs, Janaia sat. "I'm surprised the fox let you keep your gadgets."

"Perhaps," Khiruev said, "he thought I could use the reminder of my failure."

"So it was you after all."

The music box. Kel Lyu and Kel Meriki, sprawled dead. Khiruev had essentially pointed the needler at them herself. She'd written notifications to their families that she'd never be permitted to send. The one time she'd brought it up with Jedao, Jedao had quashed the idea on the grounds that it would get those families in trouble with hexarchate authorities. Which Khiruev had known, but she couldn't stop wishing otherwise. "I didn't think it was any secret," she said.

"It's done," Janaia said, unsentimental. "But that isn't what I came to talk to you about. It's the twenty-fifth day, sir."

The twenty-fifth day since Khiruev had invoked Vrae Tala. "That's something you'll have to take up with Jedao," Khiruev said.

"You're good at jeng-zai," Janaia said, "but I know a bluff when I see one. I could have gone straight to him. But I thought I'd find out what's going through your head first."

"Why don't you come right out and say it, Commander." Inside the gloves her hands had gone clammy.

"Jedao had no idea about the Vrae Tala clause, isn't that right?" Janaia said. "I thought at first that he had coerced you into it. But this last high table, there was no quarter-candle by your seat. I may be no friend of the fox's, but he respects Kel custom. He always passes the cup at high table, he wears the notorious gloves, I daresay he knows our regulations better than we do. Except, of course, the ones that came into existence after we made a hash of executing him."

"It was a command decision," Khiruev said humorously, "and one a bit late to rescind. Do you wish to lodge an official complaint?" Who was Janaia going to go over her head to?

Janaia slammed her hand down on the chair's arm. "Sir, I've served with you for fourteen years," she said, her voice utterly level. "I'm Kel, you're Kel, I'll even follow you into a fox's jaws. But I will serve you better if you help me understand what the hell we're doing." Funny how Khiruev had made the same argument to Jedao himself. "What is it that's so important that you're killing yourself for it?"

Khiruev opened her mouth.

"If you're about to make a suicide joke, don't. Sir."

"Jedao thinks he can take on the hexarchs and win," Khiruev said.

"Well, yes," she said impatiently, "that kind of delusion is what landed him in the black cradle in the first place. But, I mean, he's crazy. What's your excuse?"

Khiruev peeled back her right glove just far enough to expose the skin of her wrist, so Janaia would understand the seriousness of her intent. The Kel only ungloved for suicide missions and lovers, as the saying went. Khiruev hoped Jedao's plan wasn't suicide, but in a sense, it didn't matter. She was committed.

Janaia's mouth compressed.

Satisfied that she understood, Khiruev settled the glove back in place. "Commander," she said, "I trust you remember Raggard's Basket."

Kel Command had assigned Khiruev to deal with heresy at Raggard's Basket. The orders had changed en route. The Rahal had been making a calendrical adjustment, and they had desired a fast resolution to the matter. In response to Rahal pressure, Kel Command authorized the use of fungal canisters.

Khiruev looked for a better way, but she couldn't get around the punishing timetable. Since she could offer no viable alternative, she ordered the launch of the canisters. The resulting fungal blooms destroyed anything of human value in the world's ecosphere. It was estimated that decontamination would take upward of a century. Khiruev had a vivid memory of the first spores coming to fruit when they encountered one of the indigenous sea snakes, fungus sprouting in spongy tendrils from beneath scales until they cracked purple-red, fungus clouding the amber eyes, fungus spilling out of the agonized mouths in bloated masses. Her chief of staff caught her watching the video over and over and made her stop.

"Yes," Janaia said. "I remember Raggard's Basket. I also remember that we had our orders."

"I would like to think that it's possible to construct a society where our orders don't involve slaughtering our own people," Khiruev said. The heretics hadn't been the only ones on that planet.

"That's always hard," Janaia said. Her face did not change. "But I leave the philosophical considerations to you. My job is to fight where you point me. Tell me, do you think Jedao really has a chance, even if he isn't going to backstab us all afterward? Even at Candle Arc he was only outnumbered eight to one. The odds are infinitely worse here."

"Let me put it this way," Khiruev said. "For four hundred years he's convinced Kel Command not to kill him, despite a million good reasons. Kel Command isn't known for being slow on the draw. And then he escaped. He may not win, but I am not seeing a better opportunity." Khiruev met her eyes. "My disloyalty to Kel Command must be a terrible disappointment to you."

Khiruev shouldn't have put it to Janaia so directly, but Janaia only shrugged. "I must admit," Janaia said, "this strikes me as a singularly bad time for an insurrection."

"This is the hexarchate, Commander. There's never a *good* time."

"It's going to be blood all the way down, one way or another. And you won't be around to see the end of it."

"Someone has to decide to throw the dice," Khiruev said.

Janaia nodded curtly. "At least tell Jedao about the candles," she said.

She cared about the oddest things. "Why is this so important to you?"

"Fourteen years. Tell him. Let him do the right thing by you."

Fourteen years and Khiruev was wondering if she'd ever understood Janaia. "I'll take it under consideration," she said. "Dismissed."

After Janaia had left, Khiruev returned to contemplating the watch. She opened up the back and stared at the unmoving parts.

She was cold again, but she could get used to a little cold. It was only temporary, after all.

THERE WAS NO such thing as a routine battle, something Khiruev had figured out as a lieutenant decades ago. Even so, certain rituals made the chaos manageable. More accurately, they gave you the comforting illusion that the plan would have any relationship to reality when reality decided to stab you in the eye.

Khiruev had made sure to get to the command center as the swarm approached Minang System's inhabited worlds. The swarm alternated between two defensive formations as they traveled, in case the Hafn proved capable of coming about more suddenly than they had in the past. The Hafn swarm was going just fast enough that the Kel had to go full-tilt to keep up, which couldn't be an accident. But abandoning the chase wasn't an option, either.

For the most part, Khiruev occupied herself reading increasingly confusing scan summaries and rereading staff analyses of Hafn movements. As Chief of Staff Stsan said in private, they amounted to carefully phrased variations of 'fucked if we know what they're about.' It was too early to tell if the Hafn would make a stand at Minang, attack the wolf tower in passing, keep spearing into the Concerto March, or pull something completely new. Among other things, they hadn't left any more geese lying around. Maybe they were running low.

What worried Khiruev more than the Hafn was the fact that Jedao hadn't deigned to make an appearance. She couldn't tell Jedao what to do, but Jedao's apparent lack of interest was making the crew jittery. Janaia had glanced twice in the direction of Jedao's empty seat before catching herself.

Khiruev didn't have a pretext for sending Jedao a message asking him what the hell he thought he was doing, although she sent a restrained note anyway. It wasn't against any regulation for Jedao to be off playing cards or polishing guns or taking a nap when they weren't in combat. Anyway, it was an open question as to whether Kel regulations had meaning to an ex-officer in a rogue swarm. Note aside, it would be best if Khiruev acted like nothing out of the ordinary was going on, not that 'ordinary' meant much either, these days.

"Sir," Janaia said when they were four hours out from the tower. Her executive officer glanced at her, then looked away, troubled. Even Muris was affected by the situation, it appeared.

"Yes, Commander?" Khiruev said.

"Where do you suppose all the geese are anyway?"

It was patently not what she wanted to ask. "Your guess is as good as mine," she said.

"I would feel better if the Hafn stuck to a routine."

"The next time they consult me about their battle plans, I'll pass that along."

*Your general had better know what he's about,* Janaia's look said.

Khiruev smiled thinly at her, then returned to scrutinizing the scan readouts.

Three hours and five minutes out, Communications said, "Request from Minang Tower to speak to General Jedao, sir."

"Forward it to the general," Khiruev said. She checked the headers and was interested that a wolf tower was addressing Jedao by the rank he no longer held. Even if Jedao didn't want to be in the command center, he might wish to deal with the call.

Six minutes passed. Communications looked up, expression distinctly unhappy.

"Let me guess," Khiruev said, "the general hasn't responded and the tower is repeating its request."

"That's it exactly, sir."

While it was hardly outside the realm of possibility that Jedao had some way of hijacking a channel so he could talk to people without there being a record of it in the mothgrid, Khiruev doubted that the tower was playing any such games with them. "Forward the new request," Khiruev said grimly, appending a second note asking for Jedao's guidance. She began putting together alternate formation orders for the swarm, just in case.

Janaia had achieved the perfectly serene smile that meant she had weapons-grade reservations about their survival.

*You and me both,* Khiruev thought. Strategy had come up with three separate plans, to say nothing of contingency variations, for the defense of Minang System during the pursuit. Jedao had not approved any of them. Khiruev thought the second one might do in a pinch.

After another twenty-three minutes, the next transmission from Minang Tower wasn't a request, dashing Khiruev's hopes that Jedao was discreetly handling the matter. It came not long after Scan reported that the Hafn were changing course. If the Hafn kept on more or less in that direction, they would swing past Cobweb System, which had two settled worlds. And the Cobweb worlds weren't the only ones out that way. The possibilities multiplied appallingly with each hour the Hafn weren't stopped.

"Do we have any indication of"—she didn't say 'legitimate'—"Kel reinforcements in the area?" Khiruev said. Kel Command had to be working on the problem, although she had some idea of the logistical difficulties. After all, this very swarm had had to be scrambled for defense after General Chrenka's assassination, and the Kel were often stretched thin.

"I can't definitely identify any swarm formants," Scan said.

Communications added, "Local defenses have been scrambled, judging by system traffic, but I have seen no indication of a swarm presence."

"The message, then," Khiruev said. "Forward it."

Jedao's reply came back almost immediately, text-only: *Deal with it.* Then, a set of coordinates: *Prepare a welcoming party for the enemy here.*

With what, the threshold winnowers that Jedao had so cleverly had them discard? Notably, Jedao had given a place but not a time. The fact of the Kel swarm's presence wasn't a secret, and hanging around to launch missiles would hurt. They carried some mines for situations where you could force an enemy through an approach, but the Hafn had been merrily ignoring calendrical gradients this whole time, so that didn't work either.

"Communications," she said. "General Khiruev to warmoth commanders. I want to know how many bombs we can place for remote detonation at the following location." She gave the coordinates, and ran some calculations in consultation with a map of the system. "Head for this location." Second set of coordinates, and a set of waypoints. Then: "General Khiruev out." To Communications: "All right. While the commanders are dealing with that, let's hear the tower's message."

The message opened with the hexarchate's wheel insignia, then the gray Rahal wolf with its bronze eyes. The woman in the video looked like a standard-issue Rahal magistrate, from her immaculate upswept hair to the severe gray shirt with its bronze brooch. The bent stylus in her left hand was not, however, standard-issue, nor were the snapped pieces of two more on the desk before her. A knife's braid-wrapped hilt was just visible at the edge of the video.

"This is High Magistrate Rahal Zaniin of Minang Tower," the woman said. She had a slight melodic accent, not unattractive. Unsurprisingly, Khiruev couldn't place it. "There's a whole bunch of formulaic stuff for addressing traitors that I memorized back when I was in academy, but why don't we forget about that so I can get to the point."

Zaniin broke her stylus, scowled at it for a moment, then flung it aside. "I assume I'm addressing General Shuos Jedao and his swarm. I can only guess at your motivations, which are probably five parts head-game to one part let's-use-the-Kel-as-punching-bags. It would be helpful if you'd agree to talk while there's time, but since you're not amenable, you get the soliloquy edition.

"One of the things they made me learn before they installed me in this overgrown clock was reading scan formants. It's quite unambiguous. The Hafn are going *there*"—she stabbed with her finger, and the video was momentarily replaced by a map showing Cobweb System—"and you're apparently determined to be *here*." Another stab, this time showing Minang Tower represented by the standard wolf-and-bell icon.

"The tower and its associated stations have a population of approximately 86,000. Cobweb 4 is a fully inhabited planet, with about four billion people living there. Cobweb 3 is more like a glorified moon, but still, I don't imagine the Hafn can be relied upon to leave it alone." She appended more detailed statistics.

"As I said," she resumed, "I don't know what you're looking to get out of this. But if you're trying to preserve Minang Tower for some reason of calendrical warfare"—Zaniin's voice was almost steady—"just ask your Kel. Some of them must be able to back me up. Master clocks are fucking expensive to build and calibrate, and dealing with clock desynchronization on your end wouldn't be any fun either, I get that. But you can work around one clock. Our destruction won't set you back much, even if the Hafn leap back here. Those people in Cobweb—there's no other way to save them. Run the numbers, Jedao. Please."

Khiruev thought this was the end of the message, but after a few moments the high magistrate went on. "It's not hard to guess that you have nasty plans for the people who stuck you in a dark jar for four centuries," Zaniin said. "Judging from the propaganda, you either think the whole system is rotten or you're doing a bang-up job of faking it to make new friends. I kind of hope it's the former."

She picked up the knife, unsheathed it, and stabbed her table. "Because you know what? It *is* a shitty system. We have a whole faction devoted to torturing people so the rest of us can pretend we're not involved. Too bad every other system of government out there is even worse. You know, they say at Candle Arc you kept Doctrine from rendering a Lanterner as an on-the-spot emergency remembrance. Of course, four hundred years and one big massacre later, I have to wonder if you remember it yourself."

Her eyes flicked sideways, and she frowned. "The Hafn are still heading for Cobweb. Who knows, maybe they'll change their minds. But you're the only thing between the invaders and a lot of people who had nothing to do with all the things that happened to you during your unpleasant unlife.

"I'm going to have to turn myself in for having this conversation. In the meantime, if you have some working alternative for the world we're stuck in, by all means show it to us without spelling it in corpses. High Magistrate Zaniin out."

Into the uneasy quiet, Communications said, "Minang Tower has forwarded us scan relay data from the listening posts in the region, sir."

Four billion people and change.

Khiruev recovered the information she had sought earlier all too easily. The Sundered Spheres swarm under Major General Kel Jui had been brought up from the Rosetta March. Kel Command had pulled General Inesser off High Glass; they must be desperate. High Glass was one of the most dangerous borders, and Inesser was not only the hexarchate's senior general, she was also widely considered one of the most formidable. Whoever was taking her place at High Glass had better be good.

Khiruev called Strategy. "Colonel Riozu," she said, "double-check me on this."

After several minutes, the lieutenant colonel sent back an annotated map that matched the one in Khiruev's head. There was no way for Sundered Spheres to rescue Cobweb. They were simply too far away.

Khiruev tapped in a message to Jedao. *Request clarification of orders, sir.*

Jedao's response took longer this time. *Do you want to win? Don't interrupt me again. I will be there when I can.*

*Yes,* Khiruev thought, *but what are we winning?* No matter. She'd led swarms before she met Jedao. She could do it again.

"Approaching designated waypoint in thirty-eight minutes," Navigation said in a colorless voice.

Communications had collated the warmoth commanders' inventory of bombs and passed that over to Khiruev's terminal. Khiruev had another terse discussion with Riozu. "General Khiruev to all moths," she said, and instructed them to leave a frightening number of their bombs at the location that Jedao had indicated earlier, to be detonated at Khiruev's command. "All moths assume grand formation Knives Are Our Walls. Commander, refuse the primary pivot until we see what's coming at us."

Janaia inhaled sharply—she would have preferred to stay in a two- or three-formation shield modulation sequence—but gave the necessary orders.

"Minang Tower again, sir," Communications said. "They're forwarding updated scan reports."

"I'm impressed they're still talking to us," Khiruev remarked.

"Talking *at* us is more like it," Janaia said.

Weapons reported that the bombs had been deployed. Meanwhile, Scan was unequivocal. The Hafn had turned around and were headed back toward Minang.

All right. The Hafn had been trying to lead the Kel away from Minang, specifically from the ambush that Jedao was, in his turn, setting for someone. Did this have something to do with the scan anomalies that Jedao had been receiving reports of? And if so, why did Jedao feel the need to be so coy about it?

"They're not going to run into those bombs," Janaia said. "Or run full-tilt at us, if it comes to that."

Khiruev smiled at her. "No one's asking them to." She asked Navigation for the Hafn's projected arrival time. Navigation answered. More waiting. Minang Tower continued to send scan updates.

"Hafn swarm increasing acceleration," Scan said, and reported the new estimated time of arrival.

Forty-nine minutes before the Hafn came within dire cannon range, the cacophony began. Scan cried, "Second enemy swarm incoming!"

If 'incoming' was the right word. The formants sizzled out of nowhere, sharp as lightning, over eighty of them. Jedao's prediction hadn't been exactly correct, but it was close enough—

Khiruev gave the order to detonate the bombs, and to reorient the swarm for the engagement. The explosions showed up as a flower-chain of pallid spheres on the tactical display. They finally had the battle they had wanted.

And Jedao, who had somehow known to engineer this, was still nowhere in sight.

# CHAPTER TWENTY

NIRAI KUJEN'S ANCHOR, Nirai Mahar, was asleep when the call came. Kujen himself never slept, one of the deliberate effects of being a revenant. Jedao had hated it, although Kujen didn't much care. When he had been alive, Kujen had wondered about the long-term effects. It turned out that being a disembodied voice, and one with only a single anchor as a conversational partner, did wonders for your patience.

Ordinarily Kujen would have ignored the call until Mahar woke on his own and had a chance to eat something, but only a few of Kujen's designated agents were supposed to be able to reach him at this clandestine base. Certainly not any of the hexarchs. But the call's headers indicated that it was coming from Andan Shandal Yeng. He couldn't imagine what she had to say to him. She had never liked him, especially after Mahar had seduced that one son-now-daughter of hers, and he found her tiresome.

Kujen looked at the current object of his attention, Esfarel 12. The man was monitoring the environmental controls. Esfarel 12 had no idea who the original Nirai Esfarel had been, nor any memory of the modifications that Kujen had ordered made to his appearance. 12 had the original's slightly unruly hair and smiling mouth and long hands, but not the original's body language. Kujen hadn't bothered with that after Esfarel 5. Too much work. Besides, the variety of responses entertained him on the occasions that he was in a mood for sex.

The call indicator wasn't going away. Kujen sighed. Time to wake Mahar up. Kujen inspected the anchor's current dream. For someone who had always eaten well, Mahar was surprisingly obsessed with food. This time it was tender bamboo shoots and strips of meat in sweet sauce, bowls of fruit slices garnished with edible petals, fragrant rice, jasmine tea, everything. For his part, Kujen remembered the taste of food vividly. One of the great benefits of being a revenant was never having to starve again, although Mahar needed to remember to eat so Kujen would have a functional marionette.

Kujen inserted an image of an hourglass onto the dinner table. This time the running sand was green-blue. It changed each time. He could control Mahar's dreams in exacting detail when he cared to, but here there was no need. It hadn't been difficult to convince Kel Command that giving Jedao the same modification would be a terrible idea. Jedao had already been hard enough to control.

Kujen waited until Mahar stirred. It wasn't as though he was the one in a tearing hurry. Besides, needling Shandal Yeng was always fun.

Mahar sat up and stretched. The bedsheets were tangled in his legs. He began extricating himself from them. "Emergency?" he said drowsily.

"Just make yourself presentable," Kujen said. "It's either the Andan hexarch or her latest consort."

"Shandal Yeng doesn't have consorts so much as social rivals she's decided to take down personally," Mahar said.

"You're only sixty-four," Kujen said as Mahar dressed in silk and velvet, all black and gray and glints of silver, and agate earrings in each ear. "Isn't that a little young to be so cynical?"

"Your bad habits are contagious."

Kujen laughed obligingly.

His anchor's idea of 'presentable' was terribly involved. Kujen didn't disapprove. He insisted on beautiful, mathematically trained men for anchors where possible. If he was going to be alive forever, he might as well enjoy the view and avail himself of decent conversation. His anchors varied in their attention to fashion. This one liked ruffles and scarves, even if the taste for odd knots was a new development. Kujen had grown up paying great attention to fashion, due to his first profession. He had seen a great many trends come and go. At the moment, he supported anything that confused Shandal Yeng, and he was also for letting Mahar enjoy himself once in a while. It made for a smoother working relationship.

Kujen didn't impute impatience to the call indicator's steady blinking, once per second in accordance with the local calendar he had devised. But there was no ambiguity about Shandal Yeng's expression when Mahar activated the line. She wasn't smiling, for one. She was much less exasperating when she wasn't smiling.

"I didn't realize those high collars were in fashion again," Mahar said, "or I'd have scared up a tailor."

Most people slipped and thought of Mahar as Kujen himself, an illusion both of them worked hard to maintain. Kujen could step in and use Mahar as a puppet, but it took a great deal of concentration. In most cases Mahar did just fine on his own. (This was another black cradle modification Jedao had not been permitted during his missions for Kel Command. Naturally, Kujen had bent the rules on certain private occasions. He wasn't worried about his ability to outmaneuver a mere Shuos.) Suitable long-term anchor candidates were rare, and required extensive psych surgery and training. Kujen made sure to keep a supply on hand at all times.

The Andan hexarch was looking at Mahar with shadowed eyes. "You've done a good job hiding," she said, "and I'm glad your self-imposed exile hasn't killed your interest in making sartorial statements. But I have no heart for discussing your fashion choices right now." That had to be a first. The Andan prided themselves on using appearances against people. "I hear you have your own immortality device. Not the black cradle, a completely new one."

To Mahar, Kujen said irritably, "We need to check for leaks again, don't we." To Shandal Yeng, through Mahar: "Before you go any further with that thought, what happened to Faian? I left a perfectly good researcher in charge. I'm positive she's smart enough to follow the instructions on the technology I left for the rest of you."

Curious: she was shaking her head. "Everyone I paid to make an assessment says she's doing fine. You chose well. But I felt it was better to approach the one who trained her."

"Wonderful, a business proposal," Mahar said subvocally, so only Kujen could hear him.

"I don't know," Kujen said. "Desperation is a refreshing look on her."

Shandal Yeng straightened. "I believe you've met my child Andan Nezhe."

Kujen finally knew where this was going. "The one I slept with?" Nezhe's relationship with their mother had always been tempestuous. Shandal Yeng had not approved of her second-born fucking a rival hexarch, which was why Nezhe had done it. Nor had she approved of Nezhe's insistence on training in special operations instead of settling in for a lifetime of sycophancy.

"I want to share immortality with her. It may be my last chance to win her back."

Ah. Nezhe must be a woman these days. Mahar gave Shandal Yeng a long look. "Let me guess," he said. "Faian turned you flat down."

Unsurprising. Faian had always had a subterranean legalistic streak. "Listen," Kujen said, "last time I checked you had six living"—acknowledged—"children."

"I should think you would appreciate my restraint," Shandal Yeng said archly. "Whatever it costs—"

"I don't care about the six million ways that people wreck their lives," Kujen said, "but I happen to appreciate that eternity is a very long time. I'm going to do you the favor of giving you sound counsel, and you're going to listen. First of all, you can't bribe love out of people." He was pretty sure that what Nezhe wanted, if anything, was her mother's affection, not the latest luxury. Even a luxury as good as immortality. "Second, take immortality for yourself and forget about your children, as per the original plan—yes, I listen in when I get bored—or else offer immortality to all of them. If you're determined to be surrounded by your spawn, Mikodez will say yes because he's got a soft spot for kids, even grown-up kids, plus he'll get front seats to the ensuing chaos, and Tsoro's always been old-fashioned about family. As for the rest, you're an Andan. You can be persuasive.

"If you do it the way you propose—just the one child—she'll grow to hate you. If her siblings were expendable, she'll always wonder if you'll discard her next. Eventually she'll try to assassinate you, or if you're lucky, she'll simply leave."

Shandal Yeng narrowed her eyes. "What a droll analysis from someone who's never had to sit through a dinner with all his children squabbling over pittances of power."

Kujen had sired a couple children centuries ago, during his first life, but had no idea whether any of them had survived, let alone their descendants. He didn't particularly miss the experience. "You know," he said, "the Andan aren't the only ones who study human nature."

"That may be so," she said, "but Nezhe is the one I want. I need her, Kujen. For all the trouble she's caused me, she's the most brilliant of my children. I shouldn't have to explain to you what it's like to face a future with no family."

The number of people who had tried arguments like this on him over the years was astonishing, even if no one at this end of time knew that he was responsible for the deaths of his mother and sister. "Don't appeal to my better nature," he said. "I've spent the last several centuries brainwashing people to pass the time. I have nothing to offer on that front."

"How interesting," Shandal Yeng said, "when you just offered me family advice. For a mathematician, your grasp of logic is terrible."

"Never ascribe to irrational benevolence what selfishness will explain," Kujen said cheerfully. "Remember that you're asking me to contemplate eternity with you and your guest list. It's in my interest to have you in a good mood so I don't have to listen to the backbiting. Trust me on this. Whatever the hell your children hate about you or each other, find a way to make things right. If you want to bring them all with you into a drearily long future, you can surely win the other hexarchs' support." Good luck with Faian, stubborn Faian—but that wasn't his problem.

"And if I insist that I only want Nezhe?"

"Then I don't see that I owe you any help."

"All right, Kujen," she said. "I realize you're beyond the need for petty things like companionship—"

"I don't know, it's always nice to have an audience," Kujen said to Mahar.

"Hush," Mahar said subvocally. "I want to see if she offers us anything good."

"—but I meant what I said about payment. Don't you tire of being dependent on the goodwill of the Kel? It looks like certain of your assets are still tied up with theirs."

It looked like Shandal Yeng's analysts weren't as good at following money trails as they needed to be. Happy news.

"If I cared to find out, I'm sure I could look up how much you're worth," Mahar said. "Maybe you could offer me some museums full of paintings while you're at it?" Mahar cared a lot more about fine art than Kujen did, which was why he got to deal with interior decoration.

"If you've developed new tastes in that area," Shandal Yeng said, "I should only be happy to guide you toward pieces worthy of your interest."

"Too bad," Kujen said, playing toward her misimpression that he was still allied with the Kel, who would have given a lot to know where he was. "I'm more interested in big guns. I don't know if it's escaped your attention, but when it comes to putting holes in things, you can't go wrong with the Kel."

"Money is a much better defense than violence."

"When money's gone," Kujen said softly, "only violence will do." He had never been good at it himself, which was where people like Jedao came in handy.

"You don't want me for an enemy, Kujen," she said.

Kujen had known it would come to threats. "If you can take me down without stabbing yourself in the back," he said, "please, go ahead. Don't bother Faian again. She's strong-willed, one of the things I like about her. I'll send you some textbooks if you want to work out the equations for yourself. And don't call again. You won't find me here or anywhere. In the meantime, I have some appallingly unethical pastimes to attend to."

Shandal Yeng's expression went remote. Then she cut the connection.

"And to think she wanted us to face eternity with her hanging around," Kujen said.

Mahar yawned, then took the scarf off and looped it around his wrist. "You should have said yes," he said. "Bought her off for a few centuries."

"She'd work her way around to hating me for saying yes. With some people you can't win." Kujen considered the matter. "Do *you* want immortality? The real thing, not what we have here?" He made the offer from time to time, in case the answer changed.

Mahar scoffed. "Unlike certain people, I understand the math. Rather not be a test subject for a fucking prototype, no offense. I keep studying your design specifications, Kujen, and they ought to be correct, but I can't shake the feeling that we're overlooking something. Besides, I know about Esfarel and Jedao, remember? One functional immortal out of three is a dismal success rate."

"Esfarel was weak," Kujen said carelessly, "even though he was spectacular in bed. Jedao was a head case when he arrived. That's not a fair test. And anyway, that was the black cradle, not the new variant."

"If you say so." Mahar unwound his scarf and put it away, then had a servitor bring him breakfast. The breakfast, when it arrived, was typical Kel fare: rice, pickles, sesame leaves, and marinated roasted meat chopped fine. He ate a few bites, blinked, then eyed the food. "That wasn't what I *meant* to order. You're still thinking about Jedao, aren't you?"

Bleed-through. "He was such a good project," Kujen said. "There was always something to fix. Or break, take your pick."

"Oh, for love of stars above. Now that he's running around loose, send him a courier with a shiny gun prototype or a nice bottle of whiskey and your apologies. It'll make you both feel better. He might even forgive you for sticking him in the black cradle. The two of you can team up and conquer the galaxy."

Mahar might understand the math, but he hadn't ever looked closely enough at a certain class of weapons. Like the hexarchs, he was deeply confused as to what 'Jedao' was up to. "Someday I'll take you up on that," Kujen said. "But not just yet."

KUJEN REMEMBERED WHEN the Kel had first delivered General Shuos Jedao to the black cradle facility 397 years ago. There had been a lot of grim soldiers in Kel black-and-gold. Jedao himself occupied a plain metal casket with a transparent pane. "Held under sedation lock, Nirai-zho," the Kel corporal said, as if that wasn't obvious. "Suicide risk."

"I'll say." His anchor at the time, Liyeng, strode over to the casket and inspected the status readings. Kujen had already checked them over. Jedao was alive in there, even if he'd picked one hell of a grandstanding maneuver for his bid for immortality.

"Nirai-zho," said a different voice. It belonged to High General Kel Anien, a thin, gray-haired woman. She was shuffling a deck of cards over and over, unable to be still. "Command sent me to address any questions you might have."

"Good," Kujen said curtly, since he had a role to play. "I didn't see anything in that mess of reports about what the Rahal inquisitors got out of General Jedao. Who do I have to vivisect to get the right security clearance?"

Anien flipped a card over, made a face at it, stuck it back in the deck. At last she looked at Liyeng. "You should have witnessed the interrogation, Nirai-zho," she said. "If it hadn't been such a mess, it would have been hilarious. The wolves that Rahal-zho dispatched couldn't get anything out of him. They started a side-argument with Shuos-zho about the appropriateness of certain Shuos techniques for fooling scrying and why they should be dropped from Shuos Academy's curriculum. Watching wolves have fits is an excellent pastime when you're recovering from an incandescent disaster."

Kujen had always suspected that Anien got bored too easily for her own good. He could relate. "Nothing?" he said, because he needed to be sure that Jedao hadn't hinted at their alliance. He'd already watched the excerpts from the regular interrogation that they had deigned to send him. *Please shoot me,* Jedao had said over and over. "He couldn't have been completely brain-dead if he could form a sentence in response to stimuli. Even a very dull sentence."

"Jedao has a singularity response to scrying," Anien said, sobering. Same image no matter what the query.

"Let me guess," Kujen said. "Immolation Fox." An obvious choice, given the circumstances, if you had the ability to mask your signifier to block scrying.

"That's it exactly."

Kujen took pity on the Kel soldiers waiting to be told what to do and prompted Liyeng. "Follow Technician 24," Liyeng said, and pointed obligingly. "She'll show you where to stash the general." Anien confirmed this with a nod. The Kel and their casket moved off.

"They left something out of the interrogation files Command sent you," Anien said once they were alone. "We've been trying not to let it get out."

"Do tell," Kujen said.

"I don't have video to show you," Anien said, "and if you mention this to anyone, I'll have to deny that I ever said anything, Niraizho. But Jedao didn't start off begging to be shot. He didn't seem to understand what had happened. He—he kept asking what had happened to his soldiers. Asking if they were all right. It was only after he understood what he'd done that he started to beg."

All this time she hadn't stopped playing with the cards.

"You're worried about him," Kujen said. Interesting change from the overwhelming contingent of Kel who wanted Jedao's entrails cut into little writhing pieces and the conspiracy theorists who thought the Lanterners had devised a brainwashing ray. Kujen happened to know that there weren't useful shortcuts when it came to brainwashing.

"Ignore the blame-mongers, Nirai-zho," Anien said. "We promoted Jedao too fast and pushed him too hard, and he cracked." Her mouth twitched. "He was a great suicide hawk. Indistinguishable from the real thing."

She was getting distracted. He had to convince her to do what he wanted. "About the black cradle," Kujen said. "Are you certain? I can't guarantee that I'll be able to repair someone that badly broken."

Anien gave Liyeng a considering look. "How good are you at tactics, Nirai-zho?"

"The real kind, not game theory with perfectly rational actors? Sort of not," Kujen said. Jedao had always been annoyingly nice about it no matter how much Kujen needled him about his math difficulties. "I solve equations, not guns."

"He's good enough for the experiment to be worth attempting," she said flatly. "Who knows? He might become a useful weapon again."

"I only talked to him in passing before Hellspin Fortress, once or twice," Kujen lied. "What was he like before he lost his mind?"

"Other than his inordinate fox-like love for games and his inordinate hawk-like love for guns? Talkative. Brave. Occasionally funny. His soldiers loved him. Or they did, until, well."

She cut the deck, then showed him the top card. The Deuce of Gears. "Stupid magic trick," she said. Kujen refrained from mentioning that he had seen most of Jedao's repertoire. "He showed me how to do a bunch of them a few years ago. Honestly, Nirai-zho, I don't know what to tell you to look for. No one saw it coming. I would have suspected myself a traitor before I suspected him."

Kujen heard what she wasn't saying. "I'll do my best for him, Anien."

He could have gotten rid of her if it looked like she was going to be an obstacle, but this way was easier, and he was looking forward to taking Jedao apart.

KUJEN SHOULD HAVE known that his life would be filled with inconveniences after High General Kel Shiang was appointed his new liaison. High General Anien had died of a rare cancer, leaving him her collection of playing cards. A strange thing to offer someone who technically didn't have hands.

Shiang was a tall, tawny woman with a broad frame. The forcefulness of her movements made him wonder if the facility was going to thunder itself into rubble around her. Kujen's current anchor, a shorter manform named Uwo, found this intimidating. Kujen couldn't blame them, but it was a bit of a distraction.

Uwo had brought Shiang to the lab where Jedao was pinned. The room was drab except for a single wall devoted to a one-per-minute cycle of riotously colorful photographs of flowers. Forsythias, cosmos, moss roses, azaleas, everything. Flowers were an innocuous way of giving Jedao access to color when they switched on the portal that could, for short periods, give him a limited window into the world.

"He's in here, Nirai-zho?" Shiang asked, looking around at the terminals with their graphs and readouts. One of them was still set to a card game.

"Not precisely," Kujen said, "but this is the single point of access we've allowed him. I didn't deem it wise to give him an anchor of his own without Kel Command's approval."

"I'm authorized to make that determination."

"Of course," Kujen murmured. "Do you wish to talk to him?"

Shiang eyed him. "I did read your reports, but is he stable?"

What was Jedao going to do without a body, put nails through her eyes? "As stable as anyone is," Kujen said. "You came all this way, you might as well see for yourself. I should warn you that the time windows are dependent on calendrical mechanics—the equations were in Appendix 5—so you'll have twenty-three minutes this session if we start now."

"Let's do this, then."

Uwo flipped the switch. A chime sounded. A shadow rippled through the room. Nine candle-yellow eyes stared at them through a crack of black-silver. Then the shadow faded, and the eyes with them.

"Jedao?" Shiang said, unmoved by the phenomenon.

"I apologize for being unable to salute, sir," Jedao said, that same easy baritone with its drawl. It sounded as though he stood in the room facing them, except he'd also have to be invisible. "What do you require of me?"

"I'm here to evaluate your recovery," she said. "Nirai-zho tells me you've given no explanation for your behavior at Hellspin Fortress."

"I have none, sir."

"Do you remember what happened?" She was frowning at Uwo, as though Kujen's anchor should have an answer for her.

Jedao hesitated. "I remember it in pieces, sir. The pieces aren't in order. They showed me some of the videos, including—" His voice wavered. "Including when I shot Colonel Gized. I don't—I don't understand why I would want to do that. I can't believe she's gone."

"Can the Rahal get anything out of him now?" Shiang asked Kujen.

"Unfortunately, that's impossible," Kujen said. It had, in fact, been one of the design parameters for the black cradle. Not that Shiang was ever going to learn that from him. "Neither of us sleeps. A wolf scrying has no access."

Shiang swore under her breath, then said, "What do you think I hope to accomplish here, Jedao?"

"I imagine you're here to render judgment, sir. I'm not sure why I'm being retained as a revenant, however. There must have been a court-martial, but I can't remember any of it. I realize I killed a great many, including my own people. I am prepared for your sentence."

"We kept you alive"—Shiang's nostrils flared—"because Kel Command needs tacticians of your caliber, because you may yet 'serve' in an experimental capacity, and because the heptarchate continues to face many threats."

Uwo coughed. "About that." This would have gone better if Shiang had read the report as she had claimed.

Shiang glared at Uwo. "You have something to say, Nirai-zho?"

Kujen decided that he needed to go back to picking more physically intimidating anchors. This one was excellent in all other regards. They had marvelous conversations about homological conjectures over breakfast, but even bleed-through hadn't overcome Uwo's naturally retiring demeanor.

"Sir," Jedao said, "I—I would recommend against using me for that purpose. I have difficulty with tactical simulations now. I don't have any reason to believe that things would be any better in the field."

"That must be humbling for you to admit, given your former stature," Shiang said.

Jedao sounded puzzled. "I wish to serve, sir, but it's important that you have an accurate assessment of my capabilities."

"And if I decided that the Kel would best be served by your permanent death?"

"Then I will die, sir."

"Do you want to die, Jedao?"

"I wish to serve, sir," he said again. "It's not for me to question your orders."

"Are you happy here?"

"I am waiting to serve, sir. That's all that matters."

Shiang flipped the switch herself, banishing Jedao. Kujen hated it when strangers touched his equipment. Uwo would have said something, but Kujen held them back. He didn't want to pick a fight over this when there were more important matters at hand.

Shiang scowled. "He's respectful, obedient, self-effacing, and sounds nothing like the cocksure bastard who bet a fortune that he could get his army through the Battle of Spiral Deluge with under ten percent casualties, and who came in under seven," she said. "Congratulations, Nirai-zho, you've turned him into a sheep. There's nothing of the general left."

Kujen would have smiled. He had botched the job on purpose. "You wanted a perfect wind-up soldier," he said. "I gave you one. I can't make him any better than this. He's stable and he'll serve you no matter how poorly you treat him."

"And your report admitted that his tactical ability tests under the thirty-seventh percentile on all four of the simulators we provided. A squirrel with a bowl of marbles could do better. When they say he's never been defeated, do you appreciate what that means? We didn't send him off to a bunch of easy battles on a lark. Most of his assignments should have killed him. A Shuos officer was always going to be more expendable than one of our own. It just so happened that his choice was to be brilliant or not to die. He figured out how not to die. Kel Command expected him to be annihilated at Candle Arc, outnumbered eight to one, and he didn't just win, he smashed the enemy. This experiment is no good if he isn't *usable*."

"It was a necessary compromise," Kujen said. This was the part he had to sell. "People aren't lumps of clay. You have to work with what's already there. With Jedao, you can either have perfect obedience or you can have the little box in his head that magically tells him what his opponent is going to do so he can tie them in knots, but you can't have both at the same time. Please don't ask me how to put the little box back in while he's like this. I can't. You'd need a psych surgeon who was also a tactician." That part was even true. "If you know where to find someone like that, send them my way. I'd love to talk shop. What exactly is it that you expect of me, High General?"

Kujen had misgivings about Shiang's smile. He used to have one like it, back when he was alive.

"He seemed at peace," Shiang said. "I had a niece who served under him at Hellspin, did you know that? I'll make this easy for you. If you can't make him better, make him worse. Break him. Cripple him. He's a fucking traitor, Nirai-zho. He doesn't deserve to have his life handed back to him, even like this. He needs to suffer."

Kujen laughed incredulously. "My peach"—the Kel hated condescending endearments as much as anyone else—"you realize your operational parameters contradict themselves? Do you want a torture chew-toy, or a useful commander?"

"You're such a genius, Nirai-zho," Shiang retorted. "All the Nirai tell us so—but I guess you program them that way. Why don't you prove it to the rest of us? Find a way. Make Jedao a tactician again. Make him suffer as he serves the Kel."

"Feel lucky that I despise you, High General," Kujen said, "and that I can't wait to get you off my facility. Anything I can do to Jedao, I can do to you. Face it, Jedao's a lot more complex than you are."

"You say that like it's a good thing," Shiang said. "Try anything and some fangmoths will blow your precious equipment into radioactive little pieces. You know us Kel, we're great at breaking shit. Anyway, I believe I've made Kel Command's requirements clear, Nirai-zho, or do I need to repeat myself?"

"No, you're perfectly clear," Kujen said. He had gotten what he wanted.

"NIRAI-ZHO," JEDAO said after the eighth round of jeng-zai, "what's troubling you?"

It took a ridiculous set of accommodations to enable Jedao to play the game without an anchor, but Kujen remembered how much Jedao liked it. Unsurprisingly, Jedao's little box affected his skill at gambling. Right now he was terrible at it. Kujen was good at jeng-zai himself, but he shouldn't have been winning so easily. Between moves, his anchor was doing a logic puzzle, since revenants could talk to each other directly.

"How do you feel, Jedao?" Kujen asked.

A bemused pause. "Correct me if I'm mistaken, Nirai-zho, but aren't you sitting on top of a bunch of instruments that tell you more about what I feel than I know myself? I'd remind you what they're called, but I can't pronounce the names."

"Don't give me that," Kujen said. "I know how good your memory is, too." Except the pieces he had locked down as a security measure.

It wouldn't do for Jedao to let something slip to the Kel while he was still vulnerable. "You know what every last one is called."

"Still flunk the math," Jedao said cheerfully.

That was true. While Jedao had excellent geometric and spatial intuition, he had never developed better than scrape-by competency at the algebraic underpinnings of calendrical mechanics. Kujen had considered fixing the dyscalculia, but it was more convenient not to.

Kujen inspected the primary display. He had certain instruments that the Rahal didn't know about. In his readings, the central signifier, Ninefox Crowned with Eyes, never changed. It suggested that Jedao was not just more intact than he was letting on, but that he was manipulating the entire situation. Kujen hadn't yet caught him at it, though.

The weighted network of secondary signifiers had taken more work. Kujen had done a lot of jiggering to replace the problematic Immolation Fox in the motivational vertices with the more tractable Rose Chalice, that-which-receives. "Jedao," Kujen said, "I have to dismantle you. It will hurt."

Kujen knew how to give High General Shiang half of what she wanted. To make Jedao sane and functional, to give him back the ability he had had in life. Kujen would have to build around the latter because he didn't understand it well enough to mess with it, but it could be done. He could transmute that all-consuming guilt into a desire to make amends. The hard part would be giving Jedao some sense of proportion. The man had a judgmental streak a planet wide.

Of course, that was only half of what Shiang had demanded. If Kujen wanted the Kel to think he was in bed with them, he was also going to have to pretend to be hostage to their desires.

"Nirai-zho," Jedao said, "I was made to serve. If this is the service I am to give, then it doesn't matter how much it hurts."

The sad side-effect of making Jedao like this was that he was no longer an entertaining conversationalist. Thank goodness it was temporary. "I wish you'd shut up about service," Kujen said.

Slight pause. "What would you rather talk about?"

"Aren't you even going to ask me why I have to take you apart?"

"It doesn't matter, Nirai-zho, unless you'd like to tell me. I expect you have a good reason for it."

If Kujen wasn't mistaken, Jedao was trying to comfort *him*.

"There's one thing I can do for you," Kujen said, because it was easier to work with a calm subject and after a certain point Jedao wouldn't realize he'd been deceived. "I'm not saying you're much more than a doll as it stands, even if you have no idea what I'm talking about, but you're not out of your mind with the desire to commit suicide, either. I can take away your memory of this time. You'll be broken but you won't remember once having been patched up. It might hurt less that way."

"If it makes you happy, Nirai-zho—"

Jedao used to understand that this was a very risky line of thought. "I'm asking what you would prefer."

"I want to remember," Jedao said, his voice suddenly steady.

So Jedao hadn't entirely lost his understanding of pain or pride or ugly bargains after all. Good to know. "Fine," Kujen said. "We'll begin now."

He flipped the switch, leaving Jedao trapped in the black cradle's sensory deprivation.

Over the next week, Kujen modified the setup so he could hear Jedao without Jedao hearing him. Jedao turned out to be good about not talking to himself, unlike Esfarel. If it hadn't been for the readings, Kujen would have wondered if Jedao had died in there.

He started dismantling the work he'd done to stabilize Jedao so he could reinstall the death wish.

After seven months and three days in utter isolation, Jedao broke his silence. "Nirai-zho? Are you there? Please—" His voice was brittle.

Kujen didn't answer. Instead, he started the finicky work of suppressing more of Jedao's memories now that Jedao had cracked. If Kujen was going to spend eternity with someone, he might as well guarantee that that someone would be pleasant company. Esfarel had gone mad in the black cradle, but Kujen had figured out better techniques since then. Jedao was more resilient to begin with if he'd lasted this long.

Sixteen days after Jedao spoke, Kujen noticed the thrashing. The instruments didn't pick up on it, but as a revenant himself he could feel it. Esfarel had done that when he was newly undead and trying to figure out how to kill himself.

Eighty-three days after that, just as Kujen thought he'd be able to move on to the next phase, Jedao spoke again, very quietly. "Kujen, please. I miss you. It's so dark. Are you—are you there?"

That wasn't fear.

It was loneliness.

Kujen happened to know that even monsters seek companionship. Or an audience, anyway. "Shut up," he said, suddenly irritated. The only reason they were in this situation to begin with was Jedao's ridiculous grand strategy. "Shut up, shut up, shut up."

Jedao still couldn't hear him. Hear anything, really.

Kujen returned to work.


KUJEN CONTEMPLATED MAHAR. He'd taken a brilliant young student and ruined him utterly, done him a favor no one else could have done, promised him luxury and power and his brother's life in exchange for the use of his body. The anchor lived a restrained lifestyle, given that, but that was his affair.

Kujen had laid out the terms clearly. It worked best when he was up-front; he had figured that out early on. In a just universe, he should be a lonely pile of cinders beneath some rock, rather than hanging around to parasitize his own people, but he had never cared for justice anyhow.

A long time ago, one of his mentors had told him of the good he could do with his astonishing versatility in the technical fields. Restorative psych surgery on refugees and veterans. Better mothdrives. The occasional paper on algebraic topology. He could have done any of it, had eventually done all of it, except none of it changed the fact that he would die someday.

As it turned out, you could fix the calendar to cheat death. Even the Rahal couldn't fix calendars the way Kujen could. Granted, this didn't come without its cost. The calendar had made remembrances even more pervasive than they had been during Kujen's childhood.

Immortality didn't turn you into a monster. It merely showed you what kind of monster you already were. He could have warned his fellow hexarchs, but it was going to be more fun to watch them discover it for themselves.

# CHAPTER TWENTY-ONE

KHIRUEV RESISTED THE urge to stare at the door to the command center. Jedao's continued absence during an engagement was a problem, but Khiruev freezing up would be a worse one. Besides, Jedao's instructions to Khiruev, while requiring a great deal of faith, were unambiguous.

Hafn Swarm One (as the tactical display now tagged it) was still headed for them from Cobweb. They would be curving toward Minang Tower on the way. Hafn Swarm Two was still in disarray after the bombs that had taken out part of their lower left flank (relative to the swarm's orientation and axis of motion), but she couldn't count on that state of affairs to last.

For its part, Minang had the standard defenses for a wolf tower. The good news was that they were solidly in hexarchate territory, with friendly terrain. The irritating Hafn ability to use their native exotics in the hexarchate did not deny Minang the use of high calendar defenses. The bad news was that those defenses had never been meant for extended activation. No one had expected an invader to penetrate so deeply into hexarchate space, even in a border march.

"Shall we engage, General?" Janaia said.

"All units banner the Deuce of Gears," Khiruev said, keeping her voice unemotional. "Activate the primary pivot and close, but carefully." She specified the parameters. Like most shield formations, Knives Are Our Walls offered only short-lived protection, but it beat letting the Hafn pummel them at will. "Scan, what is going on out there?"

"Estimated thirty Hafn moths dead or disabled out of eighty-two," Scan said. "I'm distinguishing four types of mothdrives, two of them unfamiliar." The familiar ones belonged to the Lilacs and the Magnolias. "Guessing they're support vessels of some type, given their placement well back of the combat moths."

Weapons, usually reticent, spoke up abruptly. "Sir, more are coming. Look at the way they're regrouping to clear the area."

Khiruev concurred. Hafn Swarm Two wasn't gathering into the familiar dish-and-funnel configuration. Rather, its warmoths were forming a half-shell around a cluster of slower-moving moths.

The *Hierarchy of Feasts* reached the formation's pivot, and the formation's shield effect activated. It didn't show in human-normal visuals, which had made Khiruev anxious when she was younger, but the scan overlay showed that nothing was wrong. The Hafn could apparently detect the shield as well. After an initial barrage of missiles, like a stutter of wayward stars, they held their fire.

"Sir!" Scan cried. "Here they come."

More Hafn juddered into existence near Hafn Swarm Two. One group had the misfortune to arrive practically on top of a moth that had been damaged earlier. It went out in a horrible sudden sizzle, torching two other moths near it.

There were 105 warmoths in the Kel swarm. Over 150 Hafn had joined the battle, and that wasn't even counting the 71 from Hafn Swarm One that were dashing back toward them and which would be able to hit them with known exotics in twenty-four minutes at current accelerations.

The command center was everywhere awash with light, red and gold, gold and red. Sometimes Khiruev thought that the Kel had an institutionalized horror of dying in the dark, with not even a candle for your pyre.

*Deal with it,* Jedao had said. This meant, if you regarded the whole situation as a particularly lethal training exercise, that he believed Khiruev had both the knowledge and resources necessary to prevail. Ordinarily Khiruev didn't believe in applying this kind of meta-analysis to real life, but Jedao had a known tendency to think of everything in terms of games.

Khiruev had no idea what Jedao was so busy with. However, she did know what to do about the Hafn. Swarm One had done their damnedest to lead the Kel away from Swarm Two's arrival point, and she didn't think it was a feint. They had only turned back when it became clear the Kel weren't falling for it. Swarm Two couldn't just be reinforcements. It contained something vital to the Hafn. Khiruev had no intention of obliging them.

They had only another six minutes of shield protection left. Khiruev had set up new waypoints and handed them over to Janaia and Navigation. "Communications," she said, "get me Commander Gherion." Tactical Group Two.

Gherion responded immediately. "Sir," he said, unable to hide his worry.

*I don't know what the fox is up to, either,* Khiruev thought. There was no point offering an explanation she didn't have; it wasn't her place. "Commander," she said, "I'm detaching Tactical Two. I've tagged the moths Hafn Swarm Two appears to be guarding. Your job is to put pressure on them, including shooting them to cinders if you can get through. I believe the tagged units are auxiliaries, but your approach will undoubtedly bring you under heavy fire. Take whatever measures you deem necessary and don't concern yourself with the rest of our swarm until I recall you."

Gherion saluted. "Naturally, sir."

"Go to it," Khiruev said, coldly aware that if there were any ugly surprises out there, Tactical Two would run into them first. But someone always had to go in first.

"Sir," Weapons said, "shields going down in three minutes." Indeed, the shields' decay was manifesting as a lace of silver-blue light, like fractures in a hollow ellipsoid containing the swarm.

The Hafn had not been idle. Scan was reporting a storm of incoming kinetics, which blistered the shields at the points of impact. Slugs of dead metal hammered themselves into hot coins, ricocheted. Hafn Swarm Two's configuration had, if anything, flattened. Khiruev wasn't sure what that meant, nor did Doctrine have anything for her.

Khiruev said, "All tactical groups"—Gherion would know this excluded him—"reform into Mountains Never Whisper. Time the modulation to allow Tactical Two to pass through."

Tactical Two was breaking formation. The rest of the Kel moths were maneuvering to reposition themselves in compensation. Judging from the pyramidal leading element, Khiruev guessed that Gherion was going to use Winter's Eyes to punch his way into the enemy.

"Our turn," Khiruev said.

"Over or under, sir?" Janaia asked.

A trap either way, but she couldn't go in head-on. She'd run the calculations. That Hafn rupture attack would spit them if they did it that way.

"Under," Khiruev said. More waypoints. Janaia suggested an adjustment. She accepted it.

Hafn Swarm Two reacted with dismaying alacrity when they saw the cindermoth angling itself down in relation to the plane of their own movement. The Hafn moths performed a beautiful maneuver, splitting diagonally to either side in two lattices, each headed by a projecting spike. If you drew rays from the two spikes, they would intersect at a point just ahead of the *Hierarchy of Feasts*.

"Cancel!" Khiruev said. "Wheel the swarm—" She didn't have time to work out exact coordinates. Instead, she traced out the curve on tactical. Janaia translated this into the necessary evasive maneuver. The moth commanders' acknowledgment lights flickered on the panel. "Doctrine," she added, "hurry up and stab some equations until they tell us what that thing does."

Doctrine had a harried look. "Yes, sir," she said without looking up from her terminal.

Tactical Two had peeled away safely. Khiruev wished them well, but she had more immediate concerns.

Hafn Swarm One was practically breathing down Minang Tower's neck. Scan confirmed that the tower had ignited its shields. The issue was not the shields' fuel source but the fact that they would decay rapidly under any sustained barrage. A small note on one of Khiruev's subdisplays informed her that Minang Tower was continuing to forward its scan observations, not that it had a whole lot to add about the current situation. The tower's magistrate had not called for assistance, but this was consistent with her earlier behavior. Khiruev appreciated that she wasn't making a distraction of herself in the middle of a battle. Khiruev didn't think Minang was in serious danger anyway. Hafn One was going to swipe at them in passing, a last attempt to draw the Kel away from Hafn Two, then give it up and move in for real.

The Kel were partway through the wheel when Khiruev had the sudden rattling intuition that she'd done exactly as the Hafn general desired. She was just as convinced that she didn't want to stay where the spikes were pointed. That was the proper way to pin an opponent anyway, with equally terrible options.

Later, when she reviewed the combat logs, she figured out that she hadn't realized that the trap had snapped shut until nine seconds afterward.

"Formation break," Scan said sharply, while Communications reported the same alert from the commanders of Tactical Three and Tactical Five.

Khiruev knew that from the sudden disintegration of the formation's protection. Doctrine was saying something after the fact. Moot point.

"Following units are not responding to orders—" Communications, with the list. Khiruev checked it for numbers. Fourteen bannermoths were now lit up on the tactical display, marked with the crashhawk glyph. She'd never seen so many of them at once, even in a training exercise.

It would have been one thing if the Hafn attack had knocked those moths out and the interface had glitched the representation. But those moths had rolled and were now flying directly toward the *Hierarchy of Feasts*. Moreover, the crashhawks had organized themselves into what resembled a Hafn configuration, not a Kel formation.

"All moths," Khiruev said, forwarding the list Communications had handed her. "The following units are to be regarded as hostiles. Tactical Five, prioritize their destruction." They were now down to a skeleton formation. Any more losses and she'd have to step down to a formation with a smaller number of keys. "Other units assist as opportunity permits."

Tactical Five interposed itself between the crashhawks and the command moth, and opened fire.

Considering how bad it was to have fourteen *Kel* commanders go rogue on you (irony aside), Khiruev felt dreadfully calm. It wasn't fair. She was dying anyway. It was one thing for her to be unperturbed, but she should at least have some reaction on the swarm's behalf.

Khiruev's attention was caught by Janaia's hands clenching and unclenching, by the rigid way she held her head. Khiruev would not have expected it of her. Usually Janaia was hard to rattle. "Commander," Khiruev said quietly, and when she didn't respond, "*Commander*."

Janaia wouldn't meet Khiruev's eyes. "What if they can do it again, sir?" The edge of panic in her voice was unmistakable.

Khiruev barely escaped hissing an oath through her teeth. Everyone was thinking it, and the question of how to avoid another such hit was important, but that was no reason to speak your fear out loud. Janaia should know better. Even a common soldier should know better. Of all the fucking times for the cindermoth's commander to have a fucking breakdown.

"Pull yourself together, Commander," Khiruev said. If Janaia could be calmed quickly—

"Sir," she said, her voice rising in pitch, "they're coming after us again, none of us are *safe*—"

No luck. Khiruev's fault for misgauging her: always proper, always the perfect Kel, of course she'd be the most vulnerable to a breakdown. "Commander Janaia," Khiruev said, willing Janaia to meet her eyes even though she needed to be watching the scan and tactical readouts, "you are relieved of duty. Colonel Muris, you have command for the duration."

For a suspended second, Khiruev was afraid that Janaia would freeze and that she'd have to have someone escort her out of the command center. Then Janaia rose, saluted, and walked out, her face white.

Khiruev couldn't expend more attention on her, although she would have to reevaluate her fitness as an officer if they survived this. They had served together a long time. She had not realized how much she had come to rely on Janaia. While Muris took Janaia's place, Khiruev assessed Tactical Two's position.

"Sir," Scan said, interrupting her attempt to figure out just what Gherion was hoping to accomplish with Black Lens, "you should review the crashhawks' formants. Look at the comparisons—"

Khiruev didn't have to be prompted twice. She had learned to read scan under one of Kel Academy's most notoriously exacting (not to say boring) instructors, and she had a reasonable knowledge of common shapes a Kel military mothdrive formant might take. The crashhawks' formants had changed. They looked eerily like Hafn drives on scan.

"Does Tactical Five have visuals?" she asked curtly.

Tactical Five obliged. A collation of videos arrived half a minute later. The group leader's scan officer had tagged the most telling items, captured by a bannermoth that had sent out drones for a closer look.

One video frame was especially clear. The bannermoth *Tempest Countdown* should have been black painted with gold, from its name along the spine to the fire-and-bird motifs of the Kel. Instead, great swathes of the visible wing surfaces had gone green with a luster as of poisoned pearls. More worryingly, translucent veins had grown over the green area. The video showed them pulsing. Khiruev remembered the boy sewn up with birds and flowers, the endless procession of red spiders crawling through the crystalline veins that connected him to his casket. She couldn't tell if red anything crawled through the infected moth's veins. At least she hadn't wasted time on Override Aerie Primary trying to slave the rogues' mothgrids to that of the *Hierarchy of Feasts*. She had a fair idea it wouldn't have worked.

Khiruev ordered the swarm into a formation from Lexicon Secondary. The modulation was as rough as she'd thought it would be, but she kept her face impassive. The Kel ordinarily tried to avoid having hostile units materialize *inside* a formation.

Updates blinked at her, demanding her attention. What interested her most was a report from Tactical Four's Commander Gehmet and the accompanying list of units destroyed. *Dragonfly Thunder. Three Gears Spinning. Song of Blackened Stones. Stag's Blood.*

She tapped out more orders, managing swarm geometry with more grid assistance than usual. Ordinarily Khiruev relied on Janaia to fill in the blanks, but she didn't work with Muris like this often. She wanted to leave some margin for error.

"Sir, you'll want to see this," Doctrine said into one of the rare lulls. The loudness of her voice was like a hammer. "We think we've isolated the Hafn configuration."

Equations, animated diagrams. The Hafn didn't factor their configurations the way the Kel did their formations. But Khiruev could now see the traitor's lance (as Doctrine had labeled it) where it had been hidden in the spike. She had to assume they'd do it again if they could.

Hafn Swarm One was now in range of the Kel's longest-range weapons. As Khiruev had predicted, they had only struck at Minang Tower in passing. The Kel veered off to avoid being pinned between the two enemy swarms. Tactical Five was having a certain degree of success against the crashhawks and had taken out six of fourteen. Khiruev caught herself wondering what had become of the crew on those moths and made herself stop. They could figure that out after the battle.

Tactical Two under Commander Gherion had lost two moths, *Pillar of Breaking Skulls* and *Storm Chasm*. Khiruev frowned. Was Gherion doing what she thought? She lost precious seconds backtracking through the combat reports. There it was. Sacrifices, not losses.

She had authorized Gherion to do what he thought necessary. The formation Gherion was using, Kiora's Stab, was both flexible and volatile. Gherion had already used the hellstabs it generated to destroy five Hafn moths, but in the process he was burning up his bannermoths. There was some chance the whole formation would destabilize and they'd all evaporate partway through.

Either the Hafn recognized Kiora's Stab or had developed rapid respect for it. They were working very hard to keep Tactical Two from the targets Khiruev had tagged for Gherion. Encouragingly, they hadn't—yet—used the traitor's lance on Tactical Two.

Khiruev had just issued orders for the swarm to change front as it pirouetted to meet Hafn Swarm One when the command center fell silent. She glanced over and saw Jedao standing in front of the closing entrance. Jedao wasn't smiling. No one was.

Khiruev rose and saluted, not too fast. "Sir," she said, more coldly than she'd intended, although not half as much as she felt. "Your orders."

*I am not angry,* she thought. *I am not angry.* If she repeated it enough times in her head it might even become true.

"You've done well, General," Jedao said. He returned the salute. Only then did Khiruev notice that his eyes were bloodshot. Jedao took his seat. "You don't have to worry about more moths going rogue," he added without explaining how he knew this. "They were almost certainly saving that attack for a different target, but you made them panic and they blew it early."

Commander Muris had been speaking quietly with Communications about a gap: three bannermoths in Tactical Six had drifted out of alignment while evading missiles exploiting a shield breach. Muris broke off and looked at Jedao. Jedao raised an eyebrow at Khiruev, who said in an undertone, "Commander Janaia is indisposed, sir." Jedao indicated to Muris that he should carry on.

"Commander Gherion has forced Hafn Swarm Two to take the defensive," Khiruev said, "but Tactical Two will probably burn up before they reach their assigned targets. Without a counter to the disruption attack, we are unable to follow up without risking significant losses—and those losses are unlikely to bring us much chance of success."

"There's another way," Jedao said. "That's not a criticism. You had no way of knowing. Communications, get me the moth commanders, will you?" Communications signaled that the line was open. "Jedao to all units. I can tell you exactly what Hafn Swarm Two is up to. You saw them jump in. They're frantic to jump those auxiliaries back out before we obliterate them. What they're protecting is very bad news for the hexarchate. It will allow them to establish a base of operations within our borders.

"The Hafn jump requires them to be in a certain configuration. It's the trigger, if you will. The jump then takes a certain amount of time to take effect. They're feinting their way around it right now. But look at this—"

A paper showed up on one of Khiruev's displays. It had been forwarded to Doctrine as well. The diagram was a marvel of clarity, but the accompanying equations might as well have been written in seafoam. Khiruev was barely able to guess at Hafn integer keys by correlating them with what she remembered from the briefing Kel Command had given her a lifetime ago. She met Jedao's eyes, wondering where the hell he had picked up a team of pet Nirai. But now was not the time to ask.

Jedao wasn't looking at her anyway. He continued addressing the swarm. "It is possible, with good timing, to spike the jump. I require sixteen bannermoths for the operation, as the scoutmoths' drives are insufficiently powerful. When I say 'spike,' I mean that the jump translates the Hafn moths into a signal, which then travels through a space only loosely connected to ours."

The scan anomalies. Khiruev remembered.

"It is possible to corrupt the signal so that it cannot be reconstituted. We have a good idea of the limits of Hafn error correction." Almost casually, Jedao flicked his terminal. The relevant section of the paper highlighted itself.

"I require sixteen bannermoths"—Jedao's voice flexed—"but I will not order you to take on the task unless it becomes unavoidable. I am asking for volunteers." He did smile then, but his eyes were bleak. "Because if this works, nobody ever comes back out. Not the sixteen moths, not the Hafn either. You have twelve minutes to decide and to evacuate as many nonessential personnel as possible. After that, I will ask General Khiruev to pick by lottery."

Khiruev resorted to messaging Jedao privately, reflecting that if this were a training simulation, she'd be docked an entire mark. *We are Kel, sir,* she said. *Use us as Kel.*

Jedao messaged back as though they were two cadets at the back of a classroom. *You are people first. You deserve a chance to choose.*

Khiruev didn't know how any army could run on that principle, or how, for that matter, the hexarchate's oldest soldier had come up with such an incomprehensible idea.

Twenty-three seconds elapsed. Muris was doing an extraordinarily efficient job of handling swarm maneuvers. The Hafn swarms had joined up with each other. Two more of Gherion's moths were burning up.

"You have never had any reason to trust me," Jedao went on as though he had never paused. "You don't trust me now. That's as it should be. But the one promise I can make you is that I know how to win battles. It's all I can do for the hexarchate now. And this is a battle that has to be fought. Because the Hafn aren't just here to claim territory. They're here to destroy worlds; they're here to steal our service. We're in position to keep them from the things they want. Choose however you will, but choose quickly."

Khiruev had already selected sixteen bannermoths by lottery.

Communications had two calls for Jedao. Then five. Eleven by the time the twelve minutes was up.

Khiruev struck off the last eleven from her list and passed the rest over to Jedao.

Jedao had already prepared move orders. In fact, Khiruev didn't recognize the formation he called for, and Khiruev was certain it wasn't because her memory was failing her. She knew better than to ask. Jedao caught her expression and took pity. The paper Jedao passed over contained yet more advanced mathematics.

*I don't have time to check the derivations,* Khiruev thought, irritated at herself. She confirmed that Doctrine had a copy as well and asked her for a quick check if one was possible.

The Hafn wavered when they spotted the nonstandard formation. Whatever they were in the middle of doing, however, they were resolved to finish it. Light like ice and iron sprang up in a great crisscross web around the auxiliaries. A detachment headed Tactical Two off.

Gherion had been listening to Jedao's address. When the sixteen designated bannermoths sprinted for the web, Tactical Two flared up in a pillar that sliced through part of it to facilitate their passage. This had the unexpected effect of *shifting* the web laterally just as the sixteen moths plunged in, and just as the web brightened.

"It's the damnedest thing, sir," Scan said after stabbing the displays. "I've got the web on visual and all those moths, frozen like statues, but all the formants are gone. Like they're ghosts."

"Opposite of what you get with a ghost," Jedao said, very softly. "But yes."

Nothing remained of Tactical Two except a scattering of red-bronze light, rapidly diminishing.

"Hafn Swarm Two is abandoning Swarm One," Khiruev said, watching the two separate from each other. Curious: Swarm One's movements had become conservative, sluggish. Two was fleeing outright.

"Yes, I see it," Jedao said. "Communications, get me Commander Daharit. I'm detaching Tactical Six to deal with Swarm One. I don't think they're going to give you any trouble. See if you can capture anything intact for analysis. Everyone else, condense to Tide of Dragons. We're going to make sure Swarm Two doesn't get away."

As it turned out, Swarm Two didn't prove to be any trouble, either. It wasn't until the main swarm joined up with Tactical Six that Khiruev had a chance to talk to Jedao. She didn't request a meeting; she didn't have to. Jedao had summoned her to his quarters. A jeng-zai deck rested on the table.

"You have a whole list of things to say," Jedao said. "Go ahead and say them."

"The swarm deserved your full attention during the engagement, sir," Khiruev said.

"The swarm had my full attention," Jedao said. "I was in the middle of a project with implications for the campaign entire." He sat down and shoved some cards aside with his toe. Two of them fluttered to the floor. Then he put his feet up on the table.

"You put the swarm at risk."

"Are you saying you're not capable?"

"I'm saying you're the better general."

Jedao's eyelids lowered fractionally. Khiruev couldn't tell whether he was angry or not. "This isn't your fault," Jedao said, "but you're not even near the field of battle."

Khiruev refrained from clenching her hands. "I don't expect you to tell me everything, but my usefulness to you is becoming severely limited." When Jedao continued to regard her coolly, Khiruev added, "I don't know what you intend to do about Commander Janaia."

"I reviewed the transcript," Jedao said. "I agree with your assessment. She broke down precisely because she's such a good Kel. It didn't happen to you because, sorry, you're not quite so rigidly Kel yourself."

"I know," Khiruev said. Janaia believed strongly in the importance of loyalty and formation instinct. Her horror at the thought of becoming a crashhawk had been palpable. "But she's still brittle, and that's a problem."

Jedao tapped his knee. "I had better talk to her when we get a bit more breathing space, but we're going to have to retain Muris as commander for the time being. I'll have Janaia report to Medical for assessment and counseling."

Khiruev didn't mention that Jedao could have dealt with Janaia directly if he'd only been in the command center at the time. "Who provided the mathematics?" she said. "The formations and the analysis of the Hafn translation method?"

"I was in here," Jedao said, "because I would prefer not to reveal that to you."

Khiruev weighed the merits of pressing for an answer and decided it wouldn't do any good. "You asked for volunteers," she said.

"Yes, we were both there for that part."

"You originally took control of the swarm by coercion," Khiruev said. "We were both there for that part, too. Why does it matter now that we should choose our service?"

"Would it be such an evil thing to learn, General?" Jedao asked.

Khiruev looked at the cards on the floor, then at Jedao's unruffled face. "If you didn't want us to be Kel, sir, why—?"

"You're already putting your trust in the least trustworthy general in Kel history," Jedao said. "It won't kill you to follow me a little longer to see where this is all going."

"I am yours, sir," Khiruev said, and wondered why Jedao's eyes turned sad.

# CHAPTER TWENTY-TWO

Brezan was feeding the birds with Tseya, at her insistence, while *Beneath the Orchid* approached the Kel swarm. Tseya kept referring to it as the Deuce of Gears swarm. This was correct, but Brezan felt that sometimes reality needed a kick in the teeth, even if it was only in your head, and called it the Swanknot swarm to himself. They were no longer receiving active updates from Andan sources, as that might reveal their presence. Their own scan, however, told them that Jedao and the Hafn were dancing around each other. Brezan and Tseya wanted to stay close, but not too close, in case something combusted.

One of the three birds made an alarming rattling sound and tilted its head almost all the way sideways to peer at Brezan when he failed to dispense another treat. Brezan was of the opinion that necks, no matter how long and slender and graceful, shouldn't be allowed to corkscrew like that. "Seriously, we should be monitoring the situation ourselves," he said to Tseya. He tried not to think about how much the bird's beak resembled a spear.

Tseya was dangling her bare feet in a tiny creek, apparently unconcerned that her toes might get nibbled off. Today she wore her hair in braids, which tumbled down over her crocheted silk shawl. "They made me read up on a few Kel battles when I was in academy," Tseya said placidly. "Some of them go on longer than our most interminable dinner parties. The two swarms haven't even bannered at each other yet. I'd say there's no sense getting wound up, except as far as I can tell, you're always wound up."

Brezan glowered at her. The bird was looking sadly at him instead of picking on the more accommodating target, having clearly been trained to harass innocent Kel. He fished another treat out from the container and held it out gingerly. With great delicacy, the bird plucked the morsel from his grasp and swallowed it.

"I think you're more scared of a tame crane than you are of Jedao," Tseya added. "Isn't that backwards?"

Brezan glanced at her sidelong but saw only honest inquiry in her expression. "Better the enemy you know?" he said. "Although I hadn't realized just how much Kel Academy had left out about him."

During their journey, Tseya had assiduously studied their target. They had viewed a number of the records together. At Kel Academy, Brezan had become familiar with the notorious bits, such as Hellspin Fortress and Heptarch Shuos Khiaz signing Jedao over to Kel Command, repudiating him utterly. One video had even shown him being awarded some medal, very discomfiting. That had happened nearly a decade before the massacre.

As Brezan had learned, these records accounted for a fraction of the available material. For instance, Tseya had dug up a clip of some state dinner where they seated Jedao next to a Liozh poet who took a dim view of his sister's verses. Brezan had had no idea that Jedao ever had a sister, let alone one who was a poet. Irrelevantly, he wondered if she had ever annoyed Jedao as much as Miuzan annoyed him. Tseya had also found a note Jedao had written to one of his lovers, a magistrate. The letter was brief and formal, and concerned a keycard. Brezan would have considered the phrasing terribly cold, except Tseya had explained to him that this was what protocol expected back then. Even so, Brezan hated thinking of Jedao as a living man rather than an overpowered game piece. It was too disturbing thinking that someone would knowingly do the things Jedao had done.

Tseya was looking contemplative. "There's a lot on the Immolation Fox," she said, "and only so much of it was reasonably expected to be relevant to a Kel officer, I imagine. It's only a pity that the most useful piece is missing."

YOON HA LEE

The question of what had caused Jedao's madness. "I doubt he was ever crazy," Brezan said, remembering Jedao standing there in the body he had stolen, perfectly relaxed.

"Well," Tseya said, "I wish I could tell you that I hope to figure it out, but if they couldn't get anything out of him back then, my chances aren't better. Damnable Shuos."

Brezan fed the second bird a treat. It bobbed its head almost as though in thanks. "Don't these pets of yours ever fatten up?" he demanded. They showed no signs of diminished appetite.

Tseya laughed helplessly. "You're hopeless. Since my plan to relax you is a dismal failure, why don't we try something else? We can sit in the command center and depress ourselves with what we're up against by reviewing some of Jedao's old duels."

"Sure, rub it in," Brezan said. He'd told her at some point that Miuzan always thrashed him at the sport. On the bright side, being in the command center beat being pestered by unnaturally ribbony birds. "Well, since you offered, sure."

Tseya flung a last treat toward two artistically entwined potted trees. The birds strode after it. "Come on," she said.

Brezan found it alarming that Tseya went around everywhere in her bare feet. It was as though, having made the obligatory show of being an Andan, she no longer felt she had to keep up appearances. When he mentioned this, she only smiled and said, "The point of protocol is to make an impression, one way or another. Maybe I'm lulling you into a false sense of security?"

Her words reminded Brezan that when most people worried about being stabbed in the back, tangled up in an intrigue, or otherwise outmaneuvered, they didn't just worry about the Shuos. If they had any sense, they also kept an eye on the Andan. "I'm the least useful Kel general in history if you're looking for a pawn on the cheap," Brezan said. "And if you're bored, well, you're already bedding me."

Tseya snorted, but didn't respond to the jab.

They entered the command center with its aquarium. The terminals were bright with status reports. As she sat, Tseya said carelessly, "I'm sure you could kill me pretty easily if you had to."

Brezan stiffened. "Don't," he said. "That's not funny."

Tseya opened her mouth, saw his face, closed her mouth. "What's your family like, Brezan?" she said out of nowhere.

"My what?" He glanced over a status report because it was something he understood and right now he needed that. Unluckily for him, the reports revealed nothing more untoward than swarms maneuvering. The Swanknot swarm seemed disinclined to chase the Hafn, but who knew what baroque plan Jedao was executing. If it meant less chasing, he was all for it.

"Your family." Tseya had her hands on her knees and was leaning slightly forward.

He wondered why it mattered to her. *I am not devious enough for this assignment,* Brezan thought. "I'm sure we'd bore you," he said, especially since she had to have access to all the juicy bits already. "My oldest father was retired from active service by the time I was old enough to be sentient, although my younger two fathers still did most of the parental work. One of them restores antique guns, which explains his partnering with a Kel. The other does paper-cut illustrations for children's books. I once got yelled at for ruining his best pair of scissors."

He had told her about his siblings before, but she was still looking at him expectantly. "My oldest sister is Keryezan. I hardly see her anymore, and I didn't see a whole lot of her growing up, either, which automatically made her more appealing than the twins. She's rather older and she has two kids. I think she was planning on a third. As for the twins, Miuzan is the one who never lets anything rest. I could have got on with Ganazan by herself, she's pretty easygoing, but she was always on Miuzan's side by default."

Tseya continued to say nothing. Feeling hounded, Brezan said, "We fought over stupid things like who had to clean the guns and who chose what dramas to watch together. My oldest father believed that we should all watch them together, no idea why. Honestly, we're very ordinary. It's just me who's the disgrace. If crashhawks were so easy to predict, I—I'd never have made it into Kel Academy at all."

Come to that, he had no idea what, if anything, Kel Command had told his parents. He hadn't dared to ask. If he was lucky, Kel Command had said nothing. His family had probably assumed he was dead or under Jedao's control. The truth wasn't much better.

"Your family sounds very different from mine," Tseya said. "Please don't think all Andan families are about poison and platitudes. Some are and some aren't."

Brezan wondered if she meant to elaborate, and wasn't sure whether he was more worried or relieved when she didn't. Maybe she wanted a distraction. "You wanted to watch some duels?" he said, eyeing the status indicators. Still nothing useful.

"Yes, let's pick one at random," Tseya said, reviving a little.

The grid was happy to select one for them: Jedao, back when he was the commander of a tactical group, against some whippy-looking long-haired Shuos who had taken offense over a point of etiquette that Tseya undoubtedly understood but Brezan sure as hell didn't. It was strange to examine Jedao in his own body, a lean man whose face was unremarkable until he smiled; but Brezan recognized the way that Jedao-as-Cheris had moved during the takeover of the Swanknot swarm, smile included. It was also bizarre seeing Jedao with the star-and-flame tactical group commander's insignia rather than a general's wings. Brezan reminded himself that Kel Command had finally discharged Jedao, anyway.

Jedao and his opponent, Shuos Magrach, were sizing each other up in a way that made them look like siblings. "Magrach was an assassin, so they would have had similar training," Tseya said when Brezan remarked on it. "There was speculation that she was trying to injure or kill Jedao for reasons of her own."

Brezan had thought he'd had a handle on the timeline. "I thought this was when people still liked Jedao."

Tseya shrugged. "That's complicated. A lot of the Kel who served with him liked him, but others thought he was just lucky and resented how rapidly he got promoted. The Shuos considered him an eccentric. Look at it from their point of view. He was fast-tracked to his heptarch's own office straight out of academy, brilliant early career as an assassin, does some work with small units and is even more brilliant there. Then, as far as anyone can tell, he lets the military stuff get to his head and he abandons everything to chase after the Kel. Inexplicably, Heptarch Khiaz let him go. Maybe she concluded he was no good to her after all. Imagine how much trouble she could have saved everyone if she'd just sat on him until he settled down."

The match was underway, best of seven. Brezan could only follow what had happened in the slowed-down replays. He had already known about Jedao's extraordinary reflexes, but Magrach was just as fast. "I feel inadequate like you wouldn't believe," Brezan said.

Tseya kicked his shin. "I don't think you'd enjoy being an assassin."

"If I'd had an assassin's skills, I might have been able to shoot Jedao before he got this far."

"There's more to life than being able to shoot your problems," Tseya said. "We'll just have to get it right this time around. For a man so good at hitting things, Jedao has a lot of weaknesses. No; I'm more worried about getting within enthrallment range than about Jedao fighting back."

"I'm not sure this is an attitude conducive to our long-term survival," Brezan said.

She smiled at him with the side of her mouth. "One of us has to be the optimist."

The mothgrid interrupted them with a notification: Jedao's swarm had bannered the Deuce of Gears.

"We'd better get ready," Tseya said.

Brezan turned off the duel recording, noting in passing that the score was 2-2 and wondering if he was paranoid for thinking Jedao might have engineered it that way. He averted his face. More than anything he yearned to be part of the battle, yearned to fight.

"Brezan," Tseya said, "Brezan. We're fighting in our own way."

Hopeless to explain to her that being a Kel wasn't about fighting in your *own* way, as he had done during Exercise Purple 53. It was about fighting the same way as all the other Kel. Of course, as a crashhawk, he was in no position to lecture Tseya about Kel doctrine. Instead, he said, "I will do my duty," because that was always unobjectionable.

Tseya had an imitation Kel uniform for the operation. He didn't watch her put it on, couldn't bear to, but he had to concede that she would stick out on a Kel moth if she wore anything else, especially since Jedao had booted all the seconded personnel. The two of them suited up quietly. Brezan knew that the Andan cared about the aesthetics of even utilitarian objects like suits, but it was different when you had to wear one yourself. Oh well, given how his year was going, tasteful scrollwork was the least of his problems.

Of the two of them, Tseya was the better pilot. Brezan had observed her long enough to know that this wasn't just a matter of specific familiarity with the silkmoth's handling characteristics. Fortunately, she was on his side, or anyway more on his side for the moment than against it.

He was tempted to whisper as they made the approach, as if the Kel in the swarm could overhear them across vacuum. Tseya, intent on her task, seemed to feel no such impulse. Her toe was tapping loudly against the side of the terminal.

The agony of waiting didn't get any better aboard a silkmoth. Brezan was watching the Kel and Hafn swarms on scan and fretting when another Hafn swarm blinked into existence. He had no other word for it, and he didn't think that many formants, even glitchy foreign formants, could be a malfunction in their scan. "Tseya—"

"I see them," Tseya said. She wasn't changing their approach, mainly because the main body of Jedao's swarm was obdurate in threatening the newcomers. How Jedao had known they would show up there, Brezan had no idea. No one had ever said that Jedao had the ability to get extra information out of scan, but it wasn't impossible that he knew some tricks.

Brezan had difficulty not staring at the highlighted triangle in the display that represented the *Hierarchy of Feasts*. *We're going to free you from the Immolation Fox,* he thought savagely, trying not to wonder whether General Khiruev had survived. *And then I will personally kill Jedao into so many pieces you can't even burn what's left.*

One of Brezan's former lovers, a perfumer, had asked what he found so attractive about the violence of his profession. Never mind that as a staffer he didn't personally see to the violence. Brezan didn't like admitting it, but there was a certain satisfaction to kicking down obstacles.

*Focus,* he reminded himself. They weren't in position yet, and Jedao was still a threat. He glanced at Tseya. Still engrossed in her task. Good.

The battle was unfolding very oddly. He worked out that the Hafn had somehow taken control of fourteen Kel bannermoths. Jedao had caught on before Brezan did and had condensed the grand formation dangerously to release a tactical group to deal with the crashhawk units. Brezan took long, even breaths to deal with the nausea at the thought of the Kel forced to turn traitor again, something they had to be sick of—

No. That wasn't it. He remembered the shattering devotion in General Khiruev's eyes, in Commander Janaia's. Brezan himself only felt horrified because he had no formation instinct to assure him that the world was ticking along as it was supposed to. The Kel hexarch had warned him, but he hadn't been ready to heed her.

"That detached group, it's burning up?"

Brezan realized Tseya had addressed him and looked at the tactical display. "Yes," he said flatly. Which unlucky commander had Jedao sacrificed? Rationally, any commander had to send people to die. But he couldn't help the way he felt. "That group looks like it's putting pressure on the units the Hafn are trying to shield."

"I see," Tseya said. She was guiding them past the fireworks now.

They had discussed how they wanted to handle this, given that battle would complicate matters. In this case, it would harm the swarm's chances of survival to remove Jedao during the engagement. If Jedao continued to aim himself at the Hafn, they might as well allow him to complete the battle. Brezan had served under General Khiruev long enough to have faith in the woman's ability, but they had no guarantee that Khiruev still lived. For his part, Brezan didn't have the training for the task.

Instead, they were going to board the command moth and ambush Jedao when he headed back to his quarters to rest. Presumably having a body, even the wrong body, meant the bastard had to sleep once in a while. And there was a chance, however small, that Jedao would let down his guard enough to give the two of them a shot.

One thing Brezan had always hated about space combat, despite having been a moth Kel for half his career, was the illusory sense of insulation. You could almost imagine that the vast-eyed darkness was a protective shroud; you could mistake the intermittent silences for an indication that the enemy would pass you by. As it happened, the universe was very good at suckering Kel who got too cocky. During his first bannermoth posting, in an engagement against Taurag raiders, railgun shot had punched through the fading formation shields and through the moth, and sheared the woman next to him in two.

"There we go," Tseya crooned. Brezan startled, but she was talking to the moth. They were in the midst of the battle now. Tseya clearly knew more about formation mechanics than she usually let on. She had to in order to anticipate what Jedao was doing so she didn't get them shot down on the way in. Already she'd pushed them through the shields by exploiting the modulation gaps and the silkmoth's capacity for bursts of rapid acceleration.

Brezan enlarged the subdisplay devoted to optics. At this distance, only the gold paint, glimmering irregularly in the light of shield effects and incoming fire, distinguished the cindermoth from the rest of the void.

"I'll be able to mate the moths soon," Tseya said. "Ready? You'll hate it. I always do."

Both of them double-checked their webbing, and Brezan nodded. He was glad something was finally happening, even though he knew he would feel quite the opposite in a matter of minutes.

Tseya was right. For all her deftness as a pilot, the mating maneuver made Brezan's bones feel like they were going to vibrate out of his flesh. The silkmoth cobwebbed itself to the insertion point and juddered slowly closer and closer to the *Hierarchy of Feasts*. Then it released eggs that hatched to create a bridge of metalweave, and a burrower to gnaw its way through the cindermoth's hull.

The burrower laboriously extruded a blister over itself and the breach point, then got to work. They waited in silence. Brezan had the irrational urge to hit the progress indicators. Tseya showed no sign of impatience. "Everything's as good as it's going to get," she said at last, and he concurred. "Let's move."

After the silkmoth's profusion of birds and disquieting fish and graceful trees, it was almost disappointing that the airlock was strictly utilitarian. Tseya's mouth quirked when she caught Brezan's expression, but she didn't say anything. The distance between *Beneath the Orchid* and *Hierarchy of Feasts* was not large, but it was also perilous. Tethers aside, if you were careless, you might tumble through some of the openings in the imperfectly-braided metalweave. Still, it was a danger Brezan had faced before, and he completed the crossing quickly, making it onto the metalfoam blister.

Tseya hesitated for a long moment, and Brezan wondered if she had spotted something wrong. Then she, too, made the crossing. The blister opened for them, and they entered it together, forced close to each other by its small size. It closed behind them, and then the breach in the hall gaped open to admit them.

They emerged in a corridor. Brezan looked sharply around but saw no one coming. He had expected to feel something more than this knifing sense of alienation. "I'm locked out of the grid," he said in a low voice. He hadn't expected any differently. But if Jedao had gotten careless, they could at least have found out what the moth's current layout was.

Tseya's only response was a curt nod. She was breathing shallowly, and her face was too pale.

"Tseya?" he asked.

"I'm all right," she said in a faint voice.

He should have asked her about any inconvenient phobias, the kind of thing he used to vet for the general, except he hadn't been the one who selected Tseya for this mission. Plus, he'd never been allowed to see her profile, although he bet she had seen his. After all, he answered to her, not the other way around.

"We should keep moving," Tseya said, more strongly. Good: so what if she had problems with wide-open spaces or vacuum. She had made it across and they had an arch-traitor to shoot.

They shed their suits, then tucked them into the breach. If someone found the breach before they located Jedao, they were done for anyway. It was still grating seeing Tseya in the Kel uniform. As for himself, it felt as though the fucking high general's insignia was transmitting their position to the entire cindermoth.

His best guess as to Jedao's quarters took them through nerve-wrackingly identical passageways. It was hard not to read a certain smugness into the expressions of the ubiquitous painted ashhawks. *If someone ever lets me decorate a moth,* Brezan thought, *I'll have it done in a boring solid color.* More seriously, he was used to taking variable layout for granted. Being locked out of the master map's shortcuts disturbed him in ways he didn't want to name.

A clitter-clatter made them both tense, but it was only a servitor bearing a toolbox, carrying out routine maintenance of the sort that didn't require the approval of a human technician. The servitor, a deltaform, took no more notice of them than Brezan would have taken of a floor-tile. Tseya's eyes were considering, but he gestured for her to keep up, and she did. Other than the crossing, she was doing fine. He only hoped he was handling himself as well.

They ran into their first Kel outside of what had to be the dueling hall; Jedao hadn't bothered to change the painted ashhawks clutching swords. The two Kel, a soldier and a corporal, had the bleary expressions of people who just wanted to sleep. They almost walked right by Brezan and Tseya.

"I can see discipline has gone to hell around here," Brezan said caustically. He recognized them: Kel Osara and Corporal Merez. Neither was likely to give them trouble unless they were stupid enough to challenge Merez to a drinking contest. He had heard a sergeant swear that it wasn't possible to get the man drunk without resorting to additives.

The two jumped. Osara, quicker-witted, thumped a salute, her face going blank. Very Kel, and frankly the best thing she could do for herself. She could work out that something had gone seriously wrong for Brezan to be here, let alone with the rank he was claiming, but he hadn't required her to think so she wasn't going to.

Merez, on the other hand, was trying to make sense of the situation. He stared at the wings-and-flame insignia, then saluted much more slowly.

Before Merez could formulate a question, Brezan said sharply, "Is General Khiruev still alive?"

"Yes, sir," both Kel said.

He wanted to be happy about the answer, but he didn't have any guarantees as to the general's condition. "Is she well?"

Hesitation. "She's alive, sir," the corporal said.

Wonderful. He wanted to pursue this, but they had a fox to kill. "Jedao?"

No hesitation this time: "Alive, sir."

Damn. "I need directions to wherever Jedao is holed up," Brezan said, "then to the general."

Merez gave the directions. As it so happened, Jedao had given Khiruev quarters just next to his. Brezan hated what that implied.

"All right," Brezan said to the two. "Head directly to barracks and stay there. Do not speak to anyone until I countermand this order. Go."

The two Kel marched off. For a moment Osara's eyes lit with bemusement. Tseya murmured, after the Kel had rounded the corner, "We'd better hope they don't run into anyone on the way."

"Not much we can do about it," Brezan said.

They reached Jedao's quarters without further incident, even if it didn't feel that way. Brezan glanced down the hall at the doors that led to Khiruev's quarters, as though the general would come out to greet them. Hardly likely. He nodded at Tseya.

A lot could go wrong when you messed with a full-fledged mothgrid, especially if a Shuos was monitoring it, which was why neither of them had tried it earlier. But they had to make the attempt now. Tseya had grid-diving experience. She pulled out a hacking device in the shape of a ring with an egregiously large opal cabochon surrounded by diamonds, which she had previously described as 'my mother's idea of fashionable,' and cocked her head, listening to something only she could hear.

Brezan was worrying that someone would show up at either end of the corridor when the door whispered open. Tseya straightened and nodded at him. Brezan had already drawn his gun. He checked the interior from where he was, then sprinted through and broke left, sweeping the room once again. There was nothing of interest except a jeng-zai deck and some tokens on a table. "Clear," he said in a low voice.

Their attempts at stealth hadn't been good enough, unfortunately. "I'm right in here," a horribly familiar voice called out. A door opened at the other end of the receiving room. Jedao was partly visible through the doorway, including half his smile.

Brezan couldn't help himself. He aimed and fired three times. The bullets whined as they ricocheted; something in the other room shattered. Jedao had already dodged back into the room, mirror-quick.

"If you were serious about killing me," Jedao said, "you'd have blown the whole place up, just like Kel fucking Command did with the other cindermoth. Quit wasting your bullets and my time, and let's have a civilized conversation."

This couldn't possibly work to their advantage if Jedao himself was suggesting it. It had to be a ruse. But if it gave Tseya a chance at Jedao—

"I want your word," Jedao said. Now he was dictating terms. "I'll leave my sidearm in here. You can keep whatever the hell weapons you like, Brezan."

In agony, Brezan hesitated. The only thing keeping him from going in there anyway was the memory of his stinging hand, the scalding fact that Jedao was the better killer. Tseya didn't say anything and was probably remaining in the hallway until she judged that she could enter safely, so he assumed he was to stick to the original plan. "Fine," he said roughly. He holstered the gun out of a suicidal sense of honor. "Come out."

He had agreed not to shoot. He hadn't said anything about other weapons. Jedao wasn't stupid enough not to have noticed the loophole, and anyway, a Shuos would expect everyone to lie as much as he did. They both intended to betray the other. The question was who was faster.

He might not survive this. But his orders were to give Tseya her opportunity. He was going to follow the damn orders for once.

Jedao sauntered out of the room. That damnable tilted smile. Brezan clenched his left hand, wishing he could smash the fox's face in. Jedao caught sight of Brezan's insignia. His eyes widened. Then he laughed softly. "And people complained *I* got promoted too fast," he said. "Well, congratulations. How are you liking the privileges of rank, General?"

Then Jedao's eyes narrowed, and he was looking over Brezan's shoulder. Brezan didn't dare turn at first, but he heard Tseya's tread. She could walk silently when she cared to. That she didn't now indicated her confidence.

Brezan felt the heat of her presence and, to his mortification, flushed up the sides of his neck knowing she was so close, even if her attention was focused on another man. In spite of his original intention, he turned, slowly, to watch her. He wished he could run his hands through her hair, whose locks were curling free of the silver pins; marveled at how her eyes had gone rose-blue, sea-deep; wished that petal regard was focused on him instead, even knowing what it would do to him.

Then he looked back at Jedao, which was what he should have been doing all along. Jedao was watching Tseya through lowered eyelashes. Brezan wondered, very cynically, when Jedao had last known any form of human contact that didn't involve killing people. The intensity of Jedao's regard worried Brezan, except Tseya didn't give any indication that she was concerned.

Slowly, Jedao walked toward Tseya, graceful, taking no notice of Brezan. He said something caressingly in a language that Brezan didn't recognize. Tseya answered in the same language. Brezan eased into position, careful not to move too suddenly, despite knowing that enthrallment didn't break so easily.

Brezan lunged, except Jedao wasn't there anymore. He had whipped around Brezan and struck Tseya at the back of her head. The struggle was over so quickly that Tseya had slumped in Jedao's arms before Brezan could react.

Brezan discovered the gun in his hand, not that it did him any good. You'd think he'd learn.

"Don't," Jedao said, not sounding enthralled in the least. "She's alive, even if she'll need medical care. I'd rather not kill her if I don't have to. Especially not in a stupid accident."

Brezan stared at Jedao, then at Tseya, then at Jedao again. The enthrallment should have worked, unless—

Unless Jedao wasn't Jedao.

He'd been played. From the beginning, even.

Which meant he had just delivered them into the hands of someone even more dangerous than Jedao.

# CHAPTER TWENTY-THREE

CHERIS DUMPED TSEYA unceremoniously to the floor. She was already in motion. Vexingly, she still moved with the mirror-swiftness that Brezan had observed in the recordings of Jedao's duels once upon a life. Brezan fought her, but she had already gotten a crushing grip on his throat. *Wonderful,* he thought as the world sank into blackness, *I had to run afoul of* infantry *Kel.*

When Brezan came to, he had been expertly trussed up in spider restraints. Cheris had given him a chair that would, under other circumstances, have been downright luxurious. At least it wasn't one of General Khiruev's chairs, antiques that looked suspiciously like the general had a nervous habit of gouging the arms with her screwdrivers. Brezan didn't think he could have endured that.

Cheris, for her part, had draped herself over a chair with its back facing Brezan. "I was worried you were going to stay under all night," she said. "Don't bother yelling for help. No one will hear it. Formation instinct being what it is, I can't risk it yet."

She was still speaking with Jedao's accent. "We both know who you are," Brezan said in his best temperate voice, which emerged as a croak. "You can stop pretending."

"That's complicated," Cheris said, "and anyway you're confused as to who's interrogating whom. Why did you try to kill me?"

He should have kept his mouth shut. It was becoming a theme. On the other hand, the question wasn't a hard one. "I should think that would be obvious," he said. "You took over my general's swarm as Shuos Jedao. Who, in case you were asleep for that particular lesson, has a history of blowing people up. I'd have to be insane to want to leave you in charge."

Cheris smiled Jedao's smile at him. "I see that tact isn't your specialty, but you're not stupid. As you said, we both know I'm not Jedao, or your Andan comrade's attempt would have succeeded."

"What have you done with her?" Brezan said before he could stop himself.

Cheris raised an eyebrow at him. "Jedao would have killed her, but she's not dead. That's all you're getting."

Brezan believed her, but who knew what condition Tseya was in. "You put a hell of a lot of effort into being a convincing Jedao," Brezan said, remembering how this had all begun. Maybe it was better to keep her talking. She might let something drop.

"Believe it or not, it's a side-effect of something Kel Command did to me. Anyway, let's try again. Why did you try to kill me?"

Oddly, she didn't seem to be taking the assassination attempt personally. She was digging for his motivations. Why? Why did it matter? She could have killed him without any trouble. Come to that, she could have done that the first time around, too. He liked the implications less and less.

Cheris was watching him patiently.

"You hijacked my general's swarm," Brezan said, "whoever you were claiming to be. What the fuck was I supposed to do? Let you swan off with all those moths?"

Cheris tapped the top of the chair. "And what was the swarm going to be used for?"

"You know the answer to that question. Why are we even having this conversation?"

"Are all generals this bad at giving straight answers?" Cheris said tartly. "It's not even a hard question."

"We had orders to fight the Hafn," Brezan said, quelling the urge to lunge at Cheris even though he had a good idea how that would end. "Which we would have managed just fine without your intervention."

"Mostly true," Cheris said, "but there's an exception. That exception would have gotten the lot of you killed. Never mind that. You must have followed the swarm's movements to be able to board the command moth. I can only imagine you were watching its actions, too. This has undoubtedly told you all about how I've been randomly shooting up moths, or crashing them into cities, or filling them with poison gas."

"The sarcasm is much appreciated," Brezan retorted. "I'm aware of how much success you've enjoyed." He wasn't sure he wanted to know how much of that success was ascribable to someone who had, until recently, been an infantry captain. "I'm also aware that you've been fighting the Hafn just as tamely as though Kel Command had you on a leash. But I refuse to believe you're doing this for the benefit of the hexarchate."

"Yes, I imagine the hexarchate's benefit is very important to you," Cheris said, quite dryly. Her hands flexed.

Brezan wasn't thinking about her hands but her tone of voice. What the fuck had she picked up on? He didn't need her figuring out that he entertained dangerously heretical attitudes toward his government.

"You're a terrible liar," she added, although he hadn't said a word. His heart shuddered. "You care about the swarm; well and good. You will find that I have taken care of the Kel better than Kel Command would have."

"This is why you sent that tactical group out to fight in a suicide formation," Brezan said, even though provoking Cheris was a bad idea.

"That was Commander Gherion," Cheris said.

Brezan bit back an oath. He had liked Gherion, and not just because Gherion appreciated his roast stuffed pheasant, that one time Brezan had invited him over for dinner.

"He served well," Cheris said with no discernible irony. "Someone had to fight, Brezan. There's no way around it. Gherion chose how to carry out his mission. Kiora's Stab was his choice, and it did as he intended. Tell me again, then. Why did you try to kill me?"

Brezan glared at her. Too bad she was good at looking imperturbable. That must come with having the upper hand. "I am Kel," he said through his teeth. He remembered the smug ashhawks, the smoke-coil wings, the hot regard of those golden eyes. "I have my orders."

Cheris laughed soundlessly. "We're crashhawks. If you're following orders, it's because you want to. So it comes back to the question I keep asking you, and you keep dodging. Why did you try to kill me?"

He couldn't even make a fist. He had run out of facile answers. "I don't know," he said, hating how ragged his voice sounded. When Cheris didn't respond, he said, more loudly, "I don't know, all right? Is that what you wanted to hear?"

"I used to follow Kel Command, just as you did," Cheris said. "But there's a better way. I couldn't see it until Jedao showed me." When Brezan gaped at her, she added, "Jedao was evil, but that doesn't mean he was automatically wrong." She rose and began unlocking the restraints. "Here's what will happen. I'm going to give you run of the swarm, and you can talk to your comrades. I'm certain they've worried about your fate. Ask them how the swarm has been run and how you've been treated. Formation instinct will ensure that they answer you honestly." The last of the restraints snicked loose. "Then come back and tell me, to my face, why you want to kill me. Since you'll be in command of the swarm, I doubt I'll pose any threat to you."

Brezan scarcely dared to move, even though tensing his muscles surreptitiously told him he was free in truth. "They have no idea who you are, do they?"

"I thought you'd figure that out, too," Cheris said matter-of-factly. "Confine me wherever you like. I have some things to work out in my head. After all, if you had intended to kill me, you'd have managed it already."

Brezan opened his mouth, considered the fact that he'd allowed her to keep talking while he was completely unrestrained, then shut it. "Give me your word that you'll stay confined to quarters until I come back," Brezan said.

Kel Command was going to enjoy nailing pieces of him to some undecorated wall once they figured out what he'd been up to. They knew he could interpret his orders liberally, but he had crossed the line of what he could justify to them.

"You have my word," Cheris said. She rested her hand over the hilt of the calendrical sword she wasn't wearing, a formality the Kel had not used in over a generation. "You may want to start with your general. She's probably resting."

"Give me access to the mothgrid," Brezan said.

"Of course," Cheris said. She muttered a passphrase in an unfamiliar language—in his hearing, but he doubted she had any more use for it.

Brezan blinked as the mothgrid started talking to his augment again. It only took a moment to check the master map and to convince the terminal to cough up the current duty roster. "If this is part of some Shuos gambit after all," Brezan said, "I'll send you back to Kel Command in pieces."

She didn't look impressed by the threat. Considering what she had already pulled off, however doomed, that was fair.

Brezan got up. His muscles protested, but he hadn't been tied up all that long. He glanced back at Cheris, who had relocated to a couch and had called up—was that some dueling drama? With dancers? Better not to ask.

Although he half-expected to be jumped by heretic Kel when he stepped out, the hallway taunted him with its emptiness. That, and the same smug painted ashhawks.

At this point, Brezan had two choices. He could pay General Khiruev a call, as Cheris had suggested, or he could go after Tseya, assuming the grid wasn't lying to him about her location. Tseya wouldn't approve of him talking to Cheris, but she might know what the situation called for. On the other hand, Brezan couldn't help but feel that he owed it to himself to find out if Cheris's contentions held any truth.

The hell with it. Best to investigate while he had the opportunity. He walked down the hall, not very far, and paused before the general's door. "Request to see General Khiruev," he said.

A long pause followed. Brezan was about to repeat the request when the door slid open. He entered, and only then realized that he'd forgotten to mention his new rank.

"Brezan," Khiruev said, and then, when her gaze was drawn to the wings-and-flame, "sir." She had been rearranging the endless collection of gadgets on her shelves. Now she faced Brezan properly and saluted.

Brezan noticed neither the gadgets nor the salute. The white streak in Khiruev's hair had widened, and she looked thin and wan. Brezan bit down a snarl.

Khiruev's mouth twisted. "If you're here," she said, "then Kel Command sent you somehow, and Jedao is gone." She tried to reach for her sidearm, but her arm locked up, and her hand began to shake.

*She's trying to kill me for 'Jedao'?* Brezan thought incredulously. "Stand down, s—General," he said. Khiruev froze. Brezan didn't order her to hand the gun over, which was almost certainly a mistake, but he didn't want to strip her dignity away entirely. "What the hell happened to you?"

"Please be more specific, sir," Khiruev said icily.

Well, if she was going to be that way about it—"You look like you're being poisoned," Brezan said. "What's going on?"

"I invoked the Vrae Tala clause on Jedao's behalf when Kel Command revoked his commission," Khiruev said.

"He made you do *what?*" Brezan demanded. So that was why Khiruev looked ill: because she was. Because she was dying.

"No one *made* me do anything, sir," Khiruev said. "I did it voluntarily. Shoot me for it if you like. It doesn't matter anymore."

The stabbing despair in Khiruev's eyes hurt Brezan. "I'm asking the wrong questions," he said. "*Why* did you do it voluntarily?"

Silence.

Great. Brezan was going to have to pull rank on the woman who, by all rights, should have been his commanding officer. "Answer the question, General."

Khiruev inhaled sharply, then nodded. "Because he was worth serving," she said. "Because the first thing I tried to do was assassinate him with an improvised device—"

Brezan hid his surprise.

"—and I botched the job. I killed Lyu and Meriki."

"I'm sorry," Brezan said. It didn't seem quite real. Lyu with his slight gambling problem, Meriki with her crowd of children.

Khiruev went on as though Brezan hadn't spoken. "General Jedao took me aside afterward. He knew I was the culprit. Then he chewed me out for killing the wrong targets, warned me not to fuck up again, and asked for my service. I gave it to him.

"I know what the history lessons say. I know what he did. But in his time in charge of the swarm, he acted more honorably toward the Kel than Kel Command usually does." Khiruev looked away, then back. Her resistance was unraveling. "I assume you've dealt with him. You would hardly be here otherwise. Go ahead and end it, sir." Her voice softened. "For what it's worth, I'm glad you're making it out alive."

It hit Brezan, then, that Khiruev wanted to die. He was tempted to ask if it was a side-effect of Vrae Tala—there had always been the rumors—but he couldn't bring himself to do it, especially when he suspected he wouldn't like the answer. Instead, Brezan said, "What if I told you that we'd been tricked? That you weren't following Shuos Jedao after all?"

Khiruev fell silent. Then: "You were the one who pointed out that former Captain Cheris didn't possess those marksmanship skills. Unless she got lucky on short notice. If that's where you're going with this line of argument."

"I don't know a hell of a lot about how Jedao was resurrected whenever Kel Command wanted to field him," Brezan said. "Do you?"

"I never had access to that information, sir."

He could tell that Khiruev was skeptical. "I didn't come here alone," he said, which got no reaction. Khiruev would expect as much. "I was backup for an Andan agent." Her eyes did flicker then. "The Andan couldn't so much as slow Cheris down."

"It couldn't just be Jedao going crazy, or going crazier possessing Cheris?"

"I wasn't on the moth for the ride," Brezan said, thinking of how lucid Cheris had sounded. They did say the Shuos trained the knack of resisting enthrallment into some of their operatives, but Tseya hadn't thought that would be an obstacle. "You tell me. This person you've been serving. Was their behavior crazy?"

"Well," Khiruev said at her driest, "in our existence, honorable behavior *is* crazy. But I take your point, sir. Anyway, it doesn't matter."

That took Brezan by surprise. "I don't follow."

Khiruev's mouth crimped. "*Are* they dead?"

"No," Brezan said, and was disturbingly gratified to see a little of the light return to Khiruev's eyes. "She had me. She's in her quarters on parole. But she persuaded me that I should judge her actions by the state of the swarm."

"That's an interesting move," Khiruev said, "considering that I have no choice but to follow you. Are you sure she can be trusted?"

There it was, formation instinct taking hold, the switch of loyalty. *I didn't want this for either of us,* Brezan wanted to say, although he knew better than to say it. "Maybe she was hoping I would judge her the way you did," he said.

"You were set free and not killed, sir," Khiruev said, as if Brezan needed the reminder. "I'm seeing a pattern."

"I've barely looked around the *Hierarchy of Feasts*," Brezan said. "I'd prefer to do it in your company, to reduce the disruption."

"You have only to give the order, sir."

Brezan reminded himself not to pick a fight over behavior Khiruev couldn't help. "Has Cheris given you any indication as to her final objective?"

"I only know that we were to fight the Hafn, which I imagine you'd figured out, and that perhaps there was a greater game," Khiruev said. "I never received specifics beyond that."

"Even if you don't have specifics," Brezan said, "anything, anything at all—" He didn't understand when he had started hoping Cheris-as-fox had a plan. "She couldn't have possibly intended to go to war with the hexarchs with a single swarm, even one of this size."

"She did say once that I wasn't looking at the right battlefield," Khiruev said, "but that could have been misdirection."

"Do you think she was bluffing?"

"No," Khiruev said without any hesitation. "I don't think she was."

Brezan thought for a moment. "To start with, I want to see the staff and department heads, and Commander Janaia."

"Sir, you ought to be aware that the commander has been removed from duty. Muris is the acting commander. Should I reinstate Janaia?"

Just when he thought he was getting a handle on the situation. "What happened?"

"She had a breakdown," Khiruev said, without elaborating.

"I'll have to review that later," Brezan said grimly. The status of the swarm had to come first. "Commander Muris, then."

"As you wish, sir. I'll set it up."

Khiruev could no doubt tell how unprepared Brezan was for this turn of events, but she didn't comment on it. Which she wouldn't, because that would be insubordinate behavior. Brezan watched in helpless fury as Khiruev sent out the summons, not even sure who he was furious at. Himself, maybe.

They headed to the conference room early on the grounds that it would be best to be the first ones there. Brezan had to keep from flinching at Khiruev's tread, not because he heard anything wrong, but because he kept expecting to. Khiruev cleared her throat when Brezan automatically took his old seat at the side of the table. Brezan colored and decided to remain standing, while Khiruev slowly sank into a chair next to the head of the table.

First to arrive was Commander Muris. He didn't even pause before offering his salute, and proceeded to the seat across from Khiruev's at Brezan's nod. Then came most of the staff officers. Last of all was Medical, who looked at Brezan with open skepticism.

When everyone was seated, Brezan said, "I recognize that this is a damnably bizarre situation, but what I need from you is very simple. I want honest assessments of how the swarm has been handled since Jedao's takeover." He didn't explain his presence or why the fuck he wanted the information. At least General Khiruev's visible compliance lent him legitimacy. "We'll go clockwise around the table, starting with the commander. I have already heard General Khiruev's report privately."

"Sir," Muris said. He launched into his report. His crisp way of speaking hadn't changed, and Brezan had to admire his sangfroid. Brezan took notes, even though the meeting was being recorded, because otherwise he wouldn't have been able to concentrate on what Muris was saying.

It was impossible to escape the buzzing sense of unhappiness coming from the officers gathered here. But they would do as he ordered because the moment they walked in and saw him, they lost the ability to resist. Khiruev had tried, but hadn't been able to stand up to a direct order. In the middle of Muris's summation of the first engagement with the Hafn, Brezan had the idle thought that it would be horrifyingly easy to get used to people looking at you with that intent devotion, which had to be something specific to high generals, and maybe also to generals who had four hundred unnatural years of seniority. He sure as hell didn't remember anything quite like it during his regular career.

Kel Cheris had had that power over the swarm, and she had surrendered it as part of a *rhetorical gambit*. Who was she really, and what was her game?

He was going to have to return to her if he wanted to find out, that much was clear.

# CHAPTER TWENTY-FOUR

KHIRUEV HAD TROUBLE not drifting out of focus during High General Brezan's meeting, partly because, like everyone but Brezan, she knew what the swarm had gone through, but partly because of the creeping exhaustion. Barely past the first quarter of Vrae Tala and it was already this bad. How did anyone survive to the hundredth day? She felt better when she interacted with people. On the other hand, sitting in the conference room made it all too easy to succumb to the illusion that she was gradually becoming no more animate than the walls, the air, the dust that wheeled in the light.

She roused when Brezan gave orders regarding Cheris, mostly to the effect of 'if you see Jedao wandering around having broken his parole, shoot him.' Interestingly, Brezan had not revealed Cheris's identity, perhaps because the story was too incredible for anyone to believe. Then Brezan dismissed everyone else, and looked at Khiruev fretfully. Brezan had never been able to conceal what he was thinking.

"General," Brezan said, "I'd like to tour the moth, unless you consider it inadvisable at the moment."

A tactful way of allowing her to beg off, not that Khiruev intended to take it. All she'd do if she retired to quarters was dream herself into an assemblage of bones and coils and unthinking curves. "I don't see why you should delay, sir," Khiruev said. "Are you sure you don't want a proper escort?"

Brezan flinched, as she had known he would, but the forms had to be observed. "Do you think I'm in danger?" he said.

"Not from any of the Kel," Khiruev said. Of course, it was questionable whether Cheris fell in that category anymore.

Brezan didn't reply to that, although the fate of his Andan comrade had to weigh on his mind. "The command center first, then," he said. He took two steps toward the door, then stopped. Without turning around to face Khiruev, he said, "Why?"

Surely Brezan knew he wouldn't get results with such a vague query? One of the first things they taught officers was that recalcitrant common soldiers could tangle you up with loopholes if they became sufficiently motivated. Khiruev said, mostly honestly, "I don't understand the question, sir."

Brezan swung around, eyes narrowed, nostrils flared. Looking for a target. Since this was Brezan, he hadn't yet worked out that everyone in the swarm was a target if he wanted them to be. "You can't guess?" he said. "I understand formation instinct. I can't understand how you let yourself become Cheris's pawn after you were freed."

"Sir," Khiruev said, "it sounds to me like you're asking how you let her do the same to you. You already know my story. But here you are, and for all you know, the other crashhawk has already escaped to do as she pleases."

"If you'd shot her in the head when Kel Command dumped Jedao," Brezan said, voice rising, "we wouldn't be—" His mouth snapped shut.

"What exactly did you think would become of me when you were gone?" Khiruev said, tired. "I'm human, sir. People break. Sometimes it doesn't take much. If it disappoints you, I'm sorry. You can take whatever disciplinary measures you see fit. But I had decided what mattered most to me." She paused, piecing together the reasons as they had once existed; it was already difficult to remember. "I don't care if Cheris never had a chance against the hexarchs. I wanted to die having seen that someone believed in a better world enough to fight for it."

Brezan stared at her, his face unreadable, then said, "Let's go, General."

Khiruev fell in to Brezan's side. In silence they walked through the cindermoth's halls. Either Brezan had discovered his inner art critic or something else about the ink paintings bothered him. Since Khiruev hadn't been asked to have an opinion on the topic, it was none of her affair. Say what you like about formation instinct, it was soothing to know that figuring out what to do was someone else's problem. She'd only fucked up by getting herself promoted too high.

Commander Muris saluted Brezan practically before the doors opened to admit them. The grid would have informed him of their approach. Muris avoided looking at Khiruev. This was entirely sensible: for all he knew, Brezan was parading Khiruev around before executing her for high treason. Khiruev had no plausible defense against the charge.

Although the swarm was at a standstill, Brezan was able to observe Muris poring over reports on post-battle repairs and casualties, and the occasional call from the moth commanders. Doctrine and Engineering were busy taking apart the salvage they'd recovered from the Hafn in an attempt to figure out what those auxiliaries had been. The officers carried out their duties in hushed voices. Brezan stuck around for thirty-eight minutes, his expression growing increasingly remote. Then he nodded politely at Muris, thanked him for his work, and headed out.

They went through the major departments. Brezan lingered longest at Medical, although there had been few casualties on the *Hierarchy of Feasts* this past battle and one of the people in sickbay was there for a banal bacterial infection. Then Brezan stopped by the dueling hall, and Khiruev wondered if Brezan meant to challenge her. Brezan would win, no question. Khiruev was as good at the sport as she had to be, and no better, even when she'd been healthy. Brezan had some genuine enthusiasm for it. But no, Brezan seemed content to take a seat in the back, away from the other spectators, after waving away the salutes. Khiruev looked at him curiously. Brezan made an impatient gesture for her to sit by him. A few people were warming up, and only one pair was sparring, with more grit than skill.

"You've watched videos of Jedao dueling, General?" Brezan asked.

Khiruev was touched at how often Brezan addressed her by her rank, as if that could restore their professional relationship to what it had been. "Once or twice, sir," Khiruev said. "I remember that he was good, but that's about it. Why, do you intend to duel Jedao?" She assumed she was to use the cover identity until Brezan indicated otherwise.

"Jedao's colleague was supposed to be dead mediocre at it," Brezan said, meaning Cheris, "not that that's enough reason to keep someone from a hobby. But Jedao's another story."

Khiruev sensed that she wasn't supposed to respond to that, so she didn't. Whatever Kel Command had done to Cheris, they surely regretted it now.

"I should have killed you already," Brezan said abruptly.

"After a thorough interrogation, yes," Khiruev said. "It's not too late." It was Brezan's most persistent fault, his impetuosity. That, and the fact that if you put a goal in front of him, he focused on it to the exclusion of everything else. No strategic vision. Khiruev would have put Brezan in the category of a 'use with caution' Kel if he'd been a line officer: great on special missions for his ability to think unconventionally, useful in charge of a tactical group if carefully supervised, and for mercy's sake don't promote him any higher than that. Kel Command wasn't wrong: the promotion, in this case, was key to this particular special mission. As long as Brezan leaned hard on Strategy if the Hafn showed up again, he should be all right.

"I don't care if they execute me too," Brezan said after a while, although they both knew that mere execution would be the merciful option. "What I did—I wanted to do what was right. It looked simple. How the fuck do you mess up 'kill swarm-stealing mass-murderer'?" He was gazing abstractedly at the sizzle-and-flash of the calendrical swords. "I don't know enough about swarm tactics to read stylistic differences. Does Jedao fight as he always did?"

"That's complicated," Khiruev said, "since his black cradle engagements were classified and we'll never know exactly how they were handled, but I'd point out that everyone seems rattled. Sir, if you want more information, you know who you have to ask. You're going to have to hope Jedao wants to tell you the truth. It's clear that he can be a very good liar when he wants to be."

"Yes," Brezan said, "you're right." Nevertheless, he lingered another nine minutes, until two more of the duelists started a practice round. "Let's go."

Brezan stopped at a terminal in one of the lounges to verify that Cheris was, indeed, still in her quarters. "Not that Jedao couldn't have done something tricky to the grid," he said, "but if I really believed that, I wouldn't have accepted the parole."

"Let me enter first anyway," Khiruev said. "Just in case."

Brezan made a pained sound. "You trusted him once."

Khiruev couldn't see the relevance of this. "Your safety, sir."

"Look," Brezan said, "if he wanted to hurt us, we should be more worried that he'd blow the whole place up instead of shooting us up piecemeal."

"Did you leave high explosives in there with him?" Khiruev demanded.

"No, but—"

"There's no need to ascribe supernatural powers to him, sir. Or to fail to take sensible precautions."

Brezan grimaced. "The way my year's been going, I'm not ruling anything out." He strode briskly the rest of the way to Cheris's door and requested to be let in. His hand wasn't anywhere near his sidearm. Given how all this had started, fair enough.

After a few moments, the door slid open. Brezan walked in unhesitatingly. Cheris rose to greet him, although she didn't salute. She had changed her clothes: an unexpectedly festive lavender dress and a raven pendant, the one Khiruev had seen once before when she played dangerously with her gun. The pendant must have some meaning to her, but this wasn't the time to ask. Khiruev was so used to seeing her in Kel uniform that she felt the bones of Cheris's face had changed, or her silhouette; that she was someone Khiruev had never met.

"Have you decided?" Cheris said to Brezan.

"There's one thing more," Brezan said. He was—not smiling, exactly, but his mouth had an ironic twist.

"Do tell," she said.

Brezan nodded at Khiruev. "General," he said, "I'm sure you have questions of your own for the interloper. I want you to ask them as though I weren't here."

Khiruev drew a shuddering breath, unable even to acknowledge the order.

"You're learning cruelty, I see," Cheris said to Brezan.

Khiruev looked at her. "Jedao?" she said.

Her smile was still Jedao's smile, but this time sad. "If that's who I am."

"Was any of it real?" Khiruev asked.

"It was real enough," Cheris said. "I'm what's left of Shuos Jedao. Kel Command anchored his ghost to me. You can guess what some of the side-effects were. When he finally died, he passed on his memories to me. The hexarchs aren't wrong to be concerned."

Khiruev had difficulty thinking clearly. Cheris waited calmly while Khiruev formulated her next question. Not long ago Khiruev had answered to Cheris, although the memory of that loyalty was threadbare already, and would soon be gone except as a puzzling shadow. "Was there ever a chance to bring the hexarchs down?" she said. She wasn't sure what she wanted the answer to be, given that Brezan himself seemed ambivalent on that count.

"Brezan," Cheris said, "why don't you ask me straight out yourself, instead of doing this to her? I have the same incentive to give you the answers you need, either way."

"Because she's the one you hurt," Brezan said. "Because she's the one who's dying for a cause you never bothered to explain."

"Brezan—"

"You did this to her, don't you think you owe her something?"

"I didn't ask her to—"

"But she did. Don't you think you should at least give her a fucking reason before she falls dead?" Brezan was shouting now.

"Brezan," Cheris said, all ice, "*look at her*. You're a Kel. You should know better than to lose it around one of your subordinates."

Khiruev's breath was coming hard. She couldn't explain why. She had trouble looking at the high general, as though he was surrounded by fire, by death painted into the crevices between molecules.

Brezan choked back whatever he had originally meant to say. "Fine. I concede you didn't turn the swarm into a pyre. That you fought the invaders. But that's not enough justification for using people as game pieces. Tell me what the hell this plan is, what the hell made this whole crazy outing worth it, or I will feed you to a very pissed-off Andan. She'll have my head too, but at that point it'll be worth it to be rid of you. So tell me, and make it good."

"Just think," Cheris said, "all this passion for a system you're not even committed to. Imagine who you'd become in service of something you truly believed in."

Brezan visibly checked himself from hitting her.

"We need a new calendar," Cheris said.

Brezan and Khiruev exchanged glances involuntarily. Then Brezan said, "The hexarchate has spent almost a millennium crushing heresies, some of which drummed up a significant amount of local support. Hell, weren't the Lanterners heretics?"

"Technically a client state and not part of the heptarchate proper," Cheris said. "The histories tend to get that part wrong."

"It's besides the point anyway," Brezan said. "You can't possibly enforce a new calendar over enough of the hexarchate to make a difference. Not to mention—" He stopped, paling.

"Sir?" Khiruev said. Cheris had started to smile, very faintly. That couldn't bode well.

"That was the whole fucking point, wasn't it?" Brezan said to Cheris. And to Khiruev: "It's in her fucking profile. It was there all along. She's a *mathematician*. I mean phenomenally good, as in the Nirai tried to recruit her and it was her specialty in academy."

"Yes," Cheris said. "I won't deny it was often helpful being Jedao, but I meant it as a distraction. Jedao could do calendrical warfare only so long as he used a computer, or someone else juggled the congruences for him. Anytime he was in play, all people ever thought about was where the next massacre would be, not about mathematical skullduggery. Frankly, Brezan, the calendar reset is going to go off in fifteen days no matter what you do to me."

If anything, Brezan looked even less reassured. "Splendid," he said. "You've admitted that you're running around with pieces of a spectacularly bloodthirsty mass murderer inside your head. Now you're trying to convince me that this new calendar of yours will be an improvement? Because—because as bad as the hexarchate is, as bad as the remembrances are, and the suicide formations, and Kel Command getting crazier with each successive generation—as bad as this all is, I'm not under any illusion that things can't get worse. Do you have any idea how much chaos there will be if you destroy our technology base?"

"I designed the new calendar to be compatible with most existing exotic technologies," Cheris said. "Especially communications and the mothdrive."

Brezan scowled at her. "I'm not a Rahal, and I'm not a Nirai-class mathematician either, but that means the associated social structures have to remain similar. That's not an improvement."

"You haven't seen the theorem I dragged out of the postulates," Cheris said wearily. "Yes, you're right. The calendar won't make all the Vidona disappear. It won't make people forget about remembrances, or change the minds of people who think ritual torture is entertaining. It won't make the hexarchs people that I ever want to meet. What it will do is let people choose which exotic effects apply to them. That's all."

Khiruev worked through the implications. "Sir," she said to Brezan, "you have to stop her. If she can do this, she'll destroy the Kel. Without formation instinct—"

"The Kel existed as an elite before formation instinct was ever conceived," Cheris said. "I remember it, even. It could be done again, if the Kel decided it was worth doing."

To Khiruev's dismay, Brezan was studying Cheris intently. "If you're lying to me about this, any of this," he said, "I will never forgive you."

"*Sir*—" Khiruev protested.

The muscles along Brezan's jaw convulsed. "Khiruev," he said, "when she no longer outranked you, when you first had a choice between Kel Command and her, *you chose her*. You chose Vrae Tala. You saw something in her, in what she was doing. Do you remember what it was?"

It was like trying to look through a lens made of mist. "I am Kel," Khiruev said. "You are here now, sir. My service is owed to you. I understand that I was in error. I accept whatever consequence you impose."

Brezan jerked his gaze away. "I could order you to do practically anything," he said savagely, "and you wouldn't even see anything wrong with the arrangement."

"Then I await your orders," Khiruev said, because it was the most correct response she could think of.

Brezan scrubbed angrily at his eyes, but didn't say anything to that. "Cheris," he said, "just how do you propose setting off a calendrical spike? I assume it's a calendrical spike you have in mind. It'd have to be something big."

"The Rahal, like everyone else, rely on servitors for maintenance tasks," Cheris said, "including those for the master clocks." She let the statement hang there.

"You can't possibly be talking about having sway over a legion of treacherous disaffected Rahal—" Brezan paled again. His glance swept around the room, at servitor-height. "Servitors? But they're not—" He swallowed. "Can they be trusted?"

Cheris crossed her arms. "Brezan," she said, "has a servitor ever offered you harm? Or anyone you know, for that matter?"

After a drawn-out pause, he said, "All right. I'll concede that. But why? What do they want?"

"They're individuals," Cheris said tartly. "I don't presume to speak for each and every one of them."

Khiruev thought back to the servitors who had hung around Cheris's quarters back when she was being Jedao. Khiruev had never thought twice about their presence. Most people gave servitors less thought than the wallpaper. If they had wanted to slaughter humans in their sleep, they could have managed it forever ago. It spoke better of them than the humans.

Brezan hadn't finished questioning Cheris, however. "That takes care of calendar values," he said, "but you're going to have to do something pretty fucking dramatic to mark a full-on calendar reset. What are you going to do, aim some torture beams at all the hexarchs?"

Cheris gave him a look. "No torture," she said. "But Kel Command has to go."

Khiruev drew her gun.

"Stand down," Brezan hissed.

Khiruev holstered her gun, although she didn't want to. "It's high treason."

"This whole thing is high treason," Brezan said, which didn't help. "I'm not done talking to her."

"So you want to see if I can pull it off," Cheris said to Brezan.

"I am sick of serving something I don't even believe in," Brezan said. "What the hell. Fifteen days, you say? I want to know down to the fucking hour, and I want to see the math so someone who is not me can check it over. If nothing happens, if nothing changes, I'll scorch you dead and drag you back to Kel Command. And then, if they don't hang up my corpse next to yours, I will spend the rest of this rotted career helping them smash whatever uprising they point me at."

"And the Andan agent?" Cheris said. "What's her place?"

"I left her in confinement," Brezan said. His voice had gone distant. "She claimed to be disgraced, but it's always possible she was lying to get my guard down." Brezan colored. Khiruev knew then what their relationship had been. "It may not be safe for anyone, er, human to enter the room with her. We'll have to find somewhere to let her off at some point."

"Were you expected to report in?"

"They'd expect to hear from her, not me," he said. "I'm positive there's no way to secure her cooperation. As far as I know, she's loyal. And I—I don't have any leverage." His eyes darkened. "Her silkmoth is mated to the *Hierarchy of Feasts*. I'd better do something about that before we set off for wherever the hell we're going."

"I'm certain we've driven off the Hafn," Cheris said. "It's not impossible they have yet another reserve swarm, but I was looking in on the analysis that Doctrine was doing. The Hafn had a staggering number of those caskets, but they run through them fast. I looked at what we could deduce of their calendar and figured it out. Those people sewn up with birds and flowers—they're a power source. That's why the Hafn were able to use their native exotics in high calendar terrain. Fortunately for us, they were running low, and they weren't able to link up with their logistics swarm." The one with the mysterious auxiliaries.

"They use *people* as a power source?" Brezan said in revulsion. He had been shown videos of the caskets during the meeting he had called.

"So do we," Cheris said, "only we call them suicide formations."

"It's not the same."

Cheris held her silence just long enough for Brezan to get the point.

"Anyway," Brezan said, unable to meet her eyes, "since this border is otherwise wide-open, it won't kill us to be on patrol. At least until non-crashhawk Kel show up spoiling for a fight."

Khiruev listened while the two crashhawks discussed logistics, and wondered if it was possible for her world to tumble any more upside-down. In fifteen days she would find out.

CHAPTER TWENTY FIVE

# CHAPTER TWENTY-FIVE

ONE OF THE important features of the Citadel of Eyes was also one of its great disadvantages: the pervasive attention to security. It was 03.67 and Shuos Mikodez was seriously considering whether he had any chance of sneaking past his own guards and into one of the restricted sections of Archives. There had always been the rumor that one of the old heptarchs had squirreled away a collection of heretical calendrical erotica. Just how you made abstract algebra erotic was going to have to remain a mystery for the next Shuos hexarch to puzzle over, because Mikodez couldn't figure out a way past that one checkpoint without pissing off an agent whose ability to brew perfect Six Leaves tea was unrivaled. Oh well, the expedition probably only seemed like a good idea because of the hour and, all right, the fact that he'd only had five hours of sleep in the last seventy-five.

Three red lights came on in a triangle. The grid said, "High priority high priority message." Stupid phrasing, but no one could seem to fix the alert, and that was on top of the fact that most of the time it was a false alarm. He wished they were doing this on purpose to keep staff on their toes; no such luck.

Another set of lights came on. "Mikodez, wake up already," said Shuos Zehun's aggravated voice. "Someone sent in a code red nine, burst transmission, in response to a bug we planted on the Deuce of Gears swarm. Mikodez—"

"Open connection," he said. "I'm awake. In fact, you have no idea how awake I am."

"Fuck it, Mikodez, are you up scheming again instead of getting sleep like a sane person? You're not eighteen anymore."

What could be that bad for them to start swearing at him right out of the gate? "Just pipe me the damn message."

"Honestly, Mikodez, I'm going to make Istradez slip you sleeping pills."

Before Mikodez could say anything snide, the message came through. One of the bugs that they had gotten aboard the *Hierarchy of Feasts* during its layover at Tankut Primary had finally borne fruit. The report said that one High General Kel Brezan—that crashhawk who had contacted Zehun not long ago, funny how he got around—had taken over the swarm. This news wouldn't have been worth much in itself. They already knew about the Kel-Andan mission, and it wasn't surprising that the Andan half was lying low.

No: the important part was that the high general had given a briefing warning of a planned calendrical spike with an intended effect of making formation instinct voluntary. The report included some of the relevant mathematics. What was more, the spike was going to be activated by a strike at Kel Command. Mikodez reflected that Brezan was ruining things for honest crashhawks everywhere.

"Zehun, are you still there?" Mikodez said.

The link obligingly updated with video. Even at this hour, Zehun looked fresh and alert in full uniform. "You know perfectly well that the only person in the Citadel who keeps worse hours than you do is me," they said. "And before you ask, so far as I know, that report went directly to me. If someone is capable of intercepting and decrypting it, we're in so much trouble that we need to have another set of emergency meetings anyway."

"We've been had," Mikodez said after he had a chance to scan the report summary. "Ajewen Cheris has the mathematical ability to devise a calendrical spike of that order. Jedao would never have been able to put one together himself, and we'd know if Kujen had been in contact to make him a proposal."

Zehun's expression was pensive. "The hexarchate gave Cheris plenty of opportunities to reconsider her loyalties. We should have ensured that she died with her swarm at the Fortress of Scattered Needles."

"Yes," Mikodez said, "but Kujen insisted on retrieving her, and since he was checking over some critical cryptological results for us at the time, I deemed it unwise to piss him off. There wasn't any way to guess he'd take a vacation for the first time in centuries. Anyway, might-have-beens don't concern me. We have to decide what to do about the situation as it exists."

"We've got the shadowmoths on standby and we've been alerted of the situation," Zehun said. "If we're willing to lose most of that swarm, we can take out the *Hierarchy of Feasts*. As for Kel Command, I've been running a search on the report summaries and I cannot for the life of me figure out how Cheris, if that's who she is, is going to break through centuries of Kel paranoia—"

Shuos calling Kel paranoid. His day was already complete.

"—but if we inform them, they might be able to see what we're missing." Zehun's tone became deprecating. "The irony is that even if the threat gets through, the Kel hexarch will survive."

All the other hexarchs would be journeying to Station Mavi 514-11, where Faian had built her immortality device. Mikodez already planned to send a double. He didn't have any use for immortality, but it would look too suspicious to decline.

"You know," Mikodez said, "that's one option, but it's not the only option."

Zehun went dead quiet. "If that's supposed to be a Shuos joke I haven't heard before," Zehun said at last, "fine, I haven't heard it before. But it's a terrible idea, and maybe you should get some sleep."

"I'm not joking," Mikodez said. "It's true, however, that our window of opportunity is limited. I realize we only have so much information about the planned spike, but I want all our mathematicians on the problem. What will this spike do if it goes off? Formations can't be the whole story. Even Jedao with his Kel fixation wouldn't have made this play based on that alone, and even if Cheris is merely very good at emulating a dead man, we have plenty of evidence that her moves take place on multiple gameboards simultaneously. We need a fuller picture so we can make an informed decision."

"You frighten me on a regular basis," Zehun said in a low voice, "but this is something else."

Mikodez raised an eyebrow. "You could have had me killed when I was eighteen," he said, "and you didn't."

At eighteen, Mikodez had been a second-year Shuos cadet. Ever since Hellspin Fortress, Shuos Academy stopped admitting prospects who shared Jedao's signifier, Ninefox Crowned with Eyes. Never mind that for generations before that, Shuos Crowned with Eyes had managed to lead lives free of high treason and massacre. As for Shuos who developed that signifier later, they were purged.

Mikodez had entered with a Ninefox Smiling. However, during one of the periodic evaluations, it emerged that he had a variable signifier. Uncommon, but not unheard of either, especially among Shuos and Andan. The ability could even be trained in to a certain extent, which was handy for undercover work. Unfortunately, the evaluation had recorded a brief shift to Crowned with Eyes. Zehun, as a senior instructor, had been dispatched with a team of assassins to assess Mikodez.

"I think I'm being adequately punished for my lapse in judgment," Zehun said. They looked at Mikodez unsmilingly. "Forty years of stability in the Shuos. You have no idea what it was like to be Shuos before that; you can't. You're proposing turning the whole hexarchate topsy-turvy. That doesn't bother you even a little?"

"That's only if Cheris fails," Mikodez said. "Have you given the mathematicians their marching orders?"

"It's embarrassing that you're asking," Zehun said. "Of course I have. I'm also giving them whatever the hell they want for breakfast because I'm sure you don't want to rely on cranky mathematicians for urgently important policy results."

"I'm glad I can count on you to have common sense so I don't have to."

Zehun snorted.

"Well, keep an eye on the mathematicians. I hear it's easier to check someone else's work than hash it out from scratch, but it's not my field." He wasn't under any illusions that the introductory calendrical math he'd studied as a cadet qualified him to inspect whatever Cheris was up to. "In the meantime, I am going to review my colleagues' plan to see if there are any last-minute changes I should know about."

"You really should get sleep instead."

Mikodez fixed her with a stare. "Zehun-ye," he said, using the instructor honorific, "we're looking at high treason and a calendrical disruption that could be as bad as the one after Hellspin Fortress, and you think I'm going to be able to fall asleep?"

Zehun sighed. "Fine. Rest when you can, seriously, and I'll keep you apprised of any developments. I'm having breakfast sent up so you don't forget to eat yourself."

"That was eight years ago," he protested, "and I get nagged enough by Istradez as it stands. Can't you let it rest?"

"Shut up and get to work."

Mikodez grinned at Zehun. "If that's not motivational, I don't know what is." He signed off before Zehun could get in a rejoinder. He knew they hated it when he did that, so he saved it for special occasions. You couldn't get much more special than 'oh, and by the way, our government and way of life might be ending in fourteen days.'

Breakfast arrived promptly, borne by an unsmiling guard who refused the persimmon candy on the tray when Mikodez offered it to her. On any other day he would have amused himself by wheedling her to take it, but Zehun would find out and yell at him for harassing the staff. Besides, he liked the candies.

He only ended up eating a third of what was on the tray, mostly because Zehun seemed to think he needed a lot more fuel than was the case. The last time he'd suggested that he could give them a vacation so they could spoil their grandchildren (four of them, a fifth on the way), they had retaliated by scrambling his noncritical custom grid interfaces. Served him right. In the dramas people shied from Shuos assassins and saboteurs, but the ones you had to watch out for were the *bureaucrats*.

While Mikodez ate, he had the grid run some searches. He poured himself more citron tea while going over the results, applying the occasional extra filter, not that those helped much. Nothing new with the Rahal, but he liked to check them first just to get them out of the way, and also just in case they surprised him. Once some Rahal magistrate had tried to bring cooking measures in line with some obscure lemma. That experiment hadn't lasted long.

Shuos next, because the received wisdom—that the Shuos were their own worst enemy—had a lot of basis in truth. Mikodez held off on the ordinary business of approving promotions, demotions, and the occasional assassination; that could wait for later. Interestingly, the commandant of Shuos Academy Tertiary was still waffling over whether to make an attempt on the hexarch's seat. Mikodez wished the man would make up his mind already. It was hard to find good, not to say loyal, commandants. Still, nothing of crushing urgency.

Andan was more interesting. One of his senior analysts thought Shandal Yeng had discovered some of their taps and was feeding them disinformation. Shandal Yeng was also spending a lot of time in elaborate meals with various offspring and the current consort. Mikodez remembered the time years ago he had attended one such dinner with Nirai Kujen. Conversation had centered around museum pieces, and Mikodez had amused himself thinking up heists. Kujen, who could be surprisingly passionate about beautiful architecture but didn't care about the buildings' contents, spent the evening seducing one of Shandal Yeng's sons, Nezhe. As for Kujen's anchor's opinion of the whole affair, who knew. But it hadn't been hard to figure out that Shandal Yeng was cozying up to Kujen on account of immortality. Too bad Mikodez hadn't been able to eavesdrop on the conversation the two of them had late that night. Judging by the way they behaved toward each other ever after, the quarrel must have been spectacular.

As usual with the Andan, there was a lot of activity but none on the level of a code red nine. That brought Mikodez to the next faction, Nirai. The current hexarch didn't worry him. Faian had a disturbing honest streak that was going to doom her, unending life or no. Unfortunately, Nirai Kujen had contrived to vanish so thoroughly that none of Mikodez's agents had been able to sniff out his current location even now, and it was too much to hope that someone had accidentally winged Kujen with a genial gun. Mikodez was paranoid as a job requirement, but he feared few people in the hexarchate. Kujen was one of them. Until he had more information, however, he couldn't do much else. He discarded the idea that Cheris and Kujen had allied with each other, which was one small mercy. Given the personalities involved, he couldn't imagine such an arrangement lasting for long.

Kel and Vidona were business as usual. As far as Mikodez could tell, the Kel were occupied with logistics. The Vidona were having internal problems related to the interpretation of a remembrance that might have been fraudulently declared. They wanted to settle the matter before it came to the attention of Rahal Iruja. Riveting bedtime reading if you were into that sort of thing.

Zehun was right. The rest of the day passed quietly. Mikodez got through the next five days with the aid of drugs. Sleeping pills, to be exact.

The green onion was flourishing, but then, he was very diligent about watering it.

On the evening of the fifth day, Mikodez got a call on Line 6 while he was in the shower. Especially surprising because he was technically supposed to be meditating for a remembrance so he'd thought he'd at least be safe from *that* line. "Do you *mind*?" he said to the grid. "Tell them to hold and I will be there in three minutes."

It took five because that one damn button on his uniform hated him. He needed to go back to old-fashioned stupid fabrics instead of the programmable kind the Kel were so infatuated with.

"All right," Mikodez said when he was minimally presentable, "connect me." Within seconds, the five other hexarchs were glowering at him.

After examining him, Rahal Iruja said, "Mikodez, is your hair dripping?"

He'd known she'd disapprove. She sounded remarkably like one of his fathers, but he knew better than to say that out loud. "Look, Hexarch," he said, "it was either my clothes or the hair dryer. Did you really want me to pick the other one?"

"Is the whole Citadel of Eyes run like this?"

"Hexarch," Mikodez said, "be reasonable. I hire staff as little like me as possible or we'd get nothing done."

"We'll talk later," Iruja said, which made him groan inwardly because she had an excellent memory. "Hexarch Tsoro wanted to announce a change in plans."

"I apologize for the late notice," Kel Tsoro said. Mikodez wasn't the only person who started; no point hiding his reaction. Tsoro had used an archaic version of the first person pronoun, one that was specifically singular, instead of the equally archaic plural that the hivemind had employed for centuries. (The modern form of the high language rarely inflected for number.) From the sardonic curl to her mouth, Tsoro knew the effect she was having. "The deliberations took time and could not be hurried. On behalf of the Kel, I am declining immortality."

Nirai Faian looked like she'd been slapped, but then, she seemed to think immortality could serve some humanitarian purpose, rather than calcifying existing power structures or triggering wars.

"Explain yourself," Iruja said coolly.

"Rahal," Tsoro said, "I may be the will of the Kel, but I am still Kel. The Kel are made to serve. Part of that service is death. I will not order my soldiers to risk their lives when I can endure forever, nor will I stifle the officers below me by making it impossible for them to hope for advancement."

Vidona Psa didn't seem to be able to decide between admiration and incredulity. "Tsoro," he said, "that's all very noble, but few Kel have any chance of becoming generals, let alone hexarch. You may feel this way now, but decades down the line, when death comes knocking—"

"Death," Tsoro said, biting down on the word. "What do you know about death, Vidona? The scars are gone, but I once took a bullet that scarcely missed my heart. I was a junior lieutenant in a battle so small that even I wouldn't remember its name if I hadn't almost died. It was a long time ago, but I remember. I would die before I forget. If I live forever, I will certainly forget."

Iruja looked unmoved by this, and said only, "Do you wish to send someone in your place? A subordinate?"

"I refuse," Tsoro said, "on behalf of the Kel."

No wonder the argument Tsoro had alluded to had taken so long. She would have had to subdue every dissenter in the hivemind. Formation instinct was one thing, but the prospect of immortality would have been one hell of an incentive even for a component of the composite. Still, since she had won, Kel hierarchy and the hivemind's extreme conservatism now worked in her favor.

Of course, if Cheris's assassination plot was real, she would decapitate the Kel. Mikodez could warn Tsoro right now, but he had a little time yet, and he was determined to hear back from his mathematicians if possible. If he decided to foil Cheris, he could always call another meeting, this time with dry hair.

Andan Shandal Yeng spoke for the first time. "It's your pyre, Tsoro," she said, "but we'll honor it."

The scorn in Tsoro's eyes was faint, but not faint enough. "There's no honor," she said. "Only duty."

"Does anyone else have any surprise announcements we need to know about before we send Faian off to recalibrate?" Iruja said. She was eyeing Mikodez. "Why *were* you shirking a remembrance, anyway?"

It had been too much to hope she'd forgotten about that. Too bad he didn't know what excuse Kel Tsoro had given Iruja so he could use it for inspiration. "My older sibling sent me some handmade soap and I had to try it," Mikodez said. "Should I pass some on to you? Unless you're allergic to plum blossoms or something."

"Next time Wolf Hall has a soap shortage, I'll keep that in mind," Iruja said dryly. "Don't let me catch you at this again. All right. Anything else?" Silence. "Then I trust we can return to what we're supposed to be doing."

Vidona Psa was smirking at Mikodez, but that was all. The conference ended.

Line 7 was blinking at him, and if he didn't pick it up, Zehun was going to override. "Put it on," he said. When Zehun's face appeared in the subdisplay, he added, "I take it you were listening in on the whole thing."

"If you didn't want to be spied on," Zehun said unsympathetically, "you should have pursued a nice, quiet life as a hopper mechanic or a pastry chef."

"You only say that because you've never seen me try to use a screwdriver," Mikodez said. "Or a spatula, for that matter. More seriously, what's on your mind? Please tell me someone has extracted something definite from Cheris's damn equations."

Zehun shook their head. "Zhao thinks she's onto something, but the others are giving her long odds as to whether it's the right track." Then they stopped, frowning.

Mikodez's hand was out of sight of the camera and he had already begun entering certain codes, just in case. "Go ahead and say it."

"Forget the mathematicians," Zehun said. Their face was composed. "You keep putting off this discussion, but we have to have it now. Forget sending a double. Don't pull a Tsoro. You should accept immortality."

"I don't understand why you feel so strongly about this," Mikodez said. He felt calm, made of clear brittle lines inside and out. This was his punishment for taking his assistant for granted for so long. First Cheris and now this. He was getting sloppy.

Zehun smiled like a knife. There were faint lines around their mouth, at the corners of their eyes. Mikodez was abruptly reminded of their age. "Mikodez," Zehun said, "remember what I told you earlier. Four decades of stability in the Shuos. Few Shuos hexarchs have accomplished as much."

"I'm not saying that the succession isn't a very large problem," Mikodez said, "but this is not the way. Remember, Heptarch Khiaz lasted a good six decades, and she was responsible for her share of ruinous decisions."

The question was, did Zehun feel strongly enough about this decision that they'd betray him over it? Their support had been critical to his rise to power. Zehun was uniquely positioned to be able to destroy him. After all, they could throw their support to a new candidate; they had to keep a list. It was what he would do.

"If I believe you were a second Khiaz," Zehun said, "I would never have backed you. Give me a little credit. Please reconsider, Mikodez. Without a strong Shuos voice, who is going to counterbalance Andan and Rahal?"

"Zehun-shei," Mikodez said. This time he used not the instructor honorific, but an honorific used sometimes by lovers, although that was one thing they had never been to each other. "Listen. We know of three people who ended up in the black cradle. I have never been able to extract details, but Nirai Esfarel found existence as a ghost so unbearable that he convinced his anchor to kill them both.

"Nirai Kujen, on the other hand—" Mikodez weighed his words. "Kujen thinks being a parasite is so entertaining that he'll hang on until the universe's last atoms unravel. He gave us remembrances, and with them, the mothdrive. He gave us formation instinct. He will show up with more gifts. I am one of the few people in the hexarchate who genuinely likes him, but we cannot afford to accept any more of his gifts.

"And then there's Jedao. I don't know at what point Jedao stopped regarding himself as a person, but once he decided he was a gun, everyone turned into a target." Mikodez smiled grimly. "That's three immortals who should never have ended up that way."

Zehun put their chin in their hands. "The problem with your argument is the black cradle," they said. "I don't care what Kujen likes to say about stabilization effects, prolonged isolation would drive anyone crazy. That won't be a problem with Faian's method. The math seems to check out. Youth eternal, life unending, who wouldn't want it?"

"Should I send you in my stead?" Mikodez said. "I'm serious. It's not a state secret that you're the glue holding this place together. I just give bored assassins a target."

"You're the only one who believes that," Zehun retorted. "And no thanks, I'd rather leave eternity with people like Vidona Psa to those who are psychologically equipped for the job. I hear he's always late on his paperwork."

Mikodez drummed his fingers on his desk, then tapped out a few commands. The commands were simple. The multiple overrides necessary to make them go through, on the other hand, were a pain in the ass. He'd designed them that way.

"Mikodez, what are you—" Zehun's breath caught. "The *fuck*, Mikodez, I taught you never to—"

He had given Zehun access to all the emergency protocols that involved assassinating them. "I think that's all of them," he said flatly, "but it's not impossible that I missed something, and it's guaranteed that some subordinate has something creative in the works just for the hell of it. Please tell me you'd broken into some of them anyway."

"Some of them," Zehun said. "Not all of them. What is wrong with you today? You can't afford to trust anyone completely, least of all me! If you need to order my 'suicide'—"

"Zehun!" Mikodez didn't realize he had slammed his hands down on the desk until the pain hit a moment later. Considering what he kept in that desk, it was a great way to flirt with suicide himself. "You want an eternity of this? Being ruled by a man who's ready to stab anyone who looks at him sideways? Because that's what it would turn into."

"Security intercepted an attempt on you just four hours ago," Zehun said pointedly. "The only reason you didn't get the alert is that we're dealing with a bigger emergency. This *is* the reality we live in."

"And having you killed because we're having a policy dispute? Is that the reality we live in, too?"

"You've always preferred to turn people into resources and not enemies, but not everyone is going to cooperate with that."

Mikodez studied Zehun's face for signs that they were going to give up on him. He was very good at reading people, but Zehun was very good at hiding what they thought—they usually won at jeng-zai—so that was a wash. "Zehun," he said, "the black cradle's isolation is sideways to the point anyway. Thanks to Kujen's narcissistic conviction that the universe can't get by without him, we have the technology to kick death in the teeth. So sure, the unfortunate tendency of the body to give out over time has been dealt with. What I personally find infuriating is that everyone is obsessed with solving the wrong fucking problem. Granted, Kujen is psychotic so I don't expect any better from him, but what good is immortality if nothing has been done to repair the fault lines in the human heart?"

"Mikodez—"

"We're looking at an eternity of Iruja fussing over minutiae while ignoring the substance of the latest crisis," Mikodez said. "An eternity of Shandal Yeng clutching silks to compensate for the fact that she can't buy her children's love. Nirai Faian trying to solve our problems by throwing equations at them. Vidona Psa inventing more excruciating remembrances because the heretics come so close to shutting down the system each time and he thinks brutalizing them will erode their determination. Or me, sticking knives in people because ruling a faction of people almost as paranoid as I am is the only entertainment that keeps my interest. Do you think I don't know how bad my attention span is, even with the medications I take? At least Kel had the sense to opt out. Perhaps blowing up the system would be worse than having everyone be ruled by psychotic immortals, but I sure as hell refuse to become one of them."

"I'm not planning to betray you," Zehun said softly.

He hadn't asked. "I have done many terrible things," he said. "I have always done them because the alternative was worse. If I thought being a paranoid monster would help the situation, I wouldn't think twice about signing on. But I don't, and that's that."

"Fine," Zehun said. "We do it your way. I only hope you're right."

"So do I," Mikodez said.

"I'll check in with the mathematicians."

"All right."

When Zehun signed off, Mikodez began going through his desk and inventorying the cache of weapons in there, wondering when he had started losing count.

# CHAPTER TWENTY-SIX

THE SERVITOR BROUGHT Mikodez breakfast not in one of his offices, but in the Room of Guns. The room had an official designation, which nobody used anymore, not even Zehun, who was normally a stickler for such matters. The last time he'd asked them about it, they'd muttered something about bad luck. Zehun wasn't superstitious about many things, but in this case he supposed they were justified.

In his second decade as hexarch, Mikodez had challenged his infantry division to steal him Jedao's private collection of guns. During his lifetime, Jedao had usually preferred to use his own armaments rather than Kel issue, which the Kel had permitted as a courtesy to the Shuos in spite of the logistical nuisance. Jedao had accumulated guns with the sort of enthusiasm you might expect of a former assassin, even if they stayed locked up most of the time. After all, it would hardly have been practical for him to haul a private arsenal from assignment to assignment.

When Jedao had been arrested after Hellspin, the Kel had confiscated all his possessions and scoured them for clues. Mikodez knew the old sad story. Jedao hadn't done anything objectionable before suddenly going mad. He'd been a model officer. He had liked guns, which was not a crime in his line of work; he had liked alcohol, especially whiskey, a trait shared by many people who were and weren't soldiers; he had had a genuine passion for dueling. Mikodez had it on good authority that Jedao's whiskey had all been wasted on lab technicians. He could only hope that they had drunk some of the stuff rather than putting it all through tests. And there had been a modest collection of board and card games, including some plundered specimens nice enough to show off in a museum.

In any case, Mikodez had had especial trouble getting the then-Kel hexarch to take him seriously. (Tsoro would not ascend for another eight years.) Instead of brooding over the lack of respect from someone who was over 130 years old, Mikodez had decided to do something to get Kel Vaura to reevaluate him. That wasn't the only reason. He needed his own people to take him seriously as well. The assignment, widely regarded as impossible, focused Special Operations nicely once they realized Mikodez was perfectly willing to turn the division upside-down if they failed him.

("And here I thought you wanted to make friends," Zehun had remarked.)

("Sometimes fear is more motivational," Mikodez had snapped back. "Do you want me to demonstrate?" He'd had more of a temper then. The medications that improved his concentration had helped with that.)

Most of the Citadel of Eyes was not, ironically, decorated in Shuos colors, on the grounds that even if the association with assassins didn't make people tense, the color red by itself would have. Mikodez had always been amused by how many dramas depicted assassins wearing red, as if they were *trying* to stick out, instead of bundling up in ugly unremarkable coats to blend in with the locals. When he wasn't in uniform, Mikodez himself preferred sedate shades of green.

The Room of Guns, however, was in livid red with gold accents. Nothing else would have suited. The red walls with their deeper red tapestries reflected in the guns' barrels, giving them an unhealthy luster.

Mikodez paced around the room and stopped before the one he liked best, the centerpiece of the collection: the Patterner 52, which had been Jedao's favorite. Certainly he had toted it everywhere, and he had used it to slaughter his staff on his command moth at Hellspin. Mikodez had no intention of taking it out of its case to play with it, he knew better, but he studied the grip, engraved with the infamous Deuce of Gears.

The grid chimed at him. "You are so morbid," Istradez said from the door. He walked over to join Mikodez and frowned at the Patterner 52. "You should send that thing to Jedao as a gift, see if that makes him more receptive to your attempts at long-distance therapy. Face it, it's not like one lousy handgun makes Jedao *more* deadly."

"Well," Mikodez said, "there's the psychological factor. Besides, the collection's worth more if I keep it together."

Istradez snorted. "Like you're planning to sell it."

"Are you kidding? We're always broke around here." One of the things that irritated him about the Andan, if his financial spies' reports were to be believed, was that they could *afford things*. Despite a largely successful career as hexarch, he was forever juggling the budget.

"I'm surprised you don't have me sit in on Financial for you more often."

"Don't tempt me," Mikodez said. "It's too important to hand off."

Istradez smiled crookedly at him. "Of course it is." He yawned hugely and stretched first one way, then the other. "I have to admit, it's a nice collection, even if I only recognize half these things. Too bad hardly anyone has the clearance to come in here to appreciate it."

"I was hoping you'd see something here that I don't," Mikodez said.

"What, reading oracles out of a bunch of rifles and revolvers like they're tea leaves? I don't think so. Besides," and Istradez rested his hand casually on the side of the Patterner's case, causing an informational display to come up, "I have spent the last few decades learning to think like you do. It's surprisingly hard to unlearn."

Mikodez saw the subtle tension in Istradez's shoulders. Quietly but not silently, he slipped behind his brother and began rubbing his shoulders. Istradez sighed and relaxed, by slow degrees, under Mikodez's touch.

"I hope you're not going to give me one of those obnoxious memory tests after we leave this room for dinner," Istradez murmured. Mikodez could feel the vibrations through his hands. "But I promise I've been doing my homework. I'm here to ask a favor."

"More girlfriends?" Mikodez said. The Citadel was well staffed with courtesans with varying specialties. Between assignments, Istradez always took the opportunity to indulge. If he did so while being Mikodez, someone would have noticed the discrepancy. "If you're getting jaded, I'm running out of—"

"Not that." With perfect dignity, Istradez slid out from beneath Mikodez's hands, made sure they were facing each other, then sank to his knees, head bowed. "Hexarch."

The full obeisance to a hexarch looked so incongruous that Mikodez drew his breath in sharply. "Istra—"

Istradez didn't raise his eyes. "I wish to beg to be considered for an assignment. I'm not a Shuos, but I understand that there's some precedent for the use of outside agents."

Mikodez had a bad feeling about where this was going. "Get up," he said, more roughly than he had intended. "There's no need for you to do that to your knees."

"It's kind of you to be concerned about the condition of my knees," Istradez said, so straight-faced that Mikodez couldn't tell if his brother was mocking him. "I mean it, though. I realize you're holding me in reserve, Hexarch, but I believe I am uniquely qualified for this assignment."

"And what assignment might that be?" It was cruel to make Istradez say it to his face. Nevertheless, he had to be sure.

Mikodez had half-expected Istradez's composure to break, for that mirror-face to relax into the familiar wry grin. But no: Istradez's eyelashes lowered, and his hand clenched slightly on his right knee. "I have heard that an assassination attempt on the hexarchs is in the works."

"You're not authorized for that information," Mikodez said after a frozen second.

"I seduced someone on your staff," Istradez said. "Occasionally there are people who would like to sleep with someone who looks as good as we do. I don't think they even realized what they'd let slip."

'Someone' could mean more than one someone. He'd have to deal with that later. "That's very interesting," Mikodez said, meaning it, "but the answer is no."

"Hexarch," Istradez said, in the most formal mode possible, "I understand that it's a suicide mission."

"You've heard my answer."

Istradez drew a shuddering breath. "I recognize that my usefulness to you is nearing its end," he said. "I beg for one last—"

"*No*, Istradez."

"I got into the evaluation you had Spirel do," Istradez said, with remarkably little bitterness. "You're going to remove me from duty anyway, and then what will I do? Kick around here for the rest of my life? I don't think so. Let me go, Miki."

Mikodez knelt and gripped Istradez's shoulders. "You do understand that 'suicide mission' means you don't come back? Ever?"

"What were you going to do, send one of the others? I'm the best one for the job and you know it. Please, Miki."

The sincerity blazing out of the familiar eyes shook him.

"I'm your gun, Miki."

That forced a response out of him. "Don't," Mikodez whispered. "Please don't. You're no Kel."

"I'm better than a Kel," Istradez said. "Promise me you'll think about it."

"I'll think about it," Mikodez said at last. But they already knew what he had decided.

WHEN MIKODEZ FINISHED reading the report his mathematicians had coughed up, he watered his green onion three hours early. Considering what the rest of his day was liable to be like, he didn't want to forget.

Something about Cheris's contact with Jedao had given her the notion to seek a calendar that altered exotic effects so they could only affect the willing. Kel discipline might hold anyway, but the Andan would hate losing enthrallment as a crutch, even though most Andan with any sense knew it was the threat, not the execution, that was their most powerful tool. The Shuos were in the dubiously enviable position of being the only faction that didn't have a standardized exotic ability; nothing would change for them.

Next Mikodez called Kel Command, emphasizing that he wanted to be connected directly to Tsoro. The wait was longer than usual. Maybe she was being conscientious and using her hair dryer. At last she accepted the call. "Shuos," she said, deferentially, but without liking. "We understand the matter is urgent?"

"I have a personal warning to convey to you," Mikodez said, and sent over a databurst. "My analysts believe the Hafn intend a deep strike on the Aerie. You can read the details at your leisure and prepare yourself accordingly."

The Shuos's Citadel of Eyes was defended by a variable number of shadowmoths, to say nothing of the weapons installations, but its location was a matter of public record. On the other hand, the Aerie's security depended partly on secrecy. The Kel were spread thin enough that they didn't maintain a large force for home defense.

"We need to know how reliable your information is," Tsoro said. Mikodez slitted his eyes at her. "If I were having a slow day and felt like fucking with people's heads for the hell of it, I'd off a few more Shuos children. After all, there's a large supply of them. No; this information is accurate. The Hafn have already used that unnerving jumping-across-space ability once on the Deuce of Gears. If it doesn't surprise me that they'd want to use it on the Aerie, it shouldn't surprise you."

He hadn't personally forged that compilation. One of his teams had done the work, but the packet should stand up to the hivemind's scrutiny. While Tsoro didn't like him, she believed in his fundamental competence. "Tell me you have a defense swarm hanging around there," he added.

"Does it matter if we do?" Tsoro asked darkly. "We can't afford for the Aerie to fall. Your warning is appreciated."

"Splendid," Mikodez said with the particular breeziness that he knew irritated her, because she would expect it. "In that case, I'll leave you to your tedious logistical calculations." He signed off.

The problem with Cheris's plan was that it inconveniently involved blowing up Kel Command before Mikodez could, if everyone stuck to the original schedule, stab the other hexarchs in the back. First item: if marking a calendrical reset by getting rid of Kel Command was good, annihilating the other hexarchs at the same time would be even better. Second item: it would be easiest to assassinate the hexarchs if they gathered at a single location. Happily, Nirai Faian's facility would do the trick. Third item: convincing four hexarchs to change their schedules to match Cheris's was going to be a lot harder than persuading Cheris to hold off until the pieces were in place. Fourth item: calling her up and telling her what he intended wouldn't work, even if the idea had a certain appealing simplicity. He had no evidence that she was gullible around Shuos, even if she'd dated a few, and having Jedao rattling around her skull wouldn't help. So he needed a way to influence her without her realizing it.

Fifth item: nobody had figured out how the hell Cheris intended to destroy the Aerie. It would have been nice if the bugs on the *Hierarchy of Feasts* had been able to shed any light on this matter, but no such luck. At this point, Mikodez was gambling that Cheris wasn't crazy, that this wasn't a bluff, and that some method existed The crashhawk high general's faith in her was only circumstantial evidence, but better than nothing.

Sixth item: to do what she was doing, Cheris had to have some kind of intelligence network. It looked like she'd contacted Colonel Ragath at one point, but they hadn't been able to piece together specifics. Mikodez's other gamble was that Cheris's sources would alert her about Kel swarm movements and cause her to revise her timetable. At least, he trusted she wouldn't risk her swarm against the Aerie and multiple defense swarms if she could afford to wait things out.

*And people think I'm untrustworthy and dangerous on account of two cadets,* Mikodez thought cynically. But that was it: he made it a point not to get attached to any specific way of doing things. If he saw a better solution and it made sense to switch over, he was only too happy to do so.

The grid was informing Mikodez that the number of people who urgently wanted to talk to him was piling up. He fished in his second drawer until he retrieved the russet leaf-pattern lace scarf he had left off knitting two months ago. Perfect. The only thing people hated seeing more than a Shuos with a gun was a Shuos with knitting needles. As if any sane assassin would take you out with knitting needles if they could do it instead from a nice sheltered balcony with a high-powered rifle.

"All right," he said, "let's hear the first one."

CHERIS AND BREZAN were in Cheris's lounge, rotating a map of the hexarchate this way and that. Khiruev tried to concentrate on the glowing notations, the swarms with their generals' emblems, but she could only manage it in start-stop snatches. Neither Cheris nor Brezan wanted her here because she had anything to contribute to matters of strategy or logistics. Rather, the high general was afraid she would topple over dead if left unattended.

"That's six full swarms," Cheris was saying. "They must be dreadfully worried."

Khiruev marked the swarms' trajectories converging on a point in a stretch of space she had thought unremarkable, except Cheris insisted it was the Aerie's location and the high general believed her. Of the six emblems, the one Khiruev kept returning to was General Inesser's Three Kestrels Three Suns.

Cheris and Brezan weren't the only ones having a discussion. There were four servitors: three deltaforms and a birdform. The deltaforms kept flashing rapid lights at each other. The fact that the lights were in the human visible spectrum was almost certainly a matter of courtesy. Khiruev had learned that servitors cared a great deal about courtesy, and had endeavored to revise her behavior accordingly, since the high general hadn't forbidden it. The birdform either approved of this or had decided that dying generals made a good hobby. Whichever was the case, it hovered companionably by Khiruev, periodically refilling her teacup from the kettle that Cheris and Brezan were ignoring.

"If I'm understanding this correctly," Brezan said, "the servitors prefer not to take action with so many observers around who might figure out they were responsible?"

Khiruev wondered if Brezan had realized that he tended to direct his speech toward empty expanses of wall whenever he mentioned the servitors, or even when he was supposedly addressing them.

Two of the deltaforms, whom Khiruev had tagged Two and Three because she was tired, exchanged a heated flurry of lights and dissonant chords. Then Three said something in very red lights to Cheris.

Cheris frowned, then said, "That's basically it. They've already evacuated as many servitors as they could, but even so—"

Brezan bit his lip. "Cheris," he said, "if there are servitors on those defense swarms as well—" He stopped.

"You may as well come out and say it," she said.

"If they can reduce Kel Command to radioactive static, then surely a bunch of moths—"

Cheris's hands tensed, untensed. "Brezan," she said, "that's a lot of moths. Crew on the order of 300,000 altogether. Even if we had definite information that all six generals were irredeemably corrupt, which we don't, I'd rather kill as few people as we can get away with. Besides which, those aren't small swarms, and the hexarchate's enemies haven't gone away. Do you really want to do away with that chunk of the hexarchate's forces? Its senior generals?"

"That's an interesting argument from someone who's dead-set on tearing the realm apart," Brezan said.

"I'm not entirely Jedao," Cheris said, although Khiruev wondered sometimes. "The point of the exercise isn't to maximize the death toll. It's to change the system so ordinary people have a chance. People will die, yes. A lot of them. But we don't have to go out of our way to kill even more."

"I want to know how you came to this philosophy after having a mass murderer stuffed up your nose," Brezan said.

"I'm trying to fix the things he broke," Cheris said, "because I remember breaking them."

Brezan slumped. "So we wait? You're not tempted to sweep in and rescue Kel Command from the Hafn?"

Khiruev roused enough to say, "Sir, not only would they not thank us, General Inesser should be more than adequate to the task anyway."

"By 'not thank us' you mean they'd blow themselves up just to get rid of us," Cheris said wryly. "Don't they teach us to avoid full frontal assaults anyway?"

Brezan groaned, clearly thinking of any one of four hundred Kel jokes. "Fine," he said. "We wait for a better opportunity. But what if one doesn't come?"

"Then we reassess the plan," Cheris said. "What concerns me is that we haven't been able to figure out the Hafn vector of approach. The coverage of the detectors and listening posts is hardly universal, so we're going to have to wait and see."

Brezan and Cheris turned their attention to a bannermoth that was having engine problems. Khiruev was disturbed, although not surprised, that she had difficulty following the details. The gnawing cold made it hard to concentrate. The birdform chirped at her, possibly thinking that tea, even if it wasn't a sovereign remedy, would at least warm her. She smiled wanly at it and took a sip.

"I don't claim to understand you," Khiruev said to the birdform, "but considering the length of your service, I hope there's something in this for you. And I'm sorry I've never learned your language."

The birdform tapped encouragingly on the nearest wall. Cheris looked up briefly, then returned to running through drive harmonic diagnostics with Brezan. The birdform repeated the tapping, and Khiruev realized it was in the Kel drum code: *You don't have to die.*

Khiruev blinked.

*You can choose not to die.*

She couldn't remember why she had invoked Vrae Tala, except when she could. Her father crumpling into corpse-paper, the clanking bells, her mothers clutching each other afterward while she stood frozen trying not to see what was right in front of her. The cutting disappointment every time she survived a battle. She'd learned to hide it, but it never evaporated entirely.

"I am Kel," Khiruev said painfully. "Even assuming all of this works, in order to free myself of Vrae Tala I would have to free myself of formation instinct. The clause is part of the whole."

The birdform mulled this over. More tapping: *My people have served without formation instinct. Is our service not service?*

"It's not for me to make that judgment," Khiruev said.

*Would your general deny you this?*

*You chose Vrae Tala,* Brezan had said to her just days ago, trying to explain something as distant as smoke. Would the high general want her to give up what made her Kel?

It was barely possible that you could be Kel without formation instinct. Hard not to notice that Brezan was a crashhawk, after all. But this led inevitably to the question of whether it was desirable to be Kel in the first place.

"I will learn to choose," Khiruev said, "if the high general desires it of me."

The servitor's chirr might have been a sigh. It gestured toward the tea with one of its gripping limbs. Obligingly, Khiruev took another sip. The warmth wouldn't last long, but it didn't have to

SIX KEL SWARMS reached the Aerie and waited to banner.

Cheris and Brezan started arguing about what was going to become of the Kel afterward, especially once Cheris pointed out that a successful decapitation strike would leave Brezan the senior Kel officer.

"I'll resign," Brezan said.

"That will leave the Kel leaderless," Cheris said. "Is that what you want to do?"

"I hate it when you open your mouth," Brezan said. "The things you say never make the situation better."

Khiruev took to playing card games with the servitors, on the grounds that no one expected her to function anymore. The servitors usually won. She appreciated that they didn't throw the games to make her feel better.

Shuos Mikodez finished knitting his scarf. The first two people he offered it to were unable to hide their suspicion that it would come alive and strangle them. With modern fibers it was hard to tell.

Three hexarchs, Rahal, Andan, and Vidona, set out for Nirai Station Mavi 514-11. Nirai Faian was already there.

Thirty-eight days after Mikodez alerted Kel Tsoro of an imminent Hafn raid, Kel listening posts near four large moth construction yards reported Hafn moth formants incoming. Three of those construction yards exploded shortly afterward. Kel Command concluded that the construction yards had been the real targets, as two of them had been the only ones capable of building cindermoths. It dispatched four of its defense swarms to repulse the invaders. Disconcertingly, the listening posts lost sight of the formants.

Cheris and Brezan, upon receiving word of further Kel movements, held an emergency meeting and determined that this would be their best opportunity to strike. Khiruev was not present for the discussion. She had collapsed two days earlier, seventy-nine days after she invoked Vrae Tala, and had been removed to Medical.

VAUHAN ISTRADEZ REFLECTED that, on any other day, he could entertain himself by swinging by one of the Shuos academies and terrifying the everliving fuck out of innocent little cadets. Lucky for them that he didn't share his second older brother's predilection for stupid pranks, even if he was serving as his brother's double. Besides, he had a more important job to do. Mikodez's physical mannerisms weren't the hard part. It was the fact that the man was a ferret. To say nothing of the endless hobbies. Istradez was hoping no one was going to force him to knit because he had a positive talent for dropping stitches.

Istradez was aboard the shadowmoth *Eyes Unstabbed*, typical cheery Shuos name. While there had been no way to conceal the

YOON HA LEE

destination from the crew, none of them knew his identity. The ruse wouldn't stand up to serious scrutiny, but the odds were low that the commander would demand authentication, and as for the hexarchs, well, they wouldn't have a chance to think about it. At least Mikodez's notorious eccentricity would work in his favor if he did slip up.

At the moment he was in the bedroom with a tray, sticking toothpicks into honey cookies because it beat having to eat the damn things. He was considering throwing them out, even if it would be out of character, when the grid informed him that they were bound to contact Station Mavi 514-11 any moment now. He supposed he should put his shoes back on instead of padding around in his socks, even if no one could see them.

Sure enough, Istradez got a call from the moth commander. "Yes?" he said as he surreptitiously wriggled his left foot into the second shoe.

"Hexarch," the commander said, "you asked to be informed when we made our approach to the station. Protocol requires us to unstealth and inform them of our arrival at the checkpoint radius." She said that last with no particular emphasis. What she wanted to know was if they were here on an ordinary visit or if they were up to fox tricks.

"Do tell me," he said lazily, "what do we see on scan?"

She forwarded him the readings, which weren't much help. As a rule, it was hard to see much from inactive or minimally active mothdrives. They'd have to do this the hard way, then.

"All right," Istradez said after stabbing the nearest honey cookie with another toothpick, "unstealth and I'll put in a call, let them know we're here. Would you like me to send you a cookie?" Anything to be rid of them.

"That's very considerate of you," the commander said tactfully, "but if those are what I think they are, I'll never get the pine nuts out of my teeth."

*You and me both,* Istradez thought sourly. "Your loss," he said.

A brief pause, then: "Moth is no longer stealthed. We're holding position so we don't make them jumpy."

A Shuos, make someone nervous? Never. Istradez called the station, asking to be connected to Hexarch Faian. She responded very promptly. "How late am I?" Istradez asked without any contrition. He had wanted to be late—preferably the last to arrive—although she didn't need to know that. He was already entering a sequence of commands. Even if he missed the others, taking out Faian would be worth something.

"You're the last one here, Mikodez," Faian said, brows drawing low.

Splendid. He smiled his brother's smile at her, even though Mikodez had said that wouldn't work. "Well, I shan't delay us any longer. See you soon?"

"I look forward to it," Faian said, polite by rote.

Istradez entered the final override.

People sometimes got the idea that hexarchate space was so densely littered with shadowmoths that you couldn't pick your nose without one catching you at it. The truth was that space was big and the damn things were too expensive for the Shuos to use so liberally. You had to power down the stealth system to do anything useful with exotic weapons, including the devastating but slow-recharge knife cannon. To add insult to injury, once you powered it down, stealth took ages to come back up. All of which was a long way of saying that the *Eyes Unstabbed* would get in the necessary first strike, but no one would make it out alive.

Istradez did feel bad for the shadowmoth's crew, who hadn't signed on for a suicide mission. However, even he could see the problems with telling them why they were really here. Besides, he was no Kel, but he had volunteered for this. That had to suffice.

*While I'm at it, what good will this maneuver do?* he had asked after Mikodez agreed. Out of the corner of his eye he could see Jedao's notorious Patterner 52 in its glass case, but he didn't dare move his head to gawk at it.

*The Shuos will come out three moves ahead,* Mikodez said. He had returned to his customary terrifying amusement. *Are you telling me you insisted on the assignment without thinking it through?*

*I still want to do it,* Istradez said. *But I want something from you.*

Mikodez looked at him unsmilingly. *It has to be something I can give.*

*An honest answer,* Istradez said. *This time for real, not because you're giving me therapy. Is there anything you care about anymore, are you even human, or is it all games and pranks and stratagems? Not something anyone can use against you. I just—I just need to know.*

Istradez's blood chilled when Mikodez stood up, because he didn't know if this was going to turn into some contest of poison needles or garrotes or guns, and he wasn't under any illusions that the self-defense training he'd received would help him. But all Mikodez did was sink to his knees in front of him and reach for his hands. Istradez's breath stopped in his throat when his brother kissed his palms fiercely.

*I do my job,* Mikodez said. *It's like I told you before. I'll even send my fucking brother to die if it's the best way to do the job*—His voice cracked, settled. *But don't ever, ever think it's because I stopped loving you. I don't want you to go. It's not too late—*

*It was too late a long time ago,* Istradez said.

The *Eyes Unstabbed* slowed toward the Nirai station with its rings and lace of sensor arrays, engines, great whirring mechanisms with hearts that were wheels within wheels. Its commander discovered that the crew had been locked out of the controls and attempted to call Istradez on the emergency backup channel. Istradez, naturally, wasn't responding.

A few minutes before they would have docked at the station, the *Eyes Unstabbed* fired its knife cannon, scything the station nearly in two, including the central power core. Moments after that, the self-destruct sequence on the shadowmoth triggered, no safeguards, no countdown, nothing.

In his last seconds, Istradez thought that this was overkill, but it was nice to remind the hexarchate that melodrama wasn't a trait reserved to the Kel. He was looking distractedly at his palms when the world dissolved in a rush of heat and static.

\* \* \*

WHEN THE TIME came to reset the hexarchate's clocks, forty-eight servitors remained in the Aerie. The Kel hivemind didn't make a habit of noticing servitors, but they had to give the illusion that some of the complement remained. Not to mention someone had to stay behind to make sure the attack went off as planned.

Servitor sin $x^2$, one of the forty-eight, had not stayed behind on account of the sabotage. It had no particular expertise in engineering or demolitions and, in fact, ordinarily served in Medical. The other servitors had urged it to evacuate while it had the chance. The Aerie was not immune to the need for supplies. Servitors had been going out in crates, canisters, any available crevice in the moths' dark holds.

sin $x^2$ had said, *They're our Kel. Someone should be with them at the end, even if they never know or understand.* Then the others, realizing it would not be dissuaded, left it alone.

sin $x^2$ wasn't under any illusions that the hive Kel cared about it except as an instrument for necessary chores, and sometimes unnecessary ones. It knew that the hivemind became less and less sane with each passing year. Nevertheless, it considered itself Kel. Someone from its enclave should honor Kel Command's passing.

At present, sin $x^2$ was polishing a collection of musical instruments, one of the oddball duties it had taken up because no one else wanted it. High General Aurel had brought some of the instruments with her. In the early years she had come here to practice from time to time. The last time she had come in here had been thirty-one years ago. She had played snatches of a concerto. sin $x^2$ paid special attention to the viols, because they had been her favorites.

Servitor tanh $x$ sent the six-minute warning over the maintenance channel.

sin $x^2$ knew High General Aurel was part of Subcommand Composite Eight right now. It whisked quickly through the corridors so it could reach her. The doors were open, as always. It floated in to where Aurel sat on a minimalist metalglass chair. Her posture was beautiful, and her hands still had some of their strength, but the pale brown eyes saw nothing in the room except, perhaps, the limitations of light and shadow.

One minute and eight seconds later, the Aerie roared into an effusion of fire, of heady vapors, of numbers rolling backwards to the new calendar's pitiless zero hour.

# CHAPTER TWENTY-SEVEN

IMPRESSIVELY, ZEHUN GOT past the door to Mikodez's primary office without getting themselves killed. Mikodez looked up, at first not recognizing the slim figure, the somber eyes, the long red coat. With their hair pulled back from their face, Zehun almost looked as they had when he had first met them, a quiet person with unquiet ideas about how the Shuos should be run. "Go away," Mikodez said. His voice sounded as though someone had run over it with a rake.

Zehun's eyes narrowed and they stepped in. The door closed behind them. "You should have said no to Istradez," Zehun said.

"First," Mikodez said, "it didn't concern you." Patently untrue: everything he did concerned his assistant. "Second, once Istradez offered to go, I had to accept. What was I going to do for the rest of my life, coddle him while I sent other agents to die? Imagine what that would do to morale. That's bad management."

"Your *brother*, Mikodez." Zehun started to say something, changed their mind. "You're allowed to have personal attachments. As a rule, the ones who don't have any are the ones the rest of us have to assassinate for everybody's good."

"I gave up the right to sentimentality when I took the seat," Mikodez said. "The Shuos are my family now. And please don't tell me it was a poor trade, or a good trade, or anything. I can't bear it right now."

"That's not why I'm here anyway," Zehun said, although Mikodez knew better than to assume they wouldn't bring it up later. "You haven't been responding to my calls."

"What could be so urgent?" Mikodez said sarcastically.

Zehun leaned over his terminal and ran a query. "This one you need to hear," they said. A summary came up, explaining that a message had been transmitted in the clear and in all directions, from a thousand thousand sources, a storm of light. Cheris had sent her calendar and equations, plus a manifesto explaining their purpose. The Rahal were going berserk trying to suppress the information and handle calendrical fluctuations, but it was too late.

"Yes," Mikodez said, admiring the uselessness of the map showing the scintillating profusion of transmission sources: too many for the human eye to pick out a pattern, and grid analysis wasn't doing much better. "It was an obvious move. Sometimes the obvious one is the right one. I just hadn't expected it to be so thoroughly implemented."

"You made your choice, Mikodez," Zehun said. "The world doesn't stop moving forward. We have a crisis to deal with. Maybe after things settle down, we can hole up with some board games and get roaringly drunk, but in the meantime, you have a job to do."

"Yes," he said, "and you've done yours. Now get out, and fetch that Mwennin girl for me while you're at it. I won't be able to concentrate with you hovering over me."

"What's hilarious is that you think *this* is hovering," Zehun said, with the superior knowledge of someone who has raised five children speaking to a non-parent, but they went.

Mikodez resisted the urge to procrastinate by watering his green onion some more. He'd only rot its roots that way. "Call request to Shuos Jedao on the *Hierarchy of Feasts*," he said. Maybe this time he'd get through. He wondered what emblem that swarm was bannering these days. Deuce of Gears still? Swanknot? The boring temporary emblem for brand-new generals? Some crashhawk confection?

He had time for a quince candy while waiting. The stash in his desk was running low. He'd have to wheedle his staff into resupplying him. For some reason they thought he should restrict his sugar intake.

The Deuce of Gears flashed at him, and Mikodez's mouth curled. So this was how she wanted it. The emblem was replaced by Cheris's quizzical face when she accepted the call. "Shuos-zho," she said, "is this the best time? Either you have a raging crisis or I do, I'm not sure which."

"Hello, Cheris," Mikodez said, impressed that her expression didn't flicker. "I assure you that you want to be talking to me right now."

"In that case, Shuos-zho," she said, "we're both dead people miraculously able to communicate with each other. I had it on good authority that you and the other hexarchs were all assassinated at some meeting. Must have been one hell of a party to get you all in the same place. Was there any good whiskey?"

Mikodez was pretty sure Cheris didn't share Jedao's fascination with liquor. "I ordered the strike," he said, very calmly.

"Nirai-zho believed she spoke to you on the way in, before the 'malfunction.' How do you sabotage a shadowmoth, anyway?"

What the hell were Cheris's sources? This was making his entire intelligence division look bad.

"Was it a double?" she said. Her smile turned knowing. "I remember you like using those, especially after you threw that Khiaz double in my direction. Because I needed *more* reasons to stay away from a Shuos hexarch."

"Cheris," he said, "it's over. You've won. And if you must know, the double that carried out the suicide strike was my younger brother." Fuck, he didn't know why he was confessing that to this woman of all people, when he hadn't wanted to discuss it with his own assistant. But he knew after all, the way he always did, even when he didn't want to. He needed Cheris to start trusting him. That would only become possible if she believed him capable of vulnerability. A terrible way to use Istradez's sacrifice, not that that was stopping him.

Something shifted in her eyes: an intimation of shadow, a nuance of color. "I didn't realize," she said. "I'm very sorry." She waited for him to make some acknowledgment, and when he didn't, went on,

"Why would you betray the other hexarchs?"

"Two reasons," Mikodez said. "First, once I found out about your plan, I realized you had the winning hand. Second, I wish to offer you an alliance with the Shuos." His smile was hard. "Consider the deaths of my colleagues a gift to you, as a gesture of my sincerity."

"So you were the one yanking Kel Command's defenses around. To get the timetables to match up."

"Yes."

"Then it wasn't Hafn who took out those construction yards." Cheris's voice had a bite to it, and if he wondered if the outrage was hers or Jedao's. For a traitor, Jedao had always been a judgmental prick.

"That's correct," Mikodez said. "My saboteurs did the job. Don't think I wouldn't do it again, despite the death toll. People are already dying in this revolution of yours. Most of our systems would be under martial law if we weren't, you know, always under martial law. They're under *extra-special* Vidona watch now. It's always been a question of acceptable casualties."

"The price of a Shuos's assistance is a Shuos's assistance, isn't that what they say?" Cheris remarked.

Mikodez inclined his head.

"I expect the only thing I'd regret more than saying yes is saying no."

"That was the idea," Mikodez said modestly. "Running around as Jedao was an extremely well-chosen distraction, by the way. I congratulate you. But that trick only works once."

"It only needed to work once," she said.

Mikodez acknowledged the hit with a wave of his hand. "One moment. I have another gift to offer you, although it's not a very good one." Where was Zehun? He paged them but got no response. "If I can keep you on the line a few more moments, anyway. Who are you planning on blowing up next?"

"If I tried to shoot every monster in the hexarchate," Cheris said, "I'd be a monster myself."

Mikodez put his chin in his hands and smiled. "If you understand that," he said, "then you're far ahead of Jedao, and this alliance has a fighting chance.—Ah, here we go."

Zehun had returned with a teenage girl in tow. The girl had ivory-sallow skin and hair done up with enamel clasps. Her clothes, despite the striking color coordination in greens and yellows, were notable for their concession to useless practicality. Mikodez wondered just where the girl thought she needed to run off to in those sensible slacks and even more sensible boots. The Citadel of Eyes was a space station. You couldn't run far.

"Cheris," Mikodez said, "this is Moroish Nija. I don't believe you two are acquainted"—Cheris was already shaking her head—"but she is one of approximately 5,000 Mwennin we were able to evacuate. That's a pitifully small number, and I am not optimistic that your community will recover from its dispersal, but it was the most I could do without exposing Shuos involvement to the other factions."

"Wait," Nija said. She wasn't looking at Mikodez, but at Cheris's face. "This is her? Ajewen Cheris?"

"Yes, I'm Cheris," Cheris said.

Nija began speaking harshly and rapidly in a language that the grid identified as Mwen-dal. Mikodez eyed the machine translation it was providing on a subdisplay, which for all its awkwardness suggested that Nija had an impressive command of Mwen-dal obscenities.

When Nija wound down, Cheris said something haltingly in Mwen-dal, then, in the high language, "I have no excuse to offer."

"As I told you," Mikodez said, "it's a very poor gift."

"Were you planning all this even then?" Cheris said.

"No. I just like keeping my options open. And I happen to think genocide is a rotten policy anyway. Nothing personal."

"Just what are you doing with one of my people in your keeping, anyway?"

Nija spoke to Cheris before Mikodez could, to his amusement. "He offered me a *job*," she said. "Which I accepted because your shitty life choices left me so many options."

Cheris looked uncomfortable. "You're *recruiting*, Shuos-zho?"

"In a few cases, where warranted," Mikodez said mildly. "I mean, the Mwennin produced *you*. Maybe I'll get lucky."

Nija was singularly unimpressed with this line of thinking. "You mean you don't have enough former shoplifters working for you and you're desperate."

Behind the girl's back, Zehun signed, *We've located the only child in the hexarchate who isn't afraid of you.*

Mikodez signed back, *Let me know if you find any more of her.*

Cheris's mouth tightened, then: "I saw the broadcast of my parents' executions."

Amazingly, Nija kept quiet.

"I considered intervening," Mikodez said. He could offer little comfort, although the evidence suggested that she wouldn't hold it against him. Right now, he almost wished she would. "Because of who they were, Vidona security was too high. I chose not to risk it."

"I appreciate your forthrightness," Cheris said. "But what do I have to offer you? All I have is the tenuous control of one swarm, and you undoubtedly have your own mathematicians."

None of her caliber, but she didn't need to know that if she hadn't guessed it already. "Zehun," Mikodez said, "please escort Nija to lunch or gardening or handgun lessons, whatever you two find agreeable. Nija, thank you for indulging me. I'll talk to you later."

Zehun led the girl out. Nija appeared to think she should be back in school, and did the Citadel of Eyes offer a normal curriculum alongside all the Shuos refresher courses with 'deception' and 'murder' in their titles? Zehun had that 'I thought I was done raising teenagers' expression.

"I want in on your social experiment," Mikodez said to Cheris. "But there's one thing I believe only you can offer me. I'm hoping you'll indulge me, as I'm certain it will benefit you as much as it will benefit me."

"Now you're making me worry," Cheris said.

"You know more about Jedao than anyone alive," Mikodez said. "What the hell was it that drove him over the edge?"

"Ah," she said, very softly. "That."

"His academy evaluations said he was a perfect Shuos. If that's perfection, I don't want any more of it. We've been trying to keep from producing more Jedaos ever since. I was almost purged myself as a cadet for manifesting Ninefox Crowned with Eyes. But the endeavor is doomed if we don't know what the fucking trigger was."

For a moment, Mikodez saw Jedao looking at him out of Cheris's eyes, locked forever in the darkness. Then Cheris said, with Jedao's accent, "The hexarchate was the trigger, Shuos-zho. All of it. The whole rotted system. He was never mad, or anyway, not mad the way people thought he was. I'll put together a more detailed account for you. I don't think it will do anyone any harm, and perhaps it may even, as you suggest, do some good."

"Thank you," Mikodez said. He bowed to her from the waist, in the old style that Jedao would remember as a formal greeting between heptarchs. She winced, which was good. He needed her to understand what she had gotten herself into. "I am in your debt. Now, I believe we have emergencies to attend to."

"Understatement," Cheris said. "Goodbye, Shuos-zho."

It did not escape Mikodez's notice that she signed off with the Deuce of Gears.

BREZAN HAD BEEN putting off the conversation for too long, but he could no longer tell himself that he had direly important matters to attend to, even if he did. Face it, the chief of staff was better at administrative matters than he was, and Cheris seemed to have some idea of what to do about generalized crises, perhaps because she was a trouble magnet.

In an ideal world, the damned uniform would burst into flames and save him from dealing with this, but he needed to deal with the consequences of his treachery like an adult. He was almost starting to wish he could consult Jedao on how you went on with your life after turning traitor. While he could ask Cheris, it seemed gauche.

After drawing a deep breath, Brezan headed down to the brig. His shoulder blades tickled every time he passed a Kel. He could no longer take formation instinct for granted. Now he knew how other Kel felt around him. Fitting punishment, really.

On the other hand, Cheris's calendar reset meant, for the moment, that Brezan was safe from enthrallment. Terrible excuse for avoiding Tseya: he could have communicated with her remotely at any time, since the ability relied on proximity.

Tseya was being held in a standard cell, although it looked decidedly nonstandard with her in it. He wanted to offer her creeks and birds with ribbony necks and luminous tanks full of fish. Unfortunately, they were beyond the point where apologies would do any good.

Tseya herself sat calmly on the provided bench. The dull brown clothes didn't flatter her. A servitor must have cut her hair. He ached, remembering the long ripples falling through his fingers, remembering combing out the tangles.

He had expected her to try to enthrall him the moment he stepped into line of sight. Instead, she raised her head and regarded him with silent dignity. Maybe she had decided it would be better to crush his windpipe straightaway, except he had no intention of getting that close.

After an uncomfortable pause, Brezan bowed to her, very formally. She might take it as mockery, although he didn't intend it as such. "Tseya," he said. "I owed you better than this. You figured out long ago that I decided to betray you, I'm sure, and I'm probably the last person you want to talk to, but there are some things you should know."

Startlingly, her eyes glinted with humor. "You're safe, you know," she said. "I'm sure the mission's completely blown, we both know it was Cheris all along, and I can only hold onto righteous fury for so long. Not that you can afford to believe me. So what happened? What was your breaking point?"

He forced himself to meet her eyes. "Cheris offered me a better world. A better calendar. This meant a calendrical spike. All the hexarchs are dead except Shuos, who sold the others out, or something, the details aren't entirely clear to me. I have no idea what the fuck we're doing next, but we're going to let you off at—Tseya?"

Tseya was staring at him, face white. "All the hexarchs except Shuos?"

"If you want to say something cutting about my lack of character, or about how I did this because I let my promotion get to my head, go right ahead. I can't say you're not entitled."

The strength went out of her. "I think," she said, "that you really think this is for the better, although what it sounds like to me is an unbelievable amount of chaos. But that wasn't the part that—that got my attention. I'm surprised you didn't figure this out earlier. You were too polite to dig, I guess. The Andan hexarch is—was—my mother."

"Say what?" Brezan sputtered. Then, remembering simple decency: "I'm sorry. I—I had no idea."

"Well," Tseya said, regaining a little of her spirit, "she was a terrible mother. But she never stopped being my mother, if you see what I mean." Her breathing was still shaky. "Do you know, when I was little I thought Mikodez was my uncle. He always had the best candy in his pockets. Then I grew up and learned what the red-and-gold coat meant."

Brezan started to figure out that Tseya wasn't getting mad at him, she was getting mad at Shuos Mikodez. In all fairness, Mikodez was the one who'd offed Andan Shandal Yeng, but Brezan didn't feel good about himself for escaping blame. He muttered an oath, then entered the cell and started to undo her restraints. "Before you get ideas," he said, "I want your parole. We'll let you off somewhere safe, but even if enthrallment doesn't work anymore—"

"Was that what the calendar reset did?"

"Not exactly." He explained it as succinctly as he could.

"You know," Tseya said afterward, rubbing her wrists, "you should have asked for my parole before you came in here."

Brezan shrugged. "Everyone's a critic. Do I have it?"

"Why are you doing this?"

He didn't touch her, didn't catch her hands in his, only looked at her soberly. "Because you shouldn't have to grieve for your mother in here."

Tseya's mouth curved downward. "You have my parole. You've fucked up really badly, you know, and there's going to be an accounting, but I won't be the one to take it out of your hide."

"Come with me," he said, because he didn't know what to say to any of that. "I'll find you a place to have some privacy."

"Thank you," she said. It didn't make things right between them, but he hadn't hoped for that anyway.

NEITHER PRINCIPLE NOR loyalty nor memory prompted Khiruev to cast off formation instinct. Rather, it was the fact that she was mewed up in her own room in Medical and they seemed to think she should do nothing more strenuous than watch dramas or, alternately, stare at the walls. Khiruev had come to the opinion that at least the walls had better dialogue.

The birdform servitor who had taken a liking to her—she was developing a rudimentary ability to tell servitors apart—came to visit her. Khiruev greeted it with stumbling taps in Simplified Machine Universal. She didn't have much vocabulary yet, as the grid's tutorials were atrocious, but the only way forward was practice.

The birdform lit up in a dazzlement of pink and gold lights. Then it said, very slowly, *Are you well?* Just to be sure, it repeated itself in the Kel drum code.

"How do you say 'bored'?" Khiruev asked. The tutorials mostly assumed you wanted to know terms like 'toxic fungus' and 'casualty.'

The birdform flashed the word at her once, twice. In the conversation that followed, it coaxed out of her that the high general had told her to rest, but she didn't care how much her bones felt cobwebbed around with ice, her heart with frost, she wanted a diversion. Maybe some of the gadgets she had been fixing up. The way her hands shook, she'd probably mangle them. But at this point, did it matter?

*I could bring you your tools and components,* the birdform said.

*I am to rest,* Khiruev said mechanically. She looked down at her hands. They were shaking again. Some hidden reserve of obstinacy stirred up in her. *Would it be too much trouble?*

The high general wanted her to rest.

The high general didn't have to know.

The birdform whistled its assent, and left.

Not long afterward, a small procession of servitors arrived bearing Khiruev's tools, a judicious selection of broken mechanisms, and modular furniture to put everything on. She had no idea how they'd gotten all that past the medics and decided she wasn't going to ask. *Thank you,* she said, although she was certain she was using the wrong form; the grid only knew about a stripped-down, blunt dialect of the language.

They blinked amiable acknowledgments and filed out, except the birdform. It seemed to find her entertaining. Well, if nothing else, she could ask it for pointers.

Khiruev's eyes fell on the rose gold watch that Jedao—Cheris— had admired once upon a time. It took her several tries to pick it up. "This one," she said softly. She knew what she wanted to do, frivolous though it was.

She needed the servitor's help. At least the problem was the mainspring, which she knew what to do about. There must have been some reason she'd left it undone for so long, if only she could remember what it had been. No matter. She could fix it now.

By the time they had finished with the mainspring, her hands still had a tremor, but Khiruev realized with a start that the pervasive cold had slid away, and she could think more clearly.


CHERIS HAD A dreadful headache after she and Brezan went over the latest reports of riots, rebellions, scorched cities and cindered swarms. Devenay Ragath had raised an army on some planet. She hoped he wrote her a letter on how to do it because she had the feeling this was going to become vitally important information. For all Jedao's military virtues, he had always been handed his armies; he'd never had to create one from scratch.

She planned to crawl into bed and stare into the darkness, but one of the servitors, a birdform, intercepted her on the way to her quarters. It offered her painkillers, adding that she ought to have taken them earlier.

"You're right," Cheris said, sighing. "I get these moments—revenants can't get headaches. I forget sometimes I'm alive."

*You should see the general,* it said, meaning Khiruev. She knew it had taken a liking to Khiruev.

Cheris had visited Khiruev once after she was moved to the medical center. Khiruev had been dozing. Cheris hadn't wanted to wake her, not when she looked like she was disintegrating into shadows. Now—"Is she awake?"

*Yes.*

"I'll come with you," Cheris said. Companionably, they made their way to the medical center, which was marked by paintings of ashhawks entwined with snakes.

The Kel medics deferred to Cheris only as much as they had to. One of them warned her not to tire Khiruev. She promised to be careful. How bad had Khiruev's condition become? Brezan had said that he had tried a few times to get Khiruev to understand that she didn't need Vrae Tala anymore, but Khiruev had not responded. Of course, Brezan was the exact worst person to be making that argument.

Cheris wasn't prepared for the tables with their screwdrivers and different sizes of hammers and strange metal coils and small bottles of shellac. And she wasn't prepared for Khiruev sitting up, her face drawn but her eyes clear as morning. "General—?" Cheris said.

"I don't know what you want me to call you," Khiruev said. Her voice was scratchy.

"I'm Ajewen Cheris, and I'm what's left of Jedao," she said, "and from the beginning I lied to you."

Khiruev laughed a little. "Then it wasn't entirely a lie, was it?" She turned something around in her hand. Cheris couldn't tell what it was when Khiruev still had her fingers around it.

"Not entirely," Cheris said. "I remember being Jedao. That's four hundred years of him. It was hard not to drown in him sometimes. But unlike you, I had a choice. Do you regret ending up here?"

"It's still hard to think sometimes," Khiruev said. "But I'd do it again. All of it." She opened her hand, showing Cheris the watch, an antique, severe in its design. "For you," she said. "I'm not done yet. I have some more restoration to do."

"That thing must be a couple of centuries old," Cheris said. "Don't you want to save it for yourself?"

"You're a couple of centuries old yourself," Khiruev said. She was smiling. It made her eyes young. She set the watch down on the nearest table. "Three gameboards all along, isn't that right? Jedao fighting the Hafn. But that wasn't the real fight. The hexarchs thought Jedao was using the Hafn to start a revolt against them, a war of public opinion. And that wasn't the real fight either. The real fight was the calendrical spike that must have been your intention from the beginning. So that's it. It worked. The hexarchs are dead—well, except Shuos—and you've won the war."

Cheris thought of the name she would have been given if the Mwennin religious calendar hadn't been suppressed by the hexarchate. Khiruev's father crumpled into swans. Her parents' execution and her people's genocide, the riots, numbers written in pale ash. Servitors silenced for hundreds of years. Being ordered to fire on the Lanterners' children. Her swarm massacred with a carrion bomb at the Fortress of Scattered Needles.

That was only a fraction of the atrocities the hexarchate had perpetrated in her lives. And people didn't stop being people because they had choices.

She had found a gun with which to fight. It remained to be seen whether anyone had the will to use it well.

"No," Cheris said. "The war never ends."

# ACKNOWLEDGEMENTS

THANK YOU TO the following people: my editor, Jonathan Oliver, and the wonderful folks at Solaris Books; my agent, Jennifer Jackson; and my agent's assistant, Michael Curry.

I am grateful to my beta readers: Joseph Charles Betzwieser, Cyphomandra, Daedala, Isis, Yune Kyung Lee, Nancy Sauer, Sonya Taaffe, and Storme Winfield. Additional thanks to the following people from Fountain Pen Network for fielding my firearms questions: ac12, injesticate, opcnionated, ragpaper1817, and TheRealScubaSteve. All errors and narrative license taken are, of course, my own.

This one is for Nancy Sauer: yours in calendrical heresy, always.

# ABOUT THE AUTHOR

YOON HA LEE is a writer and mathematician from Houston, Texas, whose work has appeared in *Clarkesworld*, *Lightspeed* and *The Magazine Of Fantasy and Science Fiction*. He has published over forty short stories, and his critically acclaimed collection *Conservation of Shadows* was released in 2013. He lives in Louisiana with his family and an extremely lazy cat.

# FIND US ONLINE!

## www.rebellionpublishing.com

/rebellionpub      /rebellionpublishing      /rebellionpub

# SIGN UP TO OUR NEWSLETTER!

## rebellionpublishing.com/sign-up

# YOUR REVIEWS MATTER!

Enjoy this book? Got something to say?

Leave a review on Amazon, GoodReads or with your
favourite bookseller and let the world know!

# BINARY/SYSTEM

## ERIC BROWN

On what should have been a routine mission to the star system of 61 Cygni A, Delia Kemp finds herself shunted thousands of light years into uncharted space. The only survivor of a catastrophic starship blow-out, Delia manages to land her life-raft on the inhospitable, ice-bound world of Valinda, and is captured by a race of hostile aliens, the Skelt. What follows is a break-neck adventure as Delia escapes, fleeing through a phantasmagorical landscape.

As the long winter comes to an end and the short, blistering summer approaches, the Skelt will stop at nothing to obtain Delia's technical knowledge — but what Delia wants is impossible: to leave Valinda and return to Earth.

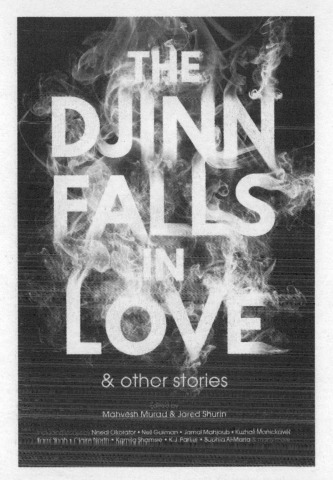

A fascinating collection of new and classic tales of the fearsome Djinn, from bestselling, award-winning and breakthrough international writers.

Imagine a world filled with fierce, fiery beings, hiding in our shadows, in our dreams, under our skins. Eavesdropping and exploring; savaging our bodies, saving our souls. They are monsters, saviours, victims, childhood friends. Some have called them genies: these are the Djinn. And they are everywhere. On street corners, behind the wheel of a taxi, in the chorus, between the pages of books. Every language has a word for them. Every culture knows their traditions. Every religion, every history has them hiding in their dark places.

There is no part of the world that does not know them. They are the Djinn. They are among us.

With stories from Neil Gaiman, Nnedi Okorafor, Amal El-Mohtar, Catherine Faris King, Claire North,  E.J. Swift, Hermes (trans. Robin Moger), Jamal Majoub, James Smythe, J.Y. Yang, Kamila Shamsie, Kirsty Logan, K.J. Parker, Kuzhali Manickavel, Maria Dahvana Headley, Monica Byrne, Nada Adel Sobhi, Saad Hossein, Sami Shah, Sophia Al-Maria and Usman Malik.

# INFINITY WARS

Featuring stories by
**Pat Cadigan**
**Aliette de Bodard**
**Usman T. Malik**
**Nalo Hopkinson**
**Christopher Rowe**
**Eleanor Arnason**
**Rich Larson**
**Lavie Tidhar**
and more

Edited by
**Jonathan Strahan**

We have always fought. War is the furnace that forges new technologies and pushes humanity ever onward. We are the children of a battle that began with fists and sticks, and ended on the brink of atomic Armageddon. Beyond here lies another war, infinite in scope and scale.

But who will fight the wars of tomorrow? Join Elizabeth Bear, Indrapramit Das, Aliette de Bodard, Garth Nix, An Owomoyela, Peter Watts, and many, many more in an exploration of the furthest extremes of military science fiction...

## WWW.SOLARISBOOKS.COM

*Follow us on Twitter! www.twitter.com/solarisbooks*

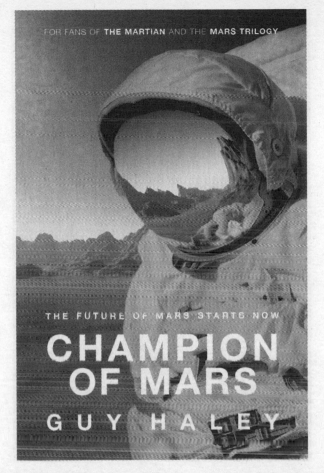

EDITED BY JONATHAN STRAHAN

# DROWNED WORLDS

with stories by
Ken Liu
Paul McAuley
James Morrow
Charlie Jane Anders
Kim Stanley Robinson
Kathleen Ann Goonan
Jeffrey Ford
and more

'Books as good as this should be of interest to any admirer of short fiction, regardless of genre.'
*The Guardian on The Best Science Fiction and Fantasy of the Year Volume Eight*

We stand on the brink of one of the greatest ecological disasters of our time — the world is warming and seas are rising, and yet water is life; it brings change. Where one thing is wiped away, another rises.

Drowned Worlds looks at the future we might have if the oceans rise — good or bad. Here you'll find stories of action, adventure, romance and, yes, warning and apocalypse. Stories inspired by Ballard's The Drowned World, Sterling's Islands in the Net, and Ryman's The Child Garden; stories that allow that things may get worse, but remembers that such times also bring out the best in us all.

Multi-award winning editor Jonathan Strahan has put together fifteen unique tales of deluged worlds and those who fight to survive and strive to live.

Featuring: **Paul McAuley, Ken Liu, Kim Stanley Robinson, Nina Allan, Kathleen Ann Goonan, Christopher Rowe, Nalo Hopkinson, Sean Williams, Jeffrey Ford, Lavie Tidhar, Rachel Swirsky, James Morrow, Charlie Jane Anders, Sam J. Miller and Catherynne M. Valente.**

## WWW.SOLARISBOOKS.COM

*Follow us on Twitter! www.twitter.com/solarisbooks*